BECAUSE OF YOU

Music City Heat: 2

Marie-Nicole Ryan

RYANDALE PUBLISHING

Copyright © 2013 by Mary Varble
Cover by Mary Varble
Edited by Linda Ingmanson
First Ryandale Press Electronic Publication: July 2013
First Ryandale Press Print Publication: July 2013
Second Ryandale Press Print Publication: 2020

ISBN: 9781393437314

Library of Congress Registration: TX 7-804-993

Chapter One

There were times like today, often occurring on a Friday afternoon, when Certified Case Manager Allison Lackey wondered why, oh why, had she become a nurse? And the answer was always simple: she'd never wanted to be anything else.

She stopped at the door that opened onto the sixth-floor terrace and glanced over her shoulder. While the terrace afforded no shade from the summer heat, it made for a fantastic viewpoint for watching the Fourth of July fireworks. It also guaranteed privacy, as long as it was deserted, which, at the moment, it was. Thank heaven.

Her friend Meryl's text had said *something fishy* was going on and to meet on the sixth-floor terrace at four fifteen. Allison glanced at her watch. She was on time, but where was Meryl? It wasn't like her friend to be late...for anything.

Waves of heat shimmered from the tile, even though the patio was on the east side of the hospital nestled between two wings. Allison shrugged off her lab coat, walked over to the wrought iron table, and set her can of Diet Coke on the top.

Five minutes. That was all the time she had.

"Come on, Mer," Allison said aloud while she drummed her fingers against the tabletop. There was one more nursing-home transfer to double-check. The ambulance hadn't picked her patient up at four as scheduled. She'd already left them one polite, but firm, message. If she had to leave a second one, it would blister someone's ears.

Friday afternoons were the busiest for getting patients transferred before the weekend, and now this curious text from Meryl—major interruption. Okay. Five more minutes, but then she'd have to get back to the floor and kick some ambulance-company ass.

Five minutes passed while she paced. Maybe Meryl, who was five months pregnant, had gone into premature labor. Maybe that was what she meant?

No. She would've just said she was having contractions and to meet her in the Family Birth Unit. As for the "something fishy"? Well, it *was* Friday.

Okay, time's up. Her patient in 804 was waiting for his nursing-home bed. If she didn't get back to the eighth-floor nursing station, he'd be spending the weekend in the hospital and incur extra expenses. The nursing home wouldn't take new patients on a weekend. So, Monday morning her supervisor would be on the warpath about wasted hospital days and ride Allison's ass all day long.

Unable to wait any longer, she left the terrace. Whatever Meryl wanted would have to wait.

Allison pulled up in front of the large stone historic Craftsman bungalow she and her fellow siblings called home and parked. They were a blended family of five—no, make it six—siblings, but no one knew where Kim, the youngest, was.

Technically, the bungalow belonged to the Lackey side of the family, since their deceased mother had inherited it from her parents long before she married Tom Holt. After her mother's and stepfather's deaths, the six Holt-Lackeys had stayed together...or they had until Kim ran away.

Allison meandered up the flagstone path, stopping long

enough to smell the purple butterfly bushes flanking the porch steps. She opened the mahogany door and yelled, "I'm home. Dinner's on me tonight."

Her older sister Caroline, usually shortened to Carrie, came down the hallway from the kitchen wearing slim-legged jeans, a white T-shirt emblazoned with a large green frog, and a confused expression in her hazel-green eyes. "I— uh, forgot. I was about to start something. Friday night's pizza night, isn't it?"

Her sister's confusion cut Allison like a scalpel. Caroline still suffered from the aftereffects of carbon monoxide poisoning. Memory loss, headaches, confusion, and an overwhelming need to count the silverware were the worst of her symptoms. Thank God.

"It's all right. It'll get better." Allison hugged her sister, then slipped a lock of her sister's honey-blond hair behind her ear.

Arm in arm, they walked back to the kitchen. "It drives me crazy," Caroline said. "What good is a master's degree if I can't even remember which nights I'm responsible for dinner without marking it on the calendar?"

"Don't be so hard on yourself. You're doing everything you can to get better. Didn't your speech and cognitive therapists say you were making great progress?" She pulled the pizza menu from under a pizza-shaped fridge magnet and set it beside the kitchen laptop. "Guess I'd better put in our order."

Caroline leaned against the granite counter and frowned. "I want—no, I need—to get back to work, but I'm afraid I'll screw something up on one of the client accounts and not even realize it."

Allison finalized the pizza order, then turned to her sister. "Why not try a couple of hours a day? Just to get back in the swing of things. What does the therapist say about work?"

"Not to rush it, but I'm scared." She blinked rapidly as if tears would soon follow. "The idea of leaving the house puts me into a panic. And that's not like me. I was never scared of anything before."

Allison put a reassuring arm around her sister's shoulder. "Give it time. It's only been three weeks." *Three* whole weeks...since a serial killer's accomplice had tried to engineer the demise of their entire family using a gas leak. Closest to the leak, Caroline had suffered the most severe exposure. Allison and her brother Justin's exposure was minor. If Scott hadn't gotten hungry and come downstairs for a PB&J sandwich—no telling what might've happened.

"Speaking of panic, I had the strangest text from Meryl this afternoon. She asked me to meet her, and then stood me up."

"Is that like her?" Caroline opened the fridge and pulled out a vegetable tray arranged with carrot sticks, celery stuffed with pimento cheese, and thin slices of yellow summer squash. "You don't mind, do you? I was craving fresh veggies this afternoon." After setting the tray on the counter, she prized the lid from a container of French onion dip. "I'm sure she's okay." She chose a carrot stick and swirled it into the dip, then leaned her elbow on the counter and waited with a quizzical expression.

Allison leaned against the counter. "It's not like her. At first, I thought it might be about the baby, but she wouldn't have been so mysterious." She picked up the phone and tried all three of Meryl's numbers—work, beeper, and personal cell phone.

"Nothing?" A worried frown creased Caroline's forehead.

"If I don't hear from her by the time we finish dinner," Allison said, "I'll run over to her condo. If she's not home... Well, I still have a key from when I dog-sat for her in June."

Caroline frowned. "Better take Scott or Justin with you."

"Come on." Allison rolled her eyes. "It's just a couple of blocks from here."

"No." Her sister's body stiffened. "Just do as I ask. Don't ask me why. I don't know why. I just want you safe."

"Woo-woo," Allison said, waggling her fingers. "Don't go all psychic on me now. I can handle anything but that."

Caroline folded her arms across her chest. "We don't need any more—" She shrugged. "You know what I mean."

"All right. All right. I'll take one of 'em." Her older sister wasn't usually so uptight, but she hadn't been the same since the carbon monoxide scare. Allison couldn't help but worry about her sister, but at the moment, Meryl's message was still bugging her. She wouldn't rest until she reached her friend.

"I just remembered." Caroline tapped the pizza menu with her forefinger. "Scott's bringing the new hire home for dinner. We'll need more pizza."

"What new hire?" Granted she didn't work *for* the family's PI agency, but as a board member, shouldn't she have heard about a new hire? "Who? Anyone I know?"

"You remember Nick Vitelli? Sure, you do. Went to school with Scott, then Western in Bowling Green. Married, moved to Atlanta. Now he's divorced and moved back here to be close to his son."

"Nothing wrong with your memory now," Allison muttered but plastered on a fake grin for her sister's benefit.

Crap. Not Nick Vitelli, Scott's *old* friend. Sheesh. She'd made an absolute fool of herself over him the summer she was sixteen...which he no doubt remembered. Her cheeks grew hot.

Stop being silly. She was a grown woman now and shouldn't be embarrassed about something that happened ten years ago. Losing a bikini top could happen to anyone.

And it had. To her.

Chapter Two

Damn. Nashville wasn't any cooler than Atlanta, despite being a good five hours northwest. Nick wiped the sweat from his brow and hunkered down for the duration. Surveillance in the sweltering record-breaking heat was for suckers.

Yeah, sucker. His middle name.

So here he was in the parking lot of the Lazee Nites Inn, no shade in sight, watching the comings and goings of one W. D. "Dub" Johnston. Dub's wife, Elaine, was of the mind her husband was fooling around because he was bringing home less money when payday rolled around. After watching Dub for two miserable days, Nick concluded their client was right. Her construction worker husband was fooling around...and he was paying for the privilege.

Attired in a UT orange T-shirt and jeans crawling down his ass, Dub had entered the Lazee Nites Inn on Murfreesboro Road at three fifteen for an afternoon quickie. The place was notorious for prostitution and frequent drug busts.

Not exactly four-star accommodations. Hell, not even one star.

All he had to do was get the pix of Dub and the working girl, then head back to the office. He patted his jeans pocket, assuring himself the tiny digital camera was ready.

Scott was testing him. How bad did Nick want to work as a PI? Bad enough to put up with shitty assignments? Hell, yeah. He'd been through worse. Undercover narcotics. Vice. He'd seen the dregs of humanity and what they were capable of. Hot 'Lanta or Nashville—didn't make much difference. But as a PI, he had better hours and more control. More time to spend with his kid.

He eased open his car door and got out, stretched his legs, then ambled over to number fifteen, where a perfect three-inch gap in the drapes made for a nice camera angle. The working girl was puffing on a cigarette and still tangled in the sheets. His surveillance subject was emerging from the john.

Click. Click. Click.

Dub's mouth opened wide like a large-mouth bass.

Crap. He'd been made. He took another snap for good luck.

The door was flung open. Nick spun and beat it for his SUV, one of the last Ford Broncos to roll off the assembly line in '96. The Bronco might be old, but it was reliable as hell. More interested in keeping the camera-ready proof of Dub's quickie than getting beat-up on his first assignment, he ignored the spate of obscenities. None of which were particularly inventive.

Mission accomplished.

Next case.

Back in the office of Holt Investigations, Nick slouched in a client chair and handed the camera card over to Justin, the agency's resident computer geek. "These should do the trick."

Justin took the camera card, gave a pleased grin, and inserted it into his computer. "Caught him in the act?"

"Right after. Working girl was already having a smoke. Warning, he's nekkid. And he ain't pretty." Nick hauled to his feet. "Guess I'll give Mrs. Johnston a call and make an appointment for tomorrow to give her the news." Never knew how a betrayed wife would react when faced with proof of her husband's cheating heart. Better tell her in person than over the phone.

"Good enough." Justin manipulated the mouse, pulled up the photos, and grimaced. "You're right. Not pretty."

"Warned you." Nick glanced at his watch. "Gonna check in with Scott and then head out."

"You don't have to check-in or out with *me*, but I'm pretty sure you're invited for dinner tonight." Justin nodded and laughed. "Printing these babies now. I'll leave 'em on your desk."

Home for dinner. That used to mean something. Not that he managed it often—one of his ex's many justified gripes.

He headed for his new office. It contained the basics. Phone, computer, file cabinet, and a couple of client chairs. A single window overlooked First Avenue; the outside wall was unfinished brick, the other walls painted plaster. Almost as barren as his life. At present, his single personal touch was a pic of his son, Ben, in a martial art pose, wearing a tiny white karate *gi*. Plenty of time for decorating. Maybe one of Scott's sisters could lend a hand.

After speaking with his client, Nick made an appointment for ten on Saturday morning so she could view the pictures. Ought to be interesting.

He ambled into his new boss's office. Scott glanced up. "How'd it go? See you're still in one piece."

Nick shrugged. "Yeah, he made me, but I had the advantage. I was dressed. He wasn't."

Scott roared with laughter. "I can see where it would." He leaned back. "First day on the job, and you're invited to the house for dinner. It's a new agency tradition."

"Got it." Nick nodded. "Since I'm the first hire who isn't

a member of the family?"

"Exactly. This is still a family agency, and now you're part of the family."

"Uh-oh." With a touch of dread gathering in his gut, he asked, "Just how many unmarried sisters do you have?"

"Hold on. This isn't a setup." Scott beamed. "I wouldn't do that to you. But if you're in the market, there's Carrie, Tamsyn, and Allison." A frown crossed his face. "We still don't know where Kim is."

"Sorry, dude. Must be tough."

"Yeah." Scott gestured, waving aside more of Nick's questions. "Anyway, let's close up shop. You can follow me home. Friday's pizza night."

Nick nodded, still a little uneasy. Three unmarried sisters. They'd just have to stay unmarried a little longer. He wasn't in the market.

His divorce from Eva had taken too much time, most of his money, and left him adrift. His ex-wife had believed in advancing through the ranks. She'd latched on to his captain and decided he was better husband material than an undercover narc who didn't make it home for days at a time. Hell, there were times when he couldn't blame her for finding someone else. Okay, so those times were few and far between. Big deal.

To make matters worse, she and her new husband, Douglas R. Mills, had up and moved from Atlanta to Nashville where he was the new chief of police.

What other choice did he have but to move back? He wasn't about to give up what little time the court said he could spend with his son. No way.

Chapter Three

Allison set the table in the large family dining room. Maybe it was pretentious to serve pizza like a formal meal, but Scott was dragging his new employee home like a surefire cure for...something. No way was she using the good china. The everyday stuff would do just fine for Nick Vitelli.

Too soon, she heard the door open and Scott called out, "We're home." She glanced toward the longcase clock in the foyer as it struck on the half-hour. "Dinner's in the dining room," she yelled back. "Pizza should be here in about ten minutes."

Scott shuffled through the arch into the dining room, picked her up, and swung her around. "It's the weekend, sis. Time to partay."

"Put me down, you big goober," she said with a huff. Her brother chuckled and complied. She straightened her cutoff jeans, adjusted her T-shirt, and did her damnedest to avoid meeting this most unwelcome—in her mind anyway— guest's gaze.

"You remember Nick, don't you?" Scott stepped aside.

Unable to avoid it any longer, she raised her chin and met the newcomer's gaze. Yes, Nick still had those steely blue eyes and wavy dark hair. It was cut shorter than the sunbleached, surfer-dude style he'd sported back in the day when it often reached his broad shoulders. A dark scruffy beard covered his square chin and upper lip. Still broad-shouldered and slim-hipped, he wore a pale blue knit shirt and a pair of jeans. The blue of the shirt matched his eyes. "Vaguely. Hope you like anchovies on your pizza."

Nick screwed his handsome face into a mask of horror, then made a gulping sound before he answered, "S-sure. Love anchovies."

She shrugged. "Too bad. I never order anchovies." All right, so she was being pissy. If he so much as mentioned the time he saw... She turned and fiddled with one of the place settings.

Breathe, girl. Breathe and forget your wobbly knees. No way should Nick Vitelli have this kind of effect on her after all this time.

But he did.

Scott frowned. "Come on, Allie. What gives? Nick's our new employee and a guest."

"Just teasing." Her cheeks heating up, she faced Nick and offered him her best I'll-smile-if-it-kills-me expression as she gazed into his eyes. "You don't really like anchovies, do you?"

"Matter of fact, I can take 'em or leave 'em." He gave her a genuine smile that made her regret her bad manners. A diversion—that was what she needed. Anything to make him forget one night at the Brady's pool.

Without warning, Nick fixed his gaze on her. "Been swimming lately?" he asked with a deadpan expression.

The blood rushed and heated her cheeks like a menopausal hot flash. Not that she'd ever experienced one at the ripe old age of twenty-six. "N-not lately. You?" She managed to get the words out. Her tongue seemed to have swollen twice its normal size.

"Not in recent memory." An amused grin spread across his face. "Nothing comes to mind except a *certain* occasion," he drawled.

"You have no business bringing up *that* occasion," she sputtered. "I was a kid. You didn't see much. Besides, it was dark."

Scott's eyebrows drew together in a frown. No wonder. He wasn't there when she'd dived into the pool and lost the top half of her bikini. On the other hand, Nick's expression was more than amused. "Oh, I saw plenty, kid, but you're right, there wasn't much to see."

Kid? She squared her shoulders. "I'm not a kid now."

"No." His gaze slid up and down her body, slow and easy like. "I can definitely see you're not." He swallowed, then smiled. "You grew up nice, Allie. Real nice."

Could her face get any hotter? Doubtful. She turned back to the table. Glasses. More glasses. Definitely what she needed. Another diversion. She ignored—tried to anyway—Nick's telling Scott all about how she'd lost her top in the Brady's pool. Let them laugh. Male humor.

Neanderthals.

After an uneasy dinner, Nick picked up his beer, followed Scott's lead, and headed to the den. He sat on the end of a coffee table. "Guess I shouldn't have teased Allison. Didn't think she'd be so touchy about something that happened in the Dark Ages."

He remembered the incident as if it were yesterday. A slight waif of a girl, all elbows and knees, with the biggest brown eyes he'd ever seen. So shy and innocent it hurt. He'd turned away as quickly as he could when she'd screeched about her top. Yes, Allison had grown into a fine-looking woman with wavy reddish-blond hair falling across her shoulders like a silk shawl. Time had certainly filled out and softened those edges. But not her sharp tongue.

"Chalk it up to the fact she's almost a redhead and tends to be prickly. Believe me, I know all about redheads and their tempers. Tess has one too."

Nick gave a knowing nod. Not much else he could say. He

glanced around the room. Like the rest of the house, the boss's den was comfortable. It was a real man cave with dark green walls, a wide-screen TV over the fireplace, leather furniture, and sturdy dark oak tables. With no raging desire to rush back to the sprung sofa bed in his brother's studio apartment, he took a pull on his beer. "Anything good on?"

Barely had the words left his mouth when Allison stormed into the den, plopped on the sofa, and launched into a tale about one of her friends while ignoring Nick as if he were another piece of furniture.

"So, I need you or Justin to go with me over to Meryl's condo. Pretty please? I still can't reach her. I'm starting to get seriously worried."

"Sounds like a job for my new employee," Scott said. "Tess expects me to bring over another load of my junk tonight—just so she can tell me there's no room for it. Justin's busy with the end-of-the-month financials."

"What?" Nick leaned back. A setup. Had to be. "Uh, sure..."

"He's our guest, Scott. Now you're trying to kick him out. And it's obvious from his expression he doesn't want to go." She sniffed and shot Nick a disdainful expression. "Did I mention she's five months pregnant? Don't let me keep you from watching your stupid ball game."

Allison stood with her hands on her hips and acted as if she had no intention of giving up. Her foot tapped in another show of impatience. "I'll just go over there by myself. That's what I intended to do anyway, but Carrie thought I needed an *escort*. But I don't."

Nick held back a groan and got to his feet. Setup or not, he couldn't take a chance Allie's pregnant friend was really in trouble. "It's getting dark. I'll be more than happy to be your bodyguard. But if your friend's just taking a nap and doesn't want to be disturbed, you're gonna owe me. Big time."

"Hmph." She glared up at him, her dark eyes flashing him a warning.

"That's what I like—a woman of few words. Rare too."

Allison snatched a pillow from the sofa, spun, and tossed it at Nick, then dashed from the room. He batted the pillow away and turned to Scott. "Sorry. Pissed your sister off, again."

"Look, it's no big deal," Scott said, shrugging. "Just run over there and see if everything's all right. Allie has a tendency to jump to conclusions. Her nerves are due to her overactive imagination."

"I'll do it. Not because you just gave me a much-needed job. I'm just warning you. Allie doesn't give a rat's ass about me...so if you have any matchmaking ideas, forget 'em."

A long, low laugh rumbled from his new boss. "That's just her way. As for matchmaking, don't give it a second thought."

A second thought? Hell, he'd never intended to give it a first, but somehow, he couldn't quite put images of her perky breasts or her eyes, warm as milk chocolate, from his mind's eye.

Allison entered the kitchen ready to load the dishwasher but found Caroline had already accomplished the onerous task. She thanked her sister, then sputtered, "Th-that Nick Vitelli is such a jerk. Scott asked Nick to go with me over to Meryl's. Clearly, the man would rather have a colonoscopy than have anything to do with me."

"Come on. You know Scott's head is up his butt over moving in with Tess and the *upcoming nuptials*." Caroline folded her hands together and intoned the last two words as if getting married were a one-way trip to the morgue, then laughed. "Nick's not such a bad guy. Just unlucky in love like some of the rest of us. And he's a helluva lot hotter than I remember."

Hot? Maybe. "Just so you know I'm not looking for any kind of a guy—good, bad, or ugly. So, don't try to palm Mr. Unlucky in Love off on me."

"You don't fool me." Her sister shut the cabinet door and glanced around the kitchen. "All this hoo-hah is over his accidentally getting a peek at your boobs—ten years ago—for Pete's sake."

"Is not." Well, maybe it was, but never in a million years would she admit it.

"Now, go on. Get outta here. Go check on Meryl. Surely you can stand the man's company for at least ten minutes. Just keep your top on."

"I'll get you." Allison picked up a napkin, wadded it, and threw it at her sister, who giggled and ducked.

"What's going on?" a gravelly male voice asked behind her.

She whirled. Crap. Nick. Had he heard every blessed word? "You shouldn't sneak up on people without warning."

The jerk clenched his jaw...his ever-so-manly jaw. Allison swallowed with a telltale audible gulp. Could she act any more like an awkward teenager? Was the condition incurable?

"Are we going or not?" he asked through clenched teeth.

"Sure. Just waiting on you, friendly PI." She waved at Caroline and tried to ignore her sister's knowing smirk.

If Allison were a dog, she'd have tucked her tail and run. But she wasn't, and no way would she run from Nick Vitelli.

No way.

"Turn right," Allison directed, "then right again into the

complex." Keep it businesslike and she wouldn't have to put up with him much longer. Truth be told, she hoped Nick was right about Meryl's having turned off her phone.

"Yes, boss. You know, you didn't have to throw a pillow at me. Can I get Work Comp. for that?"

"Really?" She glared at him. "Are you disabled? Are you in pain? It was a *pillow*."

A snort was the man's response. Few words, indeed.

They turned into the condo complex, white stucco buildings with red-tiled roofs. Meryl's unit had an attached garage, and the door was closed.

"There. Number fourteen. Park right in front," she ordered.

"You like giving orders, don't you?"

"I'm a case manager, and I'm used to ordering people around." All right, now she sounded a little on the smug side. And it wasn't true. When she needed something done at the hospital, she asked nicely—the first time, anyway.

He parked the Bronco, then shut off the motor. "If she doesn't answer the door, how're you going to get in?"

"I have a spare key." She opened the car door, exited, then raced up the brick walk to the front door.

"Hold on," he yelled. "Try knocking first. You don't want to scare her half to death and get shot, do you?" He eased from the vehicle and ambled up the sidewalk.

"Meryl doesn't have a gun," she told him with some snark. "She's not the type."

"And what is the type? She lives alone in a metropolitan city. Sounds like the type who ought to have one."

"*I* don't have one."

"And *you* don't live alone. My point."

"She doesn't live alone either." Allison inserted the key into the lock, turned it, and heard a small dog's frantic yips.

"Probably lick an intruder to death."

"She probably needs to go out." She eased open the door and peered inside. "Omigod." Her hands started trembling.

"What is it? Pile of dog poop?"

Mouth dry, she managed to get the words out. "No. Blood. Lots of it."

Chapter Four

"Get back," Nick ordered and drew his weapon, an S&W Model 4003TSW, the same as he'd carried on the job. "Grab the dog. I'll see what's inside." He turned and eyeballed her. "I know you want to rush inside, but the fewer people tracking through the scene, the better." *For forensics*, he added silently.

Allison nodded. "I know, b-but she might need a nurse." She bent over to pick up the antsy Yorkie, whose paws were covered in blood.

Optimistic, wasn't she? Missing pregnant woman and blood in the apartment didn't equal a good outcome in his experience. "If she does, I'll call you. Call 911—right now."

The tiny dog trembled in Allison's arms. He didn't want to think about what the creature might have witnessed.

She cradled the dog in one arm, nodded, then pulled out a smartphone. "What could've happened? Maybe the blood is from a miscarriage."

"Just stay here." He didn't wait for a response; instead, he eased inside the condo. The place was a wreck. There were streaks of fresh blood from the foyer to the kitchen. They stopped at another door, leading to the garage. The blood had been there long enough for thinner areas to have dried. Without a pair of gloves, he resisted the strong urge to touch the knob and open the door. Yet Allison's friend could still be in the garage. He grabbed a paper towel from the dispenser and taking care not to smudge any possible prints, he opened the door to the garage. The overhead light remained on. Empty, but with more blood.

Closing the door and taking care to avoid stepping in the blood trail, he surveyed the remainder of the unit. Nothing and no one. Not good.

Someone lost a great deal of blood and was dragged into the garage. For disposal? Have to wait for the authorities. If the perpetrator had taken Meryl away in her own vehicle, then where was his vehicle? Had he had time to return and retrieve it? Or was it still out in the parking lot?

Worse—he'd have to tell Allison what he'd seen.

Allison saw the door open and took a deep breath. "Well, is she—?"

"Nobody home. Her car's missing," Nick said with a shake of his head, then closed the door behind him. "Lotta blood. You need to prepare yourself. Something bad went down in there."

Anguish slashed through her, sharp as a scalpel. "No, Nick. Don't say it. Please..." Spots flashed black and green before her eyes. Her knees buckled. Just in time, Nick caught her and the dog before she collapsed. "I'm all right. I'm all right." Why was she insisting she was all right? She was anything but.

"Sit. Put your head between your knees."

Of all the arrogant jerks. "Don't tell me what to do. I'm a nurse. I *know* what to do."

"Excuse the hell out of me." He released his hold and stepped back.

A siren wailed in the distance. Good, someone was coming—hopefully, someone with some sense. Her vision grew cloudy and her knees weakened again. Dammit.

He grabbed her, none too gently, just in time. "Lady, you need a keeper. Sit your ass down on the step and...do what you already know to do."

Anger fueled by his dismissive attitude stiffened her spine...and her resolve. "Fine. Take her dog before I drop her." He took the dog gingerly as if the poor little creature was a package containing a bomb or worse. "What's the matter with you? Don't you like dogs?" The wail of a siren grew closer.

He headed toward the SUV. "Dogs are fine. This one is more on the order of a long-haired rat." He opened the door, rolled down the windows a bit, then shut the dog inside. "First, tell me if you're going to report me to the ASPCA for leaving the dog in the car."

"No." She glanced around. "The sun isn't high. She'll be all right...for now."

"She'd better not do her business in my vehicle, or I know someone who's gonna be cleaning it up."

Stronger now, she strode to his side and glared up at him. "Are you trying to be obnoxious? If so, you're succeeding." A second siren pierced the air, this one closer. "You're trying to distract me from what's happened, aren't you?" As if he could, but a noble attempt all the same.

"I doubt anyone distracts you for long." He paused and appeared to listen. "The authorities are 'bout a block away. Just tell them all you know. Don't make guesses. Don't try to solve the case."

"You think there's a case here, don't you?" Of course, there was. A sudden icy shiver zipped up her spine. To keep warm, she hugged her arms. A cool front had come through earlier in the evening, bringing with it the promise of rain. Leaves on the trees were turned up, showing their undersides, and the air smelled like rain. Forecasters were right. A breeze whipped through the complex, and in the distance, a wind chime rippled and jangled. She shivered. Where was Meryl? Was she cold? Was she lying somewhere in a field with no one to help her? Or was it too late?

"You're in shock," Nick said. He walked around to the rear of his SUV and opened the hatch, rummaged around, then walked back to where she stood. "Put this on." He held out a leather jacket, and, without waiting, he settled it across her shoulders. "Better?"

All right, so he wasn't a complete jerk. Matter of fact, his touch was a warm comfort, given the circumstances. She nodded. "Thanks."

No time for anything else. A police cruiser whipped into the parking area, its lights flashing blue and white, and parked. Two uniformed officers emerged. One was around thirty, tall, and thin. Allison glimpsed his shaved head before he put on his cap. The second was tall but stockier, wearing glasses, in his mid-fifties with silvered temples.

"Let me handle these guys," Nick said.

"Sure, Detective Control Freak. Go right ahead." Of course, it made sense for him to talk to them first. He was a former cop. He spoke cop-speak. Still, if they could just get a move on, it might not be too late to find Meryl.

Nick eased his way over to the older of the two officers. Hands in plain sight, he said, "I'm Nick Vitelli. I'm a PI with Holt Investigations. Used to be on the job in Atlanta." Carefully he pulled out his PI license and handed it to the sergeant, who gave it the once-over, then handed it back.

"I'm Sergeant Moore. What've we got here? Dispatch said, 'See the lady about a missing person and blood in the apartment.'"

Nick nodded. "My friend here, Allison Lackey, was worried about her friend not answering her cell. Her friend's pregnant, so we came over here to see if anything was wrong. Allison opened the door—she has a spare key—saw her friend's dog and blood in the foyer. She didn't go inside."

"What about you?"

Nick nodded. "Went inside. Didn't touch anything but the outer doorknob. Kept my big feet out of the blood. Looks like a blitz attack at the door. Lotta blood from the foyer to the kitchen and to the garage door."

"You check the garage?"

"No. Not without gloves. I know better."

The sergeant turned to the other officer. "Wells, get the gloves and booties, then take Miss Lackey's statement."

Allison waited while Officer Wells returned with latex gloves and paper shoe covers. Once attired, the older officer entered the apartment and shone his flashlight across the floor. He was lost to Allison's view, but Nick's strong grip on her wrist kept her from following. "I'm a nurse," she yelled. "If I can be of help…"

"Now, ma'am," Officer Wells began, "if you'll just tell me your relationship to the vic—the missing person?" He pulled a notebook from his back pocket.

"We don't know she's a victim yet, Officer Wells. Her *name* is Meryl Litton."

"No, ma'am. Sorry. Didn't mean to upset you."

Allison went through the entire story again. The officer rushed to get it all down, then stopped. "So, you already hired a PI to look for your friend?"

"No, Nick was having dinner at our house. He was just hired by my brother, Scott Holt."

The officer nodded his approval. "Yeah, he's all right."

At that point, Sgt. Moore emerged from the condo. "Car's gone. More blood in the garage. Gotta call forensics. Ma'am, can you tell me what kind of car Miss Litton drives?"

"A maroon Kia. I'm not sure which year it was. Not too old." Allison bit her bottom lip. "Sorry, I can't be more help."

"No problem. We'll get the rest from the DMV," the sergeant said, then jerked his head toward the patrol car. Officer Wells took off to access the DMV from the onboard computer.

The sergeant frowned. "She have any enemies?"

"No. Meryl's well-liked by everyone."

"Get in a fight with anyone at work?"

"No, I said everyone *likes* her. She gets along with everyone, except one or two doctors who don't get along with any of the case managers."

Moore grunted. "You said she was pregnant. What about the baby's father?"

"She never talked about him. And no, I didn't pry. I figured when she was ready to talk about him, she would. She's only been in Nashville for four months."

"Where'd she come from?"

"South of Nashville. Columbia, maybe."

"What makes you think she's from Columbia?"

"She mentioned something in passing about the Mule Day Celebration. So, I just assumed..." Allison shrugged. Why couldn't she have been nosier? Okay, it wasn't her style to pry into her friend's personal business. She'd always believed Meryl would share her secrets when the time was right. But if she hadn't been so patient, she could've been more help to the authorities. "You can check her work records with Human Resources," she suggested. "But they're not open this time of night."

"Right. The detectives will look into it tomorrow. Just give me your home and work numbers. Vitelli, you too. Detectives ought to be rolling up soon. They'll need you to repeat what you know. You might remember something else."

Allison nodded. She gave the sergeant her contact numbers, and Nick did the same. "Best way to reach me," he said, "is my cell. I'm staying at my brother's place."

The sergeant nodded, then turned his head in the direction of a new siren. Forensics and an unmarked car both pulled into the complex. She recognized Scott's fiancée's SUV. Tess O'Malley had caught the case. Wonderful. A sense of relief surged through Allison. Tess would get the ball rolling. She'd find Meryl if anyone could.

Allison waited until the forensics team was briefed by Sgt. Moore. They donned latex gloves and paper boots before entering the condo. Tess and her partner repeated the process. He was burly and tall with a hint of five o'clock shadow, wearing a rumpled suit and a couple of coffee stains on his tie.

Tess came to Allison's side and gave her a hug. Keeping her tone low, Tess said, "Your brother's back home and pissed off at me for running out on him the minute he showed up with two more boxes of his stuff. Are you all right?"

Allison frowned before answering. "Not really. I'm scared. I think something really bad has happened to Meryl."

By this time, the other condo residents had gathered along the crime-scene-tape perimeter. Tess pulled Allison to the side. "Kozinsky's in charge so he's going to take your statements. I'm going to canvass the neighbors and see if anyone saw anything that can help us."

"Okay. Please do something. She's five months pregnant."

"Description?" Kozinsky asked with a growl.

"Tall—probably five-ten, blond hair, blue eyes. She's beautiful. And you can't even tell she's pregnant yet. Not unless you know."

"Have a picture?"

"Yeah. I took some pictures in the department at one of

our birthday parties. I'm sure she was there that day." She pulled her smartphone from her pocket. "They're on my phone, but I haven't printed any of them yet."

"Just email it to Detective O'Malley. The quicker, the better," the sergeant said.

"Use my official MNPD addy," Tess said, reading it off. "I'll put out the BOLO."

Allison keyed in Tess's email address. "A BOLO?"

"Be on the lookout," Nick said.

Allison scrolled through the photos, found a close-up of Meryl, then emailed it to Tess.

"Got it," Tess responded. "Now all I have to do is forward it to dispatch."

Grateful he'd come along, Allison turned to Nick. If she'd been alone, she would've freaked at the sight of blood and contaminated the crime scene all to hell. Despite their history, he wasn't such a bad guy. "If you don't mind running me home, I can come back in my own car. You don't have to hang around. Sorry I dragged you into this."

Nick shrugged. "No biggie. I still have to give my statement."

Allison shivered again and pulled Nick's jacket tighter around her shoulders, inhaling the smell of the leather and his woodsy aftershave.

"You all right? You're looking a little shaky to me. Not that I'm any kind of expert."

She smiled up into his steel-blue eyes and shivered again, this time from a sensation of warmth pooling in places where it had no business. Especially now. Her best friend was missing, perhaps dead, and here she was getting turned on by a man who just happened to have big muscles and killer eyes. "I'm okay. Thanks."

*

As soon as Nick could pull Allison away from the investigation, he bundled her into his Bronco and headed back to the Holt-Lackey residence. She was just a tiny thing, about five-two, and rocked to the core by what they'd found at her friend's condo. Dollars to doughnuts, the friend was dead. He'd found a hell of a lot of blood on the floor. And what looked like arterial spray on the living room walls and ceiling. Never a good sign.

But Scott's sister was tough, admirable in the face of all that'd happened. Not the kind of woman he was usually attracted to, though. He liked them tall and stacked...like his ex. Black hair, eyes like black olives.

A woman like Allison was all fire and sizzle, convinced she could take care of herself in any situation. Yeah, any situation she could overcome by using that smart mouth of hers. His jeans grew snug at the thought of her full lips on body parts best not mentioned. Not if he didn't want to embarrass himself.

"You're awfully quiet." She hugged the rat-dog in her arms and crooned nonsense to keep her quiet.

"Been married before, so I'm well-trained," he said, flashing a smirk. "Maybe you ought to buckle your seat belt."

She shot him a quick sideways glance, but she complied.

"The boss would never forgive me if something happened to his little sister." He wished he could shield her from the pain sure to come. The authorities would either find Meryl Litton or they wouldn't. But sooner or later, Allison was in for a world of hurt.

And he hated it. In fact, given their brief acquaintance, it was a shock to realize just how much he didn't want to see her hurt.

He pulled into a parking space in front of the large Craftsman bungalow. "Want me to come inside?"

Her hand on the door handle, Allison paused and turned

to him with a frown. "Yes. You can tell Scott what we found." She grabbed the dog and opened her door.

Despite himself, he smiled. Liked to boss folks around, yes, she did. "Sure thing, ma'am." He hauled his body from the Bronco. She was already running up the sidewalk. Full of energy...or adrenaline.

By the time he entered the house, Allison and the rat-dog were nowhere to be seen. He shrugged and walked into the den, where he found Scott and his brother watching a baseball game. A frowning Scott glared up at Nick. "Well...?"

"Nothing good, that's for sure. Blood all over the place." He paused. "And this yapping creature she assured me was a dog but looks more like a wiry-haired rat. By the way, it's now living at your house for the duration, or I miss my guess."

His friend emitted a feeble laugh. "Not the first creature Allie's brought home. Most likely won't be the last. She has an affinity for small creatures who can't take care of themselves."

"Nice hobby."

"Hobby?" Justin said. "Man, you have no idea. She's a crusader. Worse than a dog with a bone. She'll find her friend and see that whoever took her pays for it."

An uneasiness twisted through Nick's gut. A crusader? Images of tree huggers flooded his mind. He shook it off. Time to get back to business. "She's done all she can do by giving Meryl's photo to the police. She'd best back off and let them do their job. This is probably a murder we're talking about. No joke. If she interferes, she'll get in over her head pretty quick."

"When I need your advice, I'll ask for it, Nick Vitelli."

Behind him, Allison stood in the doorway, hands on her hips, her chin jutting.

Nick shook his head. "Not trying to tell you what to do.

It's just that none of us wants anything to happen to *you*—"
He broke off, knowing the implication of his words.

"Like it has to Meryl?" Her eyes were red, brimming with
unshed tears. "You think she's dead, don't you?"

"Can't rule out the possibility." Hell, this was going all
wrong. How could he protect Allison from the ugly truth
when he'd all but blurted it out?

Allison's eyes flashed. She closed the distance between
them and grabbed a fistful of his shirt with each hand. "You
hear me? She's not dead. Meryl is *not* dead."

An image of David and Goliath came to mind. This was
an awesome young woman, but she didn't understand what
she was dealing with. "So, what're you going to do?"

She took a deep breath and released his shirt. "Sorry, I
just got carried away. They have to keep looking for a live
person, not... Sh-she's having a baby. Just wait. I'm calling
the hospital... Maybe she's checked into Antepartum."

"Let the authorities handle it," Scott suggested from his
chair.

"No." Her sharp chin went up a notch. "I may not be a
detective or an ex-cop, but hospitals I know. Besides, her call
to me this afternoon was work related—I'm sure it was."

"And how do you know?" Nick asked. Scott was right.
Allison was a pit bull with a bone.

"Intuition. It's real." Allison drilled him with a glare.
"Don't you dare laugh."

Nick held up his hands in a gesture of surrender.
"Wouldn't think of it. We cops *know* things in our gut all the
time. Just another name for intuition."

"Then you know what I'm talking about. All I know is we
have to find her—and soon." She sank onto the couch. "Don't
you understand? I *have* to do something."

"Agreed." Agreed? Not really. But he couldn't bring
himself to dash her hopes. Then inspiration hit him. "Why

don't you print out flyers or set up one of those Facebook pages?" That would keep her busy and out of everyone's hair.

He turned to leave. "While you're working on those, I'll check back with the authorities."

"Not without me, you're not." She sprang from the couch and grabbed his forearm, her touch a jolt that set his senses to buzzing.

Nick frowned his displeasure at her tagging along. "I'll be back. Please...just work on that Facebook page. You can reach a lot more people." He peeled away her fingers, then headed for the door, but not before he received sympathetic glances from her two brothers. "Besides, don't you have to be at work early or something?"

She rushed after him but glanced over her shoulder, clearly torn between going with him and staying behind. "It's a weekend. I don't have weekend call for another six weeks."

"What about the rat-dog? Doesn't she need someone to see after her?"

"I cleaned Roxy up, and now she's asleep in Carrie's room. She's already agreed to look after her for me. You're not getting rid of me, so stop trying."

He gritted his teeth. Crusader? More like a pain in the ass. For every good quality she had—and she had several—there were two or more that grated on his last nerve.

After Allison was gone, Nick turned to Scott. "She's impossible, but you already know that."

"Yeah." Scott frowned, then said, "I know it's not what you hired on for, but I want you to keep her out of trouble until we know something definitive about her friend."

"You're assigning me to ride herd on your sister?"

"Yeah, that's your next assignment: keep her out of trouble. Gonna be the toughest one I'll ever give you. And you'll earn every penny of your salary."

"No shit." So now, the boss's youngest sister was his client for the duration.

Chapter Five

By the time Allison and her reluctant detective reached the condo's parking lot, a full moon rode high in a night sky awash with a sprinkling of stars. A wide area was still blocked off by crime-scene tape. Allison stepped out into the warm night air and took a deep breath. Her hands trembled as she spied her soon-to-be sister-in-law. Nick gave Allison a quick wave and headed over to talk to Tess's partner.

"It's a good thing you had those photos on your phone," Tess said. "There wasn't a single photo in her condo."

No pictures? Odd. Meryl was so pretty—why wouldn't she have photos of herself and family? Most people did. "Isn't it sort of strange?"

Tess nodded. "It's as if she didn't exist before moving to Nashville."

"What about her neighbors? Did they see or hear anything?" Allison held up her hands. "Sorry. I don't mean to ask you things you're not supposed to reveal. Forget I asked." Tears filled her eyes and blurred her vision. "Sorry, it's just that—"

Tess put her arms around Allison's shoulders. "She was your friend. Of course, you're upset."

Allison felt herself being led back to Nick's SUV. "I haven't known her all that long. But we had this crazy bond almost immediately as if we were sisters in another life or something. Sounds silly, I know, but—"

"That's how it happens sometimes." Tess glanced over her shoulder. "One of the neighbors heard your friend arguing with someone last night around ten. Said it sounded like a man. Is there anything at all you can tell me about the father of her baby?"

"No. In fact, when she called me before I left work, I was sure it was something hospital related."

"Her exact words?"

Allison closed her eyes and focused on Meryl's message. "'Something fishy' sticks with me."

"Think hard. Your friend's life depends on it."

"I'm trying." Frustration racked her. Why couldn't she remember more of Meryl's message? "Wait. I'm so stupid. The text is still in my phone."

She pulled her cell phone from her belt and accessed her messages. "Here we go. This is it." She handed the phone to Tess, who read it, then handed the cell back.

"Now tell me what you think she meant."

"I think she meant Dr. Morton Ivers. He's the kidney transplant program director. Meryl was the case manager for all transplant patients. He's a little man with a Napoleon complex. Obnoxious and arrogant. He and Meryl didn't get along—professionally, that is. Nothing personal between them, as far as I know. They've had more than one argument where Meryl had to take him aside and remind him to act like a professional."

"How'd he respond?"

"He was pissed off, but he backed down when he realized she wasn't going to put up with his unprofessional behavior. Still, it's a far reach to think he had anything to do with her disappearance."

"Something hinky going on at the hospital with the transplant program? Someone with money being moved up the list ahead of someone with less money or insurance?" Tess suggested.

"I'm not close enough to that department, but someone will have to cover her caseload until she's found. I'll volunteer and do some digging."

"Careful—"

One of the CSIs ran up. "Sorry, Detective. Just wanted you to know we found several sets of prints."

"Great. Get them entered into the database ASAP." Tess turned to Allison with a speculative look in her eye. "I know you said you didn't go in this evening, but have you ever?"

"Yes, of course. Take my prints now." She held out her hands. "And Nick's too. I know you need to eliminate us."

Tess nodded. "Hand me a scanner," she said to the forensics officer. He handed her the MC75 scanner. Tess turned back to Allison. "Be very careful in your snooping around. If someone at the hospital's responsible for Meryl's disappearance, you could get jammed up."

"If someone at the hospital has done something to Meryl, I'll..." She took a deep breath. "I'll turn them over to you. How's that?"

"Better. No private vengeance allowed on my watch."

Nick strolled over to Tess. "I didn't touch anything but the outer doorknob, but you need 'em anyway. Mine are on record with the Atlanta PD and here in Tennessee with my PI license."

"Never had mine taken, but I've seen it done on TV," Allison said and held out her hands for Tess. Funny, now they trembled more than they had earlier.

After their prints were scanned, Nick turned to Detective O'Malley. "Anything else we can do to assist?" Hell. He hated being on the outside of an investigation. His every instinct said the sooner they found the father of the baby, the better the chances were of Meryl being found. Alive or dead? His money was on dead.

O'Malley shot him a no-nonsense expression. "Just leave

it to us. I'll check with Parklane's Human Resource department first thing in the morning to get her work history. Might help to know where she used to work, who her friends were, and who the baby's father is."

"They'll be closed until Monday morning," Allison said. "But you can call the hospital operator and ask for the administrator-on-call. Maybe he can get someone from HR to pull her file before Monday."

O'Malley beamed as if she liked the idea of rousting someone from Administration to assist in her investigation. "Good idea. Now, you two need to go home, but if anything comes up..." O'Malley reached in her pocket. "Here's my card. Give me a call."

Nick took the card, and O'Malley headed back to the forensics techs. Allison glared at him. Guess she wanted custody of the card. Tough.

"Let's go." He glanced toward the SUV and hoped she wouldn't resist. Dark circles had appeared under her eyes, and signs of fatigue were evident in her body language as well as written across her pretty face. The temptation to put his arm around her surged through him, but he reined it in. No point in getting his face smacked.

Appearing as if she might break down and bawl any minute, she glanced over her shoulder in the direction her brother's fiancée had taken, then back at him. "Other than printing flyers and setting up the Facebook page, there's nothing else I can do tonight, is there?"

"Right. Facebook, then you need to get some rest. You'll be fresher in the morning and maybe you'll come across something that'll help the LEOs—"

Allison's gaze widened as she raised an eyebrow. "The what?"

"Law enforcement officers. Sorry, it's cop-speak." He shrugged. How he missed being on the job. No chance in hell of being hired by Metro. Not with his ex being the new chief's wife.

"Don't patronize me, Vitelli. I'm not going to find anything to help the...LEOs tomorrow whether I get any sleep tonight or not. My friend is m-missing." She took a breath, and her body started shaking like a leaf in a windstorm.

Aw, crap. She was gonna cry. Nick slung his arm around her shoulders. "It's gonna be all right." Not that he believed one word of it. But something deep inside wouldn't allow him to dash all her hopes.

Hell. Maybe he was wrong. Miracles had happened before. Could happen again.

What he didn't expect was the vast welling of tenderness choking off his breath. In all his years on the job, he'd seen at least a hundred women cry over their missing loved ones, but Allison's tears touched him on some deep, gut-wrenching level.

And getting sucked in by a pair of dark brown eyes was the last thing in the world he needed. Scott's sister was off-limits.

She turned and buried her face in his chest and sobbed. She, sure as hell, wasn't making it easy. He patted her back much as he used to after feeding his infant son a bottle.

She sniffed, wiped away her tears, and glared up at him. "Trying to console me or burp me?"

"Aw, come on, kiddo, give me a break." Jeez. Had he called her kiddo? Really? "I don't know what the hell I'm doing. *You* need some rest. Now get in the Bronco."

"You like ordering people around, don't you?" Another sniff.

"When someone needs it as much as you do, I'm guilty." He waited for her angry retort, but she must've decided to let his comment pass. "Besides, I can't tell you what

O'Malley's partner told me with everyone around."

Interest sparked in Allison's gaze. "I'm listening."

He zipped his lip. "Not another word until you park your fanny in the Bronco."

"Fine." Another glare in his direction, but at least she'd quit crying. Couldn't handle her tears. Only one other woman's tears had affected him like Allison's. His mom—how she'd cried each time after his father beat her black and blue...until Nick had grown big enough, stepped in, and given his father the whaling of his life. No, he'd never laid a hand on his ex, not even when he'd caught her cheating with his captain.

Chapter Six

Allison sat silent and drummed her fingers against her thigh while Nick backed from the condo parking lot and nosed the SUV onto the street. "Well? What did Tess's partner tell you?"

Nick glanced in her direction. Even in the minimal light inside the SUV, his pale blue eyes glowed like a wolf's caught in the passing headlights of a car. "They already have a line on someone who could be her ex. Your friend's next-door neighbor reported hearing a loud argument last night. Apparently. the guy slammed the door when he left. So, she went to the window and checked his truck...and his license tags before he drove away. They're already checking him out with the DMV."

"Good, but that doesn't mean anything if no one saw him today or this afternoon."

"It's a no-brainer. It's always the husband or a boyfriend."

"Really?" Why on earth were men so quick to hurt the ones they were supposed to protect? Surely Meryl's ex wouldn't want to hurt his child. Then the specter of recent events flooded her mind.

"Yes, really. Look at that woman in California. Her husband killed her, and her baby was viable." He turned onto Richland. "I don't pretend to understand what drives a man to such lengths. I remember when my ex was expecting our son, she was moody and elated by turns, but I would never have dreamed of hurting her or the baby."

"No. I knew you were right before the 'really' left my

mouth. I guess I want to believe every father feels the way you do."

"That's the ideal—don't get me wrong—I wasn't an ideal husband. I worked long hours in Narco, did a lot of undercover. It didn't make for a happy marriage."

His tone was full of regret. Did he still love his ex? Not that it was any of her business.

"But you moved back to Nashville to be close to your son."

He flashed her a genuine smile. "Yeah. Ben's a great kid. You ought to see him in karate class. Those four- to six-year-olds are terminally cute." He slowed the Bronco and stopped. No parking space in front of Allison's house. "I'll let you out here. I need to get on home before my brother sends out a posse."

"Thanks, Nick." She reached over and touched his forearm. He started at her touch, then shot her a smile. A giddy sensation coursed through her brain. "You've been great. I don't think I could've gotten through all this without you." Oh no. How mushy did she sound? Next, he'd think she was hitting on him.

"Hmph." He nodded. "Thought you were about to clean my clock a couple of times."

"I was tempted a *couple* of times." She hesitated, not wanting to leave his warm presence. Nick's masculine scent on his leather jacket tickled her nose. She shrugged off the jacket. "Here. I didn't mean to keep it. Thank you." She opened the car door and—

"Hold on, Allie. Tomorrow, you keep your nose out of the case. Detective O'Malley was right. Let them handle it."

She took a deep breath. "You just ruined all the goodwill you had going with me. Don't tell me what to do. For the record, I hate it. Just because I'm next to the youngest doesn't mean everyone can tell me what I'm supposed to do or not. The hospital is where the answer lies, and that's *my* territory. You can pursue the ex-husband angle all you like, but—"

"All right." His eyes flashed with reflections from the streetlights. "I just don't want anything to happen to you. If you're right—and that would mean I'm wrong, which I personally can't conceive—then poking your nose into someone's business is dangerous. The last thing I need is my boss's sister getting hurt, or worse, on my watch." He crossed his arms over his chest while the motor idled in the background.

"Rest easy, Vitelli, I'll be careful. Your job's secure." She shoved the passenger door back and slid down to the sidewalk. What an aggravating man. All right, he was a hottie, but she didn't have time for all that. Never had. There were more important things on her agenda. Even though she wasn't scheduled to work, a little visit to the hospital was in order. If she could get into Meryl's computer, she might find something useful. Or at least find something in her coworker's cubicle that might give a hint about the reason behind her call.

Cops, or ex-cops, in Nick's case, always looked for the most obvious suspect. In her mind, it was more than Meryl's ex-husband coming to town. Much more.

"G'night," Nick called after her.

Without turning, she waved over her shoulder. "Night." Nick gunned the motor and then roared away. "Bet the neighbors liked that."

Nick Vitelli was a puzzle of sorts. Arrogant and stubborn, but basically one of the good guys—like her brothers. Still, neither of her brothers made her feel giddy like Nick, which, come to think of it, was definitely a good thing.

But how far off track could she get? Meryl was missing, and Nick Vitelli was a gigantic distraction. A little more focus was in order. And hitting Facebook was first on her agenda.

Early Saturday morning Allison eased into Case Management and slid into the chair in her personal cubicle. She dialed into her voice mail, checking for any new messages over the weekend. Now if she could just figure out her friend's PIN number, she could access Meryl's messages too.

She tried her friend's date of birth, her home phone number, and her cell number. Nothing. One more wrong attempt would lock her out of the system. Think. What about the baby's due date? Meryl was due in December, but the date? Was it the fifteenth or the sixteenth?

She entered the fifteenth, then hit the pound sign.

Bingo.

No unheard messages, but there were three messages still in her voice mail. The first was a routine request for a home health setup. No big deal.

The second was from a perturbed-sounding Dr. Ivers, who demanded she come to his office at one to discuss the new transplant critical care path. Ivers was a tyrant who felt his patients required individualized care and didn't fall into any of the hospital disease management paths. True and untrue. Of course, every patient was individual, but most transplant patients required the same regimen of meds and care as long as their progress was normal.

Basically, he didn't want to spend the time or effort required to develop an appropriate care path and resented the hospital's and the case manager's attempts to do so.

The third call was from a "Tom," and he wasn't a happy camper either, but his call was more personal along the lines of, "Sorry, I got so pissed off last night. I've just missed you so much since you ran away. And then to find out you're having my kid. Why'd you wanna run away anyway? I know we can make it. Besides, I've got a good gig here in Nashville. Just wanted you to know I'll come over to your place and wait for you to get home."

Allison played it four times and scribbled the message word for word. She'd have to turn her info over to the police, but at least it was a start, even if it did sound like Nick was right about the husband or the boyfriend being responsible, after all.

She reached for the phone and called Tess's cell.

Her future sister-in-law answered with a wide yawn. "Geez, Louise, what time is it?"

"Six."

"Just got to bed an hour ago. Whatcha got?"

After Allison related the gist of Meryl's voice mails, Tess thanked her and said she was going back to bed for another hour at least.

"Sorry. Guess I should've known you were out most of the night with this."

"Not a problem. Thanks. Doesn't look good for her ex, does it?"

"No. I guess the typical suspect is usually the one. Sorry 'bout the early call." Allison broke the connection. Nick and Tess were right. Let the authorities handle it.

On the other hand, it wouldn't hurt to check with Ivers's office staff to see if Meryl ever made it to his office.

Allison walked through the Opryland-on-steroids hospital lobby to the pair of elevators that would take her up to the physicians' offices. Most of the offices were closed on Saturday, not to mention at six-ten in the morning. You never knew who might be around, though.

The second floor, where Ivers's office was located, circled the hospital and the physician offices sides. Handy. Some employees used the large circular hallway to exercise at lunch or on breaks. If anyone saw her, that was what she'd pretend she was doing.

So, arms swinging and feet moving at a good walker's pace, she circled the second floor once. On her second trip, she slowed her pace as she neared the physician's office. The door opened, and a tall, slender blonde wearing a lab coat emerged.

Allison's heart jacked into V-Tach range. "Meryl! I've been so worried. What's going on? Where've you been?"

Chapter Seven

The tall blonde turned. "What?"

Close, but it wasn't Meryl. *H. Bane, RN* was embroidered in blue thread across the pocket of the blonde's white lab coat.

"I-I'm sorry. I thought you were my friend. She's missing. Do you know her? Meryl Litton?"

"The transplant case manager, right?"

"Yes."

"Sorry. Haven't seen her." The blonde shrugged and continued down the hall.

"Wait!"

The blond nurse stopped and glared over her shoulder, making it clear she had better things to do. "What?"

"I wondered if you saw her yesterday. She was supposed to meet Dr. Ivers in his office."

"I don't even work for Dr. Ivers."

"Then what were you doing just coming out of his office?"

Bane's face blushed a bright pink. "None of your business. I already said I haven't seen your friend. Let it go."

"I get it." And she did. Well, well, was Bane playing a game of hide-the-tongue-depressor with the good doctor? And Allison's suspicions were quickly confirmed. Ivers himself emerged from his private office entrance and made tracks for the rear elevator.

"Dr. Ivers. Wait, please. I need to ask you some questions." Allison brushed by Blondie Bane and ran to catch up with him at the elevator.

He was dark-haired, with gray threading at his temples. Brown eyes on the piggy side. Short, stout, and pompous on a good day. Today wasn't one of his good days. He glanced at his watch, refused to meet her gaze. "What's this about? Can't you see I'm busy?"

"Yeah. I saw how busy you were, but I don't care. Meryl Litton is missing, and she was supposed to meet you in your office yesterday afternoon. She hasn't been seen since."

His dark, beady eyes narrowed. "She never showed up. Most unprofessional. I have a good mind to report her," he said and dropped his gaze to the right.

Liar. Liar.

"Like it'll matter if something's happened to her." How Meryl managed to accomplish anything while working with a jerk like Ivers, Allison had no clue. She held back a growl and headed in the opposite direction.

"You would be advised to keep your nose out of matters which don't concern you," he called after her.

"Guess who just moved to the top of *my* suspect list," she muttered. Just wait until Nick heard all about it. He might have to reconfigure his suspect list too.

Nick opened one eye, then the other. Was that his cell phone? What the hell time was it anyway? He sat up on the sofa bed and rubbed his lower back. Dang, he'd better find a new apartment soon, or he'd be filing for disability.

Ring.

Could just let it to go voice mail, but no, it might be something wrong with his son, Ben. He grappled and found the cell, swallowed, and managed a raspy, "Hello."

"Let's meet for breakfast. I have lots to tell you."

"Allie?" He gave a mental groan. "Do you know what time it is?"

"Sure. It's a little after six. Don't you have a watch?"

This time he let the groan escape. "It's Saturday. And you're awake and giving me attitude already."

"Awake? I'm at the hospital, and I have news. Get dressed and meet me at Elliston Place. You know where I mean?"

To locals, Elliston Place meant the Soda Shop. "Yeah. I live just down the street. Give me time to shower."

"Will do," was her too cheerful reply. Man, who could carry on like that this early in the morning?

Allison sat in a booth in the front of the Soda Shop. The place could be called Retro except it hadn't changed one iota since she could remember. Same cracked red-plastic-covered booths. Little jukeboxes at each table—of course, they didn't work any longer. She glanced at her watch. Nick ought to be here soon. She sipped her coffee, then swallowed. Her stomach growled from the smell of frying bacon. She could even hear it sizzling in the kitchen. Onions for the hash browns. Mm.

The door opened. Nick strode inside, wearing a blue T-shirt and jeans. He slid into the booth and sat across from her. He brushed back his shower-dampened hair. When wet, his hair possessed a light wave, and it was an inch or two longer than he'd have been allowed to wear it on the job. His brown scruff of a beard served to enhance his just-crawled-out-of-bed appeal.

"Mornin'," he growled, but his expression changed as soon as a waitress brought him a cup of coffee. "Thanks," he told her. "You just saved my life"—he nodded at Allison—"and hers too."

The waitress took their breakfast orders, then left them alone. Nick stared at Allison through heavy-lidded eyes. "What on earth was so important you had to wake me up on a Saturday morning at six o'clock?"

"It was after six."

"Excuse *me*. My eyes weren't open. I might've missed a few seconds."

"If you require so much sleep, I don't see how you'll ever be a successful PI."

He rolled his eyes. "Just *tell* me. The caffeine hasn't hit my brain yet, so you're still in danger."

"Yeah, right. I'm so scared I'm shaking in my boots." She held up her hands and shook them. "See? Now, enough silliness. I managed to log into Meryl's voice mail and take off her last messages. Do you want to hear or not?"

"Sure." He took a long gulp of coffee and looked around for the waitress. Catching her eye, he pointed at his cup for a refill.

Allison glared, drumming her fingers on the table. She waited until his coffee was replenished and the waitress had left them. She said, "*Three* messages. One was routine. The second was more interesting. Dr. Ivers—he's the transplant director—was irate and demanding she come over to his office to discuss a critical care path."

"A what?"

"Not important what it is—it's a hospital deal. What I find significant is he says she never showed up."

"What?" Nick's gaze widened. "You talked to this doctor already?"

"Well, yes, as a matter of fact, I have. Some doctors make rounds early so they can get to the golf course. They don't sleep in, like some private investigators I could mention."

His gaze narrowed. His chest rose with a deep breath.

"Just kidding." Then in a rush of words, she related how she'd met the blond nurse and Ivers in the hall and their apparent early Saturday morning hookup.

"You think that's what was going on?"

She batted her lashes. "I'm sure of it. I have a feel for *those* kinds of things."

His head moved back and forth slightly as if losing patience with her. "Sure, ya do. Go on. Tell me about the third."

"Well, *you'll* like this one. It was her ex. He was all apologetic about getting angry the night before and why hadn't she told him about the baby. Get this, he said he was going to go over to her place and wait for her to get home."

Nick leaned back and gave her a knowing expression. "Told you. It's always the husband, whether current or ex. Forget about the doctor. It's nothing more than office hanky-panky. Now hold on a minute. Did any of the neighbors report seeing her ex or his truck on Friday?"

Allison shook her head. "Not as far as I overheard last night, but I'll need to re-interview them myself. If the police don't locate this guy soon... Hell, he's probably already skipped town."

"You're not—" Almost too late he remembered how she hated to be told anything. "But dammit, you ought to leave the re-interviewing to the LEOs," he suggested, hoping she wouldn't get in one of her moods again.

"Here ya go, folks." The waitress set their breakfast plates on the table and simpered at Nick. "Enjoy."

"Thank you, ma'am. Sure looks good."

Vitelli smiled at the waitress. Choosing to ignore his remark about leaving the work to the LEOs, Allison gave a little snort. "Aren't you Mister Butter Won't Melt in My Mouth? I wouldn't mind one of those smiles." Oh no. Had she said that out loud?

"*You* woke me up and brought me a headache. She brought me caffeine and food. Which one do you think deserves it?"

"A headache, am I?" She lifted her shoulders in a casual

shrug. "Well, maybe I am when I go off on a tangent."

"I can't say Scott didn't warn me," he said with a lazy grin and a glint of returning good humor in his sky-blue eyes.

His piercing gaze turned her insides to mush. "I'm sure he did." Allison swallowed her confusion, picked up a biscuit, halved it, then spread butter and strawberry preserves on each half. The smell of bacon, eggs, and hash browns wafting from her plate spoke to her Southern-fried soul. No, they weren't good for her heart, but once in awhile...

A man like Nick Vitelli wasn't good for her heart either, even if her heart rate picked up every time she was near him. All in all, he was the total package. Strong. Intelligent. Sexy. Even if more than a tad stubborn and irritating at times.

By seven, the Soda Shop had filled with the morning breakfast crowd. Nick looked around and gestured for another refill. After eating a breakfast loaded with all the bad stuff that tasted so freaking good and his brain was properly caffeinated, he could think. Maybe even tolerate the woman sitting across the table.

It wasn't that Allison wasn't attractive. Hell, with curly reddish-blond hair and brown eyes sparkling with humor and a sugar sprinkle of freckles across her elegant nose, she was cute as a new puppy. Their personalities just clashed—that was the problem.

But her lips. Whoa. She had a tiny smear of strawberry preserves on her bottom lip. Could he resist? Hell, no.

He reached across and swiped the smear off her soft lower lip with his thumb. Without thinking, he put his thumb in his mouth and sucked off the jelly.

Her gaze widened, and her jaw dropped. "Ah." Her neck and cheeks flushed a pretty pink.

What must she be thinking? He never meant to touch her, much less her soft lips. But he'd wanted to touch her. Oh yeah. But he shouldn't. Technically, she was his client. And his employer's little sis.

"Sorry. I'm so used to wiping my son's mouth like that. I wasn't thinking."

"No problem." She snatched up a napkin and scrubbed her lower lip. "Did I get it all?"

"No, *I* did." Her gaze widened at his words. Good. Her slight confusion touched and pleased him.

Man. He couldn't keep flirting with his boss's sister. When he'd stalked out of divorce court, hadn't he sworn off relationships? Yeah, Eva had walked away with his son and the house. And a month after the divorce was final, she'd married his captain.

"What's the matter, Nick? Where'd you go?"

He shrugged and cut his gaze to see her concerned expression. "No place I'm likely to go again." He glanced at his watch. "Look, I have to meet a client at ten, then I get to see my son and take him to a ball game. Later this evening, after the game, we'll come by—assuming it's okay if I bring him along—and get with Justin. We'll run a background check on this Tom guy."

"The more, the merrier." She gave him a satisfied smile. "It's probably a good thing I woke you up early."

"Yeah. I'm just not a morning person. Once I have my coffee," he said with a wry expression, "I'm half-human."

Allison wrinkled her nose. "That might be up for some interpretation."

"Yeah." He motioned for the check, and the waitress brought it over. "Thanks." He left a tip on the table and stood. "Hate to run. Don't want to disappoint my kid."

Elbows on the table and fingers laced together, she scowled up at him. "You didn't have to grab the check. I'm perfectly capable of paying for our breakfast. Breakfast was *my* idea, after all."

"No problem. Technically, you're my client. I'll expense it."

"So...you're taking my case...officially?"

He nodded. "Pro bono too, since you're part of the family." Luckily, he was on salary.

"Is that a problem?"

"No, just didn't expect my first real client to be the boss's little sister." He leaned in, lowering his tone. "You remember, the cute little gal who flashed her boobs at me at the old swimming hole."

As he expected, she started to rise from the booth. He shot her a mischievous smile, delaying her flight. "The old swimming hole? That was the Brady's pool. And *I* didn't flash you. I lost my top. I believe *that* would qualify as an accident."

"Yeah. But your cheeks get so pink, I couldn't resist."

"Jerk."

"So, I've been told, once or twice."

She glared, then her expression softened, and a tiny smile pulled at the corner of her luscious lips. "I'm sure you have. Thank you for taking my case, even if I am the boss's sister and you didn't have much choice."

"My pleasure. Besides, it'll give me even more pleasure, 'cause I'm gonna prove you're wrong about there being a hospital connection."

"Sounds like a challenge." She reached for her purse and slid from the booth. "We'll see who's right and who's wrong." Then a cloud of uncertainty crossed over her face. "It really doesn't matter which one of us is right. What matters is we find Meryl before..." She faltered, as if afraid to verbalize her fears.

Nick nodded. Fears once voiced had to be faced. Sooner

or later, Meryl Litton would be found. More than likely it was already too late to save her or her unborn child.

Allison looked up at him with the sheen of unshed tears in her eyes; her bottom lip trembled. "It's not going to be good, is it?"

He shut his for a second, then opened them and met her direct, if fearful, gaze. "No."

Eager to get Allison outside in the fresh air and away from the curious onlookers, he scooped her in one arm, pulling her close to his side. "Come on." As they brushed by the cashier's counter, he left the check and a twenty. "Keep the change."

He opened the door and allowed her to exit.

Allison sniffed. "Guess you'll expense that too?"

"Not all of it. Just wanted to get you outside. Thought you needed some fresh air."

"I'm all right. I think about the baby she was going to have, and it just feels like little pieces of my heart are ready to crumble away." She sniffed again. "She would've made a wonderful mother."

They ambled down the sidewalk. He hoped Allison would never have to see some of the things he'd seen. The darkest side of mankind. Though how the hell anyone who was supposed to be a member of the human race could do some of the things he'd seen, he'd never know.

Depravity. A mere word couldn't begin to describe the bloodied, desecrated, and rotted remains found in woods, buried under logs, eaten by insects. The children who were taken by predators... They were the worst. He hoped there was a special place in hell for child predators.

He shuddered.

"Nick?" Allison had stopped and stood staring at him, her gaze wide with concern. "Are you all right?"

Snap out of it, man. "Yeah, sure. Where's your car?"

She nodded to the silver Camry. "This one. Need a lift back to your apartment?"

Not willing to inflict his mood of gloom and doom on her any further, he shook his head. "It's not far. Coupla blocks from here."

"Okay. Thanks for breakfast and...everything." She walked around to unlock her car door.

"I'll see you later—when I see Justin."

He nodded. Would she go back to the hospital and do more snooping? "Please. Just go home and stay out of trouble till then."

Planting her feet wide apart, she set her hands on her hips. "Is that an order?"

"*I'm* the detective. *You're* the client. I detect. You *wait* for my intel."

"Do you really think this is how it's going to be?"

"This is how I *know* it's gonna be." Without another word, he took off down the street toward his apartment. Dammit. Why couldn't she take a backseat and keep her freckled nose out of the detecting side of things? There was enough pain ahead for her as it was. The last thing he needed was her digging into something at the hospital.

What if she was right and there was a hospital connection to her friend's disappearance? If Allison got in someone's way, she was risking harm or worse. She was taking a hell of a chance.

Allison watched Nick make tracks down Elliston Place. What a man of contradictions. One minute smart, the next smart-ass. Then a shift so tender and understanding, followed by a dark, brooding distance she couldn't seem to bridge. Where had he gone? And what had taken him there?

And yet, when questioned, he'd snapped back to the

present with ease as if nothing were wrong. But clearly, there was.

As for his order to go home and wait...

Nope. Not gonna happen.

She got into the Camry and started the engine, checked her side mirror, and darted out onto Elliston Place, then made a sharp left U-turn and a right down Twenty-second.

Surveillance tapes. There were bound to be some. Maybe she could get one of the guards to let her have a peek.

She whipped into the underground parking garage and parked. The garage was quiet and a bit lonely on a Saturday before the steady rush of visitors.

Determined, she headed straight to the guard station and tapped on the two-way glass. Maybe Del would be on duty today. He was all of twenty years old and had a bit of a crush on her.

The door opened. No such luck.

She glanced at the name tag. *George.* She smiled at the gray-headed man who made no pretense of being happy to see her.

"Hi, George. I was wondering if you'd heard about my friend Meryl who disappeared yesterday. There might be some surveillance footage showing when she left and who she was with—that sort of thing."

He scowled down at her over his bulbous red nose. "Police already have the tapes. No point in you nosing around." His hand was on the door, ready to slam it in her face.

Still, she had to try. "She's my friend. I just want to help."

"Told ya. P'lice already got the tapes. Go help them."

She held back an indignant snort. "Thanks for nothing," she said as sweetly as if he'd been a perfect gentleman.

Okay. New plan. If the police had the tapes, it meant Tess had access to them. Time to play the future-sister-in-law card.

Allison stopped at Starbucks and bought Tess's favorite brew. Then she texted Tess and asked for a private meeting. Tess agreed and texted she'd meet Allison in front of the CJC in five minutes.

Five was pushing it, but she managed to find a parking spot and sprinted to the front of the CJC without spilling a single drop of coffee. Tess appeared right on time. The redheaded detective wore a pale lime-green pantsuit with an ivory camisole. Sensible but colorful lime flats completed the stylish ensemble. Somehow Tess always managed to look like a fashion model even without stilettos.

Tess perched on the side of a concrete planter, her gaze focusing on the coffee. "I hope that's mine."

"Of course." She handed Tess the tall cup of coffee. "I thought it might help. Not that it constitutes a bribe or anything."

"Of course not." Tess gulped down a long swig, then sighed. "I don't have anything new on your friend."

Allison sucked in a deep breath, then forged ahead. "What about the surveillance tapes from the hospital? I have it on good authority you already have those. Is there any chance I could see them? I could help identify anyone who left around the same time she did."

Tess tilted her head and studied Allison for a second. "Okay." Her tone was hesitant. "Not a bad idea, but we're certain she was taken from her condo, not the hospital."

"Right. But someone might've followed her from the hospital or the parking garage."

"Sure, it's possible." Again, the hesitation. What was Tess trying not to say?

"I forgot to tell you what I did this morning." Allison bit her lip. "I took messages off her voice mail. One from—"

"From her ex—yeah. Administration provided us with a

transcript this morning. We're looking at him real hard."

"Oh? Found him yet?" Maybe Nick was right. It was her ex. But would he have killed his own baby?

A glint of caginess flickered in Tess's eyes. "We have a lead or two."

"Nick and I sort of disagree. He thinks it's her ex too, but something tells me there's a hospital connection."

Tess shifted uncomfortably on the concrete planter. "We're going to do our best to find your friend, but you have to know there was a lot of blood at the scene. It doesn't look good."

The blood. Like she could forget the bit she'd seen, but Nick hadn't let her inside to see the rest. Chills like icebergs slid up and down Allison's spine. Hell, even her ears were cold. And it had to be at least ninety degrees in the shade. "I-I know. I mean, intellectually I know it, but I can't help hoping."

Tess's gaze shuttered. "You have to know a leading cause of death among pregnant women is homicide."

Allison blinked back the tears. Her stomach roiled. She bit back the bitterness rising in her throat.

So much for hope.

"I'm sorry. But I've seen this same scenario too many times."

"Not ever?" Her voice cracked...much like her heart.

Tess set her cup on the edge of the planter and stood. "The blood type matches Meryl's. DNA will take another day or so. That means there's a ninety-nine percent chance she's already dead and the baby daddy did it."

Images of Meryl rubbing her belly and planning the baby's nursery flooded Allison's mind. "No! Please don't say things like that."

"I'm sorry, hon. It's the horrible truth." Snagging her coffee with one hand, Tess put an arm around Allison's shoulder. "Come on. Let's go up and have a look at those tapes."

Allison followed Tess into the small room which housed several computers and all sorts of complicated-looking equipment. She couldn't begin to imagine what all of it did.

Tess motioned for her to have a seat. "Ready?"

"Yeah." Allison hesitated. Was she ready to see the last evidence of Meryl alive? Sure. But was she ready to accept, as a fact, Meryl and her baby were dead? Hell, no.

"The tape's already cued to the footage we found of Meryl. Here she is walking to her car, getting in, and leaving the parking garage." Tess fast-forwarded the tape. "Look at the time stamp. There aren't any other cars for another four-point five minutes."

Tess removed the tape and inserted another. "Skip to footage from one of the exterior cameras. She heads up Patterson Street toward the park. This is the last we can see of her."

"Wait." Allison pointed at the screen. "What about this car? It pulled out from the front of the outpatient center. Like he was waiting for her. Can you get a close-up on the plate?"

Businesslike as ever, Tess shook her head. "Nah. Too far away."

"But on *CSI*, they just do something. They zero in on the plate and make it clearer."

"This isn't *CSI*, hon. We've already tried. The exterior cameras don't have that kind of resolution."

Frustration knotted her stomach into a tight fist. "But it was a dark SUV, one of those big ones, maybe a Land Rover, right?"

"Yeah. And before you suggest it, there are several

thousand dark SUVs registered in Metropolitan Nashville, which doesn't include the surrounding counties. Lots of footwork and man-hours just to chase down a car that probably didn't have anything to do with Meryl's disappearance. Think about it. If someone was watching for her, they would've been closer."

"I guess." Why did reality have to be so difficult? TV shows made it look easy.

Chapter Eight

As irksome as Nick found seeing his ex in her fine new Brentwood digs, he treasured his visits with his son much more. He wasn't the kind of man who could forget he had a kid just because the kid's mother was married to someone else. He paid his child support as scheduled, and on visitation days, he picked up Ben on time. No way would he give his ex a reason to go whining to a judge about his being a no-good father.

He drove up the long, winding drive to his ex's Brentwood house. Judging from the size of the house and grounds, Metro must pay their police chief well. More than Nick could earn in three years on the job.

No matter. Ben would be glad to see him.

He parked the Bronco, turned off the motor, and exited. He walked up the slate walkway and onto the porch. He rang the bell and waited.

Nothing.

He rang it again.

The door opened. Finally. His ex-wife stood staring at him as if he were a stranger. But it was just her way. She'd just as soon forget she'd ever been married to a lowly undercover cop.

"Eva." He kept his tone even. Pissing her off wouldn't help matters.

"You're late."

He checked his watch and shrugged. "Three minutes isn't late. Nashville traffic's almost as bad as Atlanta's."

A slight twitching lift of her eyebrows was her singular response. "One moment. Ben will be down." Her tone was full of contempt and dismissiveness. She shut the door in his face and left him standing.

Again, just her way of putting him in his place. The way she'd been since moving up her warped version of the career ladder and marrying his police captain.

He'd first noticed her high-handed manner after the divorce. Now that she and her captain-now-chief-of-police husband had moved to Music City, her manner hadn't improved. No one was supposed to remember she was Eva Luanne Staples who grew up in Inglewood on the wrong side of the river.

None of it mattered now. Only Ben.

The door whipped open again, and his son launched into Nick's arms. "Daddy!"

He swung his boy around in a big hug. "Hey, buddy. How's it going?"

"Bring him home in time to get ready for church," Eva said.

He halted the exuberant swing and gazed into Eva's dead black eyes. "Don't I always have him home on time?"

"See you do." She shut the door again.

"You ready for that Sounds game, fella?"

"Yeah. Oops. Mama says I shouldn't say things like 'yeah.' It's common," his son said, imitating his mother's uppity tone with perfect precision. "I'm supposed to say, 'yes, sir.' "

As much as he wanted to tell his son to talk however he wanted, he wouldn't undercut her behind her back. "Your mom's right. Manners are important."

"Must be 'cause she's always talking about 'em."

"It's okay. Moms are like that. It's up to us guys to learn manners so we can get on in the world."

"Your mom too?"

"Ye—" He hesitated. "Yes. Your Grandma Alice was always preaching about manners to all of us boys." Nick opened the rear car door, helped his son hop in, then adjusted the child safety seat.

"Did it work? Did'ja get along?"

Nick reached over and ruffled Ben's hair. "I like to think so."

Not that his ex would agree.

Allison pulled into the alley behind the house, parked, then entered the house through the French doors off the deck. Wearing cutoff jeans and a halter top, Tamsyn stood at the kitchen counter, eating a piece of cold pizza. An uncapped two-liter bottle of Diet Coke was at her elbow. No glass in evidence.

"Great breakfast, Tam."

"Can't beat it. Caffeine, carbs, and fat. What more could I want?" Tamsyn's dark eyes shone with mischief. She swung her long black hair over her shoulder, then, hefting the bottle, she took a long swallow.

"Germs. Or don't you care if we all get sick?" She shivered, knowing her sister did it to annoy Allison's always-a-nurse sensibilities.

"My mark plied me with enough alcohol last night to sink the *Titanic*. I couldn't possibly have a germ left." Tamsyn's clients were women wishing to determine whether their significant others would stray when presented with the *opportunity* in the form of one Tamsyn Holt.

"Be glad all you have to worry about is—" Allison's shoulders started shaking, and sobs erupted like waves of lava. Her knees weakened, but Tamsyn's quick arm around Allison's waist kept her from collapsing. Tears streamed down her cheeks, blurring her surroundings.

"Aw, honey. They'll find her." Her stepsister nudged her toward the dining room, then eased her into the nearest chair.

"Tess"—she gave a hiccup—"says it's already too late."

A renewed determination surged through Allison in a flurry of emotions. She shook off Tamsyn's comforting hand. "My caterwauling is getting nowhere fast. I don't care what Tess says. I won't give up on Meryl."

"That's the spirit."

"We need posters. Spread 'em all over the neighborhood. Hospital administration needs to get off their asses and offer a big reward. She doesn't have any family, so we have to be her family."

"What do you want me to do?"

"I'm going to start with the administrator-on-call. It may take more than one call if the admin gives me the runaround. Why don't you take the photo I put up on the Facebook page I created last night and print off some flyers? We can take them around the neighborhood."

"Right. It'll be better if I print a copy and take it to the FedEx store. I can make more copies quicker than our printer can print them."

"—and we can post them everywhere," Allison finished.

"I'll call Rick while I'm at FedEx. He'll give us a hand."

Rick was Tamsyn's current friend with benefits. Allison nodded and gave Tamsyn the Facebook web address. Her sister sat at the kitchen laptop and with a few keystrokes, pulled together a flyer and then printed it. "How's this, Allie?"

Allison nodded her approval. The flyer contained Meryl's color photo and her description, as well as instructions to call the police with any information. "Thanks, sis." She swallowed hard. "You did a great job."

"All right. I'm off." Tamsyn grabbed her tote bag and headed for the door. Now that a plan was in place, Allison's head cleared, and her heart seemed to start beating again.

She took a deep breath.

Okay, time to beard the lions of administration.

A frustrating five minutes later, Allison was ready to grit her teeth.

"Miss Lackey, I'm the administrator-on-call. I can't authorize a reward and a public announcement at the drop of a hat. I have to go through channels."

"Meanwhile, one of your employees is in danger, and you're going to Mickey Mouse around and quote from the P&P Manual about 'channels'?" Rage blossomed in her chest, but she tamped it down. A firestorm might be needed, but a little bad publicity might do even more if she could keep her cool long enough.

She concentrated on keeping her tone low and controlled. "Well, that's truly unfortunate, because my next phone call is to Felicity Pace at KNN Headline News. This is exactly the kind of case she likes to feature on her show. No doubt she'll be *very* interested to know how a corporation with millions of dollars in revenue refused to offer a reward for one of its employees."

"Now, Miss Lackey. Such an action would be rash. I'm sure we can arrange a reward."

"An initial twenty-five thousand ought to be enough to sweeten the pot a bit. Along with a televised PR release *this afternoon*? Otherwise..."

She could just imagine he was counting to ten—maybe twenty—before he responded.

"Yes. I'll set it up now...if you'll get off the phone." The administrator's exasperated tone left no question he was at his wit's end.

And close to hanging up on her.

But she wasn't through. No indeed. "What time do you think it'll be aired? Maybe they could do a 'breaking news' thing. There's nothing on this afternoon anyway except a ball game or a golf tournament. Yeah, that would be good. No point in waiting until the six o'clock news."

"Mm. Yes. You must understand. These things take time to set up."

"Quit *handling* me. Just see it's done. And while you're making what I'm sure will be swift and speedy arrangements, I'll just give the local TV news folks a heads-up that they're going to hear from you."

"You're like a dog with a bone," he growled.

"You know, I've heard that one before. So, it must be true. I'm very determined to see this company does everything it can for Meryl and her unborn baby."

"Consider it done. Just let me warn you this better be the last time you use these high-handed tactics with someone who has the power to fire you."

"Desperate times call for desperate measures."

"Good day, Ms. Lackey." There it was: finality and dismissal.

"I'll be watching for the news," she blurted, then broke the connection.

Okay, twenty-five thousand would get the ball rolling, plus she had about ten thousand in savings to add to it. A young pregnant mother had to be worth at least that much. Surely someone had seen or heard something. She shook her head, still not able to believe the worst. How could something like this be happening?

Next, she checked the KNN web site and made the call to the Felicity Pace show. How soon they would act on her information was unknown.

Now for the TV stations.

Allison had just made her last phone call when Tamsyn ran inside and slung her bag on the counter. "Okay, I have a thousand flyers and two new staple guns from Home Depot. Rick and one of his frat brothers are going to help us, and they're bringing their own staple guns."

"Right," Allison said, looking around for her shoulder bag. "Now let's keep our eyes and ears open, especially at the Hillside condos. Someone must've seen something suspicious."

"Way to go, girl. The family detective thing has rubbed off on you after all."

"Must be in the genes." How could she joke at a time like this? Somehow, she had to go on. Somehow, she had to believe it wasn't too late for Meryl and her baby. Her fists clenched. "It isn't fair. She never hurt anyone in her life."

"No, it's never fair."

Tamsyn's head turned toward the sound of screeching tires. "Hey, there's Rick and Pauley now."

Allison watched the two young men bound up the sidewalk to the porch. Rick Roberge was typical of Tam's real-life dates. Tall, dark, and handsome, square chin; everything about his physical appearance broadcast to one and all his genetic contributions would be more than acceptable. Pauley Schulman was dark and handsome enough, but he missed out on the tall gene, reaching Rick's shoulder.

"Y'all ready? Separate vehicles or we can all pile into my Jeep?" Rick's eyes danced with excitement, then they grew sober as if remembering the reason he was here. "Sorry about your friend. I'm glad we can help."

"We can probably cover more territory if we separate, "Allison suggested.

Pauley beamed. "Since we know Rick is hot for Tamsyn, why don't I ride with you?"

His smile was too friendly, and his gaze had a way of assessing her when he thought she wasn't looking.

"Uh, okay, but I'm driving."

He chuckled. "Like to be in control, do you?"

"Not a control issue. I just know the neighborhood better." Frankly, she'd rather have Nick at her side than this goofball. Yeah, she'd made up her mind. Pauley was a definite goofball.

"Hold on." Tamsyn's gaze narrowed. "Are you sure you'll be all right? An hour ago, you were a banana peel away from complete collapse."

"I'm fine. As long as I have a mission."

"Hey. You sound like Indiana Jones," Pauley quipped.

Allison whipped in his direction, straightened her shoulders, and poked his chest. "There's nothing to joke about. Meryl is a dear friend of mine. She's five months pregnant, and she's missing. The police don't think she's still alive."

He backed up. "Sorry."

She rounded on him and got in his face. "You should be. This isn't your average Saturday-afternoon-nothing-better-to-do lark. We're doing this to help the police. They can't be everywhere."

Pauley's gaze widened. "Man. It's true what they say about redheads."

Before Allison could kill him, Tamsyn stepped between them. "I'll ride with Allison. Pauley, you go with Rick. Might just save you from bodily harm."

Pauley shrugged, but a deep flush stained his cheeks beneath his tan. "Uh, sure."

Grateful for Tam's intervention, Allison jerked her head toward the door. "Let's get a move on."

Hillside Condominiums were mid-priced for the area and a bargain for young urban professionals. Crepe myrtles lined the green areas and were still in full bloom. The air was fragrant with the smell of their deep pink and white blossoms.

About half the units had one-car garages; the rest were more like apartments with either balconies or patios. Underground parking existed for those residents whose units didn't have a garage. Besides, there was guest parking in front of each condo.

Allison and Tamsyn parked in front of Meryl's unit; Rick and Pauley parked in the next space. Crime-scene tape still marked Meryl's front door. Her friend had been missing for less than twenty-four hours. Seemed like forever.

But under twenty-four hours, there was still hope. Right?

Allison swallowed the boulder-sized lump in her throat. "I'll take this end. Tam, take the central units. Rick, the east units, and, Pauley, the west."

Her suggestion was met with three agreeable nods. "If no one's home, slip the flyer under the door or in the jamb. Whatever works."

Tamsyn snapped a sharp salute. "Got it."

The guys headed off, but Allison shrugged when she heard Pauley mutter something that sounded suspiciously like, "Control freak."

He could think whatever he liked about her. He wasn't even close to being her type.

Unlike Nick, who apparently was.

She brushed away thoughts of his steely blue eyes and hoped he was having a great time with his son. As for being limited to seeing his son when the court dictated, she couldn't begin to imagine how much it must hurt.

A quick glance around showed her the search party had scattered to do her bidding. Best she get on with it too. How else could she keep the frightening questions at bay?

Was Meryl scared? Was the baby all right? Were they still

alive?

Two hot and humid hours later, Allison's team regrouped in front of Meryl's condo. She brushed back her sweaty bangs. "Any luck?"

"Got zip," Tamsyn announced. "But everyone I talked to was very concerned, especially the women, and promised to call the police if they remembered anything."

"Same here." Rick draped an arm over Tam's shoulder. "Don't know 'bout the rest of you, but I need a tall, cold one. STAT."

"Ditto." This from Pauley.

A tall, cold anything sounded perfect to Allison. "Come on back to the house. You'll get your brew and dinner as well, provided I can get Justin to fire up his spiffy new grill."

Tamsyn chuckled. "That's a given. He's so proud of his dang grill he volunteers to cook when it's not even his turn. And that's perfectly okay with little old me."

"Anything is better than eating your attempts at cooking." Allison elbowed her sister. Tam's cooking skills were minimal at best, but she could call for takeout with the best of them.

"Anyway, I want to thank Rick and Pauley for helping us today. Guys, I really appreciate it."

Rick nodded. "Anytime, Allie. I just hope what we did today produces a good result."

Anguish curled and grew in Allison's chest and threatened to crush her, but somehow she managed, "Thanks, guys. It means a lot."

Allison let Tamsyn drive the Camry back to the house. Now there wasn't anything to do but wait, her emotions plummeted into a nosedive to end all nosedives. Tears swam in her eyes, and her bottom lip developed a severe tremble.

She turned to Tamsyn. "I can't help it. It's just not fair."

"I know it doesn't help to say life isn't always fair, so I won't say it."

"Good. 'Cause that's the one thing I really don't want to hear."

"The police are very motivated to find Meryl. Tess is on the case, and she's an excellent detective."

"I know. And I'm so thankful she caught the case. But they need to look into the hospital angle. The last I heard from her, she was going to see Dr. Ivers, and I bet money he's involved in this somehow."

"Why would a respected doctor do something to harm your friend?" Tamsyn's expression was rife with an air of skepticism. "Doesn't make sense unless"—she turned onto Richmond Avenue and continued driving down the tree-lined street—"he's doing something illegal on the transplant side of things, and she was on to him. Maybe she was going to out him over it. You know more about transplants and all that stuff than I do, but aren't the matches all in some computer database?"

"Yes." Allison nodded. "But there are private transplants, some done illegally. Not at our hospital, of course. We have to follow the rules or we'd lose our Medicare funding, not to mention be in violation of the law. But it doesn't take into account the transplant operations performed in expensive private clinics. Those tend to fly under the radar."

Tamsyn glanced, wide-eyed, at Allison. "You know, you might really have something with this angle."

"The worst-case scenario is the type of clinic where they operate on immigrants who are desperate for money to send home to their families. The surgeon may not even be a surgeon or a doctor. The mortality rate on those is extremely high."

"Just to play devil's advocate, Ivers is a nephrologist, not a transplant surgeon—right?"

"Yes, but he could easily be in cahoots with a surgeon and direct his wealthier patients who might care more about survival than taking their chances of receiving an organ from the databank registry. Patients wait for years for the right organ. Those private clinics—the good ones with qualified surgeons—can make fortunes for their owners."

"Then you should look into it quietly—" Tamsyn pulled into the alley behind the house and parked. "No, you should give that type of background information to Tess. Let her handle it. If Dr. Ivers is behind Meryl's disappearance, then you could be placing yourself in danger...perhaps like Meryl did. At the very least, you could lose your job."

Anger and frustration building, Allison opened the car door. "Frankly, I don't give a rat's ass. If Parklane is harboring a physician who's bending the rules to line his pockets, they need to know."

Tamsyn jumped from the car and circled it to face Allison. "But nursing is your calling. Are you ready to risk losing everything? If you make a big stink and get fired, will anyone hire you? This is a city, sure enough, but the hospital community is a small one."

"I don't care." Allison clenched her fists. "All that matters is finding Meryl, and if the worse has happened—God forbid—then the person responsible deserves having the book thrown at him."

"Whew. Am I ever glad you're on the right side of the law. You'd be one implacable opponent."

A flicker of amusement tugged her mouth into a smile. "What a bizarre idea. I'd never do anything illegal. It isn't part of my genetic wiring."

Tam's brows took on a skeptical arch. "I don't know. I'd

hate to get between you and the person who kidnapped Meryl. It wouldn't be pretty."

"You might be on to something at that." Before she could ponder future actions, Scott opened the French door and waved them inside.

"Get in here. There's a breaking news segment on TV."

Heart pounding with fear, Allison slammed the car door and ran up the steps to the deck and inside the house.

"You missed most of it, but when I saw what it was, I hit the DVR Record button."

She stood in the doorway to the den, clutching the doorjamb. Sure enough, the Admin-on-call Garner was standing before three mics and a crowd of reporters. And was that Tess standing behind him?

Scott reversed the DVR back to the beginning.

"I'll read a brief statement and take a few questions."

With every word he read, her dread increased, growing and choking her.

Nothing—not even seeing the blood at the condo—had made it seem as real as hearing his bald statement of fact on TV. He finished with the offer of a reward and the bank address where additional contributions could be made.

"I'll take your questions." Garner nodded at the News Channel Nine reporter.

"Does Miss Litton have any enemies here at the hospital?"

And Garner's pat answer was, "No. Miss Litton was well liked and respected by her colleagues."

"Who was the father of her baby?"

"The hospital doesn't pry into what is a personal matter."

"Was she having an affair with someone here at the hospital?"

"Already answered. Any further details should be obtained from the police department. The corporation just wanted to offer any assistance that might result in Miss Litton's safe return." He stepped back and nodded to Tess. "This is Detective Tess O'Malley. She can address any further questions you might have regarding the official investigation."

Allison stifled her disgust. She'd had to threaten him to get him to do anything.

Tess stepped to the forefront. "I appreciate your desire to have all your questions answered. However, this is an ongoing investigation. We have several leads, but it's early days yet." Then she gave a hotline number for anyone who might have information that would assist the police in their inquiries. More questions were shouted, but Tess dismissed them with a wave. "That's all I have."

"That's a wrap," Scott said. "You got what you wanted, sis."

She fisted her hands and fought back the tears. "No, what I *want* is to find Meryl and her baby safe and sound." Rather than break down and bawl again, she fled upstairs to her room.

Everything. And nothing. It was all too late.

Chapter Nine

After the Sounds won a squeaker of a game, Nick and Ben headed to Centennial Park. Another hour on the swings and his son was beginning to look a little on this side of tired. They booked from the playground and drove down West End. Justin was expecting him at the family's home on Richland Avenue. "Okay, buddy, I need to swing by my boss's house for a few minutes, then we'll head out to dinner."

"Okay, Daddy."

Nick pulled up in front of the historic bungalow. Now, this was the kind of house he'd like someday. A house with history, full of warmth and a family. Nothing like the pricey McMansion where Eva and her new husband lived.

If he was careful, in a year or two, he hoped to have enough money to buy a small house. That way his son wouldn't have to sleep on the couch at his brother Sonny's. And Nick wouldn't have to sleep on the floor in a sleeping bag.

Thing was, Ben didn't seem to care about his surroundings, as long as he could spend time with his dad.

But Nick cared.

"That's a big old house," Ben said from the backseat.

"Yeah. Let's go see. Maybe Caroline or Allison will take you on a tour while I talk to Justin."

Up the stone steps and onto a deep porch. Before he could ring the bell, Scott opened the door. "Come on in. Just in time for dinner."

"No. I don't wanna intrude. The game ran late, and then

we headed over to Centennial Park for a while. I need Justin for a few minutes. Then we'll go."

"Nonsense. You're staying for dinner." Scott bent over and stuck out his hand to Ben. "Hey there, fella. I'm Scott, and I'm sure there are a couple of hot dogs on the grill with your name on them."

Ben's eyes widened. "Really?"

"That's right, my man."

His son's face brightened. "Good. I'm really, really hungry."

Despite Nick's misgivings about intruding, the tension leached from his shoulders. Damn. Sure felt good to be back home in Nashville and part of the doings at Scott's.

His brother's apartment wasn't a real home. More like a bachelor pad with rotating women, and not a suitable environment for his son.

Nick followed Scott through the house and out the French doors onto the deck. Good ol' Justin was manning a mack-daddy grill, and a long table was set for eight. Caroline waved a welcome and added two more place settings. "Tess called. She's on her way."

Tamsyn and her date, a basketball-player type, were coming up the back steps from the yard where they'd played badminton. A short, dark dude was bending Justin's ear while he slaved over the grill. Who the hell was he? Caroline's date? Or Allison's.

Not that it was any of his beeswax.

"Food's ready," Justin yelled over the chaos, then everyone started calling out their preferences.

Everyone except Allison.

"Where's Allie?" Nick asked. She'd better not be out investigating on her own again.

Caroline gave a quick frown. "She's kind of down. I'll take a tray up to her if she doesn't make an appearance soon."

She put on a wide smile and leaned down to greet Ben. "Now who's this big fellow?"

Ben stood straighter, his small shoulders pulled back with pride. "Benjamin David Vitelli." He added, "Everybody calls me Ben."

"Do you think you could persuade our sister Allison"—she paused, giving a quizzical lift of an eyebrow in Nick's direction—"to come down and have dinner with us? She might because you're such a perfect little gentleman."

An expression of concern flickered across his son's face. "Is she sick?"

"No. Just a little sad and worried over a good friend, but I bet you could make her smile." She raised a questioning eyebrow at Nick as if to say *okay?*

He shrugged and nodded. "Sure."

"Nick, why don't you show Ben up to Allison's room? First one on the left at the top of the stairs."

"Me?"

"Of course. I'm *sure* she'll be happy to see you again."

"Right." *Wrong.* What was the deal with the whole freaking family trying to push them together?

Ben tugged on Nick's hand. "C'mon, let's go, Daddy."

Traitor.

Upstairs, Ben pointed to one of the doors. "This one?"

Nick nodded. His son fisted his small hands and banged on the door. The result was ferocious yipping, from the rat-dog, Nick assumed, and then a wan and pitiful, "I'm not hungry."

"I'm supposed to bring you down," Ben said.

Movement and the sound of Allison's footsteps reached them. Her door opened, and her face appeared, flushed a bright pink. She gazed at Nick, her brows pulling together in a frown. The puffiness and redness around her eyes told him she was more than a little sad and worried. Hell, she'd been bawling her eyes out.

Still, she ignored him and instead smiled at his son. "I see I have a special messenger. You must be Ben." The dog slipped out between her ankles into the hall and jumped on Ben, who giggled with delight.

"That's right. There are hot dogs with my name on 'em. We might find some with your name too. If you hurry." Ben glanced up at Nick. "Can I play with the puppy?"

"If it's okay with Allison."

"Sure." Her lashes fluttered, acknowledging his presence, then she finger-combed her hair back from her forehead. "Guys, give me a second. I need to get presentable."

To his way of thinking, she didn't need to do anything. Nothing at all.

Her hemmed cutoff jeans showed slim, tanned legs. The pink Susan G. Komen Foundation T-shirt she wore was a little wrinkled, but it fit snugly across her breasts. He sucked in a deep breath and tried to look somewhere else. Ah, her toenails were painted a bright pink. "Look all right to me." He remembered the short dude on the deck and added, "Or maybe you need to freshen up for your date?"

"Date? I don't have a date." Then amusement glittered in her warm brown eyes. "Oh, you mean Pauley?"

"Short dude. He didn't introduce himself."

"That was Pauley Schulman. He's one of Rick's frat brothers. They helped us pass out flyers this afternoon. You know, with Meryl's photo and description, her car, reward info, and all that. We promised 'em dinner."

"Reward and flyers. Smart. Every bit helps. If I hadn't had..." He nodded in Ben's direction. "I would've helped." Technically, Allison was his client, although a nonpaying one since she was part owner in the family-run agency. Still, he should've been available, but time with his son was limited, not to mention precious. No way could he disappoint his boy. Not like Nick's dad had disappointed him and his brother, time and time again.

He was nothing like his dad.

Nothing.

And to this day, he remained thankful every day his mother finally grew enough backbone to leave the abusive bastard. Now she lived in a trailer park in Dundee, Florida, and cohabited with a man who was decent and worshipped the ground she walked on.

His father was in Florida too, but he stayed shacked up with first one woman and another until they got tired of being smacked around.

Thing was before his dad retired, he was a cop.

But Nick was nothing like his dad.

He often wondered if abuse was a factor in his brother Sonny's divorce. Given the parade of females through his older brother's bedroom, more likely the issue was his screwing around.

"Nick?" Allison touched his upper arm. Just a warm, light touch, but it was enough to snap him out of it.

"Sorry. Mind wandered, I guess."

"You sure everything's okay?"

"I'm fine. I wish I'd been here this afternoon...to help."

"It's all right. I understand. Your son's important." She smiled down at the boy. "Come on, Ben, let's check out those hot dogs. I'm hungry too."

From the clouded expression in her eyes, it was easy to see her heart was breaking. Still, he appreciated her attempt to put his son at ease.

As if she didn't have a care in the world, she picked up the dog with one hand and took Ben's hand with the other, led him downstairs and outside to the deck.

Smiling to himself, Nick followed. What else could he do? His son had made another conquest. Nothing new in that.

He stepped out onto the deck. The smell of grilled meat set his stomach to complaining and his mouth to watering. Allison was surrounded by her two sisters, who put their arms around her, murmuring in her ear.

"I'm fine." He watched her give a dismissive wave. "Ben here says you have hot dogs with our names on 'em, so let's have a go." She set the Yorkie down on the deck, and the pooch began to beg. She laughed and pinched a bite from her hot dog and gave it to the pooch.

He marveled at her bravery and determination not to ruin the impromptu cookout with her personal sorrows and fears. *If,* and it was a pretty big *if,* he was of a mind to get involved again, he needn't look any further than Allison Lackey.

But he wasn't of that mind. Hell, no. Allie was nothing like Eva. Still. He couldn't deny he was attracted to her. But that was just his 'nads doing the talking.

Allison was pretty and smart...and a mite too young for him.

Caroline clapped her hands together. "Everyone, grab your plates and find a place to sit. Just because we have company doesn't mean we're formal around here."

Nick settled at the table with Ben at his side.

"I want Allison—"

"Miss Allison, young man," Nick warned, even if he dreaded whatever Ben was about to say.

"I want Miss Allison to sit next to me...please?" He cut his gaze up at Nick. "Was that all right, Daddy?"

He nodded. "Much better." He glanced at Allison. "If it's all right with you?"

The sadness still in her gaze, she smiled down at Ben. "Of course."

"Good. 'Cause my daddy's divorced and needs a new wife to look after him."

Said all in innocence, of course, but Nick was glad he didn't have anything in his mouth.

Flame-faced and choking, Allison spewed lemonade in a fine mist across the table. She clapped a hand over her mouth. "Sorry."

Nick's face burned at his son's bold remark. Pretty funny, or so everyone else at the table seemed to think. He swallowed the urge to laugh too. "Thanks, son. I believe I'm capable of looking out for myself, but I appreciate your concern."

Did he dare catch Allison's eye? No. Diversion. "Here, son, you're about to drop ketchup on your T-shirt."

Ben held up the end of his hot dog and licked the dab of ketchup with a quick flick of his tongue. "Got it."

Dinner passed in a blur of laughter and familial teasing. The exceptions were Allison, Schulman, and Nick himself.

When their parents were killed by a drunk driver ten years ago, the Holt-Lackeys had been handed a devastating blow, but you'd never know it to see them now.

The solidity of the blended family was apparent in how they treated and cared for each other.

Nothing like his family.

After dinner, Allison walked with Nick and Ben out to the Bronco. The sun was hovering low on the horizon in the western sky, and the ever-present mosquitoes were droning a warning buzz. Nick carried his son because the poor little tyke had fallen asleep right after polishing off two hot dogs and a whopping piece of devil's food cake.

She opened the back door for Nick. He turned and met her gaze, his expression grave.

"Thanks for dinner. I really appreciate how good you were to Ben." He settled the sleepy boy into his child safety seat and secured the belts, then eased the door until it closed.

She folded her arms across her chest, an almost unconscious maneuver. Did she really need to protect herself from Nick? "It's a madhouse, but tonight was fun. I'm glad you brought Ben with you."

The corner of his mouth turned up. "Uh, sorry about his little comment."

A somewhat self-conscious chuckle played havoc in her throat. "He's just a kid. That's the best and the scariest thing about kids. They say exactly what's on their minds. Self-editing doesn't come until later." She glanced away. Too many feelings surged. Meryl. Her baby. And Nick.

Most of all Nick.

"I have to have him home tomorrow morning in time for church. After that, your case will have my full attention."

"I understand. You have a right to a life, Nick."

"I know, but...the harder we work the case—"

"I know. Tess has already given me her prognosis." She hugged herself as a cold chill shook through her body. "It wasn't good." Her bones seemed to turn to sand. With speedy reflexes, Nick caught her before she could fall.

She glanced into his eyes. "Sorry, I seem to be doing a lot of that lately."

He held her close, her head rested against his chest until she could hear the rapid beat of his heart. "'S all right."

He held her until she steadied. "I'm okay, now. Just— sometimes it gets to me."

"You need to get some rest, sleep even." His tone was low. Tender. It resonated through her body as surely as the chill.

"I know. Nurse, heal thyself." She forced out a bitter laugh.

"Allie... Go to bed. You've had a long day." He leveled his sky-blue eyes at her. "Or do you want me to pick you up and carry you back to the house?"

She drew back. The very idea. "Absolutely not. I'm fine." Truth be told, it wasn't such an unpleasant idea. Just inappropriate. "Really."

Nick's lips twitched, and a twinkle of amusement flickered across his sculptor's dream of a face. "Just makin' sure."

Damn, but the man had a way of making her feel like a giddy teenager again. She mustered all her willpower. Back to the business at hand. "You and Justin had your heads together after dinner. What's the game plan?"

Nick walked around to the driver's side of the black Bronco. Allison followed. "He's running background on Meryl. Seeing what we can find out about the father of her baby. We'll go from there. He also took a look at the Facebook page you did. Lots of support, but nothing of value."

"Yeah, still it keeps her face out there. You just never know when someone will turn up with something," she said. "In the meantime, I'll keep snooping at the hospital. I know Dr. Ivers has something to do with her disappearance."

"Don't waste your time," Nick said, shaking his head. "It's always the husband or boyfriend."

Arrogant, that's what he was. Cops, PIs, and their gut instincts. She had a gut too. "But Meryl lived alone. And I would've known if there was a man in her life."

"Come on, Allie. There's a man somewhere in her life...or was. She's pregnant. She didn't get pregnant by herself."

"Well...she could've gone to a sperm bank."

Nick erupted with a raucous groan. "No *tube* of frozen sperm showed up at Meryl's door and kidnapped her."

"And I say her disappearance has nothing to do with her

being pregnant. You're looking for the obvious."

"There's a reason for looking for the obvious. Nine times out of ten, it's the answer."

"This time it's different. I just know it."

"That's because you—" He broke off, shaking his head.

"Because I don't want to face the truth? Is that what you mean? Meryl's dead?"

He took a deep breath. His mouth thinned to a mere line, but his gaze softened before he uttered the one word she did *not* want to hear. "Yes."

No matter how many times Tess or anyone else said the same thing, that single word almost stopped her heart. "I won't accept she's already dead. She has to be alive. *Someone* has her, but they wouldn't kill her and her baby. Who could do something like that?"

"Are you gonna get weak-kneed again?"

"No. I'm fine. I'm mad—"

"What did I do now?"

"I'm mad at you and everyone else who's given up on her." She whirled around and stalked back to the house, leaving Nick and all his doubts behind.

Let 'em give up. But she wouldn't. She'd show 'em.

Chapter Ten

Sunday morning, at nine sharp, Nick drove Ben home. Eva met them on the porch. "Guess what, sugar? Mama's bought you a big surprise."

Ben danced up and down, his small body vibrating with excitement. "What, Mommy? What is it?"

"A brand-new puppy, a Golden Retriever," she said, her tone dripping with the saccharine sweetness Nick knew too well. "He's in his crate in the family room."

At the word puppy, his son gave a squeal. Nick watched him run off to play with his big surprise. He didn't begrudge his son a new puppy. After all, he'd seen how taken Ben was with the little rat-dog, but damn—a new *puppy*. Now the boy wouldn't ever want to leave home, and there wasn't a chance in hell of finding an apartment complex that would allow a pet without a huge deposit.

Way to go, Eva.

A smirk replaced the good-mommy expression she did so well when someone was watching. Apparently, he didn't count. "So, did Benjamin have a good time? Did you feed him properly?"

Nick repressed a mental groan. "Took him to a Sounds game, to Centennial Park, and then we went over to my boss's house. One of his sisters is my first client."

Hands on her hips, Eva scowled. Too bad her face couldn't freeze with that expression.

"His sister? What do you mean you took him to some broad's house?"

"Allison isn't a broad. I told you, she's my boss's sister, and she's an RN. Besides, it was my *boss's* house. He and his brother and three sisters all live there. It's my job. You expect me to pay child support, don't ya? I *have* to work this case." Actually, he was on salary, but that was information Eva didn't need to know.

"On his *sister's* case?"

She couldn't be jealous. After all, she was the one who strayed. "A friend of hers disappeared. Maybe you heard about it on the news. The nurse at Parklane Medical Center."

"The pregnant one?" She nodded. "Yeah, I heard about it."

"Yes. From all the blood I saw, it doesn't look good."

"What business did you have on the crime scene? You're not a cop anymore."

"Dammit, Eva, I don't owe you any explanations, but here goes. Allison couldn't reach her friend. We drove over to her friend's condo. We checked things out. Saw the blood, so we called the police. As for Ben, he went with me when I went to see Justin—he's the other brother in the firm. Ben ate two hot dogs and some chocolate cake. They treated him like little Lord Fauntleroy. There was nothing for you to worry about."

She took a deep breath, her expression saying *bored.* "I know you have to have a life, but I'd appreciate it if you wouldn't drag him around on the days you have him. Surely every other weekend, you can manage to be celibate."

"It wasn't a date. I had to see Justin about a background check, and they invited us to stay for dinner. Most definitely *not* a date."

"Just see you don't. And I don't like him sleeping on the couch at Sonny's either. When are you going to get your own place?"

"As soon as I get a couple of paychecks under my belt."

"Fine. Just see you pay the child support on time."

"Haven't I always?"

"So far."

"All right, then. Quit bustin' my balls." He spun on his heel. Why did he let her get to him? Every time he brought Ben home, it was the same litany of complaints and warnings.

But this was the first time Ben had been around another woman. Maybe Eva picked up on Nick's interest? She always had a sixth sense when it concerned other women. Not that he'd ever been unfaithful.

Tempted a time or two, but he'd never acted on it, even when things between them were at their worst.

He turned back for another go at setting her straight. "And you're right. I do have a right to a life. So, get used to it." Without another word, he ambled down the steps. Fuck it. She was the one who wanted the divorce. Not that he blamed her. Being assigned as an undercover narcotics cop didn't lead to any kind of a happy home life or any kind of schedule a wife could depend on.

On the other hand, she didn't have to have an affair with his captain. For Ben's sake, he hadn't fought the divorce. His marriage had been over for a long time.

The high-rise condominium on West End where Dr. Ivers lived was brick with windows irregularly placed in a hodgepodge arrangement which made no sense to an external viewer. The underground parking for the residents didn't include Allison and her Camry. She folded her arms and scowled at the other occupants of her car, namely, Caroline and Pauley.

"Allie, this is the screwiest idea you've ever had," Caroline protested. "I tried to talk her out of it as soon as she mentioned it."

"Don't look at me," Pauley said. "I don't have any influence on her."

"Don't talk about me like I'm not here. I am *so* going to march right up on the elevator of this fancy high-rise and demand to see him. I'll bang on his door and make so much noise they'll have to let me in just to keep me quiet. He needs to see what he's responsible for."

Caroline's hands went to her head. "No. No. No. You can't. You'll get this doctor all mad or worse. If he's responsible for Meryl's disappearance, he could come after you."

"I'm not afraid of that weasel. I'm as tall as he is."

"I'm here to look out after you girls." This from wannabe backseat driver Pauley, who had the most irritating habit of clearing his throat every five minutes. The man was a drag. Whatever possessed him to show up at nine to assist in the search?

"Appreciate that, Pauley, but I know how to handle doctors. Been doing it for several years now."

"Why don't you just let Nick handle the investigation? Better yet, the police." A tone of terminal frustration had crept into her sister's voice. "I know they're—"

"—barking up the wrong tree."

Caroline emitted a long sigh. "What I was going to say was, I know you feel helpless, but pissing off one of the doctors isn't going to help you at work, is it?"

"Frankly, I couldn't care less. All I care about is finding Meryl and her baby. Finding them safe and sound." Yes, she had to keep repeating it, because everyone else had given up on a positive outcome.

Maybe it was a fool's hope. But it was all she had.

Her sister jerked her purse from the floorboard and started rummaging through it. "I'm calling the house. Isn't

Nick supposed to come over sometime this morning?"

"Yes, but this is my deal. Don't go calling for reinforcements."

"We don't need anyone else," Pauley said.

All right, so he was agreeing with her, but don't think she wasn't up to his game. Waste of time. Not her type at all.

Not like Nick, who was. If he weren't so darn pigheaded.

"You can sit here if you want to." Allison grabbed the door handle. "Frankly, my dears, I don't give a rat's ass."

"You're losing it, Allie. If you're not careful, you're gonna get arrested."

"Then you'll just have to come along and charm the gatekeeper or whatever they—"

"Concierge," Pauley said with a smug sneer.

"That's right. Come on, Carrie." A little begging couldn't hurt. "While you charm the concierge, I'll sneak up the elevator."

"You don't know his floor number, much less—"

"Show him some cleavage. I'll sneak behind him and look in his computer. They're bound to have one."

"Deliver me..." Caroline sighed, shutting her eyes. "Why do I suddenly feel like I've been dropped smack-dab in the middle of an *I Love Lucy* episode?"

Pauley let out a harsh bark of laughter.

"Don't laugh," Caroline said. "You're either Fred or Ricky, and neither one of them could do a thing with Lucy when she had one of her harebrained schemes."

"That's it." Allison opened the door and jumped out. "See ya."

A groan emitted from Caroline too, but along with the sound of another car door...and a third. Good. The posse would back her up after all.

*

All the good citizens on Richland Avenue must be at church. Most of 'em anyway. Nick deduced this since he had no trouble finding a parking place. He pulled in behind a boxy, puke-green 1950s vehicle and parked.

He'd bet money the vehicle belonged to Scott's brother. The quirky computer whiz—yeah, it fitted his personality. On the other hand, how the lanky Justin squeezed his body into a vehicle not much bigger than a baby's porta-crib was a question for another day.

He hopped from the Bronco, strode up the walkway, bounded up the steps, then rang the doorbell.

The door opened. Tamsyn, the hot sister, stood there in cutoff jeans and a T-shirt. His gaze swept her hotness up and down, then stored it away in his rusty memory bank. She definitely rated as his type. Too bad her little sister had wormed her way into his heart first.

She gave him a lazy smile. "Come on in, cowboy. Justin has something for you if his recent 'Yahoo' is any indication. Of course, it might just mean the Sounds scored a home run."

Anticipation and the desire to get to work fizzed through him like New Year's Eve champagne. Anticipation and more than a touch of dread. He dipped his head and stepped inside. "Thanks. How's Allison?"

Hottie lifted her shoulders in a casual shrug. "You know how she is. She's out papering fifty city blocks with more posters of Meryl. Caroline went with her this morning."

"Good."

"And Pauley. He showed up and volunteered for another go." A quick, knowing smile flitted across her face. "Personally, I think he has the hots for our little nurse."

Without another word, Tamsyn swept from the foyer but stopped at the doorway and turned. "Justin and Scott are in the den."

Hots for Allison. That runt? One thing he couldn't abide was a man—any man—taking advantage of a woman. And she was raw and vulnerable over her friend's disappearance. She had the softest heart of anyone he'd ever met.

Still, they didn't need another woman to disappear. Maybe it was better if this Pauley guy went along with them and kept them out of trouble...if he could.

Nick stood in the doorway of the den. There was a ball game on the wide-screen TV, but the sound was muted. Eyelids drooping, Scott set down his cup of coffee on a table and yawned a sleepy, "Morning."

Justin kicked back. "Dude, you're right on time. I've located Meryl's ex-husband. Name's Tom Buckley. Seems the baby daddy's right here in town trying to make a name for himself, twanging on his guitar down at the Cannery on Friday nights. Rest of the time he's bartending at the Wildhorse."

"Meryl changed her name to get away from him. Fits the profile—"

"It's *always* the husband or boyfriend." Tamsyn's low-pitched tones interrupted behind him. "Honestly, anger-management classes ought to start in the womb for boy babies."

Given his father's rages, Nick grunted. "Agreed. But your sister's off on a tangent. And gonna get her cute butt in trouble if she's not careful."

Hottie shot him a seductive smile. "I'll be sure to pass on the compliment."

Hell. What had he said? "You know what I mean."

"Yeah, we all do." This from Scott. "She *is* my little sister, you know."

"Didn't mean anything by it," he said, protesting too much. Desperate to change the subject. "Where's this Tom Buckley camping out?"

"No official address yet. Have a feeling he's hanging with some fellow musicians. Probably parked on someone's couch or floor."

"Right." Who was he to judge, being as he was in the same situation? "I'll check his workplace. They're bound to have a way to reach him."

Notes of classical music interrupted the planning session. "Mine," Scott said, glancing at the caller ID. "It's Caroline." He answered, listened, then said, "Okay. Okay. Try to hold her down till Nick can get over there."

"What?"

"Allison's ready to launch a full-scale invasion of some doctor's high-rise condo, but the concierge won't let her in. She's raising Cain, and they're going to call the authorities if we don't hightail it over there." Scott gave him a nearby West End address.

"'Nough said." He held up his hand and booked for the door, muttering to himself, "Crazy broad."

"Don't let her hear you call her that. She'll kick your ass," Tamsyn offered.

What the hell had he gotten himself into? Allison Lackey and her big brown eyes and pink lips were a pack of trouble, even if all he wanted to do was kiss those pink lips and dry her tears.

The tony West End high-rise was less than five minutes away. Cooling down Allison could be more difficult than subduing a druggie high on PCP. He pulled into the parking lot and parked with a screech of tires to announce his arrival. He hopped from the Bronco and strode toward the entrance.

Sure enough, she was in full freak-out mode. Her sister had her arm around her, trying to calm her down. Useless-as-bat-shit Pauley was leaning against one of the marble walls, trying to pretend he wasn't there. A heavyset woman—make that one very red-faced woman—had gotten off the elevator and was marching toward the trio. Whoever she was, she was pissed off.

Time to swoop in and carry her out—bodily, if need be.

Caroline threw up her hands. "I give up."

"Allison." He kept his tone low, hoping to calm her like a child. Hey, it worked with Ben.

Her body tensed, her shoulders were as stiff as a coat hanger. She raised her pointed chin at him. "I can't believe you thought you had to rush over here. This is *my* business, not yours."

"If you don't take this young woman out of here right now, I will summon the police. You cannot harass my husband in such a manner on his weekend off. I won't have it."

"Mrs. Ivers"—Allison's tone sweetened until it was one note beyond thick honey—"I just want to give him a poster personally. You see, the concierge won't let me post one in the lobby."

"I should think not. My husband had nothing to do with your friend's disappearance. He's a respected physician. And believe me, he knows who *you* are. The hospital administrator is going to hear about your unconscionable behavior as soon as I go back upstairs."

"Allison." Hell, he had to try again. "We're leaving right now." He nodded at the doctor's wife. "Ma'am."

"I'm. Not. Ready. To. Go." Each word was enunciated with a corresponding sideways bottle of her head as if he were incapable of understanding.

"You have a choice. Now—under your own power—or I'm picking you up and carrying you."

Allison's gaze widened, her jaw dropped with disbelief.

"You wouldn't dare."

Stubborn? The woman exemplified the word. "I will...if you make me."

"Looks as if he means business." Caroline paused, then added, "And not a moment too soon."

Nick widened his stance and set his hands on his hips, ready for who the hell knew what she would do next. "Is she always this crazy?" he asked the calm and collected Caroline.

"Not usually."

"All *right*." Allison sighed with a flair for the dramatic. "I'm calming down. Mrs. Ivers, if you will just give this"— with a prissy gesture she held out the poster with her fingertips—"to Dr. Ivers, I'll certainly appreciate it. I'm turning to go now." She pasted on a fake smile.

A smile was a smile, even it wasn't real—right? Nick started to let out the breath he'd held.

She started toward the exit, then turned for just one more word. "Just make sure your husband knows if he had anything to do with Meryl Litton's disappearance, he'd better come forward now."

The doctor's wife shrieked and lunged at Allison. Nick stepped between the two women just in time to keep the doctor's wife from raking her claws down Allison's face. He nudged his client none too gently toward the exit.

"I'm going." She bristled and glared at him. "Don't have to go all alpha on me."

"Wait just a freaking minute." This warning came from good old Pauley, who was as useless as a sack of cowpats.

No point in responding. The dude had no influence on her. Nick raised a hand and gave him a dismissive gesture. "Keep moving, Allie, and I'll share the latest on your friend's ex."

Her eyebrows arched, and her lips formed an O. "Really?" She quickstepped toward her Camry. "No. You're going with me. Your sister can drive your car. Get in."

She frowned, then nodded. "How could I refuse such a gracious invitation?"

He opened the passenger door. "Need a boost?"

She cocked her head. "I'll have you know I'm perfectly capable of getting in this vehicle of yours."

"You *are* a little on the short side."

"Like that's really news to me. Thanks for the insight." She sniffed and clambered up without a problem.

Nick ran around to the other side and climbed in. "Whatever the hell possessed you to go to this doctor's residence? He could sue you for harassment or get you fired. Or both."

"Forget about him. What about Meryl's ex?"

Nick found an opening in the traffic and pulled onto West End while giving her a quick rundown on what Justin had learned and Nick's plan of action.

"Take me with you."

"No way." He turned on his turn signal and moved into the left lane. "I'm taking you home."

"No, I have to be there when you interview him."

"And have you go off like you went off on the good doctor? I don't think so." He shook his head. "No way."

"He's not the good doctor, but I know you don't believe me."

Keeping his gaze focused on traffic, he hung a quick left off of West End. Drove a block and took another left on Richland. "Just so we're clear, I'm the investigator. You're the client. Keep your nose out of it."

"I can fire you."

"Go ahead. You weren't my first choice for a client, more like the last. You've been nothing but trouble. If I had any doubts, the way you acted today confirmed it."

"Now, Nick. I was just bluffing." She rested her hand

lightly on his thigh. Jeez, what was she trying to pull now? "You're the man for this case, and I'm glad Scott hired you."

"Now *you're* bluffing. For what it's worth, I'm not buying your one-eighty."

He parked in front of the house. Waiting for her to get out...waiting. He drummed his fingers against the wheel. "Come on. The meter's running."

"Get moving, then." She raised her chin a notch. Reckon she was determined on staying in the Bronco.

Why? What had he done to deserve such an impulsive and stubborn client with the nicest rack he'd seen in a long time? He tamped down a surge of lust. "Not until you hoist your butt outta my vehicle."

"I'm not going anywhere but with you. I'm the client, and that means I'm the boss."

"Boss, hell—a major pain in my ass is what you are." He groaned his disgust, and, shoving the Bronco into gear, he pulled away from the curb.

The Wildhorse Saloon had been a Nashville fixture ever since it opened its doors on Market Street in the mid-nineties. And it was still a popular tourist spot with food, entertainment, and atmosphere. Allison had taken a line-dancing class one Saturday night while she was still in college.

They parked in the closest lot with an open spot and walked down the street to the Wildhorse. Nick held the door for Allison. She entered, and the cool AC sent a shiver down her spine. Whew, but it felt good after the late-August morning's heat outside.

The air was full of yummy odors of barbeque and grilled meats. A bartender was wiping down the bar, and a couple of waitstaff were setting the tables and chairs to rights. The bartender looked up. "We don't serve until eleven."

Nick cut his gaze to the clock behind the bar. "It's ten till, and we're not here to eat." Nick moseyed over to the bar and hitched a hip on the stool. "Got some questions about one of your employees."

The barkeep's right cheek twitched. "Figured as much. You got cop written all over you."

"Used to be, but I'm private now."

"Have to talk to the manager. I don't know anything. Anyways, a bartender's like a doctor or a priest."

"Yeah, right. Tell your manager Nick Vitelli needs to speak to him."

The bartender shrugged and took his good old time leaving. "Will do."

Allison sidled up to Nick, climbed onto the tall stool beside him, and whispered, "You should've let me try to pump him first."

"You?" His brow shot up. "Honey, I've seen you in action. The only thing you'd get from him is us kicked out of here."

"I'm sure there's an insult in there somewhere." Still, he'd called her *honey*.

"You catch on quick." He nodded knowingly. "Yes, you do." He shot her a sideways glance with a bemused expression flickering in his cerulean eyes and a faint smile curving his lips.

"I'll have you know I can be seductive...when it's called for."

"Mm." Another sideways glance. The corner of his mouth twitched.

How could she blame him for not taking her seriously? Maybe she'd been a *little* over the top at Ivers's high-rise.

But time was running out for Meryl and her baby. If it hadn't already.

No. No negative thinking allowed.

The bartender returned and jerked his head toward the back door. "She'll see ya. Down the hall. Second door on the right."

Allison scooted off the barstool. "Thanks."

"*You* stay here."

"No." She raised her chin and set her hands on her hips

His face morphed into a mask of resignation. "Fine. Come on." Shoulders straight, he strode away, forcing her to run to keep up with him.

The hallway was dark, but the rich smell of barbeque sauce was even stronger back here. Her taste buds twanged and her stomach rumbled. Not much of an operative, was she? Hungry and not even eleven o'clock.

Was Meryl hungry? Was her captor feeding her? A shudder rippled through her body, but she shoved the painful visions away.

Otherwise, she couldn't face what everyone else accepted as fact.

"Down the hall, second door on the right," Nick muttered, then knocked on the door.

"Come in." A low voice, but a female one.

He opened the door. Sure enough, a big blonde with big hair and big boobs to match sat behind the desk. So much for Allison's being seductive.

"You wanted to see me. What about?"

"One of your part-time bartenders, Tom Buckley. We'd like to question him, but he doesn't have a local address. I figure he's camping out with someone from here."

"And who are you?" She raised her brows, a speculative expression at best. "You look like a cop. Smell like a cop." She stood and slithered around her desk, then placed a manicured claw on his upper arm. "Mm. Feel like a cop too."

"Nick Vitelli. I'm a PI. Working a missing-person case."

The blonde shot a sneer and looked askance at Allison. "And who's she?"

"My—uh, partner, Allison Lackey." No point in telling the manager Allison was the client. No self-respecting PI let his client trail around with him. Not that she was a typical client.

He glanced at his partner and smiled. She nodded, straightened her shoulders, and tried—and failed—to assume a casual stance. Women. Amazed, he shrugged. No one would ever know she'd been two degrees from full-on hysterics not thirty minutes earlier.

"Like I said, I'm looking for Tom Buckley. Either you can give me his home address, or you can't."

"Well, sugar, I might be able to help you, or..." She paused and batted her lashes. "I might not. Why don't you send your partner to have a drink at the bar?"

"Don't drink on duty, ma'am," Allison responded, quick, edgy, and to the point of pissed off.

Hell, it wasn't his fault if the broad kept coming on to him. Having his *partner* along was definitely a liability in more ways than one. Without her along, he'd be tempted to work the manager for more info.

"What does Buckley have to do with your missing person?"

"You might've heard about the pregnant nurse from Parklane who went missing on Friday? He's her ex."

"The police are working the case, aren't they?" Her voice was low and sultry, like a blues singer. "What do *you* have to do with it?"

"She's my best friend." Allison advanced a step. Nick noted her rigid shoulders and sensed the waves of anger vibrating her body. "And if you know something that will help us or the police, you'd better spill before I lose my temper." She smacked her small fist on the manager's desk.

Crap. The crazy woman's back.

The manager's gaze widened and flickered with amusement. "Temper. Temper."

"Settle down...partner." Nick put an arm around Allie's waist. "Take a deep breath, or you're out of here."

"But—"

"But nothing."

She took a deep breath, her body sagging against his.

"You gonna help us or not?" Nick asked.

"All right. I have a feeling I'm not going to get rid of you unless I do." She sashayed her way around the desk, then sat. Her fingers flew over the keyboard, the claw-like nails clicking. She squinted at the screen. Did she need glasses? Too vain to wear them? "This is a temporary address. No idea if he's still here or not. Employees are supposed to let us know when they move." She shrugged. "But you know how that goes." She clicked the mouse a couple of times, then the printer started chugging. She pulled the sheet of paper off the printer. "Hope this helps you find her."

Nick took the paper, glanced at the address, a familiar one, then folded it in quarters and stuck it in his jeans pocket. "Thanks."

He turned and tugged on Allie's elbow. "Let's move it."

She stumbled over the doorsill, then brushed away his helping hand. "I'm fine, even if I am clumsy. Just leave me the hell alone."

Instead of shaking her, he gave himself a mental shake. Allison followed him out through the bar. The restaurant was already filling up for the lunch crowd. He dipped his head and spoke low, "You can't keep going off on people like that. You need some serious downtime."

"It's just... I keep seeing her body all cut up and bleeding. I can't help it. I get so angry when people act like they don't care." She started to cry.

God, he hated it when women cried. "Now come on. We're a step closer." Eyes full of tears, she gazed up at him. He pulled her closer, and damn if he hadn't underestimated what holding her would do to his heart rate.

Dang it. She was a sweet armful. No doubt about it.

His mouth dried until he couldn't have spit a drop. Okay, diversion needed. And quick.

"Barkeep, how about a couple of bottled waters?"

The bartender snickered, then nodded. "Sure."

Nick threw a ten on the bar and grabbed the two bottles. "Here, you need to hydrate."

"Thanks." She sniffled like a kid but took the water. "I know all about keeping hydrated. I'm a nurse."

"Yeah, yeah." He twisted off the cap and emptied half the bottle with a long drink. "Come on. I want to catch this guy before he knows we're looking for him."

They headed out into the hot-as-hell day. "You think he might try to leave town?"

"If the man's got half a brain and he had anything to do with Meryl's disappearance, he's long gone."

"And if he's still here, then that'll mean you're wrong, and I'm right about—"

"You're not right. Even if he's stupid enough to stay in town, stats are on my side. It's always the husband."

Allie frowned and stuck her nose in the air. She had to be the most stubborn woman he'd ever come across. "We'll see."

Chapter Eleven

Buckley's address was easy to find. First, a straight shot down Murfreesboro Road, then onto Briley Parkway. One short block and they found Tom Buckley living in a small two-bedroom apartment on Saturn Drive, made smaller because of all the crap Allison could see when Buckley opened the door.

Meryl's ex was a scrawny scarecrow of a guy with limp brown hair and a three-days'-growth beard. He stared at them with red eyes. "Who the hell are you?"

"Nick Vitelli. I'm a private investigator." He pulled a card from his jeans pocket. "Like to ask you a few questions."

Meryl's ex shrugged, stepped back, and allowed them to enter. "Sorry about the mess. Roommates aren't big on picking up." He swept a pile of discarded clothes from the sofa onto the floor. "Have a seat."

Allison declined his kind offer. If "picking up" was synonymous with a grave need of a John Deere tractor with a scooper on the front, then he was exceedingly accurate.

Meryl's ex swiped at his nose with the back of his hand. "This 'bout Meryl, isn't it?"

"What about her, Buckley?" Nick asked, stepping between Allison and their quarry. "She's been missing for a day and a half. Where do you fit in?"

"I didn't have nothin' to do with her taking off. And believe you me, that's what she's gone and done. Done it before too."

"To get away from you, no doubt." Okay, so she couldn't keep her mouth shut. Whatever had Meryl seen in this low-life skunk? She must've married too young before she knew any better.

Buckley shrugged. "Maybe. She divorced me and took off without telling me she was carrying my baby. You'll find her. Mark my words. She's hiding, trying to keep my kid from knowing his rightful daddy."

Allison nudged Nick with her elbow. She wasn't afraid of Tom Buckley and had no intention of letting Nick treat her any way other than as an equal. "Listen, you dumbass. There was blood found at her place. She didn't just run off somewhere—not that I'd blame her one little bit."

Two strong hands settled on her shoulders, her body shuddering from the sudden contact from Nick's body. And his heat.

"Cool it," Nick's tone was low and calming. "Look, fella, we're just trying to find some answers. We know you left a message on your ex-wife's voice mail. And the neighbors heard her arguing with someone fitting your description the night before she disappeared. Make it easy on yourself and tell us what you argued about."

"You used to be a cop, right? Yeah, I can always tell." Buckley sprawled back on the ratty sofa and scratched his head. "Just the same old stuff we always fought over. How I was useless and no-good. She had the kid to think of and all that. Done heard it all a dozen times, except about the kid. She never bothered to tell me 'bout that."

"Have the police talked to you yet?" Nick set his hands on his hips. He was definitely in cop mode.

"No. Say, how'd you find me anyways?"

"He's a PI," she said with a snap, "and he can find anyone anywhere."

"Might not have too long to wait. I'll be real visible soon. I'm gonna be a star." Buckley reached over and pulled out his guitar from another pile of the apartment's detritus.

"Wanna hear a sample? Wrote this one myself." He strummed the strings, ready to serenade them.

"What time did you see Meryl?" Nick asked, interrupting before Buckley could launch into song. Thank heavens. Somehow, she didn't think he'd be any good.

The never-would-be star sighed and set his guitar aside. He scratched his scraggly chin. "Thursday night right after she got off work. Didn't stay long 'cause I had to work my shift at the Wildhorse. And Friday night I had an early gig at the Cannery. I opened for the Baker Boys."

Nick pulled out a notepad and pen. "We'll be checking your alibi. What time did you get to the Cannery?"

"Gig's from quarter to seven to quarter after. Got there around six, had me a tall one."

Allison drifted around the living room but kept her gaze on Nick. His eyes were shuttered, revealing little. "What about the afternoon before work?"

Meryl's ex twitched, cut his gaze to the ceiling, scratched his chin. "Um, caught me the matinee at the Cineplex."

"What was showing?"

"Danged if I know." He shrugged, giving them an embarrassed expression. "Fell asleep. Good thing they woke me up and booted me out, or I would've been late for my gig."

"Have the name of the person who woke you up?"

"Hell, no. Just beat it outta there and headed back downtown."

She'd had enough of his guff. She stopped drifting to eyeball him. "You really expect us to believe you fell asleep and don't even remember what movie you went to see?"

"Makes me no never mind what you believe. You're not the police."

"No, but my future sister-in-law is, and this is her case. She'll be happy to know where to find you." She shot him a smug grin. *Yeah. Let the slug squirm.*

"No need to get all huffy, ma'am, but I 'spect you get huffy a lot." Buckley sniffed and rubbed his nose with a forefinger. She'd bet even money he was a cokehead or a tweaker.

"Tell me about it." Nick's response was low, but she wasn't about to let him get away with his snide remark.

"I *heard* you." She gave Nick's ribs a quick jab.

Totally ignoring her, Nick continued. "Have you seen or heard from Meryl since you argued Thursday night?"

"Hell, no!" Buckley straightened up, his eyes flickering with realization. "I know how you cops are. You always go after the husband—"

"*Ex*-husband. She divorced you," Allison said.

"I was going to say 'or ex-husband.' That's why you're really here."

"We're just trying to eliminate you as a person of interest." Warming to her role, Allison bristled, setting her hands on her hips. "Yeah, you—"

Nick interrupted her flow of words with the tiniest shake of his head. The sharp flicker of anger in his cool blue eyes stopped her dead anyway. Fine. He could play good-cop. Crazy-bad cop was much more her style.

"Yeah, you got that cop talk down all right." Meryl's ex leaned back, relaxing under Nick's professional way of handling him. "Do whatcha have to. I don't want anything to happen to her or my kid."

Allison watched Nick make his notes. If she weren't so sure the good Dr. Ivers had something to do with Meryl's disappearance, her ex made as good a suspect as anyone. And if she didn't quit flying off the handle at *persons of interest*, Nick wouldn't let her keep riding shotgun on his investigation.

But there was no way she was going to sit on her hands and allow Nick and the police to do the investigation alone.

Nick closed his notepad. "If you hear from Meryl, you know to call me or the police right away—right?"

"'Course I know." The never-gonna-be-famous musician dragged himself from the sofa. "If y'all don't mind, I gotta get to my shift at the Wildhorse. You got any more questions, you know where to find me."

Nick leveled his gaze on Buckley. "Don't be leaving town."

"*You* can't tell me that, but I know the police can. Anyways, I'm sticking around 'cause I'm on the verge of getting a recording contract...and for Meryl and the kid."

Meryl and the kid were just an afterthought to him. A strong urge to fly at him with nails bared surged through her, but she gritted her teeth and resisted, then headed for the door. "We're through here." Maybe the disgust in her tone would shame him.

But she doubted it.

After leaving Buckley's apartment, Nick headed the Bronco down Murfreesboro Road to downtown. For once, Allison was quiet. Good thing too. A little more quiet contemplation on her part was exactly what the doctor ordered. Hell, it was crazy to let her ride shotgun. Left unsupervised, she was a loose cannon. A lightning rod for trouble.

And she was more than one kind of trouble. The boss's little sis. Cute as hell. Sharp and prickly as a thorn. Unpredictable as a tornado.

Yeah. Trouble like her he didn't need.

"Why don't you call O'Malley and ask her where we can meet," he suggested.

"We could go to the station house."

"No. Reckon she'd rather meet us off-site."

"And this is because you know her so well and have ESP

besides?"

"Detectives like to protect their sources. Doubt she'd want the entire squad to know we're working the case too."

"Right. Because you're a former cop and you know all things copperly."

"*Copperly*? That's not a word."

"So now, you're an English major too?" She emitted a ladylike snort but bent over and pulled her cell from her purse. "Fine. I'll do it."

"You will if you want to keep riding shotgun."

"That's the real reason. You don't want anyone to see you with me. Another non-copperly thing to do."

"Stop using that word. I hate it."

"Fine." She punched in some numbers and waited. "Hey, it's me. Any news?"

From the corner of his eye, he saw her shoulders drop. No news.

"We have something for you. Nick wants to know where you can meet us." A pause. "Okay. Starbucks it is. Ten minutes. We're on Lafayette now." She snapped the phone shut. "Happy?"

"Very." He zipped through the yellow light onto Eighth. "Thanks."

Luckily, when she decided to behave herself, she was tolerable. Her tagging along wasn't procedure—not at all. Keeping his mind on business was twice as difficult. Besides being a heap of trouble, she was a major distraction.

And if they ran into trouble, his distraction could endanger their lives.

Nick set his cup of coffee on the table and handed Allie her green tea with lemon, then nodded at the window. "There's Tess now."

With a jacket slung over her shoulder, she entered the coffee shop looking better than any homicide detective of his previous acquaintance had ever looked. Given she was about to marry his boss, he'd leave it at that.

When Allison wasn't getting on his last nerve, she was pretty damn hot herself. Even so, there was an air of innocence about her that was long gone from the homicide detective's gaze.

For some strange reason, Allison's innocence appealed to him. Granted, she drove him to nuts and back, but he couldn't help but wonder what she'd be like in bed. At twenty-six—probably not a virgin. But the young woman had more on her mind than the next party or hookup.

"I need a refill," Tess said on her way to the counter.

He nodded.

He waited until Tess returned and scooted a chair up to their table. "What's up? I can see from your expression you have *something*."

He gave Tess the quick-and-dirty version of how they found and interviewed Meryl's ex and handed over his notes.

Tess glanced over them, chewed on her inner cheek, then her bottom lip. "Why didn't you tell me first? I don't like the idea of you two getting there ahead of me." Her cheeks flushed and her tone rose a notch. "Now you've tipped him off. I bet Buckley's on his way out of town right now. You might've revealed something about the case and compromised everything."

"Hold on, Detective. I'm not a rookie, and I don't appreciate being talked to like one. I've interviewed suspects before."

"Geez, Louise, I know. But it's not fair. You have Justin as a resource, and all I have is an overworked computer system, which takes forever to spit out a report." O'Malley picked up her cup and drained it.

"Did I hear a 'thank you' in there somewhere? We gave you the ex-husband's address and everything he told us." He glanced at Allison. "Did I miss anything?"

"Nope." Allison shook her head. "And I don't think he's gonna skip town because he's here to become a *star*. Meryl and her baby, or 'the kid,' as he calls their baby, are secondary."

Did he imagine steam coming from Tess's ears? "Those dreams are a dime a dozen," she said. "For your sakes, I hope he doesn't wake up and skip. Obstruction of justice comes to mind."

"Hey!" Allison slapped the tabletop. "You're both wasting time on her ex anyway. You need to investigate Dr. Ivers. And that's all there is to it."

"Come on. What possible motive could the doctor have for kidnapping Meryl Litton?"

"I think she came across some irregularity in the transplant program and was going to expose him." Warming to the task, she continued. "There's money to be made in black-market organs. Plus, that very afternoon she called me and said something was up and that she had an appointment to see him."

Shrugging, Tess made a face. "He says she never showed up."

"So he *says*, but I don't believe him."

"Is that why you took it upon yourself to show up at his condo and make a scene?"

"It's exactly the reason. I don't want him to think he can get away with this." Allison's gaze darted from him to Tess.

"*If* he had anything to do with Ms. Litton's disappearance," Tess said, "we'll find evidence and he'll pay for it. But in cases like these, it's almost always the husband."

"Her ex says she's run off before. Maybe she has."

"Allie..." Nick set his hand on her shoulder. "You don't believe that for a minute. We both saw the blood."

"It was a lot of blood. I'm a nurse I know there was more blood than someone could safely lose, but if Dr. Ivers had anything to do with it, he could've taken her somewhere and cared for her."

"Did you see him at the high-rise?" Tess raised an eyebrow, her expression bordering on skeptical.

"No, just his wife." Allison groaned. "His very pissed-off wife."

"She could be an accessory in this wild idea of yours."

"It's not that wild."

Before Tess could continue, a country tune sounded from her cell phone. "My partner just texted me. I need to call him back to verify...something." She stood and left the coffee shop to stand on the sidewalk.

Something was up. Never much of a lip reader, he still made out the words "car" and "where?"

He held his breath and cast a low glance at his partner in crime. Her jaw was set, but her bottom lip quivered. She watched Tess too, trying to make out what she was saying.

"This could be it. Maybe they've found Meryl. I'm sure she's fine. Thank goodness."

Brave words backed by fear, no doubt.

This could be it, all right. They'd found the car. And maybe Meryl's body. How would Allison react if the news was bad? All the positive thinking in the world wouldn't keep her tender heart from breaking.

And it might just send her over the edge.

Tess re-entered the coffee shop, her face schooled in a mask of neutrality. "I shouldn't tell you this, but Meryl's vehicle has been found."

Allie's gaze widened. She started to rise from her seat.

"And?"

Nick braced, ready to catch her, just in case.

"Uh-uh," Tess said. "Don't know anything else. I'm headed over there now." She grabbed her jacket from the back of the chair and slipped it on. "You all need to go home, and I'll call you as soon as I know something for sure."

"Sit at home? And wait?" Allison squared her shoulders. "No way. We'll follow you."

Tess shrugged, no doubt expecting Allie's reaction. "Free country, but you will *not* cross the perimeter."

"I understand. But I just can't sit at home and wait." There was the slightest quaver in her voice, but she held it together for the moment.

"Patience isn't one of your better virtues, is it?"

"We're *working* on it," Nick said. His hand was heavy on her shoulder, stopping Allison from bolting. Or something more? "Can you at least tell us where it was found?"

Tess frowned, but a touch of resignation flickered with a quick upward glance. "Found in the Farmers' Market parking lot just off Buchanan. Stripped. Don't ask me anything else. That's all I know." Her gaze darted toward the door. "If you're coming, come on."

"I'll be on my best behavior. I promise." She glanced at Nick for his reaction.

The corner of his mouth lifted in a wry smirk. "I'll see to it," Nick said. "No point in leaving her behind unless I handcuff her to the bed."

Had he really used handcuff and bed in the same sentence? Allison's jaw dropped. "The very idea."

O'Malley rolled her eyes, muttered something under her breath, then opened the door.

Nick leaned close to Allison's ear. "Not a bad idea, but there's no time if we want to keep up with Tess."

"I'm not the one standing here yammering about

handcuffing my client to the bed, which, I might add, is inappropriate, all things considered. Maybe you've forgotten..."

"Haven't forgotten anything. Move it."

It wasn't far. Meryl's car was in the far corner of the Nashville Farmers' Market parking lot. Bright yellow crime-scene tape was already in place. All Allison could make out was the maroon Kia with the trunk popped. She wasn't close enough to see anything else. Dammit.

Nick stood at her side. His hand beat a nervous tattoo against his thigh. So, she wasn't the only one eager to see what was going on or what, if anything, was in the trunk.

Was there—she shuddered—a body? At least there wasn't a coroner's wagon, merely a wrecker sitting off to the side.

She was ready to slip under the tape when she saw Tess headed her way.

"Come here. There's something I want you to see. Tell me what you think it is. We'll take the entire vehicle into the garage and have it analyzed, but I thought, since you're a nurse, you might have an idea."

Puzzled, she followed Tess to the car.

"There's more blood, but there's something else."

The gray carpet liner in the trunk was marked with a Rorschach swirl of blood and a thinner fluid. She took a whiff and turned her head from the characteristic odors and from the certain knowledge of what its presence meant. "Amniotic fluid. It's not fresh. The odor's from sitting and baking in the sun."

Tess sighed, but her face remained impassive. "Was afraid of that."

"Because it means Meryl's lost the baby?" Of course, she'd lost the baby. It was too early in its gestation to have survived. But it didn't mean…

Tess blinked, then turned away.

The detective's slow, stoic blink said it all: what everyone had already accepted, what Allison couldn't—or didn't want to. Meryl was dead.

The bleak, uncompromising certainty her friend was dead seeped into her consciousness, obliterating all hope of a positive outcome. Her heart pounded. Breathing…impossible. An icy sensation of cold suffused her body. She started to shake.

First her hands. Her arms. Her knees jittered, weakened, and gave way.

Chapter Twelve

Nick closed the door to Allie's bedroom. Never had he ever seen anyone go from strong and professional to poleaxed in a matter of seconds. He'd tried to console her at the scene, but nothing he'd said or did helped. So, he'd brought her home. She needed her family. Not him. He headed downstairs and found her brothers in the den munching chips and downing a couple of tall ones.

Scott stood. "Beer's in the fridge. Help yourself."

Nick nodded. "I could use one. I'm two hours past empty."

When Nick returned with his beer, Scott asked, "How is she?"

He shrugged. "Guess she's all right. She's awake. Crying her heart out. Carrie's with her."

"Hey!" Justin shouted. "Get a load of this." He gestured at the TV.

"We're coming to you from the Criminal Justice Center. Tom Buckley, the ex-husband of missing nurse Meryl Litton, has just emerged after being questioned by homicide detectives, and he's consented to give us an interview about his ex-wife's disappearance."

Buckley nodded at the camera and mugged. What did that bastard have to be so happy about, anyway?

"Mr. Buckley, do the authorities consider you a person of interest?"

"Don't reckon they do. I'm free to go, as you can see." He smoothed back his straggling hair and again mugged for the camera.

"Looks like a person of interest to me." Nick sat on a corner of the coffee table, his gaze glued to the screen.

"Ditto." This from Justin.

"I got me one of those ironclad alibis. I wouldn't harm Meryl or my kid. Won't say I wasn't mad at her for running away from home. Columbia—that's where we're from."

A pure pissed-off surge of anger slammed through Nick's chest, no doubt sending his blood pressure through the roof. "Ironclad my ass. Bastard said he fell asleep at the Cineplex."

"You're kidding." Scott reached for a bowl of chips.

"You followed your ex-wife to Nashville?"

"Sort of. You see, I got me a gig opening for the Baker Brothers at the Cannery on Friday nights. Folks, you come on down. I start at—"

The TV journalist broke in before he could complete his blatant burst of self-promotion. "Where were you during the time your wife went missing?"

"I was at a movie. Good movie too."

"Lying son of a bitch." Nick jumped up and started to pace. "His ex-wife's dead, and here he's drumming up publicity for his singing career. Somebody needs to put him down like the dog he is."

"If he's giving different stories to different people, then he's bound to be lying."

The reporter wasn't ready to let him go. "What movie did you see?"

He responded with a hangdog expression. "*The Lorax*."

"You went to see *The Lorax*?" Disbelief was written across the reporter's face. "That's a cartoon."

"But it's a good one like I said."

"Quick," Nick said. "Let's check if *The Lorax* was really on at the Cineplex."

Justin grabbed his laptop from the side table. "Hold on."

The computer whiz's fingers flew over the keys.

The Tom Buckley show continued to play out for all of Nashville to see. "Do you have any idea where your wife could be or why anyone would harm her?"

Buckley waggled his straggly head. "No idea at all. She was a good person...mostly."

"Mostly?"

"She had a temper on her when she got all het up."

"Neighbors reported hearing the two of you arguing the night before she disappeared."

"Yeah, we had us a disagreement, but it don't mean I killed her. We was about to make up. I think we coulda gotten back together if she was still alive."

"Then, in your opinion, she's dead?"

"Most likely. Leastways, that's what the police tell me."

The reporter turned from Buckley to face the camera. "You heard it here first. Kendra Wilson reporting for News Channel 9."

"Un-fucking-believable." Never had Nick seen anyone who disgusted him more. That jackass was one bare step above a pedophile.

"Hot damn," Justin interrupted. "*The Lorax* was on Friday's matinee."

Nick sat, his mind racing. "Crap. He must've checked the listings before O'Malley and her partner interviewed him. No matter. He's already told two different stories about where he was. If he keeps talking, he'll slip up again. Bound to." He leaned forward, determined not to miss another word. "TiVo?"

"Yeah." Scott snatched the remote from the chair arm and pressed the Record button. "Save it for posterity."

"I don't know about Allison," Scott said. "She was all gung-ho about that doctor having something to do with Meryl's disappearance, but this slimy piece of crap beats all

I've ever seen. If he's not guilty, he oughta be."

Worry about Allison's reaction if she ever saw the interview sat heavily on Nick's shoulders. "Can't jail someone for being 'a slimy piece of crap.' Can't say there haven't been times I wished I could."

Scott's expression grew sober. "I don't want to question your tactics, but are you sure Allison ought to be riding shotgun on this case?"

"Hell, no. She's got no business being involved in any of this. But *you* try keeping her out of it. If I've learned anything in the last couple of days, it's that she'll go off on her own and do heaven knows what. She's *your* sister. You have to know what she's like. For Allie, *this* is a crusade. She won't back down for anybody."

"Yeah. You're right." Scott leaned back. "It's a good thing tomorrow's Monday. She has to work. What are you going to do about her then?"

"What can I do? It's not like I can put a leash on her. Hang around the hospital and give a correction whenever she starts to get excited?"

A low chuckle rose from Justin's corner. "Man. I'd like to see that. Allie on a leash."

"I don't *think* so."

Great. The lady in question stood in the doorway. How long had she been there? Long enough to hear his leash joke.

Too long.

Caroline stood beside Allison with a protective arm around her shoulder.

"Relax, fellas," Allison said. "Scott's right. I have to go back to work. First of all, Monday is one of the two busiest days of my week. If any of the weekend transfers fell through, I'll have to get on those the first thing. I'll have to screen the new admissions. Set up home health and order any durable medical equipment. Don't worry about it. I won't have time to do anything but my job."

"I don't pretend to understand half of what you said, but it's good to know. Maybe I can get some real work done, then." The last words slipped out before he could stop them. Would she consider them a challenge or let him slide?

"Plus with Meryl...out, we're a case manager short, and I'm her back up."

Okay, slide. "You gonna have contact with Doctor Ivers?"

She huffed and gave him the evil eye. "I'll *try* to keep it to a minimum, but I might have to talk to him about a patient. My best bet is to let a social worker handle him and not have any direct contact."

"Sounds like a plan. Good thinking. What time do you go in and what time do you get off?"

"Since I'll be covering two assignments, I'll go in around six-thirty and probably get off around five if I'm lucky. Six or seven if I'm not."

Her arms were folded across her breasts. Why was she being so defensive?

"What's the matter, Nick? Don't you trust me?"

Her expression was innocence personified, but he didn't buy it. "Not as far as I can throw you, darlin'."

"How long do you think it'll take the authorities to"—she paused and swallowed before continuing—"to find Meryl?"

"Depends on how hard they sweat Buckley. He's the one."

She shrugged. "I guess."

Perhaps in an attempt to diffuse the situation, Caroline spoke up. "Guys, we're going to grill some chicken. Any takers?"

Three hands rose; Caroline nodded and headed back to the kitchen. He glanced at the brothers, who indicated with sideways glances he should be the one to tell Allison about Buckley's TV interview. They stood and followed Caroline's example by beating it for the kitchen, leaving Nick alone with Allison.

Chicken shits.

Bad as he hated it, he might as well find out if she caught any of the interview. "Uh, before you came in... Buckley was on TV—"

A scowl wrinkled her face into a displeased mask. "Yeah, I caught the end of it in my room. Imagine using Meryl's disappearance to further his so-called music career? He needs to go to prison just for being barely human."

"Before this is over, he will. For sure."

"Someone has to pay." She set her hands on her hips and gave a determined nod. "Someone *will* pay if I have anything to say about it."

"That's all the *law* can do now. See that he pays."

"Don't think I didn't hear the warning. You want me to stay out of it? Right?"

"You have to. Whoever's responsible—they don't want to go to jail. Understand?"

She nodded thoughtfully. "You think I could be in danger if I keep pursuing this."

"Exactly."

She threw her hands up. "Fine. I'm out of it. I'm just so tired." She leaned against the doorjamb as if needing support.

He wanted to go to her, give her some of his strength, but he held back. She might take it the wrong way.

Her face paled, and her eyes grew shiny. "I try not to think of what she must've gone through. Being afraid. Knowing her baby would never draw breath. I'm sure she fought for her life. And her baby's."

"Allie, stop it." He moved to her side, still uncertain how she would take his actions. This wasn't a case of her collapsing and needing to be caught. No, this was more like she needed someone to hold her and tell her everything would be okay, even if it was a lie. "You're torturing yourself."

"Maybe if I'd just gone over there earlier and not waited until after dinner?"

Dammit. Standing there like an armless tree wasn't an option. He pulled her into his arms. She buried her face in his chest, hiccupped, and sobbed like a child. He inhaled the citrusy fragrance of her shampoo, even as the softness of her hair tickled his nose. Being so close sent an eddy of emotions swirling through his mind.

And body.

God, she was soft and pliant in his arms. He held back, still unable to surrender to the surges of sensual need this one woman, part nutcase, part crusader, but all woman, had unleashed.

She let out a deep sigh, pressing her round breasts into his chest.

Deliver me. He cleared his throat. "Better see if you can help your sister with anything. I'll check with your brothers."

She nodded and pulled away.

How stupid was he? How could he send her off to the kitchen as if nothing had passed between them? Maybe it hadn't. Maybe it was just him.

Allison had picked at her dinner. In fact, her stomach roiled at the smell of grilling chicken the entire time it cooked. Thankfully, Carolyn and Tamsyn cleared the plates, excusing her from KP duties. All she could think about were Meryl and Nick. Two very different situations and both unthinkable.

For very different reasons, of course.

She leaned her elbows on the deck rail and stared into the

night. If only things could be different. So many things.

A hand touched her elbow. She glanced up and smiled.

Nick.

"Let's take a walk in the backyard." He placed a steadying hand at the small of her back, and they walked down the steps. He led her over to the water feature and nodded she should have a seat on the stone bench. "The flowers are nice."

"Yeah," she murmured. "Tamsyn really has a green thumb."

"Tamsyn?" He chuckled. "Somehow she doesn't seem the type."

Insects buzzed in the growing darkness. Allison slapped her upper arm. "Mosquitoes are out." What did he want? Another chance to press bodies? She'd felt him harden. Not that she was offended, just surprised.

"We won't stay long," he said. "I just need to know if you're all right."

She relaxed against him. Maybe she could absorb some of his solid strength and alleviate the utter sense of helplessness gnawing at her night and day. "It just doesn't seem possible something like this should have happened. Not to anyone I know. Especially not to Meryl."

"I'm really sorry about your friend. I'm sorry you have to deal with this, and there's no good way to go about it."

"You saw cases like this—in Atlanta, I mean?"

"More than I care to remember. I wasn't in Homicide, but everyone on the job was always aware of the cases. Ninety-nine percent of the time, it was the husband, the ex, or the boyfriend."

"Scott said you worked in narcotics—undercover?

"Most of the time."

"I guess it made things difficult at home?

"You could say that."

He seemed uncomfortable. His shoulders hunched, and she could just make out the muscles in his jaw clenching. Prying into people's personal lives wasn't part of her nature, so she changed the subject. "Ninety-nine percent of the time, I'd agree with you about it being the husband. I've seen abused wives come in knocked around and bruised and battered. Then they turn around and go right back to the same old situation. It doesn't make sense."

"Nah." He shook his head. "I never could understand why my mom let my dad smack her around the way he did. She had an idea it might keep him from hitting us boys."

"And did it?"

"No. Well, maybe sometimes. He sure was a mean SOB."

"What happened between them?"

"My mom, she finally got up the gumption to leave him. They're divorced now, living in Florida, both of 'em—on opposite coasts. Seen the same thing, time and time again when I was on patrol. Always the same deal. They call the police. We show up. They're bleeding and bruised, but they won't press charges. And all the time, you know the next time might be too late."

"Wife beaters are the second lowest form of humanity, the lowest being reserved for those who abuse children. My personal opinion, of course." She rubbed her hands back and forth on her thighs, seemingly unconscious of what she was doing.

"No argument here." Nick continued staring into the warm August night. In the distance, a neighbor's cat yowled a mournful complaint.

"But I still think there's something else at work in Meryl's—uh, case." No, she still couldn't bear to say death, dead, or body when referring to Meryl.

He cocked his head and gave her a knowing nod. "The doctor angle? You're still thinking about him, aren't you?"

"Can't help it. She was going to see him. And now she's gone."

"Have an idea—a way you can still help with the investigation but at a distance."

A way she could help. Her heart hammered, and her mouth grew cotton dry. "Sign me up. I'm listening."

"Since you're convinced this doctor had something to do with it and I know next to nothing about his specialty—hell, about anything medical—do some online research. You mentioned the black market in organs. Find out all you can on the Internet."

"Yeah, it'll keep me out of everyone's hair. Won't Justin do that?"

"He's involved with researching other aspects of the case. Besides, he doesn't have your medical background. And if there's any way you can research Ivers online, go ahead. Do it. Just don't go showing up at his home or his office."

"I was stupid. I shouldn't have gone anywhere near him. Now he knows we're on to him."

"No. If he's guilty"—Nick aimed his forefinger at her chest—"he thinks *you're* on to him. That's not a situation I'm comfortable with."

She let out a huff. "Understood. Keep my distance."

"Yes. That way, both of us will live through this and come out the other side."

There was a hint of wry humor in his tone, but Allison couldn't forget. "The irony is we can, but Meryl can't."

"I know." He nodded, his expression softening as he met her gaze. "Think you can manage some research time while you're at work?"

She thought for a moment. "Not on a Monday. I might find time to Google the topic and print something on my lunch break, but I'll have to bring it home to study."

While they talked, the sky had darkened to an inky black

with pinpoints of stars the only illumination. The fountain bubbled, and an energetic cricket chirped. She leaned closer to Nick. The woody scent of sandalwood tickled her nose. "What will you do tomorrow—while I'm at work?"

He stirred beside her, stretched his neck, and rotated his shoulders as if his muscles were growing stiff. "Reckon I'll chase down Buckley's alibis. See how firm they are. I'm definitely dropping by the Cineplex to see if anyone remembers him."

"Yeah, his falling asleep in the movie sounded bogus." A sense of unease grew. Why? Nick was as comfortable as could be. Most of the time, anyway.

He must've felt it too. He stood, his body positioned for leaving. "Guess I'd better go."

"You all right? Did I say something wrong?"

"Nah. I need to get home in time to call my son and tell him good night."

"You really miss him, don't you?"

"Yeah. Not that I got to spend much time with him when I was with his mom, but..." He broke off with a shrug.

"Sorry. Didn't mean to stick my nose in your business." Was that what she'd done or just brought up a painful subject?

"That's not it. Just need to get going." He took off and loped up the steps to the deck. What had just happened here? Not twenty minutes ago, he was kind and considerate, and then, with an abrupt about-face, he couldn't get away fast enough.

Men.

Nick said his good-byes to Scott and the rest of the family, then beat it back to the Bronco. Allison was nowhere to be seen. Relieved, he sat in the SUV for a moment. What the hell was he thinking? She was his client *and* his boss's sister. Bad business for him to get all hot and bothered every time she came within five feet.

But she smelled like summer sunshine and had a heart every bit as big as Texas. Lips, eyes, and a slender body he wanted to wrap in his arms and hold on to forever.

Smart too, even if she was wrong about Ivers being responsible for her friend's disappearance.

Fuck it. He'd get no sleep tonight. He jammed the key into the ignition and turned on the motor, then cut his gaze toward the house.

She was standing inside the front door, her hand raised in a wave.

Pay no attention to the beautiful gal behind the window, fella.

Get the hell out of Dodge.

More conflicted than ever, Allison watched as Nick drove away. The man was rapidly becoming more than the PI assigned to her case. More like he was her go-to guy. For everything.

Need help finding your best friend? Call Nick.

Need a broad shoulder to cry on? Call Nick.

Need someone for love and understanding? Call Nick?

No. Love wasn't on his agenda. Nick was just a good-hearted guy doing his job. Nothing more.

Chapter Thirteen

The first thing Monday morning, Allison booted up her computer and checked her email for any issues that might've arisen over the weekend.

Hm. Already an email marked *urgent* from her boss, Carol Waller. She quickly read the cryptic message. *See me as soon as you come in.* No worries. Carol was one of the best department directors and always fair. She'd come up through the ranks and had the respect of her case managers and Administration too.

Seeing nothing else that needed her immediate attention, she walked down the hall to Carol's office and knocked.

"Enter."

Allison opened the door and found her boss scowling over what appeared to be a file. "Good morning. What's up?"

Carol pushed back from the desk, adjusted her glasses with one finger, then leveled her gaze on Allison. Uh-oh, something was definitely up. Carol's usual good humor didn't seem to be at home.

"Have a seat." Carol's tone was crisp and in her no-BS mode.

What else could she do? She sat.

"I know you and Meryl were close." Her nails beat a light, rapid tat-a-tat on the desk. "All of us in the department are upset, but you've got to—" Carol blew out a puff of air, blowing up her poufy bangs. "I received a call from the admin-on-call this weekend. Needless to say, Dr. Ivers and his wife are less than pleased that one of my case managers showed up at their residence and took it upon herself to harass them and make all sorts of accusations."

Allison took a deep breath, using the few seconds' time to frame her words. Of course, they'd reported her. She'd expected nothing less. "I was a little out of control this weekend. I'm sorry they involved you."

"You know how it is. These doctors act like they own this place. Truthfully, some of them have a big stake in it...*and* they have influence. This can't happen again." Carol sighed, then continued. "As for now, I have no choice but to make note of our conversation and to place a record of verbal reprimand in your file." She tapped said file with her forefinger.

"I understand. And if he actually had something to do with Meryl's disappearance? You know the police are certain she's—" She couldn't bring herself to say more, the idea still too horrific for words.

"Let the *police* take care of it." She closed the file. "If anything like this happens again, I'll have no choice but to terminate you."

"I understand. It won't happen again—I promise. I've come to the realization there's nothing I can do anyway."

Liar. Liar. Yes, her job was important, but not more important than her friend's life.

Allison stood and tried not to grit her teeth. "Is that all?"

"Yeah, go on." Carol seemed to relax now the painful interview was over. "Go on and get to work." She said the last with a half smile.

"I see the on-call case manager had a quiet weekend."

"Quieter than yours, anyway."

Allison nodded, headed back to her cubicle, then pulled a ton of new orders off her printer. Today was going to be worse than usual. At least the work would keep her out of trouble.

She spent the morning assessing the new weekend

admissions for any possible home needs on discharge, set up nine discharges for home health care, and ordered more DME than she'd ever ordered in a single day before.

At lunchtime—not that she had time for anything more than a Diet Coke and a bag of chips at her desk—she Googled "black-market organs" and printed out five articles as fast as the printer could print. She'd take them home to study later, but now back to the two floors she was covering. She found the transplant social worker and pulled her aside for a private confab.

"It's probably all over the hospital, but I had a dustup with Dr. Ivers and his shrew of a wife over the weekend. I've set up Weems in 506 for his first office visit on Wednesday, and if you'll let the good doctor know, it'll probably make everyone's life go a lot smoother."

Mischief sparkled in SuEllen Mason's dark eyes. "Might've heard something. You've got big ones, girl. But I'll keep in touch with him. Have the police found anything yet?"

"No, and I've got to go back to Meryl's floor and tie up some loose ends."

She headed to the elevator, but her cell phone rang before she could hit the Up button. The number was unfamiliar, but she answered since she often gave patients or their family members her number.

"Hi, Allie, it's Tess. Can you come down to the office when you get off work? I have some CCTV footage I want you to take a look at."

"I've already seen the footage."

"No. This footage is from the parking lot where we found Meryl's car. It's not very clear, but I thought—what the hell, I'm clutching straws, I know, but another set of eyes..."

"Sure. You know I'll do anything I can." She bit her bottom lip, then forged ahead. "Anything back on the lab work?"

"Same as Meryl's blood type. Takes longer for a DNA match, and you were right about the presence of amniotic fluid."

Allison swallowed the clot of grief hanging in her throat. "I don't know if I can ever truly accept it until we find her."

"Believe me. I understand."

The phone beeped in her ear. "Got another call. Gotta go." Another unfamiliar number. She answered, "Lackey."

"How's it going?" Nick's sexy low voice sent a quick thrill up her spine. "I still have that leash. Do I need it?"

"Considering I'm covering two assignments and I've already been threatened with losing my job if I don't back off, I'm having a hunky-dory day. How 'bout you?"

"Spent all morning running down Tom Buckley's alibis."

"Right. By the way, Tess has some additional CCTV footage she wants me to see from the Farmer's Market."

"Why don't I pick you up? I'd like to have a look myself."

"Sure—" She broke off, remembering his abrupt escape the night before. "I mean, you don't have to go with me. I'll be fine."

"No. I really need to see it. Buckley has a limp. Maybe the footage shows—"

Attempting to lighten the mood, Allison interrupted. "A limper?"

He snorted. "Uh, yeah. Someone with a limp—you know, someone who limps."

This time, she almost smiled. "Right. And I have some articles on what we discussed last night. I'll look at them after work and let you know what I've learned."

"We could go over them together. You could explain whatever medical jargon's over my head."

So, he wanted to go over her material. Maybe he wouldn't run off like last night. "Did you talk to your son?"

"Made the call just in time. Eva gave me some guff about calling so late and started grilling me about where I'd been—like we were still married—but she finally quit busting my chops and put him on so I could tell him good night."

"You're working a case, for Pete's sake." Granted, Allison had never been married, much less divorced, but there were limits to how much interference a man should have to put up with. Having a child complicated things for both exes.

"None of her business anymore." He paused, then asked, "What time do you think you'll get off?"

"Five thirty should do it."

"See ya then."

Nick disconnected. Hm. Whatever was bothering him last night didn't appear to be bothering him now. Okay, no more calls. Back to the fifth floor. Maybe Ivers was through with his rounds and she could relax. Dealing with his wife was bad enough, but the doctor himself was Napoleon on his good days and Attila the Hun on his bad ones.

Before she could head back to the floor, she heard an overhead page. She called the operator and asked them to connect the call to her cell number, then answered, "Allison Lackey, case manager."

"Well, Allison Lackey, *case manager*, there are a few things you need to know about your new boyfriend."

"Pardon? Who *is* this?"

"Eva Mills, formerly Vitelli. You need to know what Nick's really like before it's too late."

Oh, great. Now his ex-wife was calling. "If it's any of your business, Nick isn't my boyfriend. He works for my family's PI agency. It's a professional relationship, not a personal one." Okay, so that wasn't quite true, but it wasn't any of his ex's business.

"See here, honey, I was married to him for seven years, and he's most definitely not your knight in shining armor."

"And you were a fair maiden? Looks to me like you made your choice and moved on."

"Yes, I left him. He was physically abusive, and I have the scars to prove it."

Abusive. Scars? The words whipped like a red flag through her mind. Of course, it all fit. In the garden, he'd told her how his father abused his mother, but he'd neglected to tell her he'd followed his father's example.

Still, she'd never seen anything but kindness from him. And she'd put him to the test with her antics at Dr. Ivers's condo.

"I don't hear you saying anything. Just remember I warned you. He has a terrible temper. Don't cross him, or you'll be sorry."

With that parting shot, Nick's ex hung up.

Allison's knees weakened, and she had to lean against the wall for support. Disbelief warred with anger. Their history notwithstanding, she'd known Nick a few days. He'd been letter perfect with his son. With her, supportive but calm and strong when she'd gotten a little out of control over the last several days.

How could he be the kind of person who'd abuse his wife, the very person he'd vowed to love and protect?

Her beeper prevented her from dwelling on whether his ex was lying. Work waited for no woman. She stiffened her spine and jabbed the elevator button.

Nick drove under the hospital portico and left the motor running. Allison emerged from the hospital promptly at five-thirty, wearing tan slacks and a matching jacket. Even in a suit, she looked damn good. Must work out somewhere. Scott had told him the agency had a discounted rate with the Y. Maybe they could work out together sometime.

She slid into the passenger seat and fastened her seat belt, her face a stern mask and her gaze fixed straight ahead.

Hoping for a warmer response, he asked, "How was your day?"

"Fine." She averted her gaze. Her nails drummed on her knee. What was up with that?

Never one to let things go unsaid, he forged ahead. So, what if she bit off his head? "You don't sound fine."

A sideways glance in his direction... Some response.

"Come on. Out with it. How have I managed to piss you off? I swear I don't have a clue."

"I *said* my day was fine."

"Yeah, but your body language says otherwise."

"You don't have any business reading my body language. You're blocking the drive. If you're not going to take me to police headquarters, then I'll get out and drive myself."

He inched forward and then pulled onto Patterson. "Whatever the hell happened?"

"You're not going to drop it, are you?"

"Nope." He hung a right on Twenty-second. "Just say it. I can read body language, but I'll be damned if I'm gonna try and read your mind."

"I had a hell of a day. Covering for my best friend, who's probably... A million phone calls to deal with, one of which was from your ex-wife."

He held back on the urge to stomp the brake. "*Eva* called you?" Allison's face was red, and she might be a second or two from another of her hissy fits if her rapid breathing was any indication.

"Yes, indeed she did. Want to hazard a guess why?"

"Eva's like the dog in a manger. She doesn't want me anymore, but she sure as hell doesn't want me to be with anyone else. She was making noise last night like she was jealous. I told you about it when we talked earlier." He turned left onto Elliston Place.

"First of all, you're not *with* me. You're an agency employee who's working on my case. I hope I made that clear to your ex."

"And to me too. Thanks for putting me in my place, *Ms. Lackey.* Just so there are no misunderstandings, no, we're not together and not likely to be, given you are my boss's sister and a major pain in my ass besides."

Another quick glance to assess her response. Arms folded across her breasts, nice ones.

"It's what else she said."

"I was never unfaithful. I don't care what she told you. That was her excuse for leaving me."

"She said she left you because you were *abusive*"—she spat the word at him—"just like your father."

"What?" He slowed and pulled into a strip mall's parking lot, then faced her. "I abused her? She said that? Really?"

Allison eyeballed him, her piercing gaze full of steel. "Furthermore, she warned me not to cross you. Said you had a terrible temper."

"You're testing my temper now. I told you how my father treated my mom. Remember that?"

"Yes, and I also know it's a proven fact abusive parents frequently have children who grow up and tend to be abusers themselves."

Her accusation he was like his father rankled through every fiber of his being. He tamped down the outrage and the memories of his mother's bruises and tears. "I would *never* hurt a woman or a child. *Ever.*"

Her gaze faltering, she blinked rapidly. "I-I want to believe you."

"How can you *not* believe me?" His jaw clenched so tightly it was difficult to spit out the words. "Have you seen me do anything that lends a speck of truth to Eva's claim?

Have you?"

She shook her head, and a little slow she was about it too. "N-no..."

"I get it. 'No, not yet.' Isn't that what you're thinking?"

"Let's get this straight. Just a minute ago, you couldn't read my mind. So, now you *are* a mind reader?"

"No, what I am is a crazy man. You're driving me nuts, Allie." He slammed the gear into Drive and backed out of the small lot and headed east on Church. "Anybody ever tell you that you jump to conclusions faster than a jackrabbit? Well, lady, you do."

"But—"

"If I didn't need this job, I'd put your ass out of my vehicle and quit. But I took this case—not like I had a choice in the matter. You don't respect my opinion. You go off on crazy tangents, and you won't listen to anyone but the voices in your head."

"Voices in my head?" she said with a squeak. "I'll have you know I'm not schizophrenic in the least. You are opinionated, arrogant, and"—her intonation moderating to a more level tone—"possibly correct about everything you've just said about me."

"What?"

"I admit it. I'm all those things. Under normal circumstances, I keep the impulsiveness under control, but this thing with Meryl has done something to my sense of what's appropriate."

Understatement of the year. "It's understandable."

"Mind you, just because I'm aware of my faults, it doesn't mean I'll behave from now on." She shot him a quick glance. "Because I probably won't."

"Yeah, well..."

"And I'm sorry I jumped to conclusions about—you know—what your ex said. I have a real sore spot when it comes to abusive men."

"Hmph. I gathered that." He kept his gaze on the traffic flow, as much to hide his relief at her apology as to avoid crashing into the driver who turned in front of him without so much as a signal. "My ex is hard to figure. If I didn't know better, I'd say she was jealous."

"That's the second time you've said that. But why? We have a business relationship."

"Believe you mentioned that before too."

"Is there something more—between us, I mean?"

"I'm not having this conversation now. How 'bout later, when I'm not playing kamikaze with Music City's worst drivers?"

"Excu-use me. I guess it's true men can only do one thing at a time." She completed her chauvinistic statement with an evil chuckle.

"What?" He bristled, then recovered. "Men focus on the project at hand and don't waste their resources trying to multitask."

"It's a scientific fact women's brains are hardwired to multitask. Yours aren't."

"Feminist claptrap," he countered.

"Look." She pointed to the left. "There's a spot. Pull in there."

"Backseat drivers too."

She wrinkled her nose. Kinda cute too. "The species would've died out if it weren't for women telling you men where to park and reading the directions."

He parked, put the car in gear, then turned to Allie. "Darlin', if you're not the biggest pain in the ass I've ever known, I don't know who is. But you're kinda cute, even if you never shut your mouth."

"Make me."

"I will." He leaned in and caressed her neck, pulling her

closer to him. He kissed her, not knowing if she'd submit or scream bloody murder.

She gave in. Boy howdy did she ever. Her arms went around his neck.

The sweetest lips. Soft and responsive. They parted.

Oh, God.

His heart revved like a Harley.

Then she pulled back. Her eyes wide and those luscious lips still parted. "What was that?

"A kiss."

"I mean what are we doing, Nick? You and me."

"It was a kiss, not a freaking marriage proposal."

Allie jerked back, her face blazing and lips trembling. "You arrogant ass. As if I'd consider marrying someone like you." Head averted and staring out the side window, she folded her arms across her chest, which rose and fell with each breath.

God, he was such an ass-wipe. What made him say something so freaking stupid?

"I sounded pretty crass, didn't it?"

"You think?" She jerked open the door and took off.

"Hey. Hold on a minute." He jumped from the Bronco and headed out after her.

One pissed-off little sister equaled his job was history as soon as she talked to her brother.

Still shaken by Nick's kiss and asinine non-proposal, Allison tried her level best to hide it. She kept her gaze on the monitor, waiting for Tess to cue the Nashville Farmers' Market footage. Nick leaned back in a chair, his long legs stretched out before him, his hands clasped behind his head.

"It's clear, but the camera was so far away it's impossible to see their faces," Tess said. "There was a new moon that night, so other than a parking lot light there's no other source of illumination. We've already amplified it to the best of our equipment's ability. So, here it is. I want both your impressions."

Allison zeroed her gaze on Meryl's Kia, sitting in the far corner of the lot. Impossible to see if it was occupied or not.

No matter. Another vehicle pulled into the lot beside it, and someone emerged. The door to the Kia opened, and another figure stepped out.

"Two people," Nick said. "Someone needed help with—" He broke off.

"—disposing of Meryl's body," she finished for him. "That *is* what you were going to say, isn't it?" Her speech was clipped, tense. Couldn't help it, though. She'd clenched her jaw to keep it from trembling.

"Yeah."

"Now it looks like they're arguing. See, one of them is waving his hands around. Oh, wait. The other one just opened the trunk." Afraid of what she might see, she averted her gaze. "I can't watch." Her heart pounded so hard and so loud deafness was a possibility. Her entire body heated and burned with the increased blood flow.

"Want me to describe?" Nick asked.

"Not really. But go ahead."

"Individual from the second vehicle has a blanket-like object. They're covering something in the trunk of the Kia with the blanket and they're making wrapping motions. Now they're lifting a heavy object from the Kia and carrying it to the other vehicle. What model SUV is that?"

"Looks like your basic SUV," Tess said. "Can't tell the make." She stopped the tape. Allison glanced at the screen again and squinted at the SUV's image. "Doesn't it look similar to the one that left the parking area right after Meryl pulled from the garage?"

"I guess," she said, shrugging.

"Is there any way to enhance the license plate on it?" Nick suggested.

Tess fiddled with the resolution for a couple of seconds, then gave up. "The SUV's parked at an angle to the camera, so this is as good as it'll get."

"I don't suppose you have a database of vehicle profiles?"

"This isn't *CSI*, Allie."

"No, but—" Nick sat up straight, then leaned his elbows on the desk. "What are the chances of my getting a copy? Maybe Justin can dig up something."

Tess's expression changed from flat to devious. "I'm a step ahead of you." Pulling a DVD from her jacket, she said, "You didn't get this from me. I added a snip of the Parklane footage as well."

Nick took the disc, flipping it back and forth while he and Tess, the professionals, discussed the mechanics for further lines of inquiry.

Allison forced down her hurt feelings. Screw Nick Vitelli. He might be the person her brother hired and assigned to Meryl's case, but she'd be a fool if she let him kiss her again.

No way.

Chapter Fourteen

All the way back to Nick's Bronco, Allison marched along, ignoring—okay, trying to ignore—his presence as he kept pace with her. Once they were inside the vehicle, she faced him. "New ground rules. This is a purely professional relationship. From your actions, it's obvious you're only interested in fooling around. And I'm not. However, if I've given you the wrong impression, I'm sorry. That's all I have to say on the matter."

"Come on, Allie. So, I was an ass. Sorry. Fooling around with you never entered my mind."

"Like hell, it didn't. What was the kiss about? Huh?"

"I acted on impulse, and I'm sorry. I screwed up."

"Apology accepted." She nodded with a satisfied air. "Now take me back to the hospital so I can pick up my car. It's late. I'm hungry, and tonight's Carrie's night to cook. She's the only one of us who actually knows the difference between crudités and croutons. And that includes my brothers, who have delusions of grandeur and think they're cooks because they happen to commandeer the grill."

He nodded, humoring her, no doubt. "Fine. Just don't go off on me when I show up to give Justin the disc."

Going to be at the house...again? She let out a sigh. "I didn't know you were going to be a permanent dinner guest, but I guess it's unavoidable."

His jaw clenched, and he bit out, "Y'know what? Your brother doesn't pay me enough to have dinner at your house...again." He jammed the key into the ignition and revved the motor. "As for the disc, take it and give it to Justin yourself."

She bit her bottom lip. What was the matter with her? Why was she making such a big deal over a little kiss? Might as well overlook his insolent "not a freaking proposal" remark. "I'm being ridiculous, aren't I?"

"Ya think?" he said, pulling from the lot onto the street as if he'd expected her to calm down all along.

"Then stay for dinner. You and Justin can spend the night figuring out what model the SUV was. And then maybe we'll be another step closer to finding what happened to Meryl."

He shot a quick sideways glance in her direction. "You're sure?"

"Yeah. I blew up. Exaggerated the importance of an...*impulse*."

"I had no business kissing you." He paused, and a smile played around his mouth. "Just couldn't help it. Have to admit arguing with you is kinda fun."

"You *like* arguing with me? Seriously?"

"Yeah." There it was again: I'm a bad boy expression. Bad boy or not, the ice in his blue gaze was definitely melting.

To make matters worse, she *wanted* him to kiss her again. Her heart hitched at the memory of his lips on hers. The kiss was tender and hot. Hot. Beyond hot.

He cut a glance in her direction. "Don't look at me like that."

"Like how?"

"Like you're a hungry puppy, and I'm your first T-bone steak."

"I'll have you know..." What was she about to say, that she'd already had her first piece of steak, and while it was plenty tasty, it wasn't enough to make her jump into the sack with just anyone?

"Yeah?"

"I'm not anybody's hungry puppy...and steak is overrated."

His head went back. He roared with laughter until his shoulders shook.

"I wasn't trying to be funny."

"Can't help it. You were." He turned onto James Robertson Parkway and circled behind the state capitol building complex. "Maybe you just haven't had the right cut, or maybe it wasn't properly prepared." He winked. At least she thought he did; maybe he just had a twitch.

"And you think you're some kind of expert in...steak?"

He hung a right on Church. "Different circumstances? I could show you the difference between choice and prime."

"You are as arrogant as any man I've ever known." Okay, so she'd only *known* two. And yes, there was a self-assured challenge in his tone. Maybe... Her breath caught. Her mouth dried until she didn't have a drop of saliva to spare.

"Like I said, different circumstances. And like *you* said, our relationship is purely professional."

Considering the truth of his—no, their—situation, she chewed the inside of her cheek, then admitted, "Sometimes I talk too much."

"No argument here."

"You always argue."

"Not this time, doll." He sent a smirk in her direction, then slammed on the brakes. "Freaking SOB stopped in the middle of the street!" They'd reached Elliston Place, where cars parked on both sides of the somewhat narrow street, a half of a block from where they'd shared breakfast on Saturday.

"You're supposed to keep your eyes on the road—at least that's the general idea when driving. Now when you get to the hospital, just let me out at the back garage entrance."

"No way. I'm taking you to your car."

"There you go. Arguing again."

"Argh!" he groaned. "One nurse has already disappeared. Not gonna risk letting you out of my sight."

"It's a few minutes after seven—time for shift change. There'll be plenty of people around. I'll be fine."

"I'm not dumping you on the street. Parking garages are dangerous if you're not paying attention to your surroundings." He gripped the steering wheel, knuckles white.

"All right!" she said with some heat. The man was overly cautious, but somehow his protective nature comforted her. She was just arguing with him for the heck of it anyway.

"Where's your car parked?"

"Second floor on the side next to the park," she said, then added, "I wish you'd just pay attention to the traffic and quit bugging me about the parking garage."

"You don't take the stairs, do you? Security-wise, they're the worst."

"I *always* take the stairs—for the exercise."

"That settles it. I'm driving you to your car."

"You're such a nervous Nellie." She tamped down the urge to laugh.

He looked askance, confusion written in his gaze. "A what?"

She emitted a groan of frustration and crossed her arms across her chest, then changed position again and drummed her fingers against her thighs. "You know. Overprotective. Nervous. Like a mother hen with her chicks."

"Why are you so agitated?" he asked.

"I'm hungry. I had a granola bar for breakfast and a bag of chips for lunch. Forgive me if I'm a little cranky."

"You'd think a nurse would take better care of herself."

She groaned. Couldn't the man cut her a little slack? He turned up Twenty-second Avenue, drove by several doctors' office buildings, the Lentz Public Health Center, then hung a left on Patterson. "Between the two buildings, then left," she said. "The employee garage is on the right."

He followed her directions and pulled inside the parking garage. "Second floor, the park side?"

"Right. Silver Camry."

He found an empty spot beside the Camry, pulled in, and braked. He jumped out and circled her car and even checked under it.

She eased from the Bronco and walked around to watch him with a smile. "I'll say one thing. You're thorough."

His gaze of steel was back. "This is what you should do every time you come out here."

"I'm careful. Just not obsessive—like you."

Allison didn't have a clue when it came to protecting herself. "Until we find whoever's responsible..."

Still smiling, she sauntered into his personal space. The closer she stood next to him, the more his heart sped up. He did his best to ignore the rush of blood to his groin. It was late afternoon, yet she was fresh and clean. Her hair smelled of the citrus-scented shampoo she seemed to prefer. He glanced toward the park and dragged in a deep breath.

Relax. Doing the boss's sister is never a good idea.

She dug in her purse for her keys. "I'll—uh, see you at the house."

"I'm right behind you."

The tiny tip of her pink tongue flicked across her upper lip; the corners of her mouth twitched as if she wanted to smile. "That's very reassuring. I'm sure."

"Not taking any chances. You're so blasted stubborn. "

"Being stubborn gets things done, Vitelli, on the job and in life."

Just what he needed—a motivational lecture. "Like I said, investigate in the background. Don't be so obvious. Don't draw the attention of Meryl's kill—"

"Killer," she spat out the word as if it left a bad taste in her mouth. "Don't bring myself to the killer's attention."

"This isn't a game. I need this job. *And* I need to keep you alive."

"I know it's not a game. But I can't sit back and calmly paint my nails when I'd rather be useful."

Her passion and determination—code word for stubborn—never failed to stir his protective instincts. She was fast becoming more than an assignment.

Much more.

"Dammit. Get in your car and lock the door. With "lock," he swatted her ass. Her very fine, round ass.

Her brown eyes shone with sparks, first with anger, but then her gaze softened. "I'm not a child, and the next time you try spanking me, you might want to think twice."

"If you don't get in your car, I'm gonna do it again and no thinking twice about it."

Strong as the temptation was to pull her over his lap and give her another swat, Nick waited and watched for her reaction. Her jaw dropped, her luscious lips parted, tempting him more than he could bear. "If you weren't Scott's sister, I'd turn you over my knee."

"I'll have you know I'm not into any of your Atlanta-city-boy kinky stuff."

"And I'll have you know kinky stuff is the last thing on my mind." He shook his head, unable to believe she'd jumped from the just-kidding threat of a spanking to kinky goings-on. "Kink isn't a place you'd ever want to go. Those places aren't for nice girls like you."

"Nice girls like me?" She set her hands on her hips, and her pointed chin raked up a good thirty degrees. "Does 'damned by faint praise' mean anything to you?"

"I don't get it." He cocked his head. "You're insulted

because I think you're a nice girl?"

"First of all, since you apparently haven't noticed, I'm not a girl. I'm a woman—"

"W-O-M—" he started to warble, but the *woman* in question wasn't having any and punched his shoulder.

"As for 'nice'—nice is as boring as white walls or chips without salsa."

Her face turned a brilliant shade of stoplight red, and, strangely enough, it pleased him. He hadn't lied when he said he liked arguing with her. He could get used to her hissy fits, entertaining as they were. There was more than a touch of Lucille Ball's zaniness in this little strawberry blonde. And for the umpteenth time, he wished she wasn't Scott's kid sister.

Fuck it anyway.

"What's wrong?" Her eyes were nearly crossed in fury. Unable to stop himself, he watched, mesmerized. Covered by a light blue knit top, her perky, round breasts rose and fell with each exasperated breath like juicy, ripe oranges. Through the material, he could just make out the hint of pearl-size nipples. Lust slammed his gut and settled south of his belt.

"Eyes on my face, Vitelli," she snapped, then glanced around—to see if anyone had heard her?

"Sorry." His face heated. Okay, so she'd caught him leering like a perv. Leering was the least of what he wanted. More and more, *she* was exactly what he wanted.

"You're being such a guy." She twitched her shoulders for emphasis. "I don't know why I'm so surprised. It comes with the XY chromosome. And if my brothers are any example, the condition is incurable."

"Besides being a nice girl—woman—you're a very attractive one, with all the important parts in the right places." Oh, God. How deep a hole could he dig with his mouth?

She wrinkled her nose. "Thanks for your clinical assessment. I'll be sure to add that to my résumé." She turned and unlocked her car. "Now, unless you've any more asinine comments you'd like to make, I'm going home."

Careful to keep his gaze above the seductive blue knit, he shoved his hands in his jeans pockets. "I've said enough."

More than a little uncomfortable, he watched a smug smile spread across her pretty face. Without giving him another glance, she backed out and took off. He beat it for the Bronco and caught up with her on West End.

Dude. All you had to do was keep your eyes in your head and not act like a teenager on a testosterone high.

He parked on Richland right behind her Camry. Allie was already in the house by the time he made it to the porch.

"Come on in," Caroline called. "It's about time you two got here. The rest of us are starving, and if dinner gets cold, I won't be happy. And you know the rest of that tune."

"Nobody's happy," the entire group, including Allie, good-naturedly chanted in unison.

"Sorry. Sure looks good," Nick offered by way of apology. "We—uh, got hung up."

Caroline's eyes widened into pools of near jade. "Oh, really?"

"Hmph." Allison averted her gaze, then shrugged. "It was nothing. He's exaggerating as usual."

Nick gestured with his thumb. "The nurse here thinks I have an incurable condition."

"Oh?" Caroline's tone was rife with amusement.

"Yes," Allison responded with a bit of heat. "He's afflicted with an XY chromosome. So there." She glanced through the French doors onto the deck where the picnic table was already set with plates and glassware. "Don't know about the rest of you, but I'm ready to eat."

"Guess your Diet Coke and bag of chips didn't go very far," he muttered just loud enough for her to hear.

"Guess not." Again she wrinkled her nose in his direction.

They stepped out on the deck. The tangy, smoky aroma of barbeque chicken set his stomach to growling, reminding him he hadn't eaten all day either. A platter was piled high with corn on the cob and veggie kebabs. Caroline brought out a large bowl of potato salad and set it on the long picnic table. "Oh no! I forgot the rolls. They're still in the oven." She ran back inside to retrieve them.

He waited until Allison took her place and chose one opposite hers. He just didn't trust his flagging self-control. With a table between them, he might have a slim chance of not making a fool of himself, for once.

Dinner had been a watchful affair. Allison was well aware of Nick's furtive glances in her direction. She'd caught Caroline watching, her gaze darting back and forth like someone watching a tennis match. Was her sister trying to figure out if anything was going on between the two of them? After dinner, the Holt-Lackey clan gathered around the fire pit and laughed about the absurdity of a fire pit in late August.

Allison swung her legs over the bench seat and surveyed the remains of barbequed chicken, corn on the cob, and kebabs. She reached for the last yeast roll, one of her weaknesses. "It's a good thing you only cook like this once a week," she told Caroline.

Her sister looked up from her task of gathering the dishes and smiled. "Since I'm sidelined, the one thing I don't have any trouble remembering is how to cook. I'm here all day. Besides, cooking makes me feel useful and not a burden on the family."

"A burden?" Nick shook his head in apparent disbelief. "No way. From what I've seen, you're the only sane one in this bunch. They couldn't function without you."

"Thanks a lot, dude." This from Justin, who didn't appear at all offended.

"None of you is certifiable like Allie here, but then, I have to admit—" He shot a furtive glance in her direction. "I'm about to swallow this foot in my mouth. Someone, please stop me."

A phone chimed, or rather it played something by Rascal Flatts. "Sorry. Gotta take this." Nick pulled the cell from his jeans pocket and answered, then listened, his face growing red. "What difference does it make where I am?" He stood and walked toward the French doors. "Come on, Eva. Please put Ben on. I know he's not asleep yet."

His ex must be a real witch. No man should have to beg to talk to his son. Nick's jaw tensed; the muscles jumped. His foot did a quick heel-and-toe tap dance, then he headed back into the house, so she couldn't hear the remainder of the conversation.

Divorce was hard on everyone, but Nick's ex seemed intent on making him suffer by placing their son in the middle, yet just out of reach.

He returned. "Sorry."

"Everything okay?" she asked, wishing she could comfort him.

"Yeah. Just hate jumping through her hoops. I don't get it. She's the one who moved on." He jammed his hands in his pockets and basically appeared uncomfortable.

Not knowing what else to say, she started to clear the table. "Uh, I'm going to load the dishwasher, and then I'll read over the material I brought home."

"Good." He turned toward the house. "I guess Justin and I are ready to do a database search on vehicle profiles."

"Okay. I'll let you know what I come up with."

He stopped at the door and turned to face her. "Fine, but it's still a waste of time. The SUV won't be a legit lead unless we can just narrow down to the model."

"Oh, so it's all right for me to waste my time while the real experts chase down real clues?"

A quick half smile flashed. "Darlin', *anything* that keeps you out of trouble and out of my hair is all right with me."

As if she were still in third grade, she stuck out her tongue and made a face.

Too late. He'd already headed back inside.

Chapter Fifteen

Two hours later, Allie set the fifth article on black-market organ transplants on the kitchen table and yawned. It was almost ten. Nick and Justin were probably still in the den, aka man cave, yakking about databases and security cameras. Scott and Caroline were out on the deck, talking about her return to the office. Tamsyn had come in from an assignment and was upstairs in her room, reading the latest Nora Roberts.

Allison headed down the hall to the man cave. "Hey there, guys. Want to hear how the black market in organs works?"

Justin brushed his hair behind his ears and leaned forward. Nick rolled his eyes and gave her his here-we-go-again expression. "Sure. Enlighten us."

She sat in the oak rocker across from her brother and Nick. "This isn't China or South Africa, so I have to wonder how the supposedly respected director of a transplant program, like our Dr. Ivers, manages to fly under the radar here in the States."

"Good question. So, does he enlist hookers to drug tourists and leave the donors in a bathtub full of ice?" Justin cackled and leaned back.

"Smart-ass. That's an urban legend, but there might actually be something to it."

"So, how do you think he could work it?" Nick's response, at least, was more sensible.

"He'd have to have his own facility and staff. At the very least, it would take a surgical team, an anesthesiologist, access to donors who were either paid donors and rewarded handsomely for their services or..." A shudder shook her body. The very thought of involuntary donors. "Maybe that's what happened to Meryl. She was on to him, so he killed her and stockpiled her organs."

Nick shot her an eye roll. "If, and that's a big *if*, Ivers is responsible for Meryl's disappearance, what happened at her condo was disorganized and spontaneous. Later, at the parking lot, the cover-up showed a better sense of planning had come into play. I doubt the good doctor came prepared with a cooler. And if he had, would he have bothered to remove her body? What's his alibi for the time frame of her disappearance?"

"I don't know," she said, pouting. "You wouldn't let me stay at his place to ask him."

"You don't have to confront him to find out where he was. He's a doctor, right? Has office hours. Surgery—that kind of thing."

"Yes, I can check his office hours on the QT. But he's a nephrologist, not the transplant surgeon. That means he manages their medical care before and after they're dismissed from the hospital."

"Now you're using your head for something besides banging it against a brick wall."

"Point taken."

Scott stepped into the den. "Tess just called, said to turn on the ten o'clock news."

Justin grabbed the remote and fired up the plasma.

In disbelief, Allison covered her mouth with her hand. There he was again: Tom Buckley swanning around like he was some sort of minor celebrity. He was headed into his crap apartment, smiling and nodding to the reporters who kept shouting and asking whether or not he had anything to do with his wife's disappearance or knew who did.

"Look, dudes, I'm on my way to change for a gig. New gig too. Guess I'm sorta famous now. Making my mark here in town."

"Is it true you abused your ex-wife?"

"I never laid a hand on her unless she asked me to. She liked it a little rough, ya know?"

Bile rose in Allison's throat. The very idea he would say such a thing, smearing her friend in front of the world. Tears sprang to her eyes, but she blinked them back. "I *know* he hit her, and it wasn't some kinky sex play."

At the same time, a red-faced Nick jumped up and strode from the den. Swallowing her own emotional reaction, she followed him outside to the deck. He stood staring into the night, his chest rising and falling with obvious emotion, his large hands clenched in fists. Scott and Caroline eased back inside, giving them a semblance of privacy.

"Nick..." She touched his shoulder.

He shrugged off her hand. "Not now." His response was muttered through clenched teeth. She stepped back. The underlying ferocity of his reaction shook her to the core. Maybe his ex was right about his temper...and being an abusive husband.

Still, there they were—the doubts she couldn't quite overcome. The rage was there and plain to see. But he wasn't breaking furniture or faces. He was just out on the deck taking some mighty deep breaths.

Like her brother and sister, she backed off and headed inside. Better to leave the man alone and let him deal with whatever demons Buckley's interview had unleashed.

Once he'd cooled down, Nick wandered back to the den. "I'm heading out."

"I'll walk with you." Allison rose and, without saying a

word, followed him. Was she still thinking about his ex's out-and-out lies?

The cool night air was dry and a welcome relief from the hot mugginess of the August afternoon. "You're awful quiet," he said.

"Got a lot on my mind." Her tone was soft, neutral, and determinedly nonjudgmental.

They walked down the front steps. "I never denied having a bad temper." He swatted at a whining mosquito. "That bastard Buckley reminds me of my father. Used to brag to his friends my mom asked for it. His smug face pushed my buttons to hell and back."

"I'm sorry. I can't imagine what Meryl ever saw in him. At least she was smart enough to leave."

"Yeah. And now he's grabbing his fifteen minutes of fame."

"By dancing on her grave...wherever she is."

The sound of tears and choked-back emotion hurt him as much as his mother's sobs once had. Couldn't be helped. At least Allison was beginning to accept the inevitable outcome. Nick stopped when they reached the Bronco. "The man's either completely innocent or a complete fool."

"Or absolutely convinced she'll never be found." She set her hands on her hips. "What does *he* drive anyway?"

"'05 White Chevy pickup. Only thing I haven't nailed down is his alibi when he was at the Cineplex. Whoever took her had an accomplice after the fact. And that's our perp's weak link. Got to find the SUV and its owner."

"No luck yet?" Her expression was wistful, the streetlights reflected in a dazzling array of sparks in her dark brown eyes. If only he could erase the grief from her eyes and, even more, protect her from the gut-wrenching knowledge which would surely come, sooner or later.

"Not yet. Program's still running. Should have something

by morning, if we're lucky."

"Do they often take this long?"

"Lot of SUV models to consider. Everybody and his brother in Nashville drive one." He rolled his shoulders to loosen them and relieve the tension cramping them. Being alone with Allison served to remind him how much he wanted to protect and comfort her. He fisted his hands, more to keep from touching her than any other reason.

Her shoulders twitched, and she seemed to jump. He forced his hands to relax. She still didn't trust him. Screw Eva and her underhanded lies.

"I guess I'd better go in." She hugged herself, and he saw her shiver again. Did he make her that uncomfortable?

What did he have to do to prove he wasn't the ogre Eva said he was? "Right. You're shivering. Tomorrow's another day."

"Meryl's been gone three days now. It doesn't seem possible." Her trembling increased.

He touched her shoulder, tentatively first, then scooped her closer. "We'll find who did this."

"But will we ever find *her*?"

"If we're lucky."

"I've seen those forensics shows. I know what happens."

He'd seen it for real. No TV screen between him and insect-ridden corpses. Depending on where Meryl's body was dumped, she could already be unrecognizable. "Stop it. Put it all out of your mind. Don't remember her like that."

She buried her head in his shoulder, her tears falling on his shirt, warm and damp through the knit.

What else could he do? He took a deep breath and cuddled her closer.

"I-I try not to think about her, b-but I have nightmares. She's calling my name, but when I see her—" She broke off, and her entire body shuddered against his chest. "She tells me it's my fault. I should've looked her up Friday afternoon before I left the hospital. She could've told me what she'd found. Don't you understand? I have to find out who took her."

"It isn't your fault, and it's just a bad dream." Holding her set his heart to hammering. Could she feel his reaction?

He put his other arm around her. "I'm taking you back inside. Carrie can put you to bed and give you some warm milk or something."

She emitted a sound, half laugh, half sob. "*I'm* supposed to be the nurse. The nurturer. Some nurse. I can't even take care of myself."

Nick guided her up the walk to the house, then stopped at the front door. "This isn't one of your normal everyday occurrences. Your friend—her loss is a tragedy, and you're grieving."

She gazed up at him with eyes glazed with tears. "I know—intellectually, but— "

"It's different when it's a friend or family. I know, darlin'. I know." The endearment slipped out, but she was too distraught to notice.

The front door opened. Scott stood there, watching them. "Problem?"

"She's upset. She needs to go to bed. And a glass of warm milk wouldn't be such a bad idea." Nick flashed what he hoped was a brotherly smile.

"Thanks. We'll take care of her." Her brother held out his hand. Hesitating, she took it as Nick released his hold.

"Night, kiddo."

Eyebrows raised, Scott's gaze raked over Nick with an unasked question—or two. Nick turned and beat it down the walkway, cursing himself for being ten kinds of foolish.

"Night," she called softly after him.

He climbed inside the Bronco and sat there for a

moment, then glanced at the house. The door was shut and the porch lights already turned off.

Screw it. He was losing focus and objectivity all because of one little strawberry blonde.

He started the engine and pulled out into the silent residential street, but he couldn't forget the rush of emotions from holding Allison in his arms.

She was so different from Eva. Not just different, more like a one-eighty-degree change in attitude, personality, and heart.

Was Allie even aware of the depth of his attraction? Doubtful. There was still a thread of distrust in her mind as if she were waiting for him to lose control and start smacking her around.

Never. Never would he stoop as low as his father. He hit the steering wheel with his fist. Never.

He headed down West End back toward his brother's studio apartment.

God, he had to get out of that dump soon. Like before Ben's next weekend visit.

Not to mention an abject lack of privacy. There was no way he and Allison could be alone.

Alone? Hell. What was he thinking?

Just as well, dude. Just as well.

Up in her bedroom, Allison had pulled on a long T-shirt nightgown. A glass of warm milk had appeared on her bedside table while she was in the bathroom.

"Allie?" Scott tapped on her door. "You decent?"

"Always."

He ambled inside and pulled up a chair. Straddling it, he leaned on the back. "Something going on with you and Nick?"

"Meryl's case." What was her brother getting at? Were her feelings so transparent to everyone?

"You know what I mean. Something more personal than professional."

"Of course not. It's just I feel a little overwhelmed at times, and Nick understands. He's a good guy. He has a way of settling me down." She glanced away from his direct gaze and straightened the duvet. "Why would you ask me something like that anyway?" *Just because you found me in his arms?* She glanced back to meet his hawkish gaze.

His mouth lifted at the corner. "Just a hunch."

She laughed, albeit a little self-consciously. "You're not allowed to have hunches. That's for us womenfolk."

He stood. "Yeah. Yeah. Get some sleep, sis."

She picked up the glass of milk and wrinkled her nose. "I hate this stuff, but I know it works." She took a sip, swallowed, then shuddered. "Good night, big brother."

"Night," he said and eased out the door, closing it behind him.

Alone. Finally.

The deep sense of contentment she'd felt earlier in Nick's arms resurged. Still, if Scott had noticed a change in her behavior... Surely he was the only one. Nick was kind and good and protective because she was his client. And, other than a natural body reaction, that's all there was to it.

Wasn't it?

No sleep tonight. Not with all the Vitelli scenes playing in her head.

Chapter Sixteen

The next morning, Nick checked at the office before heading out to nail down Buckley's funky alibi. Tamsyn was in Caroline's usual spot, looking very fine but a little on the harried side. "What's up, Tamsyn? Aren't you having fun yet?"

"I'd shoot myself if Carrie wasn't coming back part-time next week. Number crunching and ordering supplies aren't high on my agenda." She swept her fingers through her long, dark hair. "By the way, Scott wants to see you before you head out."

"Sure." He ambled over to Scott's office and knocked on the door, then opened it. "You wanted to see me?"

A cup of coffee in hand, Scott glanced up and sort of smiled. "Yeah, come on in. Close the door." He gestured for Nick to have a seat.

With some trepidation, Nick complied. *What now?*

"What's going on with you and Allie?"

Nick held up his hands in a gesture of surrender. "Not a thing. I mean, she's impulsive and in left field as far as this investigation goes, but—"

"No, there's some chemistry sparking between you two. Have to be blind not to see it. Just wondered, that's all."

"Look, dude, I'm not about to fool around with your sister. Guy'd be crazy to—well, you know." Talk about breaking the cardinal guy rule.

Scott lifted his shoulders in a resigned shrug. "Allison's a grown woman and, as I'm sure you've noticed, has a mind of her own."

"We're friendly combatants—sort of." Shit. Screwed, that's what he was. "But I respect her and the client relationship as well." Did he sound as bogus as he thought he did?

"You like her?" Scott continued to eyeball him over his morning cup of coffee.

"Sure. What's not to like?" *Dude, keep your trap shut.* This was another one of those holes he was digging with his mouth.

"Look, we've been friends for a long time." A smile flickered on Scott's face.

Uh-oh. What was the smile about?

"I just don't want to see my sister get hurt."

"Are you asking me about my intentions?" He rose. Where was the door anyway?

Moving too fast. Moving too fast. Way too fast.

"Not exactly." Scott shrugged again.

"Then what?"

"As you said, she's impulsive and headstrong." Scott's expression was thoughtful as he set his coffee on the desk. "And she's fixated on this doctor's involvement. If it hadn't been for you, she would've lost her job last weekend. You got her out of there just in time. Appreciate it."

Nick shrugged. "Barely."

"Just keep an eye on her. With the wedding coming up so soon, I'm not as hands-on as usual. Tess is going freaking nuts with menus, seating charts, and bands, and, lucky me, I'm along for the ride. Eventually, I'll end up with a wife then maybe things will settle down."

Nick tried not to chuckle but failed. "No chance of eloping?"

"Slim to none." Scott's expression was dead-on *please, help me.*

"O'Malley's pretty sharp, though." Nick nodded his approval. "You're a lucky man. I just hope you know what you're getting yourself into, marrying a cop."

Scott took another swallow from his cup. "Pretty good idea. Late dinners. Calls at all times of the day or night. Worrying about her when she leaves every morning. My dad was a cop before he retired and opened the agency."

"Yeah. You sound pretty philosophical about it." Talk of marriage, not necessarily the best way to start the day, even if it wasn't his marriage under discussion.

"Tess is..."

"Say no more, dude. You're getting too warm and cuddly for me."

Scott blushed, then laughed. "A man in love is kind of a pathetic creature when you come to think about it."

"Or awful lucky." *Too much information, dude.*

"Yeah. So, what's on your agenda today?"

Good. Back to business. Some of the tension leached from his shoulders. "Going to check out the Cineplex again. The usher who was working Friday afternoon is supposed to be on duty today. Allie's occupied at work. She's researching the black-market organ deal."

Scott nodded. "Should keep her busy."

"Exactly."

Scott leaned back. "How's your apartment hunt going? Still at your brother's place?"

"Yeah. Figure I'll have enough money put aside in a couple of weeks for deposits."

"If you need an advance... No, consider it a relocation bonus. Just tell Tamsyn how much you need."

He held up his hands in protest. "You don't have to do that. I'll be fine."

"Take it. You don't look like you're sleeping too well. I need my operatives sharp and rested."

The unexpected offer took Nick back. "Thanks. Ben'll be glad to have a place to sleep instead of a pullout." He shot Scott a quick two-fingered salute and headed to Tamsyn's desk. The advance check she wrote was generous enough for a first and last month's rent as well as a utility deposit.

Holy shit.

Still, a little stunned by Scott's more or less asking his intentions and then his generous offer, he stuck his head in Justin's office before leaving." How's it going?"

"I've narrowed down the model SUV to three, but there are about a zillion registered in Metropolitan Nashville."

"Crap."

"You said it, dude."

"What do we have in the way of bird dogs?" he asked Justin.

Justin smiled. "Only the very latest in GPS tracking systems. It's equipped with real-time tracking. All you have to do is attach it to your target's vehicle and access the site on the Internet." He scooted his chair back and spun around, then opened a file drawer. "Here you go." He handed Nick the unit. "Small. Handy-dandy and very reliable. Battery lasts a good thirty days. Just download and install the software from the agency's cloud account. You're good to go. And the agency foots the bill."

"Thanks. Figured you'd have just what I needed. My iPad's in the Bronco." He shoved the tracker unit into his jeans pocket.

"Then you're set." Justin flashed a wide grin. "So, who's your target?"

"Who else but that piece of shit Buckley?"

"Think he'll lead you to the dumpsite?"

"Always possible. He doesn't strike me as particularly smart."

"Have fun, dude." The computer whiz turned back to his

bank of monitors.

Fun wasn't exactly what Nick had in mind. More like catching the killer who'd murdered a pregnant woman and her baby...and seeing he paid for it.

The day proved a busy one for Allison. It was midafternoon before she received a call back from the transplant social worker. SuEllen Mason shared that Meryl had asked her some of the same questions the day before she disappeared.

"Which questions?"

"Like how a doctor could scam the system. I told her running a privately owned facility would be expensive and impractical, considering how many people would need to be in on the secret."

"But—" Then it hit her. "He could do the transplants here in the hospital, collecting his money upfront. Both donor and recipient would be in on the scam, but that's it."

"Meryl also asked about his rate of LRDs—living related donors. It's higher than average.

"How much higher?"

"Usual rate of LRDs is around twenty percent nationally of all the transplants done. The majority are still cadaveric donors. The doctor in question has a rate of forty percent."

"Twice as high."

"Well, it's possible, but we would've caught on before."

"Thanks. It's high, but just how significant is it? I need to do some more research."

She hung up the receiver. Maybe there was something in the last few medical charts that tipped off Meryl.

She accessed the surgery schedule and made note of the last five LRDs. It stood to reason Meryl's suspicious were recent. She read through the case manager notes. When

Meryl set up the discharge plans, a couple of the living related donors didn't seem to know the recipient as well as donors usually did. Frequently, it was a mother or father, a sibling, and sometimes even a husband was a viable match. Of the last five cases, four were documented as cousins from out of state. That must've been what alerted Meryl something was "fishy," as her last call had said.

"Wow." Allison leaned back and let out a deep sigh. It was suspicious, but was it enough?

Time to check the op schedule for Friday. She pulled up the schedule and scanned through the list of procedures. No kidney transplants on Friday afternoon, but there was one that morning. Ivers would be keeping close tabs on the patient as well as the transplant surgeon. Perhaps someone in ICU had seen him on rounds Friday evening.

Wouldn't hurt to check. She stood and opened the door to her small office and stopped.

Detective Tess O'Malley stood in the hallway with her fist raised, ready to knock. "Got a minute?"

Nick drove to the shopping center where the Cineplex was located. Stepping from the Bronco, he wiped the perspiration from his forehead. Waves of heat rolled off the blacktop parking lot.

Inside the Cineplex, the AC was on high. The manager pointed him to a plump twenty-something behind the candy counter. "Can I help you?"

"I'm Nick Vitelli. I'm a PI, and I'm trying to substantiate an alibi for a client of mine." He fudged the truth. So what? Not like it was the first time. "Have you seen this guy?"

She gave it a cursory glance. "Seen a lot of scroungy shits in my time, but I don't remember him. Wait. Saw him on the TV news. He's the husband of the missing nurse."

"Ex-husband. Think hard. You haven't seen him at the Cineplex?"

She looked at the picture again, cocked her head from side to side, screwing up her mouth as she considered his questions. "Nope, I tend to notice the pervs. And that's what he looks like, a perv who gets off on feeling up little girls."

"Thanks." At least now he knew Buckley's alibi was bullshit.

Time he quit chasing a bogus alibi and pin Buckley like the bug he was.

He got back in the Bronco and headed toward Murfreesboro Road and then to Buckley's squat. Buckley's white Chevy pickup was there, all right. Nick parked a few spots away. After he pulled the GPS tracker from his pocket, he palmed it. He exited the Bronco and walked to the rear of the Chevy, pretending to check the tires, then attached the small unit inside the rear fender. Getting back in the Bronco, he turned on the iPad and accessed the tracking site.

Hot damn. There it was, the corresponding lighted dot indicating the location of Buckley's rust bucket. Now he could track Buckley in real-time on the Internet anytime he wanted without having to tail him all over Nashville.

Fearing Tess's presence at the hospital meant the worst, Allison took a deep breath. "I didn't know you were coming by today?" She hadn't meant to form it as a question, but her rising inflection made it so. She gestured for her future sister-in-law to have a seat.

Tess sat and pulled out her casebook. "It's like this. Meryl has a rare blood type—AB negative. The DNA's still pending. Things are always backed up at the state lab, but with a type that rare, it's almost certain to be her blood. M.E. says given the amount of blood in the apartment and in the back of her car, it's almost certain she expired."

Expired. That was the detached clinical word medical personnel used instead of saying the patient died. Allison grabbed for her chair and sat. Hard.

"Guess it's settled, then," she said, her throat so clogged with emotion she could barely breathe.

"We found some unidentified fingerprints at the scene. No match in the AFIS database."

"And that just means the person hasn't been charged with a crime or fingerprinted by law enforcement—right?" Allison asked.

"Right."

Allison straightened her back and took a deep breath. "Who's your main suspect?"

"Her ex is good for it in my book. Bastard told us he was shopping at Opry Mills that afternoon, and he told you and Nick he was at the movies. Lying this way doesn't help his case."

"And that makes you and Nick both suspicious of her ex." No one gave Allison's suspicions a second thought. She picked up a pen and fiddled with it, trying to slow her heart rate. "So, how do you think it went down?"

"Someone either followed her from the hospital or was waiting for her at the condo and followed her inside. Appears like a blitz attack. Unpremeditated, since the weapon was a knife from Meryl's kitchen. No doubt there may be some of the killer's blood mixed with Meryl's. But sorting it all out takes time, given the current backlog. There were definite signs of a struggle. Footprints in the kitchen and garage show she was forced into the garage and into the trunk of her car."

Allison nodded. "I'm sure she fought for her life and for her baby's. Then she probably died in the trunk."

"Yeah," Tess said, "I'm sure she did."

"Died. All shut up. Knowing her baby didn't have a chance of surviving." Overcome with the 3-D images playing in her mind, Allison lay her head down on the desk.

"Crime of passion. Unorganized."

Allison straightened and banged her fist on the desk. "We have to find whoever did this. I know you don't think the doctor's a viable option, but look at what I've found. You have to look into what he's doing. At the very least, it's illegal, but he's getting away with it. Mark my words, this is the reason Meryl was killed."

Allison handed Tess the case manager notes on Ivers's last five LRD patients. "These all have the same thing in common. Distant relatives, not first degree or even second. All the donors are from out of state, as far away as New York."

Tess flipped through the documents. "These aren't admissible, but if we find anything else connecting Meryl to the good doctor, we'll subpoena the official medical records."

"You think I'm obsessing over this, don't you?"

"Not at all. You'd probably make as good a detective as the rest of your family. It's in your genes. Anyway, your reaction is quite common. Most families or friends of a victim aren't able to move on until the body's found. The chances of finding her body aren't great. I could quote you stats, but I won't."

"Unless we find her killer and he tells us."

"Contrary to what you see on TV, all you get from the majority is, 'I want a lawyer.'"

"But what about the accomplice?" Allison cried with frustration. "You said *he* was the weak link."

"Yeah, he could get by with a smack on the wrist if he gives us the killer and the location."

"So, he'd be charged as an accomplice after the fact,

improper disposal of human remains, obstruction of justice. And most of that could go away if he cooperates?"

Tess nodded. "'Fraid so."

Allison headed up to the fourth floor where the Med/Surg ICU was located. As a case manager, she was in the unit frequently, evaluating patients, and talking with their families. The unit was divided into four sections of eight beds each, but all the charge nurses knew her, which should make her questioning them easier.

She'd already checked the bed assignment for the Friday AM transplant. Sector B it was, although the patient had done well and was already out on the surgical floor. It wasn't one of Ivers's LRD patients but a cadaveric kidney recipient instead. Having already reviewed her chart, the patient was doing well and had already been set for discharge the next day. Her nurse from the day shift, seven to seven, was on duty today.

Another piece of good luck.

She approached the nurse, Rhonda. She was a short pudgy redhead, who was bright, caring, and took excellent care of her patients.

Allison picked up a chart and waited until the nurse was free. Rhonda leaned against a counter and made a couple of notations in a chart, then glanced at Allison. "Need me?"

She sidled up to the nurse, asking in an offhand manner, "You worked Friday—day shift?"

"Yes, six-thirty A to seven P. Why?"

"Was Ivers in here his usual time for rounds—between four and six?"

The nurse frowned as if trying to remember. "Friday—seems like he was called to the phone, then rushed out. Emergency, I guess."

"Did he come back? Know what time?"

The redhead's gaze narrowed. "What's this really about?"

"Just curious, y'know. Did he come back?"

"If he did, it wasn't while I was here. I left right after seven." Her expression turned cagey; she lowered her tone to a whisper. "Is this about Meryl Litton?"

Allison lowered hers as well. "Did they ever have words?"

"Well, par for the course, he tried to intimidate her when she first took on the transplant patients, but she took him aside in one of the storerooms and set him straight pretty quick. They tolerated each other afterward."

"No more disagreements?"

Rhonda chuckled. "Once he found out she wouldn't take any crap from him, they got along okay."

"Okay, thanks." Allison turned to leave.

"No, wait. They did have words once more. Friday, right after lunch."

Words on Friday. "Know what it was about?"

"No. I was coming back from the cafeteria. Just saw his body language. He was all stiff and red-faced. I couldn't hear what was being said, but she stalked away." The nurse's eyes widened. "Hey, you don't think he had anything to do with...?"

"Oh no. I-I was just curious about what her last day was like."

"Uh-huh." The nurse's underlying tone of skepticism sounded like Allison hadn't fooled her.

Hell's bells. She might as well pump Rhonda for all she was worth. "Look, don't say anything. I could lose my job if it were spread around. It's just a hunch, and I don't have any proof. But the last thing Meryl said to me was she thought he was up to something fishy."

"What do *you* think?"

Should she express her exact thoughts or not? Not for the

first time, Allison let her tongue overrule her brain. "Maybe—just maybe—there's this tiny possibility of black-market organ transplants going on here at Parklane."

"That'd be worth killing someone over, all right." The nurse nodded. "Yeah. You better be careful. You wouldn't want to get on anyone's hit list."

"Right." Allison shivered. Bringing attention to herself was the exact situation Nick had warned her against. Here she'd gone and spilled her guts. Okay, she had to trust someone.

Right?

Chapter Seventeen

Nick spent the remainder of the morning looking at two-bedroom, two-bath apartments on the west side of the city. Damn, but they were too pricey for his pocket. He aimed the Bronco west toward Bellevue and found several which were in his price range. He signed a year's lease for one located at the top of a steep hill. Might be hell in the winter, but he liked the semi-isolation of those few units up there.

The complex was older, built in the seventies, and clad in very weathered cedar. The rooms were larger than the newer high-priced ones that, granted, were closer to work.

The one he chose had a living room with a corner fireplace, a separate dining room that would make a good office since formal dining wasn't his style, an eat-in kitchen, two bedrooms, and two baths. The master was huge and opened onto a deck that ran the entire length of the apartment. From the deck, his view was trees, trees, and more trees. If he didn't know better, he could've been in the middle of the woods with no one around for miles.

Plenty of room for his son to spend his weekends and the swimming pool was on the hill section of the complex as well.

Now all he needed was a shitload of furniture, and he'd be settled by the time Ben came for another weekend.

Back in the Bronco, he pulled out his cell phone to tell his son the good news.

Naturally, his ex answered, "He's over at a friend's house for a play date."

"Why aren't you with him?"

"It's none of your business. He's in good hands. Where are you and why are you calling him in the middle of the day anyway?"

"I just rented an apartment and wanted to tell him he'd have his own place next time when he comes to spend the weekend."

"Hmph. It's about time you got your own place. I'll tell him. Anything else?"

God. He hated the whine in her voice. "Yeah, don't go around telling people I was abusive when you damned well know I wasn't."

"No, *you* weren't around long enough for anything like that to happen."

"Why'd you lie?"

"What's the matter, big boy? Did she dump you?" He could hear her gloating over the phone.

"If she did, it wouldn't be any of your business. Besides, she's my client. That's all."

"Oh well. Too bad, so sad. Now, I'm outta here. I'm due for a mani-pedi, and I'm running late." She hung up.

Blast it. Why had he ever married her?

Oh yeah, because she'd said she was pregnant and conveniently miscarried as soon as his ring was on her finger. Had she really been pregnant? To this day, he didn't know.

But if he was a betting man, he'd lay money on not.

By four-thirty, Allison was ready to call it a day. Her cell phone sounded; she retrieved it and read Nick's name on the caller ID.

More than a little puzzled by his call, she answered. "Hi."

"About time for you to get off?"

"Yes. I was about to leave. Why?" Apprehension gathered in her throat, making it difficult to speak. "What's happened?"

"Nothing major. Thought you might want to go furniture shopping."

"What?"

"I rented an apartment today and have nothing to put in it. Plus, I'm no good at stuff like that, so I figured..."

She smiled. "Sounds like a serious problem."

"So, will ya?"

"Uh, sure." She sweetened her tone. "Then you can bring me up to speed on the case, and I can do likewise."

"I'm already on West End. I'll pick you up at the Patterson Street entrance in about five minutes," he said, obviously ignoring her hint about bringing her up to speed.

She agreed to meet him, hung up, then panicked. Crap, she was in everyday work clothes, not a uniform, but a lab coat. She jerked off the institutional white jacket, hung it on a hook, grabbed her purse, and headed for the ladies room.

When she'd showered and dressed for work, she hadn't dressed with the thought of seeing Nick or going furniture shopping. Tan slacks, pale blue light sweater, and comfortable beige flats made up her not-so-memorable ensemble. Good thing her hair was clean. Rushing, she ran a brush through it, freshened her lipstick, and that was it. Nothing else could be done.

Hopefully, she wouldn't scare any animals or small children.

She left the restroom and headed for the front entrance. Two nurses in scrubs walked by, whispering and casting glances at her.

Oh well. There still wasn't anything else she could do about her appearance.

*

Nick pulled under the large glass-roofed portico. Allie exited the hospital, right on time, looking as fresh as if she'd just stepped out of the house. Her long reddish-blond hair fell to her shoulders with a slight wave. Her blue sweater fit her in all the right places, showing off her tiny waist and perfect breasts. Her unwrinkled slacks fit just tight enough to accentuate a fine ass.

She opened the door and got inside. "Hi." She sounded a little breathless as if she'd been running.

"Didn't mean to make you rush."

She smiled and fluffed her hair. "Oh, you didn't."

He waited for a car pulling around him, then moved out. "Where's this new apartment?"

"Bellevue. One of the older ones."

"Great. Now tell me what else you've been up to."

Woman had a one-track mind—down to business. Might as well get it over with. "Interviewed this gal who was working when Buckley said he was at the Cineplex. I showed her his picture, but she only remembered him from the news. After that, I drove over to his apartment and put a bird dog on his truck so I can track his location on the Internet."

"Come up with anything good yet?"

"Not yet. But give him time. If he's the guilty party, I figure he'll recheck his dumpsite or maybe move her if he gets nervous. What about you? How was your day?"

"Busy as usual, but I talked to a nurse in ICU who said Ivers and Meryl argued the morning before she disappeared."

"About?"

"She didn't know. Wasn't close enough to hear them."

"Doesn't mean it was anything other than usual nurse and doctor disagreement."

"You are *so* determined to be right."

"No more than you are."

"Oh, by the way, Tess came by. I gave her copies of some case notes Meryl made about the LRD patients."

"LRD?" he asked.

"Living related donors. I'm more certain than ever our Dr. Ivers is running a black-market organ program right here in this hospital—right under our very noses."

"And you're keeping your suspicions to yourself, I hope."

"Yeah..."

He cut his gaze toward her. Her uncertain tone trailed off, and she chewed on her bottom lip. He didn't like the tentative tone of her answer at all.

"Allison, have you said anything to anyone besides Tess?"

"Well, just this one nurse, but she'll keep it quiet. No one likes Ivers. He's a real horse's butt."

He maneuvered the Bronco onto West End, merging with the rush-hour traffic. "Somebody could tell him what you're up to."

"But you don't think he's the one responsible for Meryl, so I could actually be saving the hospital's ass. If this hits the papers, it could be a major scandal."

"If it hits the papers without any real proof, you'll lose your job."

"I can find a job anywhere. Don't you know there's a nursing shortage?"

Time to change the subject. "Furniture."

"Right. And I know some great consignment shops. In the right part of town, you can pick up some cool stuff for a lot less money."

"Furniture's one thing, but I need a new mattress and springs."

"No problem. We can pick those up after we see what size bed you buy."

At least he'd gotten her mind off the case and, more importantly, off the doctor.

"Where're we headed?"

"Brentwood and a place called Finders Keepers. Moore's Lane exit."

Given the state of traffic, it would take at least thirty to forty-five minutes to get there, but she kept up a steady flow of inconsequential trivia, including way too many details about Tess and her brother's upcoming nuptials. Must be a female thing. If he ever married again... He gave an involuntary shudder.

Elopement. Now that was the ticket to sanity.

One thing Allison shared with her sisters was the shopping gene. Granted, she didn't shop as much as Tamsyn—who shopped as if it were an Olympic sport—but since Allison was spending someone else's money, it was even more fun.

They stood in front of the shop. She grabbed Nick by the hand. "Come on."

"Hold on. There's no rush."

Ignoring his feeble protests, she dragged him into the consignment shop.

"Now look," he said, lowering his voice, "my budget's slim. All I need is bedroom furniture for Ben's room and a small desk to use in my office. I'll add the rest later."

"Pfft," Allie replied. "You need a sofa for the living room and a TV too." There wasn't a man in existence who could manage without his TV and remote. At least her brothers couldn't.

Nick shrugged. "Nah, the main thing's to take care of Ben's needs first. I don't need much."

Stubborn man. Thoughtful man. "You need a bed too.

I'm telling you there are some deals to be had."

"I don't even have my first paycheck yet. Your brother went overboard and offered me a signing bonus so I could go on and rent the apartment."

"Good for him." She dropped her tone as well. "I'll extend you some cash if you're short. My monthly expenses are minimal."

"No way." He jammed his hands in his pockets. "I'm not taking money from *you*. Besides, I already had set some aside."

"Oh, male pride and all that." She rolled her eyes, then nodded. "I get it."

"No, you don't." He glanced around as if concerned someone would overhear their bickering. "Well, maybe you do, but I'm not about to take money from any woman. That's just how I am."

Admirable, but still stubborn as a slow-healing wound. "Hold on, didn't your ex contribute to the family income?" Not wanting him to think she was judgmental, she hastened to add, "Of course, if she was a stay-at-home mom, that's very admirable."

"Eva worked, but that was different. We were married. The apartment doesn't have to be turnkey. I've been sleeping on a sofa for two weeks. I can handle a mattress and springs on the floor."

"Okay, out with it. How much do we have to spend today?"

"About six-fifty."

"Tight, but it's doable. I'm not going to embarrass you if I do a little old-fashioned haggling, will I?"

His steel-blue eyes shone with good humor. "Haggling is an honored Southern custom."

"Well, you dudes may corner the market on haggling to get a better deal on your car or tricked-out truck, but leave the furniture haggling to me." She stopped to catch her breath. "Okay, the first priority is furniture for Ben's room—right?"

"Yeah."

"Okay, here we go. This way." She headed down the aisle, then stopped in front of a twin bed. "Nice, simple straight lines, Mission style. Masculine, and he can grow up with it unless he grows to be six-feet plus like his dad."

"Mission style? I like the look of it."

She ran her hands over it, assessing the quality of the wood. "It's solid oak with a dark stain. And there's a bookshelf that goes with it. And a chest and a side table." She checked the price tags. "Well, five hundred—but that's for the bed and dresser. We can ditch the side table and use the chest with a lamp as a bedside table."

He glanced around. "This place is too expensive."

"Hold on. I haven't worked my wiles on the owner yet," she said, not telling him she and the owner's daughter were sorority sisters.

She flagged down the nearest clerk, a tall, thin scarecrow of a woman with mannish-cut hair and black-rimmed glasses that kept slipping down her nose.

"We'd like to buy the bed and chest of drawers, but five hundred's too much. Would you take three-fifty and throw in the small bookshelf?"

The clerk's gaze widened. She stopped and adjusted her glasses. "Oh no, that's entirely too large a reduction."

"Is there someone I can talk to? Mrs. Owens, perhaps? Otherwise, we'll just have to keep looking."

"Maybe we should," Nick said, turning to leave.

"Now wait." A look of desperation crossed the woman's face. "Since you know Mrs. Owens, I'll give her a call and see what we can work out."

"That'll be so sweet. Just tell her it's Allison Lackey." She winked at Nick, who rolled his eyes, his expression bemused.

Ten minutes later, the deal was struck, and Nick forked over the agreed-upon three-fifty. "Will all of it fit in your Bronco?" Allison asked.

He eyeballed the furniture. "Nah. But my brother has a pickup. He'll give me a hand one night this week."

"All right." She smiled her best and brightest at the clerk. "You'll hold it, won't you?" *Of course, they will.*

The clerk nodded.

Allison took Nick's hand and started pulling him toward the exit. "Now we need to find a discount store for some linens, and then we're off to buy you a mattress."

By the time they made it to the mattress store, Nick questioned his sanity. What the hell was he thinking, asking for Allie's help?

Here she was in the middle of a mall store, lying on a plush mattress, patting the space beside her. "Come on. You have to test it. Personally, I think it's fine. Very comfy."

The salesman stood at the foot of the bed, quoting stats and telling Nick the price was actually lower than it was marked because of a special sale.

"Looks too soft," Nick said.

Allie grinned up at him. "You won't know unless you lie down."

There, she did it again. Patted the mattress in a clear invitation to lie down beside her. What the hell was she thinking?

She appealed to the salesman. "Tell him it's the only way to buy a mattress."

Nick took a deep breath, then said through clenched teeth, "This isn't the first mattress I've bought. I like a firm mattress, but this one's too soft." He pointed at a mattress two beds over from Allie. "What about that one?"

"Yes, sir," said the salesman, eager to make the sale. "This is our luxury firm. And without a nasty old pillow top, it's a bit less expensive too."

The linens from Target and the small, yet-to-be-assembled desk had taken the rest of Nick's cash. He pulled out his billfold. Plastic would have to do for this purchase, since he was short several hundred, despite the sales price.

He walked over to the firmer mattress, sat, then bounced a couple of times. "This'll do."

"That's it, then. We're done." Allie sat up, shook her hair into place, and set her feet on the floor.

"Free bed frame with the mattress too," the salesman offered.

Nick nodded once. "Even better."

After the delivery date and time was set up and the paperwork completed, Nick yanked her toward the exit. "What's the matter? Weren't you having fun in there?" she asked with a playful expression.

"I was until you started acting like..."

"Like what?"

"Hell if I know." Just being her cute, sweet self—make that sexy, sweet self.

"Are you always so rigid and uptight? Look what we've accomplished. We have furniture for Ben's bedroom. And they threw in the twin mattress and springs, for good measure." She ticked each item off one by one on the fingers of one hand. "Linens for both beds and a desk from Target. Now I think you ought to wait until Saturday morning and hit the yard sales. You're bound to pick up a decent sofa. Lamps, some artwork. You know—stuff to make it homey." She shot him a brilliant smile, showing her even, white teeth, then wrinkled her nose. "Hasn't this been fun?"

They walked toward the Bronco. He held back a groan of frustration. "Had about all the fun I can stand. How about some dinner?" He opened the door for her and gave her a little boost inside.

She curled her lip. "Hmph. Not the most gracious invitation I've ever received."

"Not an invitation." He frowned, even though she was just yanking his chain for the fun of it. "I'm talking about food—a necessity." He shut the door firmly, then walked around to the driver's side and got inside.

"I guess a strong man like you must have food to stoke the fires." She batted her lashes at him, like some sort of femme fatale.

He leveled his gaze on her. "Come on, Allie. Cut it out."

Resigned to his lacking a sense of humor, she sighed. "Fine. How about we take all this stuff back to your apartment and..."

"Why don't we head back to town and have something to eat, then I'll drop you off at your car." He started the engine and backed out of the parking space, then headed for I-65 and the Bell Road exit, opposite the main traffic flow.

"Right. I'd forgotten about my car." She made a face. "I'd say from your behavior this evening shopping isn't high on your list of things to do?"

He stared at the road, not about to let his gaze wander to his talkative passenger. "Nope. Fun is chasing down escaped felons," he said, slanting a wry smile in her direction. "And putting bad guys behind bars."

"So, you've been tortured all afternoon. You could've said something."

"Aw, kinda fun," he muttered, halfway hoping she wouldn't hear.

"What?"

She tapped his thigh with her fist. Her slight touch sent a

jolt of heat to his groin. *Ignore her.*

"I didn't quite make that out."

"Okay. It was fun watching you haggle. Happy now?" The stoplight ahead turned red. He slowed and stopped.

"I have a confession to make." Her tone was playful. Just what he needed. *Not.*

He shot a quick glance in her direction. Oh no—batting those long lashes again. Her flirting was getting to him, not that he wanted her to stop. "Yeah?"

"The—uh, consignment shop owner's daughter is a sorority sister of mine."

"I get it now. You just pretended to haggle. You cheated."

"Maybe I did. But it was more fun watching you roll your eyes and get ready to walk out."

He cut his gaze in her direction. "I'll have you know walking out is a necessary part of haggling strategy."

"You were perfect, then." She patted his leg. His thigh muscles jumped involuntarily.

The car behind them honked. What the hell! She had him so distracted, the light was green and he hadn't noticed. He waved a thank-you at the driver behind them and hit the gas.

"Just wait till you see me at the yard sales. I'm a terror." There was a hint of laughter in her tone. Laughing at him, no doubt.

"Presuming I allow you to herd me all over Nashville."

"Why change now?" She awarded him a smug smile. "We need to get an early start. Pick me up at seven."

Too mesmerized by her energy to fight the inevitable, he gave in—not that he wanted to resist. "All right. Seven." For all her craziness, he enjoyed her company way too much for his own good.

Unaffected. Frank. Honest to a fault. Allison Lackey still possessed more than her share of that mysterious something every woman he'd ever known possessed to one degree or another.

He wouldn't be getting much sleep tonight. An image of Allison curled beside him sent another curl of lust straight to his groin.

Get your mind out of the gutter, dude. Change lanes.

"You like Chinese?" he asked.

"Mmm, second only to *Italian*." How could one woman make such a simple statement sound so sexy? Nah, she didn't mean anything about the way "Italian" rolled off her tongue.

He swallowed hard. "PF Chang's it is, then."

Allison's cell phone rang. "Home," she said. "Sorry. I know I should've called. Didn't mean to worry you, but Nick and I were shopping for his new apartment."

She was silent for a moment while she listened. "Okay... Okay. Sure. We're on West End now, but my car's still at the hospital." She listened some more, closed the phone, then turned to him, her eyes wide. "We need to get home ASAP. Carrie says Tess is on her way over...with news."

"Sounds like there's a break in the case."

"Maybe they found Meryl."

He reached over and covered her trembling left hand with his right. Wishing he could do more to comfort her, he stroked the back of her delicate hand. "Just hold on."

Chapter Eighteen

Allison marveled at Nick's tenderness. True, his hand was callused, but his touch was gentle all the same. This was *not* a man who abused his wife. No way.

They took Bell Road over to Harding Road which turned into West End. Nashville was infamous for having more than one street with multiple names, depending on which part of it you were on.

"Turn down Craighead and go past Richmond to the alley behind the house. The front spaces are bound to be taken already."

"First come, first served."

"Usually." She fell silent. What else was there to say until they heard Tess's news?

Always understanding, Nick seemed to sense she needed some quiet time. He followed her directions and parked the SUV in the area behind the house.

Dusk had already fallen. The buzzing sounds of cicadas high in the trees were so loud she couldn't hear herself think. Without waiting for Nick, she ran up the walk and bounded up the steps onto the deck.

Tamsyn, her face fixed in a frown and arms folded, greeted her on the deck. "Dude, you could've called. We were about to call out the troops."

"Sorry. Nick rented a new place and—what's this about a break in the case?"

The party in question strode up behind Allison. "My fault. Sorry."

"Who said there was a break?" Tamsyn's dark brown eyes widened. "Yes, Tess is coming over, but, hell, I don't know what's going on around here. No one tells me anything."

They walked inside to the kitchen. Caroline was wiping off the granite counters. "Have y'all eaten? Justin brought home enough Chinese to feed an army of hundreds."

Allison took in the scattering of Chinese food containers on the dining room table, and without warning, her stomach growled. "Perfect. We were about to go to PF Chang's. Any General Tso's? Pork-fried rice?"

"I thought *I* was the hungry one." The corner of Nick's mouth lifted.

"Might as well eat something while I still have an appetite. Tess isn't here yet." She started checking the various yummy-smelling containers. "Chopsticks or forks?"

Her "might as well eat" remark was a vain attempt to hide her misgivings. As much as she wanted Meryl found, she didn't want it to be tonight. Shopping with Nick had been fun. Forgetting about Meryl, even for a while, had refreshed her outlook on life.

And now it was over. Back to grim reality.

The French doors opened, the sound catching Allison's attention. Tess, her face set in a grim mask, entered the house from the deck. "No place to park out front." She glanced around the kitchen. "Let's go into the den. I want to give you a heads-up before it hits the news."

Caroline, Justin, and Tamsyn followed Nick and Allison into the den. Tess cased the group, and a mounting unease collected in the pit of Allison's stomach.

"Where's Scott?" Tess asked.

"Stakeout at some sleazy motel. Work never ends," Caroline said, giving a matter-of-fact nod.

They settled in the den and waited. Allison's heart sped up. Mouth dry, she tried to swallow the anxiety choking her and grasped the arm of the sofa, her nails digging into the leather.

With everyone's gaze on her, Tess stood, her back rigid, her face composed but stern. "What you're going to hear shortly on the news is another nurse has gone missing. She resembles Meryl. She's tall and blond, not pregnant, though, as far as anyone knows."

A memory nagged at the back of Allison's mind. "The nurse's name? What's her name?"

"Bane. Harmony Bane. You know her?"

"Yes." Allison sat straight. "She's the nurse I saw coming out of the transplant office last Saturday morning. You're right about her resembling Meryl. From the back, they're dead ringers."

"So, now you're thinking serial killer?" Nick asked.

Tess frowned. "Too soon to tell. The funny thing is there's no sign of foul play at this one's apartment. She just didn't show up for work yesterday. She's not at home. No one has seen or talked to her since Monday evening. Still, it could be a case of her getting scared and taking off."

"What about her phone records?" Nick asked.

Allison stirred on the sofa, crossing and uncrossing her legs. No way could she keep still. Here was another nurse with some kind of connection to the transplant program. Ivers *had* to be involved. Why couldn't anyone else see that?

Tess paused as if choosing her words. "Her phone records are still under review. Nothing definite yet."

"But you must have an idea?" Allison insisted, trying not to disintegrate into an out-and-out whine. Her gaze traveled to Nick, who shook his head, warning her. "But—surely..."

"Tess *can't* tell us everything." Nick's tone was reasonable but annoying because he spoke the truth.

"I hate this." She jumped up from the sofa and began to pace around the room. "What you mean is she can't tell me because I'm likely to fly off the handle and do something rash?"

"Exactly." Tess reached for Allison's wrist. "You *have* to stay out of it. You could compromise evidence or other witnesses. If there is, as you believe, a common thread, you're putting yourself in danger."

Nick eased off the chair arm where he'd perched and pulled Allison into his arms. "You know she's right. You have to leave this to the police."

His arms around her felt so right. So, what if a few of her family exchanged some startled glances. Her chin notched upward. "What about you? You're not going to stay out of it, are you?"

He shot a wary glance at Tess. "I'll continue pursuing lines of inquiry that don't conflict with the official investigation." His reply came out like canned text. And rehearsed.

She shoved him away and faced them all, arms akimbo. "I don't like being double-teamed. I can take care of myself in most situations, and I can outrun anyone in this room."

Tamsyn's eyebrows rose. "Faster than a speeding bullet?" came her pithy reply. "Allie, you're verging on reckless, and if anyone in this room agrees with me, raise your hand."

Allison took a deep breath. Everyone in the room, Nick included, raised a hand. "Well, I certainly see what you all think of me." Tears welled up and threatened to reveal just how devastated she was by her family's betrayal. She blinked them back.

Concern written across her face, Caroline, the family peacemaker, spoke first, her tone even and assured. "Honey, we all love you"—her gaze darted to Nick, then back to Allison—"or care what happens to you. The rest of this lot—

we've been in the investigation biz for a long time, but you—you're our rebel. You chose nursing as a career. You have a job you love, and it doesn't include chasing down bad guys. Or guns. Or knives."

"I'm a grown woman," she said with a sniff. "I'm *not* the baby of the family, but that's how you're treating me."

She stormed from the den. Man, was she escaping an impromptu family intervention or what? Outside on the deck, the night sky was as dark as it ever got in the city. The temperature had dropped. The night air helped clear her mind as she waved her hands to cool her burning cheeks.

Screw them all. They had no right to treat her like a total incompetent. She was tough and she *could* take care of herself, no matter what they said.

"Allie?" Nick.

His tone was soft, almost pleading for her understanding. His warmth and light sandalwood scent swept over her. But no, she was determined. He slipped his arms around her, but she shrugged him away, refusing the very comfort she wanted and needed, then turned to face him.

"You can just go back inside with all the grownups," she told him with a touch more heat than she intended.

"Excuse me." He hooked his thumbs in his jean pockets and leaned against the railing. "I thought I was invited. Isn't this where the pity party's being held?"

She raised her fists as if intending to beat his chest, but he captured her wrists in one hand and held them close to his heart. "Allie…"

Pain sliced through her like a scalpel. "I *need* to help," she said. "If I can't find Meryl, the very least I can do is bring her killer to justice."

"Listen to yourself. Every day you sound more like an avenging angel." He wouldn't release her. Part of her didn't want him to either.

"She was my friend. And now she's gone. I can't just go my merry way and forget she ever existed."

"No one's asking you to forget your friend. Do you think she'd want you to put yourself in danger? That's what you're doing. You're risking your life...everything."

"N-no."

Nick pulled her closer, so close he felt her heart hammering against him. Her hands splayed down his chest, tugging at his shirt.

"No," he said as gently as he could. She pulled away. Dammit, he might be powerfully attracted, but she was too vulnerable, and he wouldn't take advantage. Too many old wounds. "Sorry."

He was a very physical person, and he figured that tendency might just scare her...just a bit if she admitted the truth. His ex and her claims of abuse probably still nagged her. The old "where there's smoke, there's fire" theory.

"I'd never hurt you. You ought to know this by now. You're still thinking about Eva's lies. That's all they were. Lies."

As if ashamed he'd read her so accurately, she averted her gaze.

Anger flared and flashed through his brain like a bolt of electricity. "I knew it!" He released her wrists and strode to the other side of the deck. He willed his fists to unclench. "Women are all alike. And you—you're the worst. You're a freaking crusader. Yeah. Deliver me from do-gooders and crusaders. Not what I need." He raked his fingers through his hair, leaving it in spiky rows.

"A crusader, am I? I've seen plenty of abused women in my career. You know what they have in common? They think it's their fault for getting beat-up."

He drew in a deep breath to force his heart rate to slow. "Don't waste your breath. No need to give me a psych profile on battered women. I grew up with one." As if they had a mind of their own, his fists clenched again at his sides.

"Which makes it all the more likely..." Her voice trailed off, perhaps realizing, she realized she'd said too much.

"I *know* the statistics, Allie." He forced his hands to relax. "You don't have to quote 'em. I've made a concerted effort all my adult life not to repeat my father's mistakes. And I never laid so much as a finger, much less a hand, on my ex."

"That's good to know," she murmured.

He shut his eyes for a brief second. "And no matter how much you aggravate me, I'll never lay a hand on you. *That's* a promise. But sometimes, you can be the most infuriating woman I've ever known—bar none."

Her gaze widened. "Oh..." She breathed the word so softly he could scarcely hear her.

Emotions balanced on a razor's edge, he took another deep breath. "Now if you'll excuse me, I need to work off some tension."

"Scott beats up weight bags at the Y." She studied him carefully. "What do *you* do?"

Honestly, the woman's moods had a sharper turning radius than a kid's scooter. *Patience, dude.* "Before I sold it, I rode my hog. Now I run."

She gave a little jog in place. "I run too."

"So?"

She shot him a tentative smile. "We could go for a run together."

His jaw dropped. "You want to go on a run...with *me*?" He gestured with both hands to his chest. She actually thought she could keep pace with him?

"Besides, I was helping with your decorating."

"Tell you what." If she was serious about running or

decorating, he'd soon find out. "Tomorrow after work, come over to the apartment. We'll run around the complex a few times. Then you can decorate to your heart's content."

"That's a big hill."

"Yeah. If you can't manage it, I'll understand." He gave her a smug smile, knowing his response would aggravate her. Teasing her was the only enjoyment he would allow himself.

She squared her shoulders, challenging him. "Oh yeah? I'll call you when I get off."

"Don't chicken out. I'm gonna run you into the ground."

She set her hands on her hips. "I'll have you know I ran track in school."

Nick winked. "So did I, short stuff."

Instead of taking his bait, she smiled up at him. "You're good for me, Nick. You really are."

Her sweet, honest gaze unsettled him. It would never work. His life was too complicated. But he cared about her. He did.

Before he could say anything, Meryl's Yorkie ran onto the deck to Allie, bouncing like a rubber ball. Smiling, she bent over and picked up the dog. "I think he needs a nice long walk to drain some of that energy."

Maybe running would drain some of *her* energy too, since she seemed to have enough for three people. Nick raised a brow. "He's a runner too?"

She nodded. "I'll just go find his leash."

"I'll go with you."

"I'll be fine," she said in an I-mean-business tone.

"But I want to. It's safer—I know you think you're Wonder Woman and Xena, Warrior Princess rolled into one, but I'll lose my job if anything happens to you." If common sense and Allie weren't on speaking terms, then maybe he could guilt her into not going off on wild-ass tangents.

"Can't have that," she said wryly, then nuzzled the top of the terrier's head. "I give up. You can go. You don't mind, do you, Roxy?" she asked the dog, ignoring him.

A smile tugged at Nick's mouth. They were right about dogs having a calming effect on people. A woman like Allie needed at least two.

The night air was fragrant with the scent of crepe myrtle. Feeling safe and secure with Nick at her side and the rambunctious Roxy darting ahead, Allison couldn't help but wonder what life would be like if Nick was around because he wanted to be. Not because it was his job.

He made no move to touch her, but she felt the comforting air of his presence. Other than a chuckle when the dog's antics amused him, he made no sound. No idle chatter. That was her department, after all.

And yet the silence was comfortable, not oppressive. She was glad he'd offered to come along. No matter how safe she'd always felt on this street lined with large yards and stately homes, she'd lost her sense of security.

Once in a while, her gaze darted from side to side, imagining a dark figure lurking between the vehicles parked on the street. But as long as Roxy was content to frolic at the end of the leash and Nick was by her side, she could relax.

After walking five blocks, Allison turned north. "We can circle the block and head back through the alley."

"Think the rat-dog has had enough?" Nick asked.

"It's been a long day. I thought maybe you'd had enough too."

"Let's see. Interviewing witnesses. Riding herd on you. Apartment hunting. Shopping. Yeah, it's been a full day."

She heard the teasing tone in his voice and smiled. "I'll

be more careful," she promised. "At least, I'll try."

He chuckled. "Yeah, I know how hard you try."

"Really. I will."

The remainder of their walk passed in companionable silence until they reached Allison's backyard. "Thank you," she said.

"For what?"

"For giving me a chance to calm down. As I said, you're good for me."

"Nah. You calmed down as soon as you picked up that rat of a dog." He reached down and scooped up the squirming terrier and handed it to her while trying to avoid its licking tongue.

"Roxy likes you. Otherwise, she'd have already bitten you."

He smiled down at her. In the scant light from the back of the house, she saw his lips part as if he were going to say something but didn't.

Her mouth grew cotton-ball dry, even as her heart rate ventured into the tachycardic range. More than anything, she wanted to feel his lips on hers. Instead, she sighed. "G'night, then."

He glanced toward the deck. "Call me tomorrow. We'll run."

So, he was ready to call it a night. Fine. She nodded. "Get ready to lose," she said. With the terrier still in her arms, she headed up the yard, determined not to look over her shoulder. When she reached the door, she allowed herself a final glance.

He was still there, standing by his SUV. With a nod and a two-fingered wave, he waited until she entered the house before climbing into his vehicle.

Somehow she'd break through his cool façade. She closed the French doors behind her, set the dog down, and unfastened its leash. True, Nick's breakup was still fresh, but she wasn't anything like his ex. Imagine ever wanting to cheat on a man like Nick Vitelli. No way.

After seeing Allison safely inside, Nick sat in the Bronco for a minute, his thoughts whirling with the contradiction who was Allison Lackey. When she wasn't bouncing off the walls or running her motor at full throttle, she was easy to be with. Too easy. Gentle even. But when she set her mind on something, she was relentless. Boy howdy, just bar the door.

He started the motor and backed into the alley. Somehow he had to keep her safe and investigate her friend's disappearance at the same time. Then he remembered the tracker he'd placed on Buckley's truck. Might as well see what the dude had been up to. Nick braked and turned on his tablet. Sure enough, the bird dog was working fine. Plus, the updated software had a backtrack feature. Keeping the motor running, he reviewed where Buckley's truck had been since he'd placed the tracker.

Son of a gun.

He revved the engine. Buckley was in for a surprise visit.

Nick sat at the Wildhorse's bar and sipped on a beer while he waited for the Tuesday-evening crowd to thin out. He'd have to be careful when he pumped Buckley. No point in letting him know his vehicle had a tracker on it. The wannabe singer was a dab hand at pouring drinks. Not up to Tom Cruise *Cocktail* standards, but good enough. There were a couple of hard-looking groupies hanging on his every move. Big hair, tons of makeup, and slightly worse for wear.

"Ready for another?" Abandoning his groupies for a

minute, Buckley sidled over to where Nick sat.

Nick declined. "Would rather talk to you when you've got some free time."

Nodding, Buckley curled his upper lip and shot Nick a fishy gaze. "I remember you now. You were with the nutty broad who knew my wife."

"Yeah." Allison would hate being characterized as a "nutty broad," but he wasn't about to argue the point—not when it contained a grain of truth. And then there was Buckley's use of past tense when referring to his ex-wife. Gotcha.

Granted, it was assumed by all involved that Meryl Litton was deceased. Even Allie.

"Don't get much free time," Buckley said, swiping the bar top with a rag. "Got nothing much to say—to you, anyhow."

"So, you're cooperating with the authorities? Taken a lie detector test?"

"I'm a-going to. But getting my career going keeps me busy. Know what I mean, jellybean?"

Nick clenched his jaw and fists to keep from popping Meryl's ex a good one. The SOB couldn't care less about her or his unborn child. Taking a freaking lie detector test was the least a decent human being could do.

He could think of one main reason to delay the test. Buckley was guilty.

No point in wasting any more time with Buckley. Nick slid off the barstool and left a ten on the bar. "See ya."

"Not if I see you first." Buckley cackled and pointed at Nick, his hand folded like a gun.

Back in the Bronco, Nick sent Tess O'Malley a text message outlining the results from the bird dog he'd placed on Buckley's truck. Let the authorities handle it.

Otherwise, if Nick had stayed any longer, assault charges would be a possibility.

Chapter Nineteen

Ready to break for lunch, Allison headed back to Case Management. The department's administrative assistant, by habit a cheerful person, was at her desk, frowning. She gave Allison a sideways glance from her keyboard. "Carol wants to see you—right now."

"Sure." She walked down the hallway to Carol Waller's office and knocked. The moment she opened the door, she started to speak, but the words stuck in her throat. The boss's face was set in a mask of displeasure. What now?

She gestured for Allison to take a seat.

Allison did, but a sense of uneasiness crept through her.

"Allison, I warned you. Administration has come down hard. I have no other choice but to let you go."

"What? Let me go? I haven't been near Dr. Ivers or his residence."

"No, but it's all over the hospital you're investigating Meryl's death."

"But—"

"Gossip and innuendo have no place at Parklane. Accusing a respected member of our staff of dealing in black-market organs..." Carol shook her head.

Thank you, Rhonda. "We're already one case manager short."

"Yes. And you picked a very bad time to play amateur detective. Fortunately, we have someone who's familiar with transplant patients and can step into Meryl's place. She'll follow your caseload as well. It's a double load, but I'm sure

Rhonda Siebert will manage."

Rhonda Siebert. Bless her heart. Talk about a knife in the back. Ruined my plan and stepped into my job to boot. Talk about a lesson learned. Don't trust anyone and keep your mouth shut.

"Well, she certainly did a fine job of spreading the news. I'll say that for her. I'm sure she'll do just fine in my place."

Carol's stern expression didn't change. "You have a choice. You can leave quietly, or I can call security to escort you out."

"Hmph. I thought they only did that for the bigwigs." *Crap. Haven't you said enough?*

Determined to proceed, Carol said, "I need your ID badge and your office key."

"But I have a couple of cases to add notes to. Do I have time for that?"

"No. You no longer have access to the hospital computer system. Your computer codes have been deleted. And I have your final check." Carol opened a desk drawer, pulled out an envelope, then handed it to Allison.

"That's it?" Disbelief settled heavy on her shoulders, weighing her down like concrete blocks. She took a deep breath. If she couldn't access the computer systems, how would she ever be able to investigate Ivers?

Answer: she couldn't.

Carol leaned over and picked up an empty file box. "Here. Don't even think about taking any files, just your belongings."

"Sure." Allison took the box from her former boss.

"I hate this, Allison, but you gave me no choice. Administration gave *me* no choice. Dr. Ivers has a lot of clout here. Besides, you're guilty of violating patient confidentiality, a serious HIPAA violation. You accessed his patients' records. Patients who were being followed by

Meryl, not you."

Allison sucked in a deep breath. "Then just maybe you or Administration ought to do a bit of investigating yourselves and find out what's going on here—right under your noses. *Two* nurses are missing now. How many more have to go missing before someone takes me seriously?" With that single, feeble parting shot, she turned and got the hell out.

Her belongings consisted of family photos, certificates, and a stuffed dog of an indeterminate breed she'd received on her last birthday.

Less than five minutes later, she shut the door to her office.

Fired.

At least Carol was kind enough to let her leave under her own power rather than be escorted out like a criminal.

Out in the parking garage, she stowed the box of her pathetic belongings inside the Camry's trunk, then slammed the lid.

The shaking—and the tears—started as soon as she fastened her seat belt.

Fired.

She couldn't say she hadn't been warned...by just about everyone in existence, or so it seemed.

Way to go, dumbass.

Now, what would she do? Her brave words about the nursing shortage were a load of bull. Being fired was the end of everything. What hospital would hire her once they discovered the reason for her dismissal?

How could she face her family, especially Scott? He'd sacrificed law school and slaved to make the agency a success just so she could have an education.

And Nick. Oh, he'd just *have* to say *I told you so*. Like she needed to hear that again...from anyone.

In a daze, Allison drove to the nearest McDonald's. Their low-fat ice-cream cone was calling her name. Getting fired definitely called for some frozen consolation.

After a lick or two of the creamy goodness, she pulled out onto West End. Home was a few blocks away, but she wasn't ready to face Caroline. Nine thirty—what the hell could she do with the rest of the day? Maybe she should just go ahead and call Nick. That way she could get his *I told you so* over with. Was he at his new apartment, waiting on delivery of some of last evening's larger purchases?

There wasn't any place she could pull over on West End or Harding, so she waited until she reached the Belle Meade Plaza to make the call. She glossed over his surprise at her being off with: "It's a long story. I'll tell you all about it when I get there."

He responded rather cryptically he had something related to the case to tell her as well. When she pressed him for details, he fed her own words back to her.

"Fine. Be that way," she said, ending the call. But she'd let him have his say first because once he heard she'd been fired, he'd go ballistic.

Before Nick had time to wonder why Allie was off so early in the day, someone knocked. He opened the door. Two hulking men stood on his doorstep.

"Vitelli?"

Great. His new mattress and springs were here. Finally, a decent night's sleep. "That's me. This way." He motioned the deliverymen toward the larger of the two bedrooms. His son's room was already set up. Earlier that morning, he and Sonny had picked up Ben's furniture from the consignment store.

The rest of the previous day's purchases were still in the bags they came in. As it was, the apartment had a very divorced-dad style. That was to say bare.

Allison had her work cut out for her if she was going to make his apartment resemble anything like a home for his son.

But it was a giant leap over the pullout sofa in his brother's apartment with rotating girlfriends.

Following Nick's directions, a mere fifteen minutes later, Allison hung a left into Nick's apartment complex. She wove her way through the twists and turns of the property until she reached the rear portion and one helluva steep hill. Feeling like she was nosing her Camry up a Coney Island roller coaster incline, she held her breath until she reached the top. Whew.

She spied a single row of apartments. Nick's was second from the far end. His Bronco was parked next to a delivery truck. Two men emerged from the back of the truck. Hefting a mattress between them, they carried it into his apartment. She found a spot behind the Bronco and parked.

Reluctant to admit she'd been fired, she remained in the Camry until the deliverymen hopped into their truck and left. She ate the last bite of her ice-cream cone and then sucked in a deep breath. Might as well get it over with.

She hopped from the car and waltzed up to his door. Ready to knock, she raised her fist when the door opened. To say Nick stood there in all his male glory might be trite, but cliché or not, it was *not* an exaggeration.

His clothes were casual—moving day and all. His sable brown hair was mussed, and his usual facial scruff was scruffier than usual. A pale blue T-shirt, reflected in the faded denim of his blue eyes, was tucked into tight-fitting jeans. He'd jammed his bare feet into running shoes. Best of all, he wore a wide smile that said he was glad to see her.

"Through taking inventory?" he asked with a teasing tone.

Whoops. Her survey of his muscular bod had taken a bit longer than she'd intended. Her cheeks heating, she managed to stammer, "Uh, hi—" and tripped over the doorsill.

Nick caught her before she embarrassed herself by falling flat on her face.

"Walk much?"

"Apparently not." Heart racing, she gazed up into his eyes and noted a sparkle of amusement. "Thanks."

"No. Thank *you*. Not every day a beautiful gal throws herself into my arms."

"Very cute, Vitelli. I did no such thing." She walked inside and found herself in the living room. There was a fireplace in the far corner and boxes everywhere. Good thing she was here to help him get organized.

She followed him into the kitchen. Crossing his arms over his broad chest, he leaned back against the counter and smiled. "Then you're okay with being unable to walk and eat an ice-cream cone at the same time?"

"You saw that?"

"Yeah, just wish you'd offered me the last bite." He winked.

Well, his good humor wouldn't last long when she dumped her big news on him. "So, what have you learned?" She set her purse on the laminate counter, hoping to delay her reveal as long as possible.

He arched one dark brow. "First, tell me why you're off so early in the day."

"No." She held up a delaying hand. "You go first. My explanation is a little more complicated."

"Uh-huh." His gaze widened as he launched into his tale. "Remember the bird dog I placed on Buckley's truck?"

She nodded.

"Last night, after leaving your place, I checked it. Wanna make a guess where he's been?"

"Nashville's a big city. Enlighten me."

"Yesterday. Early morning hours, he was at the Farmers' Market. He went back to make sure he hadn't left any evidence behind."

"But Meryl's ex drives a truck," she insisted. "Besides, that wasn't what was on the video."

"Right. In the video, he had an accomplice. One of those vehicles was most likely borrowed. But that's not all."

She gave him the eye roll. "So..."

"He drove out to the Moss Wright Park in Sumner County."

Finally, something they could do. She squared her shoulders. "What are we waiting for? Let's go!"

"Steady on. I sent the information on the coordinates to O'Malley. This kind of thing is better investigated by the authorities. They'll re-interview Buckley first. Determine if he has an alibi or a convincing reason to be in both areas."

"What are we standing around for? At least *we* should re-interview him." She turned, ready to rush from the apartment.

Nick blinked, then shook his head slowly as if she were an impatient child. "I already talked to him last night at his job. Didn't find out much—"

"And why not?" Honestly, did she have to do everything herself?

"First, I didn't want to spook him by letting him know I'd placed the tracker. It could still come in handy."

"Then let's search the park."

Again, he brushed off her suggestion. "I know what

you're thinking, but the park is too large an area for two people to cover. If the authorities think there's any value to the information I sent, then they'll do a search with—uh, dogs."

Her mouth grew dry, but she managed to get the words out. "I won't fall apart. Go ahead and say it: cadaver dogs."

His gaze softened and grew regretful. "Right. Besides, it's a long shot. Buckley may have a very good explanation for his early morning drive."

"As ready as I was to rush to the park a minute ago, I still think Meryl's disappearance is related to something at the hospital and Dr. Ivers. But we need to eliminate all the other possibilities, don't we?"

"Yeah." He eyeballed her, his gaze penetrating and focused. "Now is this where you're going to tell me why you're off early today?"

"I got fired." She tossed the words out into the universe. What happened to her intention to lead up to the news bit by bit?

"What?" Nick's gaze widened. His jaw dropped, then he shut his mouth. Good thing he did, because she wasn't in the best of moods.

"Apparently, I asked a few too many questions at the hospital, and it got back to my boss and Administration. Go ahead. Say it—I know you're dying to."

He moved away from the counter and stood facing her. Slipping his arms around her, he murmured, "Allie, I'm sorry—"

"Yeah, you warned me." She stiffened her spine. "I don't have anyone to blame but my own big mouth."

He pulled her close. The warmth of his body was comforting and his lack of condemnation reassuring. But this display of unexpected tenderness caused all the emotions she'd denied for the last forty-five minutes to overflow like a flood-breached dam. Clinging to him, she burst into tears, turning his T-shirt into a soggy mess.

Nick let her cry until she quieted in his arms. Truth be told, holding her felt good. More than good. More like she belonged. And more than anything, he wanted to sweep her into his arms and take her to bed.

But taking advantage when she was this vulnerable... Well, he wasn't that kind of man. She deserved so much more than a divorced dad who had all he could do to pay child support and keep a roof over his head.

She sniffed and gazed up with puffy red eyes. "I'm sorry. My mascara—I ruined your shirt."

He glanced down. In addition to her tears, she'd left one small dark smear. "Don't worry about it. I reckon it'll come out in the wash."

"I can't believe you're being so sweet about it. I figured you'd bless me out for getting fired."

"Now what good would that do? Your job's history. I don't suppose there's any chance you could apologize and get it back?"

She wrinkled her nose. "I pretty much burned my bridges there."

"So, you gave 'em a piece of your mind, did ya?"

"'Fraid so." She shrugged. "And...they've already hired someone in my spot."

He nodded. "Let me guess. I know this game. The way it usually works is the one who reported you is your replacement."

"Yeah." A smile started to relax her pretty face. "I see you've played before."

"Affirmative." Had he ever. "How about a run? Seems like I remember a certain someone challenged me." Now that her mood had lightened, it was time to put some—not much, but some—physical distance between them. A diversion.

"I'm not exactly dressed for running." She pulled away from him and spun around. "In case you hadn't noticed."

Allie was wearing slacks, a pink knit top, and an official-looking lab coat. "Right. You're looking very hospital-ish."

"That's what happens when one is fired at nine-thirty," she said with some of her sassy attitude returning. "Don't worry. Since it was my intention to help you get settled after I got off work, I have a change of clothes in my car."

"Would you rather go to lunch?"

Her head tilted to one side while she appeared to ponder his question. "Actually, the run you suggested sounds great. Maybe I can eliminate some of this stress."

"A run always helps me."

She squared her shoulders. "Then come on. I'll run you into the ground."

"Yeah?" he scoffed. "You and whose army?"

Chapter Twenty

After changing, Allison and Nick first ran down the hill. They didn't have much choice in the matter since they were already at the highest point on the property. She managed to keep a nice steady pace with him. Once her muscles loosened, warmed by the heat of the day, she even managed to pull ahead. Granted, he was a mere half stride behind her.

Laughing over her shoulder, she told him, "Told you I'd run you into the ground."

"Not through yet," he said, "and we still have the hill."

Yeah, that hill was going to be the make-it-or-break-it of their run. Would her steady pace keep her chugging along, or would he beat her by charging up the hill like a commando taking a sniper's nest?

They circled through the property several times. Traffic was beginning to pick up as people returned home from work, making the run more hazardous.

"Had enough?" he asked, not even breaking a sweat.

"Why? Getting tired?" *Say yes.*

"Nah. Just don't want you so whipped I'll have to carry you up the hill."

The nerve. Just because she was female and on the petite side, he had no reason—other than typical male arrogance—to think she couldn't make it up the incline. "Don't worry about me. I'll be fine."

If she admitted the truth, that her thighs were starting to feel like sodden bags of cement, he'd laugh and take advantage.

As it was, he increased his pace and now was two strides ahead of her before she'd realized what he was up to.

Still, she had a nice view. His powerful body glistened as his thigh muscles pumped smoothly. They reached the back of the complex and started up the steep hill. No time to give up now. She shortened her stride and let sheer determination power her upward.

He glanced over his shoulder. "You okay? Need some help?"

"I'm. Fine," she said, even though she gasped with each word.

Of course, he reached the door to his apartment before she did. Smiling with his easy triumph, he leaned against the door with his hands on his hips. "Now I'll say it: I told you so."

Laughing, she stumbled and fell into his arms. "Yeah, you did."

Suddenly, she couldn't breathe. He was so close. So warm. And so undeniably sexy. Without thinking, she slid her arms around his neck. A little hop and her legs wrapped around his waist. With a chuckle, he held onto her while he used a free hand to fish the key from his shorts pocket. He turned, unlocked the door, and carried her inside.

After shutting the door, he set her feet on the floor and pressed her against the wall. "You're sure about this?" he asked, his voice so low and husky with emotion it staggered her.

She gave a quick nod. "Very."

He sucked in a deep breath and dipped his lips to hers. His kiss was salty. His tongue battled with hers. Tender at first, then hard as if he wanted to devour her. Come to think of it, she wanted the same. And she'd wanted it for a while.

He slid his hands under her T-shirt and sports bra. She mewled, her breath hitching as he caressed her breasts and tweaked her nipples.

"Your brother's gonna have my head on a platter."

"Forget about him and kiss me again." Cradling his face in her hands, she said, "No regrets. It's no one's business but ours."

Over her head went both garments, landing somewhere on the floor. She ripped Nick's shirt over his head and then splayed her hands down the tan, muscular planes of his chest. Sliding her shorts down over her butt, he pressed a palm to her damp heat. Desire shot to her core, eliciting a gasp. Her lace bikini panties were soon history. Off and tossed over his shoulder.

God. She wanted him. She skimmed her hands under the elastic of his running shorts and pulled them down. His erection sprang free and jutted hard against her belly. She took him in her hand, marveling at the texture of steel covered in silk.

"Protection," he gasped and dug a condom from his pocket, then ripped it open with his teeth.

"Hmph," she said with a bark of laughter. "Prepared. I *really* like that about you."

"That all you like?" he murmured into her ear.

His erection was hot and hard as she sheathed him. "Well, I like—"

"Ya know ya talk too much."

With her hand to guide him, he adjusted his stance and thrust home. She gave a hitch and wrapped her legs around his waist, her thighs trembling as she took his full length.

She wanted it hot and fast. And that was what he gave her. They rode hard and exploded over the crest together. Laughing and gasping for air, she said, "Whew, I needed that."

"You blew me away, babe. Slower next time," he said. "Promise."

*

How or when they ended up on Nick's brand-new, bare mattress wasn't quite clear, but Allison didn't mind. Waking from a quick nap cuddled in Nick's strong embrace left her a little discombobulated. Making love—hot, crazy, frantic love—up against a wall had never been her style. Until now.

As she smiled at the memory of their lovemaking, she felt him wake. He stirred, pulling her closer. "This is nice."

"Just *nice*?"

"Okay," he said. "Fantastic."

"That's better." Still snuggled in his arms, she rolled to face him. "Fantastic is a great place to start." Then, realizing he might not be on her particular wavelength, she hurried to add, "Of course, I don't mean this is the beginning of..."

No. That sounded worse. "Uh, I just mean *no* expectations."

"No expectations? No regrets?" His blue gaze grew clouded with confusion. "Was this just a hookup for you?"

"No, that's not what I meant either. Oh, crap."

"Then say what you mean."

"Well, obviously, I'm having some difficulty at that." She sighed. "To be clear—clearer—I don't do casual. Never have. But you might be in a different place. You're newly divorced. It's only natural..."

One brow raised, he waited. "Go on."

"You're not being very helpful."

Levering onto one elbow, he bit back a grin. "It's more fun watching you stutter around."

"I'm *so* happy to be the cause of your amusement," she said with some sass.

"For the record"—he brushed away a damp curl from her forehead—"I don't do casual either. And I never assumed you did."

Allison swallowed.

"I enjoy your company—at least I do when you're not going off on some wild tangent or other."

"And *you* are a master of the left-handed compliment."

"Feel free to respond in kind."

"Well then, I enjoy *your* company—as long as you're not being an arrogant know-it-all PI."

"Speaking of being a PI, your brother's my boss."

"Whatever we have going on is none of his business. I don't tell him how to manage his relationship with Tess, and he doesn't have to know about us unless it becomes necessary."

"You're okay with not telling your family?"

"Hey. I'm the almost-a-virgin little sister. No one will ever suspect we've done the wild thing." Not close to being true, since one and all said her face was an open book. She'd have to guard her emotions when they were around her family.

Nick whooped with laughter. "Almost-a-virgin? That's good."

"You *know* what I mean."

"I know this, if there was any doubt, you're definitely not a virgin now."

"Then you don't want to hear about my wild college days? The stories I could tell." Okay, so she was exaggerating. Most of the time, she'd kept her nose buried in her textbooks, unwilling to let Scott and Caroline down when they were working so hard to pay for her education.

"Not unless you want to hear about mine."

"I'll pass unless it was significant—disease-wise."

"Always the nurse." His tone was tender, teasing.

"Yeah." She gave a heavy sigh. "The *nurse* without a job. What am I going to do?"

"You don't have to decide this minute, do ya?"

"No."

He shot her a cheeky grin. "Now you have more time for the rat-dog of Meryl's you adopted."

"Omigod. It's getting late. I've got to get home and feed her." She swung her feet over the side of the bed and onto the floor. Now, where were her clothes? She stood, then asked over her shoulder, "Wanna come with?"

He leaned back, hands laced behind his head with a wide, satisfied smile that spread across his face. "And miss the best show in town?"

"You." She grabbed a pillow, tossed it at him, and then ran from the bedroom. Her clothes had to be around here. Somewhere.

Still, a little stunned by their unexpected bout of lovemaking, Nick stepped into his jeans. Before he could do more than zip, he heard first a short swear word, then rustling noises. "What's going on? Are you all right?" He padded into the living room. She was already dressed and in the throes of decorating his apartment. In the interval since she'd left his bed, she'd opened several boxes and plastic bags.

"This decorating stuff can wait," he suggested. "And you have a dog to feed."

"True." She faced him, her hands on her hips. "My purpose here today was—"

"—to get laid." He ducked behind the doorjamb, still teasing.

Her cheeks flushing a pretty pink, his partner in crime let out an exasperated huff. "To get you settled."

"Don't know about you," he drawled, "but I'm feeling pretty settled. We broke in the mattress."

She cast him a sheepish grin. "I guess we did at that."

Before he could close the distance between them, his cell phone rang. He disconnected it from the charger. It was an unfamiliar number, but local. "I'd better take it."

"Vitelli," he answered.

"This is O'Malley. I'm calling from my private cell. Have you seen Allison?" Her tone was tense, guarded.

"She's right here." He handed the phone to Allie. "It's Tess."

He noted a slight tremor in Allie's hand as she took the phone.

"Tess? Sorry. I had it turned off." Allie's face paled as she listened. "Are you sure?" She hit the Disconnect button, then handed back his phone. "They've found them," she said, her throat sounding clogged with emotion. "Meryl...and her baby."

Chapter Twenty-one

Allison clenched her jaw, determined not to break down yet again. "She wouldn't tell me anything more than they'd been found."

"Are they sure? Has she been formally identified?"

"Tess said she was still wearing her lab coat with her name badge. She must've been killed right after getting home." She forced out the words, each one a bitter pill. Too bitter to swallow.

Nick pulled her into his arms and placed a gentle kiss on her forehead. "What do you want to do now?"

"There's nothing I can do but wait until Tess can give me more information." Her eyes stinging with unshed tears, she said, "I want to go home. We can finish this"—she made a sweeping gesture—"later."

"Sure. I'll drive you."

"No." She shook her head. "I'm fine. Really."

"You are. But I'll take you home all the same."

Allowing herself a single sniff, she cuddled in his arms. His gentle expression of tenderness made her feel safe. And so comforted she couldn't imagine experiencing the sensation with anyone else. "Thank you—but what about my car?"

"I'll bring you back to pick it up whenever you want...once things settle down."

"You're a good man, Nick Vitelli. A really good man."

*

On Richmond Avenue, Nick and Allison opened the front door. A pale-faced Caroline greeted them with, "You've seen the news?"

"Nope," he responded, assuming she meant the bodies being found.

"Tess called," Allison said, her expression grim and her slender shoulders squared. She glanced around, walked into the kitchen, and called the dog.

The Yorkie yipped and darted out from the laundry room. The pooch danced on her hind legs, and he watched with amusement as she scooped up the little dog. After a few sloppy dog kisses, Allison seemed to relax. Apparently, she wasn't ready to face the TV news—or drop her job-loss bombshell. He watched her snatch the leash from one of the hooks the members of the family used for their keys. "We're going for a walk."

"But don't you want to—" With a puzzled expression, Caroline walked over to the counter where she'd been chopping vegetables and resumed the task.

She waved her sister away. "Later."

Nick caught Caroline's gaze and shrugged. "Want me to come with?"

"Not this time." Her chin notched upward as if daring him to argue. "Roxy and I need some time alone. She needs to know."

"Needs to know what?"

"About Meryl."

He stuffed his hands in his pockets. "You honestly think that dog is gonna understand?"

"Yes." With a single word, she left him standing and shaking his head in disbelief.

He watched as she left the house, and then turned to Caroline. "Is she nuts?"

"No, she's just being Allison... Maybe a little more than

usual. Are things all right with the two of you?"

"Yeah." He shrugged. "Why?"

Caroline's gaze pinned him like a bug on display. "Something's different. I noticed it when the two of you were coming up the walk."

What? He'd been careful to keep his hands to himself, difficult as it was. "She's just tired. We ran a couple of miles this afternoon. Thought I'd have to carry her up the last hill." He chuckled, showing he was exaggerating. "Then we—uh, worked on the apartment."

"Uh-huh." If the skeptical expression on Caroline's face was any indication, she wasn't buying his worked-on-the-apartment spiel. But it was the best he could do on short notice. When and where Allison told her family about the change in their relationship was up to her. Fine with him too.

"Crap. I lost count," Caroline said, ending with a growl.

"Count?"

She laughed, then rearranged the chopped peppers, onions, and mushrooms she'd been chopping. "Oh, you haven't heard about my obsession with counting. It's one of the lesser-known side effects of the carbon monoxide poisoning I had a couple of months ago."

He nodded. "Right. Scott mentioned something about the poisoning."

"The aftereffects drive me crazy, but I'm learning to live with them."

"Can I help?"

She glanced over her heavily notated calendar. "You could set the table." She pointed first to an upper cabinet. "Plates," then to a second, "glassware. Justin will be home soon. It's his night to cook. Basically, it means he'll grill the chicken breasts and veggies I have marinating in the fridge. The veggies are for kebabs."

"Sounds great."

"You'll stay?"

"Uh—" He started to object, but Caroline gave a dismissive wave. "Of course you will."

By the time Nick had set the table, Allison reappeared, carrying the dog, who appeared none the worse for hearing bad news. But he couldn't say the same for the object of his affection. Clearly, she'd been crying. Again.

Restraining the urge to rush to her side and comfort her, he contented himself with a simple, "You okay?"

"Yeah." She set the dog down, walked over to the sink, and washed her hands. "What can I do?" she asked her sister.

"Put the veggies on the skewers." Caroline motioned with her butcher knife. "That way I won't have to keep counting these dratted peppers."

Nodding, Allison gave a little chuckle. "Will do."

Nick envied the sisters' easy camaraderie as they moved busily around the kitchen, never bumping into each other. Obviously, they'd prepared many a family dinner together. His memories of family dinners before his mom ditched his abusive father were anything but easy. He couldn't help but wonder what kind of life he might have with Allison. Best get his mind off the future. Caroline was already suspicious. As for his desire to sneak up behind a certain nurse and nibble on her slender neck... Not gonna happen anytime soon.

In quick order, the house filled with Holt-Lackeys. Tamsyn and Justin came in together. Tamsyn gave Allison a hug. "I'm so sorry. It's just awful." Five minutes later, Scott followed. "Tess called and said she'd be here later...maybe," he said on his way to the man cave. Allison heard him turn on the TV, but she still wasn't ready to listen, much less watch, the breaking news. Hearing it wouldn't make it any more real.

Meryl and her baby were dead.

With more people—meaning more distraction—and less attention focused on her, Allison began to relax. For the moment, Nick was with Scott, watching the local news. Justin was presiding over his mack-daddy grill, and already the aroma of grilled chicken set her stomach to growling. As for Tamsyn and Caroline, they were whispering and sneaking not-so-surreptitious glances in Allison's direction.

"Anyone ever told y'all it's not nice to whisper?"

Tamsyn leaned back on the counter and directed a knowing smile at Allison. "What's with the beard burn? When did you and the blue-eyed hunk get *that* close?"

Automatically, Allison's hands went to her cheeks. Leave it to eagle-eyed Tamsyn to spot the rash left by Nick's scruff.

"It's sunburn. I forgot the sunblock when we went for our run this afternoon."

"And then, *they worked on Nick's apartment*," Caroline said, using those tacky finger quotes. "Like we can't see what *that* was about."

"Dammit, y'all." Her cheeks heated until they felt like they were hot as blazes. She aimed a skewer of veggies at her sisters. "Grow up, will ya?"

The last thing she needed was for her brothers to ferret out the truth too. She'd never hear the end of it from Justin, who was the biggest tease on the planet. As for the always protective Scott, he might not appreciate hearing his newest employee and his younger sister had done the deed.

Fortunately, everyone's attention was further diverted as soon as Scott's fiancée Tess blew in. "Where's Allie?" she asked.

Allison's stomach knotted. She headed toward the back stairway. *Gotta get the hell out of here.* Gory details, she didn't want or need.

"Hey!" Tess called, stopping Allison in her tracks. She turned.

The redheaded detective stood in the doorway to the kitchen. "I thought you'd be more interested."

She sighed, easing onto a stool at the counter. Blinking back the threat of tears, she shrugged. "They're dead. That's all I need to know."

"Can't tell you much, anyway. It's an ongoing case," Tess admitted. "A farmer found Meryl's body in his field about fifteen yards from an access road."

Forty-five feet from the road? "Doesn't sound like they went to very much trouble to hide her." Was Meryl's killer just lazy or perhaps impaired in some fashion?

"No, they didn't." Tess shook her head, her tone subdued. "I'm sorry. But we knew this day would come. I didn't expect a result so soon. Usually takes longer."

"The baby? Could you tell…?" She faltered, unable to continue. But she watched Tess for her reaction.

The redhead schooled her expression into a neutral mask as if choosing her words. "As far as we could tell, at the scene, the baby was still contained within the womb. This wasn't one of those kill-the-mother-and-take-the-baby scenarios."

"No, Meryl was only five months' gestation. For what it's worth, she didn't look like she was that far along."

"And now we have this other tall, blond nurse who's gone missing. What else can you tell me about Harmony Bane?" Tess straddled the stool beside Allison. "I've interviewed her supervisor and two of her friends, but they're completely unhelpful. Sometimes people are more inclined to talk to a fellow employee. Could you talk to some of her coworkers?

Casually. Not like an interrogation."

Great. No time like the present. Might as well get it over with.

Allison took a deep breath, then spit out the news. "No can do. I got fired today."

Tess's gaze widened. "Ooh. That's bad—for the investigation and you too."

"It wasn't among my favorite moments."

"Guess not."

"You got *fired*?" Tamsyn's voice went up an octave. She rushed to Allison's side. "Are they freaking nuts? You practically ran that department."

"Apparently, I talked to one too many people about Meryl and the good Dr. Ivers. Then I might've threatened to go to the media—I still might."

"That's exactly what you should do," Tamsyn said, then turned and stuck her head into the den. "Those idiots at the hospital fired Allie today. Can you believe it?"

Caroline worried her bottom lip between her teeth, then stepped to the French doors to announce the news to Justin, who was turning the chicken breasts over on the grill.

Just great. Broadcast it to all the neighbors too.

Within seconds, every member of the family gathered around the kitchen island. If only a hole would open in the kitchen floor, she would've gladly taken the plunge just to get away from their solicitous encouragement.

She'd failed. Failed her family and herself. Most of all she'd failed Meryl.

She waved them away. "I need some air, folks. Give the poor pitiful slob some air."

"Let's walk." Nick's hand grasped hers as he pulled her away from the crowded kitchen.

Somehow, the warmth and strength of his touch centered her. She gave a quick nod. "Yeah, let's go."

*

Outside, the sun was still high on West Nashville's horizon. Allison matched Nick's longer stride as they strolled along the sidewalk. The dense shade of mature trees on both sides of Richland Avenue was a welcome relief from the stuffy kitchen.

Now she could breathe.

"It's done. Your family knows and still loves you. You haven't failed anyone, Allie."

She raised an eyebrow and shot him a skeptical glance. "Reading minds another one of your many talents?"

"Maybe just reading yours." He squeezed her hand. "Another of my talents—if it is a talent—focus. There's still a lot we can do, even if you're not at the hospital. Don't let this setback define you."

She gave him a major eye roll. "Now you're sounding like a shrink." She popped him on the shoulder with her fist. "Who *are* you, and where's my favorite PI?"

"He's still here."

She came to a dead stop. "You did *not* just refer to yourself in the third person. You think you're royalty?" She pulled her hand from his and took off ahead.

"Wait up, brat."

She turned and gave him what she hoped was a shamefaced grin. "I *am* a brat, aren't I?"

"You have to ask?"

He held out his hand, and she took it gratefully. It never failed. His easy manner and calm strength seemed to stem her emotional outbursts.

Hand in hand, they ambled along for several minutes. Conversation didn't seem necessary. Most of the time she nattered enough for two people...maybe even three. Tonight, his touch was enough.

"Ready to go back?" he asked, slowing the pace.

She nodded. "Might as well. Can't dance."

"Who says? I cut a mean rug, don'tcha know," he said, affecting a Cajun drawl and pulling her into his arms.

"You stole that line from *The Big Easy*. It's one of my favorite movies."

"Mine too." He winked. "What was your favorite part?"

Remembering the exact oh-so-sexy scene, she grinned. "I'll never tell."

He twirled her around until they were headed back to the house. Still a little giddy, she stumbled on a crack in the sidewalk and fell into his strong arms again. Her breathing gave a hitch as she gazed into his warm eyes. "Don't say it," she warned. "Sometimes, *if* the occasion truly calls for it, I *can* walk and chew gum at the same time."

"Was beginning to wonder 'bout it myself."

Tucking her head so he couldn't see, she smiled. His dry sense of humor was another thing she loved about him. Whoa. Was she ready to settle down? True, she'd dated some in college, but her social life since graduation hadn't exactly been on fire. Even if she was ready, he was newly divorced. Being his transition woman wasn't anywhere on her bucket list.

Maybe it was time to put the brakes on.

A little late for that. Not after an afternoon of steamy lovemaking.

Nick felt her tense for a second, then pull away, yet her withdrawal seemed more a mental one than physical. What was going on in that head of hers? They walked along in an uncomfortable silence until they reached the brightly lit Holt-Lackey house. As bright as the house was, he was still mired in the darkness of her mood change. And, as usual, he had no clue why.

"You okay?" he asked as they stepped onto the wide porch.

"Fine."

Great. She was giving him the "fine" answer, which, if he'd learned anything at all about women in his seven years of marriage, meant she was anything but.

"You sure?" Come on. What had he done?

Hesitating a moment, she nodded and gave him a tight smile. "Yeah."

Unsure if he should follow her inside, he opened the door. "I don't have to come in if you rather I didn't."

"You don't have to if you don't *want* to." She said that with a little huff.

Great. Now she was pissed off.

"That's not it," he said in an attempt to smooth her ruffled feathers.

Sighing, she gave him an eye roll. "Oh, come on. I have to watch the news sometime. Besides, I'd rather have you with me than not."

Not quite a ringing endorsement, but he'd take it. "Good. I'd rather be with you too."

She shot him a quick smile, grasped his hand, and tugged him inside the house.

The rest of her family, minus Justin, who was still manning the grill, was in the den gathered around a huge sixty-inch flat-screen TV. What he wouldn't give for one. He gestured for Allison to take the last available seat. Instead of taking it, she smiled. "You're my guest. You take it."

He shrugged, then sank into the cushy soft leather sofa. She perched on the sofa's arm beside him, and he covered her hand with his, giving a little squeeze. Music cued that there was a local news update. "You ready?"

"Not really." Her eyes were shiny with unshed tears. If

there was any way he could make this easier for her... Hell, he'd do anything to banish the pain and sadness from her gentle gaze. And the questions would haunt her for a long time: how much did it hurt; how scared was she? And how long had Meryl suffered, knowing she and her baby were doomed?

Truth was her friend probably hadn't suffered long or known much of anything. But then, would come the guilt. Yeah, guilt. He knew all about it. He'd lost a partner once. Still blamed himself too, on those long nights when sleep wouldn't come.

She'd wonder if there was anything she could've done. Maybe if she'd gone over there sooner. Maybe. Maybe. Who the hell knew the unfathomable answers to unthinkable questions? He sure didn't.

Beneath Nick's strong hand, Allie's clenched hers into a tight fist. She sucked in a breath and squared her shoulders, ready to hear the worst. A gasp escaped without her volition, and she straightened her back into a rigid line when the TV showed a body bag being placed on a stretcher. Poor Meryl. Who else could it be? Not the other nurse, surely.

The news journalist from one of the local affiliates was pretty, blond, and solemn-faced as she gave the basic facts— nothing more.

"The authorities tell us a woman's body has been discovered in a field off Hurt Road, north of Hendersonville." A map of the area flashed on the screen. The news journalist continued. "As you can see, the site is at least twenty-three miles from where Ms. Litton disappeared. The medical examiner says it's too soon to tell if the body is that of the missing Parklane Medical Center nurse case manager, Meryl Litton. Ms. Litton was five months pregnant at the time of her disappearance last week." Video footage from inside Meryl's condo flashed on the screen.

God. So much blood. No wonder Tess and the other authorities had expressed so little hope of finding her friend alive. No wonder. Nick had kept her from going into the condo, so it was Allison's first view of the absolute carnage the killer had left behind.

Her breathing grew ragged, and her shoulders began to shake. "Enough. I've seen enough." She stood...or tried to. She felt Nick stand and slip his arm around her waist. Physically—and emotionally—he steadied her. More and more, she needed his presence and support. Like her brothers, he was fast becoming a man she could depend upon. Maybe even *the* man.

She allowed him to lead her from the den and into the kitchen. He pulled out a stool, and she climbed onto it. He wrapped his arms around her shoulders, comforting her. Leaning back against his chest, she felt his heartbeat speed up. So, she definitely had an effect on him. Good.

"Hungry?" she asked. Her nose twitched as the aroma of grilled chicken wafted through the French doors.

"I could eat."

A hand, smaller and lighter than Nick's, touched her shoulder. She turned. Tess. "You okay, hon?" Tess asked.

"Yeah."

"Any questions?" Tess's expression was sympathetic and kind, but there was a weariness in her gaze as if she'd been through this situation too many times.

"So many questions, but I can't bear to ask them." She shook her head. "Besides, I know you can't discuss an ongoing case. I understand that."

"I will...for you. If there's anything you want to know."

Recalling the bloody crime scene, she swallowed the

lump in her throat, then murmured, "She never had a chance."

"No."

Nick backed up a step. "I can go if you two want to talk."

Grateful for his consideration, she smiled and clung to his hand. "Stay."

"Let's go outside and sit on the deck," Tess suggested.

Out on the deck, Justin was already taking the chicken breasts and kebabs off the grill, piling them onto a large platter. "I'll get out of your way."

"We won't be long. Don't wait dinner," Allison said, wondering if she'd ever again feel like eating.

The lanky Justin nodded and carried the platter into the kitchen.

She sat on the top step, with Nick on one side and Tess on the other, and stared out into the dark Nashville night.

She rested her head against Nick's shoulder and gazed at her brother's fiancée. "How do you do this job, Tess? How can you look into the unspeakable faces of death and not let it drive you crazy?"

Tess seemed to give the question some consideration before answering. "Think about it like this. It's sort of like being a nurse. All-day long, you take care of patients, some of whom might die soon. You do the best you can to make them comfortable. My job is to speak for the victim. The way I see it, a murder victim whose killer isn't caught can't rest. And if the victim can't rest, neither can I."

"But the nightmares—how do you sleep at night?"

"Sometimes I don't." Tess reached over and patted Allison's hand.

She turned to Nick. "What about you? You were a cop."

"Tess is right. Crime, whether it's murder or drugs, is just shit to be cleaned up."

His plainspoken statement brought a sharp bark of

laughter from Tess. "Yeah, that too."

"I get it." Allison gave a world-weary sigh. "The world is one big bedpan full of crap, and someone has to deal."

Just when Meryl's future had seemed rosy and bright, she'd fallen victim to the ugliness of that world, along with her unborn baby. A baby who would never take his first steps. Go to school. Or marry and raise a family of his own. Who knows what he might've accomplished or the lives he might've affected?

More unanswerable questions.

She got to her feet. "I'm whipped. I think I'll turn in."

Nick stood and wrapped his arms around her waist, pulling her close. "Wish you'd eat something."

The very thought of eating made her stomach lurch. She shook her head. "I'm not hungry, but you go ahead. There's plenty." Overwhelmed by the grisly reality of Meryl's last moments, Allison hoped he would let her go without protest.

His dark brows drew together in a frown. "But—"

"Honestly," she said, easing from his embrace while still clinging to his hand, "I just need some time alone...to process." She released her hold, then headed inside before either of her companions could react.

For now, she needed to get away from everyone. Even Nick. Although she couldn't imagine what she would've done without him thus far.

Chapter Twenty-two

That evening, Nick shot a pleading glance at Tess. "She oughta eat. All she's had is an ice-cream cone, and that was hours ago."

Tess gave him a sympathetic smile. "Let her go. She's not gonna starve."

As reluctant as he was to let Allie go, he was eager to hear what Tess might reveal about the investigation. He raised a brow and leaned back on the deck railing. "So, what *can* you tell me?"

She shot him a wry expression. "It's early days, and if you hadn't been on the job, I wouldn't tell you anything. But here's what I know. It was your basic body dump. Ms. Litton was wrapped in a rug from her condo. There was no attempt to bury her body. Considering she was killed on Friday and not found until today, there was a lot of decomp and some animal predation. But she was still wearing her lab coat with her name badge. He had to have killed her right after she got home from work Friday afternoon."

"Allie won't have to ID the body, will she?"

"No, thank God. We'll bring in her ex for that chore and then have another go at questioning him."

"Whew," Nick said with a sigh of relief. "Who found her?"

"The farmer who owned the land where she was found. Says he was walking his fields, looking for a missing calf. Saw the buzzards circling." She lifted her shoulders in a shrug. "Figured it was the calf, but it turned out to be Ms. Litton."

"What about access to the area?"

"There's a private road off Hurt Road. Body was about fifteen yards from the road. CSU is still working the scene. Didn't appear to have any drag marks."

"Someone local, then?" he asked. According to the TV news broadcast, the site was a good twenty-five miles from Meryl's condo.

"Makes sense it could be someone familiar with the area. I interviewed the landowner and his wife. They were visiting their daughter and son-in-law in Bowling Green from Friday morning until Sunday after church. We've checked their alibis and cleared them. They also have a hired hand who rents the small house on the farm and helps with the farm work. So, we're looking for him, but he seems to be in the wind."

"Is there any connection between him and Meryl Litton?"

"Too early to tell," Tess admitted. "Frankly, I'm more interested in her ex-husband. That bird dog you placed on his truck tells us he was in the vicinity."

"He would've needed an accomplice. You said no drag marks, so someone helped him carry her body. So, he called one of his buddies. They met up at the Moss Wright Park?"

Tess shook her head. "Don't think so. Remember the video from the Farmer's Market? He already had help."

"But the park is only five or six miles from the dumpsite, and her ex was at that park."

"I agree. It's a troubling coincidence. And I don't like coincidences."

"Me neither."

Further discussion was cut off by Justin's reappearance. "Eat now or forever hold your peace," he said.

"Hold your horses, Jay-man," Tess said.

"Jay-man?"

"Yeah, that's my special name for him. Justin just sounds

too formal."

"Can't disagree." The agency's tall computer geek was anything but formal. Almost shoulder-length blond hair and a holey Grateful Dead T-shirt made him look like a reject leftover from the seventies or a rock-star wannabe. Couldn't fault the younger man's mad skills, though. According to Scott, the FBI had even tried to recruit him once, after he'd hacked into several federal databases in the course of an investigation.

Nick followed the detective inside the house. No sign of Allie. Guess she had already turned in. "I'd like to take her something to eat. No matter what she said."

"I'm a step ahead of you." Caroline handed him a small plate of grilled chicken and vegetables. "Maybe you'll have more influence over her than I did," she said, giving him a wink.

"Hope so." He took the plate of food. What he hoped was that Allie wouldn't toss it at his head for ignoring her wish *to be alone*. That sentiment might've worked for a film star in the thirties, but Allison Lackey was no Greta Garbo.

Allison lay on the bed and cuddled with Roxy. How could she tell the little terrier her mistress was no more? The little pooch seemed content enough, but she had to wonder if the dog missed Meryl as much as Allison did.

The dog-whispering guy on TV always said, *"Dogs live in the now."* She certainly hoped it was true for Roxy. Too bad people couldn't.

Before she could ponder further, there was a light tap on her bedroom door. "Allie?"

Damn. It was Nick. Persistent, wasn't he?

"I'm all right." Roxy wasn't any happier either. The little dog yipped and spun around on the bed.

"Carrie sent you a small plate. You know you have to eat something."

She gave a theatrical groan and swung her legs over the side of the bed. "Oh, all right."

She opened the door. Nick stood there in all his male yumminess. She tried to wipe away the images of the hot bod underneath his jeans and T. "I told you I wasn't hungry." Actually, the aroma of grilled chicken teased her nose, and her traitorous stomach chose that moment to growl.

The corner of his mouth kicked up in a half grin. "Your stomach says different." He stepped inside the room, and it seemed to grow smaller. And an awareness of how girlie and young her pink room and canopy bed were hit her. Time to redecorate?

No—time to get real. Her friend was dead, and the mere sight of Nick Vitelli in her bedroom was a distraction from grief. That she'd allowed it—the distraction—for even a second. Unforgivable.

"I know you mean well..."

He set the plate of food on the faux French Provincial desk she'd had since childhood and pulled her into his strong arms, weakening her knees. Her mouth dried. "You're not helping anyone by starving yourself—least of all Meryl."

She met his tender gaze and saw acceptance, more than acceptance. "I know. It's just..." Without warning, a single tear ran down her cheek. She took in a ragged breath, and all the strength leached from her bones.

"It's okay," he said. "No one expects you to be brave. Go ahead. Cry. I'm not going anywhere."

Sobbing, she sat on the foot of the bed, where the dog wriggled her small furry head under Allison's hand. Nick sat beside her and slipped his arm around her waist. Comfort, both canine and human—of the warm male variety—eased her sobs. She leaned her head against his shoulder. Amazing just how much she'd come to depend on his strength and presence in a few short days.

His breath was warm on her neck. Shivering, she reached to caress his cheek. "Nick..." She stopped, not quite knowing what to say. Just because they'd shared an afternoon of steamy sex didn't mean he was ready for another round. And how could she even think about sex at a time like this?

Before he could react, she heard raised voices from downstairs. What now?

A little reluctantly, it seemed, Nick stood. "Stay. I'll see what's going on."

She nodded. Funny, but it seemed natural to let him take over—for a while, anyway. Not that she was anyone's pushover, not by a long shot.

Waiting until she heard his footsteps on the stairs, she gathered the Yorkie in her arms. Creeping to the door, she opened it and listened.

Nick sped downstairs and found the Schulman guy arguing with Allie's brothers in the foyer. What was the dude doing here anyhow?

"I just wanted to see if Allison's all right, considering they just found her friend's body," the short dude said.

"She's fine," Scott insisted. "Her family's all she needs right now."

Schulman glared when Nick entered. "So, what's *he* doing here?"

"Allie and I are *together*." Nick set his hands on his hips. For the moment, he ignored her brothers' raised eyebrows.

Schulman's face darkened. His upper lip lifted in a sneer. "Oh, really?" He glanced around as if uncertain whether to stand his ground or haul ass. "Just wanted to offer my support."

"Much appreciated," Scott said, "but we have Allison's back. You understand she needs some time to grieve. We've got it covered."

"Yeah," Schulman muttered. "Guess so."

Justin opened the front door, and with nothing else to say, Schulman took the hint and left.

As soon as Justin closed the door, he turned and said, "You're *together*. Really?"

A brief scowl flickered across Scott's face, then he assumed a more neutral expression.

Just for a second, Nick considered hauling ass himself. "Well, what I meant to say was…" Crap, he hadn't quite meant to blurt it out that way.

Scott tilted his head to one side. "Just what *did* you mean to say?"

"Allie and I have spent a lot of time together this week. We've grown closer. She's great, a little crazy sometimes, but she's a great—uh, person."

Justin flicked a floppy strand of his long hair behind his ear. "Yeah, that's Allie, all right. Yeah, she's a *great* person."

Nick's mouth was Mojave dry. Hell's bells. He'd broken at least two, or maybe three, guy rules: Never sleep with your friend's little sister. Never sleep with your boss's little sister. And if you do, don't blab it. "I care about her…a lot."

"So do we," the brothers said in unison. They took a step toward him, again in unison. What were they, freaking twins?

"Now hold on," he said, taking a judicious step backward. "I respect your sister a lot. We've spent a lot of time together. We've grown close."

Scott's gaze darkened. "Believe you already mentioned that."

Damn, he was already repeating himself. Just how deep a hole could he dig with his big mouth? "I really care about her, guys."

The brothers took another step forward, but Justin's stern expression broke into a wide grin. "Dude, Allie's all grown-up. She makes her own decisions."

"Just don't hurt her," Scott added, "or then I'd have to fire you right before I *kill ya*."

"Rightly so." Nick nodded. But dang, just because the situation with Allie was good now, there was no guarantee where their new relationship would go. He'd been through too much crap with Eva to believe in happy ever after. No guarantees in life, at all.

Never should've let his guard down. Never gotten sucked in by her big puppy-dog brown eyes. Never tasted her sweet lips.

Smiling, Allison stepped back from the door and eased it shut. She set the little pooch on the foot of the canopied bed. "Did you hear that, Roxy? Nick *cares* for me. Thinks I'm a *great person*. What a hoot. Couldn't he see Scott and Justin were just yanking his chain?"

Still, she couldn't help but smile. Who knew what might happen in the future? For now, she'd just take advantage of the way he steadied her and take her time getting to know him. Of course, they'd already taken a big step in the really-getting-to-know-each-other direction. As for rushing out for the latest issue of *Brides*, it was definitely too soon.

Definitely.

On the other hand, watching Tess go through the hassle of trying to plan a wedding while managing her career as a homicide detective made Allison wonder if she would ever want a fancy wedding at all. All that fuss and money down

the tube for one day. Nah. Elopement was the way to go.
Clean. Quick.
And uncomplicated.

Chapter Twenty-three

The next morning the sun beamed through Allison's window. Time to get ready for work. She rolled out of bed with alacrity. Then stopped as the realization hit her.

Work?

Her spirits plummeted. For the first time since she'd graduated from nursing school, she didn't have a job to go to. What would she do without a job? Being a nurse was part and parcel of who she was. And what about the rest of her life?

Okay. Shower first. Then coffee.

Asking existential questions before her first cup was an exercise in futility.

She grabbed her robe and padded down the hall to the bathroom she shared with her sisters. As the earliest riser, she didn't worry about either one of them beating her to the hot water. Caroline would be up next, and Tamsyn an hour later, before she moseyed into the family's Market Street office. Scott had the master bedroom with bath, and Justin had the second hall bathroom all to himself. As soon as Scott moved in with Tess, Caroline could take over the master, and Allison would only have to share a bathroom with Tamsyn.

After adjusting the water for a steamy hot shower, Allison stepped in. The water sluiced down her back, allowing the heat to ease the uncommonly stiff muscles. The memory of how those muscles received some unaccustomed use brought a smile to her lips. Nick was a very thorough lover, and he hadn't neglected any of her erogenous zones.

Perhaps she should go into the office like the rest of the gang and proceed from there. Finding a new job while things were so unsettled in the case didn't hold much appeal. The idea of sprucing up her résumé and applying at the other hospitals in town held even less. No, find Meryl's killer first and then worry about finding a job.

If she could even find another job.

Dressed in light blue slacks and a white short-sleeved sweater, Allison headed downstairs for the kitchen. From the tantalizing aroma filling the air, someone, probably Caroline, had already started the coffeemaker.

"Coffee—c–c–c." Allison lay over the granite counter as if too weak to go any farther. "I need coffee."

Her sister looked up from reading *The Tennessean*. "It's ready." She held her cup up as proof. "Are you strong enough to pour your own cup or do you need me...?" She paused, elevating one perfectly arched brow.

Allison sighed. "I suppose I have just enough energy to do it myself." She grabbed a mug from the cabinet, then poured herself a cup of the fragrant brew, carried it over to the breakfast nook, and sat across from her sister. She added creamer and sweetener, swirled the mixture with her spoon, then took a quick sip.

"I'm going into the office this morning."

Caroline's gaze widened. "Really? That's pretty ballsy after they canned you yesterday."

"That's not what I meant." Allison took a sip. "I mean downtown. I can help out with the office stuff until you're ready to come back."

"Yeah." Caroline gave a knowing smirk. "*And* there's this PI who works there, the one you're kinda fond of..."

"Pfft..." Allison shrugged, then said, "I have an idea. Why don't you come in to give me some in-service training? You don't have outpatient therapy today, do you?" She took another swallow of coffee.

Ah, simply heaven.

Her sibling's lips pursed as she considered Allison's offer. "The occupational therapist did recommend I try going to the office a couple of half days a week. Things have just been so unsettled here, I haven't gotten around to it. It slipped my mind—such as it is."

"Great. We can help each other."

"Drink your coffee while I brush my teeth and change. I won't be long."

Allison laughed. "Right." She checked her watch. "I bet you a mani-pedi at the spa that it'll be at least forty-five minutes before you show your face again."

Laughing, her sister dashed upstairs, then called, "I'll take that bet."

Settling down to sip her coffee and scan the headlines, Allison turned to the pages for local news. Her heart skipped a beat when she read: *Missing Local Nurse in Hiding*. It went on to say Harmony Bane, RN, had contacted the paper to tell reporter Bill Dudley she was hiding at an undisclosed location in fear for her life. Ms. Bane indicated she felt Meryl Litton, whose body was discovered the previous day, had been killed because of mistaken identity. The article published photographs of both nurses side-by-side, and their features were similar—something Allison already knew.

The article went on to say Ms. Bane wouldn't reveal why she thought someone might want to kill her, but she wasn't taking any chances.

Allison snatched up her cell phone and called Tess's number. "Have you seen the paper?" she asked without giving Tess time to do more than respond.

"Yes. Bill Dudley called me last night after Scott and I went back to the loft."

"You know the reporter?"

"Sure. He's on the crime beat, so our paths cross frequently."

"Good deal," Allison said, ideas sparking left and right.

"Anyway, after citing a reporter's constitutional right to maintain confidentiality, he refused to elaborate other than to tell me Ms. Bane is alive. At least that rules out the possibility of a serial killer targeting nursing professionals."

"But it doesn't rule out a personal motive"—Allison paused for emphasis—"*or* someone from the hospital being involved."

"That would be your favorite candidate, Dr. Ivers?" Tess finished. "No, it doesn't rule him out. Or her ex. Or anyone. And as shallow and self-centered as it sounds, I have to clear this case, or Scott and I won't be able to take our honeymoon."

"No one would think you're shallow or self-absorbed. I'm sure your family has spent a lot on your wedding, but surely you can at least take a day off to get married. Besides, the wedding isn't for another week. Anything could happen."

"Huh," Tess said. "I'm not sure I can even make it to the bridal shower you and your sisters are throwing for me. Now how would it look if I don't show up?"

Through her phone, Allison heard Tess's phone alert. "I gotta go," she said. "It's the case."

After her future sister-in-law disconnected, Allison sprang from the stool and fumbled through the abandoned *Tennessean* to find the reporter's email addy. There it was. Right at the end of the article.

She opened the email app on her phone and fired off a brief message to the tune of having information about a possible hospital connection to Meryl's death. "There. That ought to pique his reporter's curiosity."

Less than five minutes later, she received an email from the reporter requesting a meet. She instructed him to swing by the PI agency any time after eight-thirty.

She smiled. *Done deal.* How could it hurt to put good old Dr. Ivers's feet to the fire? No doubt he'd been instrumental in getting her fired. Time for some payback.

After parking the Camry in the Market Street parking lot, Allison and Caroline headed toward the office building.

"You're looking awfully pleased with yourself—sort of like the fat cat who ate the canary," her sister commented.

"That's because I am." Allison flashed her sister a grin over her shoulder and opened the massive oak door to the lobby. Foot-thick oak beams ran up the inside of the historic brick building. It wasn't difficult to visualize the massive oaks from which they'd been cut over a century earlier.

"Are you going to tell me why, or is it your plan to torture me and make me guess?" Caroline punched the Up button once, then a second time. "Yes, I know. It only takes one punch."

Allison laughed, sliding through the opening doors. "Wait till we get into the office. Then I'll spill all."

Her sister followed into the elevator. "What's the big deal?"

"Patience, dear Caroline. Patience." She pressed the button for the second floor.

The elevator stopped, and they emerged in front of Holt Investigations. "We'll use Tam's office," Allison said. "More *private.*" She let the cryptic phrase hang in the air, refusing to say more.

Caroline deposited her purse in a file drawer and, instead

of following, headed to the small kitchen.

Allison set her hands on her hips. "Where are you going? I thought you wanted to know what I'm up to."

"Coffee first. I always make the coffee first if one of the guys hasn't already started it. I need to get back into my usual routine. There's less chance of my forgetting something important if I take care of the little stuff."

Nodding, Allison reined in her impatience. That was what she got for teasing her sister earlier. That bitch karma, again.

"What can I do to help?" she asked.

"While I start the coffee, you can check the storeroom and see if anything needs reordering. I have a list tacked to one of the shelves with par levels."

"Easy-peasy." With a quick nod, Allison turned to go to the storeroom, then called out, "By the way, I have a reporter coming by to see me. He'll be here after eight-thirty."

Caroline popped out of the kitchen, still holding a coffee filter in her hand. "A reporter? Is *that* why you're acting so smug this morning?"

She shot her sister and enigmatic smile. "Could be. Did you see the article about the other nurse who went missing? It was on the local news page."

"I didn't get that far."

"It seems she's in hiding, so I emailed him I might have more info relating to Meryl's death and a hospital connection."

"You did not. Tell me you're kidding."

"Oh, yes, I did."

"I guess you know you're kicking a hornet's nest."

"And why not?"

"Because someone *killed* her, and he might take exception to a certain nosey ex-case manager's shining the spotlight on him."

"I'm not doing this alone," she said, shrugging. "Nick'll watch my back."

"Someone mention my name?" Looking better than any man had a right to, Nick strolled into the storage area and leaned against the doorjamb. "What're you up to now, Allie?" His brows drew together in a frown, but his frown didn't detract from his broad, black-T-shirt-covered shoulders tapering down to his slim jean-clad hips and muscular thighs.

She held back an appreciative sigh and countered with, "I have a plan to flush out Meryl's killer."

"Do ya now?"

Caroline sniffed. "She *thinks* she does."

"I do." She turned and went through the motions of checking the stock, ignoring the naysayers.

"A reporter is coming to interview her. That's all I know," her sister said, then glanced down at the coffee filter in her hand. "I guess I'd better make the coffee since *she* doesn't seem to be in the mood to share."

Allison waited until she could hear Caroline puttering in the kitchen before turning back to Nick. "I'm merely going to share some of my hunches with a reporter."

"Allie..." He placed his hands on her shoulders and drew her into his arms. "Not a good idea interfering in Metro's investigation."

"I'm *not* interfering." She settled into the comfort of his warm embrace. "This is all stuff I've already told Tess. I just want someone to really hear me about Dr. Ivers. Tess doesn't take my suspicions seriously."

"You don't know that. It's a matter of police procedure; she can't reveal all the avenues of their official inquiries— not even to her future sister-in-law. And what if you're right about a hospital connection?"

"I've already been fired, so I might as well go ahead. And

if I can't find another job, I'll find something to do at the agency."

"You're worried about career plans? What about your freaking life?"

"Oh, I know," she said with a sigh. "Caroline was just saying the same thing when you came in. You'll keep me safe. Won't you?" Giving him her most innocent smile, she fluttered her lashes for effect.

"Only if you promise you won't go anywhere without me."

"Easy enough."

"Right," he scoffed.

What? Now the man didn't trust she'd keep her promise?

"I promise. *Okay?*"

His blue gaze grew cloudy with his skepticism. "If you say so." He pulled her so close she could feel the steady beat of his heart. "Don't know what I'd do if I lost you."

"You're not going to lose me."

"Noted." He dipped his head and gave her a light kiss, then patted her bottom. "Time you got to work. No more PDAs in the office."

"And I thought Scott would be the slave driver."

He nodded. "Now you know." He left her in the stockroom and swaggered away, giving her a great view of his firm glutes.

What a guy.

Chapter Twenty-four

A few minutes after eight-thirty, Allison ushered the reporter into Tamsyn's office. "Coffee? Tea?"

Dudley nodded. "Coffee'd be great. Thanks."

After pouring a fresh cup and handing it to the reporter, Allison shut the door. "I'll go over everything I know and what I suspect led to Meryl Litton's murder." She sat behind the desk and motioned for the reporter to have a seat.

"Go ahead." Once seated, Dudley pulled a smartphone from his belt clip and set it on the desk. "If you don't mind, I'm going to record this interview."

She leaned back. "That's fine with me."

"How well did you know Ms. Litton?"

"She's—was—my best friend. We both worked in the Case Management Department."

"In your email, you indicated you had information about a hospital connection. What makes you think someone from the hospital is responsible for her death?"

"It all started with a text message on Friday afternoon." Allison went on to tell him everything from mistaking Harmony Bane for Meryl, her suspicions about the transplant program, to Allison's getting fired when she started asking too many questions. She even gave him a copy of the questionable transplant-cases list.

"So, you think her suspicions about the dodgy transplants are what got her killed?"

"I certainly do." She slapped the desktop with her hand for emphasis. "And you can quote me." He took a sip of his coffee. Dudley frowned. "No direct quotes without proof. We could all get sued for libel by the hospital and Dr. Ivers if we can't substantiate your charges."

"So I'll have to be one of those so-called *unnamed sources*?"

"Better that way." He nodded. "Reporters never reveal their confidential sources." He took another sip, his expression guarded. "I understand the detective on the case is engaged to your brother..."

She nodded. "Yes, Detective O'Malley is marrying my brother Scott next week.

"Then why give this to me instead of your future sister-in-law?"

"Oh, she knows all about my suspicions, but I don't think she takes them seriously. After all, I'm a nurse, not a detective."

Gazing at her over his reading glasses, Dudley leaned back, the fingers of one hand fiddling on his knee. "But you have the resources at hand here with a PI agency at your disposal."

"My family doesn't want me to get involved. And Scott doesn't want to piss off his fiancée this close to the wedding." She leaned forward. "I need someone independent to dig into the case and find the connections between these dodgy transplants and Meryl's murder."

"You're aware it's usually the husband or boyfriend in cases like these?"

"Yes, I know all about the conventional wisdom," she said with a huff. "And truthfully, if it weren't for Meryl's text the day she died, I'd probably go along with the conventional wisdom because her ex is *such* a sleaze. Please, just this once, we have to think outside the box. Let the police focus on her ex while you dig into this angle."

Dudley pushed his glasses up on his nose. "You do know

I don't work for you? What I decide to 'dig into' is up to me."

"Of course...but you'll let me know what you find, won't you?"

Sitting up straight, he shot her a cagey expression. "You can read about it in the paper with everyone else."

Taken aback, she let out an exasperated groan. "After I've gone to the trouble to hand over all—"

"Listen, hon," he interrupted, "you want that kind of access, hire a PI. I figure you know where to find one—or two." Standing, he tucked the transplant list into his coat pocket, then grabbed his smartphone.

Ready to do battle, she rose from her seat. "You patronizing shit!"

His brows arched as he replied smoothly, "Such language." He headed toward the door. "Thanks for the intel, hon." He gave a cheeky salute.

"It's a good thing you're leaving, or I'd have one of my brothers kick your sorry ass out of here."

Breaking into a loud laugh, he opened the door. "I've been kicked out of worse."

"Ewww!" Allison rushed from behind the desk, ready to encourage his swift departure.

Overhearing loud voices, Nick strolled into the agency waiting room. "What's going on?" He eyed the newspaper reporter. What had he said that upset Allison?

"Just leaving," the reporter said, exiting the office with a new burst of speed.

Nick turned to Allison. Her face was flushed, and her breasts rose and fell with each breath. "You okay?" He gathered her into his arms, still ready to protect her from one and all.

"Yeah," she said with an exasperated sigh. "He's just an

arrogant asshat."

He held back a chuckle. "What's the matter? Couldn't you bend him to your will—like you do me?"

She gave him a shamefaced grin. "Something like that. I mean I gave him all the information I had, and he blew me off. Totally."

"And you thought he'd come back and share his results with you."

"He had the nerve to tell me I could read about it in the paper. And he said I ought to hire a PI."

"You already have one...or have you forgotten?" he reminded her. "Maybe you don't think I'm up to the job?"

"You're definitely up to the job, but like Tess, *you* think her ex did it. What I really wanted..."

"You wanted him to pursue the hospital angle. You wanted him to write what you wanted him to write."

"And what's wrong with that?"

"Reporters go where the story leads them. If he's any good, he'll follow up on your theory. If he finds anything, he'll keep you out of it. And that's definitely okay with me."

"You just don't want me involved. In case you haven't noticed, I'm already involved." She wrinkled her nose.

Wisely, he refrained from laughing outright. "Hold on. Let's call a truce. How about we—that's you and me—let the authorities follow up on the ex. Then I'll do some digging into your transplant theory."

She gazed up at him, her brown eyes shining with emotion. "Would you? Really? Just for me?"

"Damn straight. You just have to promise no matter what I find, *you* won't go near the transplant doc. Either I'll clear him or I'll discover something incriminating. And if I do, I'll turn it over to Tess."

"But you'll tell me if you find something...won't you?" She pulled her brows together in a frown.

Now here was where things got tricky. "Not necessarily."

She snuggled closer, running her fingertip over his bottom lip, a move guaranteed to make him hot.

"But if you're my PI, then you should."

He threw up his hands. "No way. Besides, you're not paying me."

As if looking for her purse, she glanced around. "I could."

"Save your money. You're gonna need it if you don't find another job."

"Jerk!" She rolled her eyes and threw her hands in the air. "I'm surrounded by jerks."

"Does that include us?" Scott, with Justin on his heels, entered the office. "What's going on? Honeymoon over?"

"My remark includes *all* of the male species." She grabbed her purse and flounced from the office.

Justin shot Nick a bewildered glance. "Who pissed in her cornflakes?"

"A reporter." Nick shrugged. "And me."

Caroline, who'd apparently watched the entire scene from her desk, laughed. "Long story, fellas. Don't ask."

He scratched his neck. "Scott, I need to go over something before..."

Scott nodded. "Let's talk." He jerked his head toward his office.

He followed Scott into his office and shut the door.

"So, what did we walk in on?" his boss asked.

"Allie called a reporter and gave him her theory of Dr. Ivers being involved in Meryl Litton's murder. Then she got pissed off when the reporter wouldn't agree to follow up on her information or let her know what he found if he did."

Scott perched on the corner of his desk. "That's it?"

Nick chuckled. "He might've told her she could read about it in the paper like everyone else."

"Should've warned you. Our Allison expects people to do

her bidding. Comes from being a case manager."

"Tell me about it." Nick gave a bark of laughter. "I'd almost convinced her to stay out of it. Let the authorities focus on the ex-husband and let me follow up on the hospital angle. I warned her to stay away from the transplant director. I don't want her on his case. No way."

"Right. Whoever killed Meryl could get nervous and decide to get rid of the big thorn in his backside."

"She wasn't too happy when I told her I wouldn't share whatever I find unless it cleared the doc. She seemed to think I should bring my findings to her first."

"Not good. Normally my sister is as steady as a rock, but this thing has thrown her for a loop. She's too close to the situation. Her usual common sense is on vacation."

"I wanted you to know I'll be digging into Ivers. His alibi. And whatever else I can find about his dealings in the transplant program."

"If you can keep her out of trouble. So be it. That said, I've a wedding coming up in a week. And if this case is cleared, Tess and I have our honeymoon planned. We'll take a couple of weeks, provided she can tie everything up."

Nick nodded. "Sounds good to me. Justin and I can hold down the fort."

"With Caroline back part-time and Allison to help, things should be okay. Tamsyn will be glad to be back to managing her clients. But she'll need backup when she goes out to seduce some unsuspecting slob of a husband or boyfriend. Justin usually acts as my backup, but occasionally he's busy after hours."

"Not a problem. I'll be glad to watch her six." Indeed, watching Tamsyn Holt's six would be a pleasure. Still, despite Tamsyn's lush, dark beauty, it was the sweet, and sometimes prickly, Allison who'd found her way into his heart. With her fresh beauty, what you saw was what you got. And more and more, he loved what he saw.

"That's *if* Tess closes the case. A very big if."

Nick blew out a puff of air. "No pressure then, boss."

Scott grinned, holding his hands up in surrender. "Not meant to be. Honest." He shrugged. "Trip's already paid for, though."

"Yeah, I get it." Nick nodded. "I just have to get off my ass and dig into Ivers's background."

Scott leaned back and leveled his gaze at Nick. "If you think that's the way to go?"

"I don't." Frowning, he pinched the bridge of his nose. "I still like Meryl's ex for it, but I don't know any other way to keep Allison out of it."

"Tess and her partner are hot on his movements, so don't concern yourself with that avenue of inquiry. I intend to keep Allison busy here in the office with gofer stuff."

"Agreed," Nick said with a quick nod. "And Justin can give me a hand with the computer research?"

"Damn straight."

Nick turned toward the door. "Now I'd better find Allie before she tracks down Ivers for another go."

"If it's not too late."

Nick ran a hand back through his hair. "Perish the thought."

Allie strode along Second Avenue, muttering and not giving a rat's ass who heard her. "Men. Always trying to control. Always—"

All right, always trying to protect her, if she would just admit the truth. Overall, not a bad thing, but still, this was the freaking twenty-first century, not the eighteenth. Women had come a long way, baby—yeah, she was starting to sound like a cigarette commercial from the sixties.

Having a tantrum and storming out—not very mature. Truth was, not having her job left her at loose ends. And running errands and making coffee for the office crew wasn't going to cut it as a career.

Her pace slowed. She found herself in front of one of the many food establishments on Second. Peering at the display window at an arrangement of freshly baked goods, she licked her lips and her mouth watered. Then she discovered Nick reflected over her left shoulder. She whirled to face him. "Are you stalking me?"

Now, why had she come off so snarky? She hadn't meant to. In fact, she'd been more than glad to see his handsome face as he watched her.

"Hi, to you too," he said. "You really need a better awareness of your surroundings when you're blazing down the sidewalks. If I was a stalker, I could've grabbed you anytime in the last five minutes."

Knowing he was right didn't help her feelings of embarrassment. "You're right. I wasn't paying attention. And I'm really glad you're not a stalker." She smiled, hoping it would soften his response.

"In fact, I'm pretty sure you scared a couple of folks with all your muttering."

He stepped into her personal space. She took a quick breath to steady her pulse, but it was no use. The memory of their lovemaking was too fresh to ignore.

"How about we grab a cup of coffee?" he suggested.

"I'm not sure I'm ready to face everyone in the office again. I was such a brat."

"Let's try neutral territory, then. Aren't there a couple of Starbucks around here?"

"Yeah." She chewed her bottom lip as she considered their next move. "And I could bring some pastries back to the office...as a peace offering."

"Sounds like a plan." He held out his hand. She entwined her fingers within his, finding comfort in the warm strength of his callused hand. With Nick, she felt safe and secure. Wherever their relationship was headed, somehow she knew he would never hurt her...on purpose.

Allison leaned across the table and inhaled the steamy aroma wafting up from her latte. "Did you know Scott first met Tess in this very Starbucks?"

"Love at first sight?"

"No way. She threatened to arrest him as a public nuisance."

Nick took a swallow of his coffee—black, of course. "For real?"

"Yeah." Lest he thought she expected a similar result, she hastened to add, "Not that *our* being here is of any particular significance." She took a quick sip of the latte, then checked her phone to see if she had any messages...to keep from meeting Nick's direct gaze.

"You're deflecting."

Her gaze shot back to him. "What do you mean?"

"Instead of looking me in the eye, you're playing with your phone. It's a delaying tactic. Criminals use similar tactics when trying to avoid answering questions."

She jerked her hand from the phone. "You're comparing me to a criminal?"

"Not at all. I pay attention to body language—force of habit—and right now, I'd say you're trying to avoid the conversation we need to have."

"I know I was a brat this morning. I'm sorry." Averting her gaze again, she stirred her latte and took another tiny sip. "Man, it's almost too hot to drink."

"Allie..." His tone was one of patient exasperation.

"You're doing it again."

"I apologized. What more do you want? Honestly..." Shaking her head, she shrugged.

"We need to talk about where our relationship is headed."

"I don't want you to think just because we—uh, were together..." She paused, glancing around to see if anyone could hear them.

"Why *wouldn't* I think something? You're not a one-night-stand kind of woman. I know a lot of guys are real horndogs, but I never was. Being with you means something to me, Allie. You're special."

The sincerity with which he delivered these simple words sent the blood rushing to her face. Indeed, she could feel the burn of a full-on blush. "I don't know what to say." She reached across the table and covered his big hand with her smaller one. "It's just I don't want to be the transitional relationship. You're newly divorced. You have a wonderful little boy, and seeing me might make things difficult. I get the feeling his mother won't be happy you're moving on."

"*She's* already moved on."

"But she seems determined to make your life miserable. I don't want my presence to make things worse. And I most definitely don't want to be the one who gives her a reason to deny your visits with your son."

"I admit my life's complicated. Eva's not a bad person, not really."

"She tried to convince me you abused her. In my book, a lie like that makes her a bad person."

"You've heard the expression 'dog in a manger'?"

She nodded. "She doesn't want you but doesn't want anyone else to have you either. Well, she's just selfish and immature."

"Yeah, but it's something we'll have to deal with if we decide to go forward."

She brushed her hair back from her face. "I thought men didn't like having the relationship talk," she said, using finger quotes.

His broad shoulders lifted in a shrug. "I'm an upfront kind of guy."

"I'm beginning to see." She smiled at his use of "we" and sipped her latte. Even so, certain misgivings remained. If she knew anything about women, Nick's ex might be more of a problem than he anticipated.

A lot more.

"So, what're you thinking?" he asked.

After a careful pause to consider her next words, she said, "That we should take things one day at a time."

"I'm okay with that."

"Good. Now let's buy some pastries and take them back to the office."

"Sounds like a plan."

Chapter Twenty-five

Skipping out from the office after lunch, Allison drove home and spent the remainder of the afternoon finalizing the arrangements for Tess's bridal shower. While Caroline and Tamsyn would assist with the actual shower, recording the gifts and serving refreshments, Allison had signed up for the bulk of the planning.

The idea had been to keep things simple, so despite the many elegant venues available, she'd decided to have the shower outside on the deck. Last month, Scott and Justin had a beautiful retractable awning installed.

Quite satisfied with her arrangements, she smiled. Despite being in the middle of the lazy, hazy days of summer, the party guests should be quite comfy and relaxed on the deck, as long as it didn't storm.

The catering service would deliver the chicken and fruit-salad plates an hour before the event. One of her friends from high school was a stay-at-home mom who baked the most fantastic cupcakes. Sara would deliver the delicious lemon-sponge cupcakes in plenty of time for the six o'clock party. For the icing, Tess had chosen a lime buttercream. Allison's mouth watered as she remembered tasting the icing which was rich and sweet with just the tiniest hint of citrusy tartness.

After confirming everything was in place, she grabbed her bag from the counter and dropped her phone inside. Just enough time to run to Target for swag bags. And decorations.

*

"Allie!" A child's voice rang out. Allison stopped short in the party-favors aisle and turned. Nick's son came running toward her, his mother in tow. Nick's ex-wife was a tall, curvy brunette with long black hair and very well turned-out in designer casual wear. She wore a not-too-pleased expression on her otherwise attractive face as she tried unsuccessfully to corral her son.

Wishing she hadn't run out in faded jeans and a Parklane Medical Center-logoed T-shirt, Allison crouched down to his level. "Hi, Ben. How are you?"

His dark eyes sparkled with excitement as he shifted from one foot to the other and back again. "I'm good. My puppy needs some toys. Mommy's going to buy some."

"That's really cool."

"Benjamin, come here this instant. You know what I told you about talking to strangers."

"But she's Allie."

Straightening to her full height, Allison held out her hand. "I'm Allison Lackey. I'm a friend of Nick's."

Ignoring her outstretched hand, the brunette gave Allison the once-over, the corner of her mouth lifting a bit. "Eva Mills. My husband's the chief of police."

"I've heard. You have a great son."

"I *know* I have a great son," Eva said in a tone meant to wither. "You'll have to excuse us."

"Yes, puppy toys. Have fun, Ben." She wasn't any more interested in continuing the awkward conversation than Nick's ex was.

"Bye." The boy took off running toward the rear of the store, but Eva remained long enough to say, "You'll find out I wasn't lying. Nick was abusive, and that's why I left him. No matter what he tells you."

"Oh? And here I thought it was your having an affair with his captain," Allison replied, doing her level best to keep the snark from her tone.

The other woman's lips compressed into a thin line, her eyes flashing with anger. She let out an exasperated sigh, whipped around, and took off after her son.

She watched Nick's ex's departure with a sense of puzzlement. Why would Eva Mills stubbornly continue to insist Nick was an abuser? Allison had seen Nick so pissed off by the accusation he'd been ready to spit nails. But he'd never lifted a hand. Still, the woman's allegations left an uneasiness Allison couldn't quite resolve.

Maybe it was time they addressed the issue again, whether Nick wanted to or not.

At Nick's apartment, Allison turned on the faucet, rinsing a head of romaine under the stream of cold water. Glancing over her shoulder, she asked Nick, "The Chinese should be here in about fifteen. What do you like in your salad?"

Nick was hunkered behind the TV, connecting the Blu-ray player she'd bought as a housewarming gift. He looked up and shot her a heart-stopping smile. "I'm not picky—the usual stuff."

"Good thing. Because I'm kind of picky myself. I'd be happy to eat the lettuce and dressing alone."

"I'm shocked." He got to his feet and ambled toward her, amusement making his sky-blue eyes glow. "And you a nurse. Haven't you heard? Vegetables are good for ya."

"I know." She turned to face him and smiled. "But I was a picky eater long before I was a nurse."

He backed her against the sink, leaned down, and nipped her ear. "If you don't eat all your salad..." His voice low and husky, he continued, "You'll be sent to bed without your supper."

Need rushed through her, stunning her and weakening her knees. Her arms went around his neck. "That's fine with me," she managed to say.

"It's a bad girl who wants to go to bed without her dinner," he teased.

She favored him with her sweetest expression. "You have a lot of experience with bad girls, then?"

"Some."

"I can be bad...sometimes. Do you *like* bad girls?"

"Depends." His blue eyes deepened to sapphire as he gazed down at her.

"On what?"

"On *how* bad they are."

He cupped her bottom, pulling her close enough to feel his erection. "I don't mean illegal bad," she said, rubbing against him.

"Didn't figure you did. However, I don't like *Chinese interruptus*."

The term caught her off guard. "And exactly what would that be?"

"Being in the middle of something hot"—he reached behind her and unfastened her bra—"and heavy when the doorbell rings with the Chinese takeout."

"Ahh," she said, trying to swallow the freaking lump in her throat. "*That* kind of interruptus." She grinned, enjoying the slow tease of foreplay. "Not that I've ever experienced the panicked rush to redress decently enough to answer the door. I do live with four siblings, after all."

"I can see where having so many folks around would tend to dampen things."

"That's why *you* needed to have your own apartment. And here I thought you were concerned about Ben's having a place to sleep."

"Oh, I was, but I might've had an ulterior motive or two."
He bent down and nipped her earlobe.

Her breath caught in her throat. "Seems to me you did."

He pulled her top over her head and tossed it aside. "It's
worked well so far, ya think?" He smiled, then slipped the
bra off her shoulders.

"Oh yeah."

Unzipping his jeans an inch at a time, she could feel his
erection arrowed straight up. She gave a low laugh, then
insinuated her hand inside his briefs. "No point in my being
the only one exposed here."

"Guess not," he groaned. In return, he unbuttoned her
jeans and slid his hand inside her panties, flicking her clit.

Moaning and biting her bottom lip, she squirmed against
his hand.

"Like that?"

"Oh yeah." She let out a sigh. "But there's something I like
better."

"How many guesses do I get?"

"Just two. And the first doesn't count."

"Now I wonder what it could be?" Smiling, he licked his
bottom lip back and forth in a sensuous manner.

Her inner muscles clenched. "That's it. You win."

"Then take off those freaking jeans."

She unzipped and wiggled out of them. "Gone."

He ripped the T-shirt over his head then tossed it to the
floor. He dropped his jeans and kicked them away. Picking
her up, he carried her into the bedroom and rested her on
the edge of the mattress. He knelt before her as she opened
to him. He parted her labia and flicked her clit with his
tongue. She writhed and moaned her pleasure. "Oh, God."

"I guessed right, then?"

"You did." Her skin seemed to catch fire as he licked the
seat of all sensation. Her thighs quivered as the pressure in

her core grew and spread through her body in waves of pleasure. She cried his name as the orgasm tore through her. "More," she gasped. She could never get enough of this man. Not just his lovemaking but the man himself.

"More?" Nick needed no encouragement. Grabbing a condom, he ripped open the package, and Allison quickly sheathed him. About to burst, he positioned her legs over his shoulders and plunged into her slick hot depths. Her inner walls gripped his cock as if she'd never let go. He pumped into her core, his love for her pouring from him. He groaned with the ripping force of his climax and collapsed. Before he could catch his breath, the doorbell rang. "Shit."

He got to his feet, scrambling to find his jeans. "Just a minute!" he yelled. He should've known this would happen.

Seemingly still dazed, Allison remained on the bed. He forced his legs into the jeans, zipping as he stumbled to the door.

By the time Nick returned from paying the delivery guy, Allison had hurriedly dressed and was toeing on her sandals. The savory odor of Chinese takeout wafted into the bedroom, causing her stomach to rumble. "I'm ravenous."

"Good. You ordered a mountain of food. And I'm starving." He started setting out the various containers.

"That's because you eat it and thirty minutes later, you want more."

"I've heard that about you." He wrinkled his nose. "Always wanting more."

"I was talking about Chinese food, not myself." She wrinkled her nose in return and opened one of the containers, inhaling the goodness. "Ah, cashew chicken...

My favorite."

"Can't say I'm surprised. You're a bit on the nutty side, on a good day."

"Am not." She tossed a chopstick in his direction. "Okay, maybe I am a little high-strung...sometimes."

"Sometimes? Lady, you are high-strung most of the time."

Unable to wait, she dug into the chicken and downed a bite. "Gosh, this is delish. By the way, I ran into your ex today."

"And...?"

"Same old tune and second verse of he's an abuser."

"Why bring this up now?" His voice was tight. "Do you still doubt me, even a little?"

"No. I don't." She took two plates and added fried rice to both. "I absolutely don't believe her. But why is Eva still harping on it?"

"Like you said before, she's selfish and immature. She hates me. She wants to break us up. Take your pick!" He spun around, heading for the door.

"Where're you going? The food's going to get cold."

"I need some air." He slammed the door behind him.

Should she follow him? No, give him some time to cool off. The man had a temper—no doubt about it. But he wasn't an abuser.

Was she afraid of him? No.

All right, then, show him. She opened the door and spied him, his back to her. Time to make a stand.

Outside, Nick sucked in a deep breath, let it out, and sucked in another. To hell with Eva and her meddling. And Allison—if she didn't trust him, or worse, if she was afraid of him, he couldn't deal. They might as well break up now. Save himself the grief of another failed relationship.

Lost in thought, he started when he felt the warmth of a smaller hand slipping into his.

"It was stupid and tactless of me to bring it up again. I shouldn't have said anything. I'm not afraid of you, Nick. And I'm falling in love with you."

He pulled her into his arms. "You are?"

"Yes."

"Good. 'Cause I'm already in love with you. I want to protect you and erase all the sadness from your life." *And keep you out of trouble.*

She gave him a shy grin, but humor glittered in her chocolate eyes. "Good because the Chinese is getting cold."

"Unbelievable!" Crazy woman, but, for now anyway, she was his woman. "Here I've gone and told you I love you, and you're worried about your stomach."

"Not entirely." The corner of her mouth twitched as she snuggled into his arms. "How about if I promise dessert will be served *warm*?"

"Warm—huh? Yeah, that'll work."

Chapter Twenty-six

The next morning, the landline phone rang awakening Allison from a steamy dream about a certain PI. She glanced at her bedside clock. Damn. 10:30. She'd overslept. Rubbing the sleep from her eyes, she grabbed the receiver and mumbled, "Hello."

"Allison Lackey?" a woman's voice asked.

"Yes, this is she." Where had she heard that voice before?

"I need to talk to you about my husband. I'm afraid of him."

"No," she said, ready to hang up the phone. "You *need* to talk to the police."

"You don't understand. This is Harriet Ivers, Dr. Ivers's wife. As soon as I read the paper this morning, I knew you'd be the one to help me."

"The paper? I haven't seen today's paper yet. What are you talking about?"

"It's that article on transplant organs and their donors. It's true what the reporter's implying. I have proof my husband is mixed up in something very unsavory."

"Hold on while I find the article. I'll have to go downstairs." Allison set the receiver on the bedside table. She drew on a housecoat and flew downstairs to the kitchen. Everyone had already gone to the office. She found the paper folded neatly on the counter—Caroline's doing, no doubt. After spreading out the newspaper, she picked up the kitchen extension. Bingo.

The headline read, ILLEGAL TRANSPLANTS IN MUSIC CITY?

"Still there?"

"Yes."

"Okay, give me a second." She scanned the article. "Are you confirming Dr. Ivers is mixed up in dodgy organ transplants?"

"Yes, and more. I think he killed that case manager too. He was acting very suspicious around the time she disappeared."

"That was just last week, and it was just *this* week you and your husband got me fired for suggesting he might be involved. Why the big turnaround, Mrs. Ivers?"

"He forced me to complain to your boss. I'm so sorry they fired you. But now I'm afraid he might kill me too. You *have* to help me."

"No. I don't. You really, really need to call the police. Let me give you the detective's number. She'll see you're protected." The nerve of the woman.

Why on earth would she expect me, of all people, to help her?

"I'm afraid the police will arrest me for helping him. I have proof about the transplants. Bank account records. His account in the Caymans. Everything. I could give it to you, and you give it to the detective. I wouldn't have to be involved."

"You're not thinking clearly. Just how am I supposed to have come by this documentation? You *have* to be involved. The police will understand you were under duress. They'll protect you." Whether or not the authorities were understanding would depend on the degree of her involvement.

"Just meet with me. I have all his files on a flash drive, and I'll turn it over to you. You can give it to the detective and tell her I gave it to you. Then I'll leave town until he's arrested."

"That won't work. They'll need your written statement at the very least." As much as she'd like to see what was on the flash drive, she wasn't about to jump when Mrs. Ivers yelled, *Froggie*.

"I can't go to the police. He's watching me. I'm afraid." She gasped, then whispered, "Oh no. He's back. I've got to go. Help me, please."

The doctor's wife disconnected, leaving Allison gazing at the receiver. What the hell was she supposed to do now? The woman certainly sounded scared of her husband. Maybe a quick run by the high-rise where the Ivers couple lived? After her previous performance, would they even let her in the front door?

She sprinted upstairs, pulled on a pair of sweatpants and a T-shirt. Before leaving, she forwarded calls to her cell.

She was already driving down West End when her cell phone rang. With one hand, she dug the phone from her purse. She answered, "Allison Lackey."

No answer.

"Mrs. Ivers?"

"Yes," the woman answered. "I got away from him. Will you meet me in the park?"

"Centennial? Sure."

"No. Too many people. I don't want anyone to see me as I hand over the flash drive. Do you know the Nature Center in Edwin Warner Park?"

"Sure." She flicked on the turn signal and changed lanes. Morning rush was over, and it shouldn't take too long to get to the park.

Once she had Mrs. Ivers's evidence in hand, she'd turn it over to Tess and then still have plenty of time to go back home and get everything ready for the bridal shower.

*

The sky was darkening with low-hanging clouds when Allison pulled into the Nature Center's drive and parked. Frowning at the ominous clouds, she turned on the radio and listened to a weather report. Great, a tornado watch was in effect for Davidson and surrounding counties. Rolling down the window, she yawned and wished she'd taken time to stop for coffee. She pulled her phone from her bag. Might as well check in with Caroline and see what was going on in the office.

Her sister answered before the second ring. "Well, Miss Stay-Out-All-Night, it's about time you emerged from your bed. When Nick came in, he said you'd probably want to sleep late."

"Oh, he did, did he?" She'd left after they made love a second time, even though Nick had asked her to stay, sweetening his request with an offer to make breakfast. But it was too late to call home and risk waking everyone. Simpler to pull on her clothes and ease out the door. No point in complicating matters.

"So, are you coming in or are you just too tired to make the effort?" Her sister's tone carried a note of amusement. "Honestly, why don't you just stay home today and get ready for Tess's shower tonight."

"Fine. Be amused. I've had a break in the case, and all you can think about is my love life."

"So, spill. Does it have anything to do with the lead article on page one?"

"It rattled someone's cage for sure."

"What?"

A hand reached through the open window and snatched her cell phone. "Hey!"

The next sound she heard was her phone crunching as

Mrs. Ivers stepped on it, smashing it into several pieces. Allison opened the car door and jumped out to face the woman. "What the hell are you trying to pull, lady?"

But she faced the woman's big old handgun instead. "I thought you wanted my help. In case you're wondering, this isn't the way to get it."

"Get in my car," Ivers's wife ordered tersely. "You drive. Just remember I have this gun, and it's fully loaded."

She took a single step toward the woman's black Cadillac Escalade, then stopped and turned. "Be sensible. When you so rudely interrupted me, I was talking to my sister. They'll come looking for me. And it won't take long."

"Just shut the hell up. I've had enough of your smart mouth."

"Before I shut the hell up, one more comment. I'm guessing you don't have a flash drive full of evidence incriminating your husband to give me."

"I said shut it!" Harriet aka Bonnie minus Clyde shrieked and unsteadily waved her nine mil around.

The weapon looked too heavy for the short, stocky woman. Maybe...

"Don't even think about it." The woman's face pulled into a mask of ugliness. Now, *this* was the Mrs. Ivers Allison remembered all too well. "I know how to use this thing."

Allison rolled her eyes. "Great. Because I really hate to think you might shoot me by accident."

"The car. Get in." Harriet jerked her head toward the SUV. "Otherwise, I'm going to shoot you where you stand."

Allison cut her gaze toward one of the parking lot's security cameras but kept her tongue still.

Right. Go ahead. At least, the video will play well at your trial.

Harriet shoved the gun into Allison's right kidney area. "Now move it. I'm sure you don't want any innocent bystanders getting hurt—like that group of school kids coming out of the center."

Allison glanced over her shoulder. Harriet wasn't bluffing. A group of six- or seven-year-old children were already trouping outside, ready for an exciting nature hike.

"All right. I'm going." Dread gathering in the pit of her stomach, she opened the SUV's door and slid behind the wheel. Her captor flounced into the passenger seat.

She favored her captor with a wide I'm-so-hating-you smile. "So, Miss Daisy, tell me where do you wanna go?"

"You are *such* a smart-ass. It will be a pleasure to kill *you*." Then almost as an aside, she said, "As a murder weapon, a knife is so messy. That other bitch bled all over me."

That other bitch? The three words thudded Allison's gut like sucker punches. So much for her theory involving Dr. Ivers. Somehow she managed to keep calm, turning the SUV around to head out the drive onto Hwy 100.

"Speaking of my best friend Meryl, why *did* you kill her?" she asked through clenched teeth. "And her baby?"

"None of your business." Her eyes widened. Her lips pulled back in a snarl, showing a perfect set of crowns. It was all a mis—" The woman broke off midsentence. "Turn left and drive. Try anything, and I'll get your blood all over my SUV."

Her hands gripping the steering wheel until her knuckles whitened, Allison swallowed the lump in her throat. "A mistake—that's what you started to say, isn't it? You meant to kill Harmony Bane, didn't you? She and your husband were having an affair. But Meryl had a meeting with him that afternoon. What did you do—follow her from his office, thinking she was your husband's mistress?"

"Never mind what I *thought*," the woman shrieked, jabbing her weapon in Allison's ribs. "Drive."

"But where?" Allison asked as calmly as she could. Better dial it down. Getting shot wasn't on her day's agenda.

"I don't care where. I need some time...to think."

Obviously, the woman's tenuous hold on reality was starting to slip. Acting on impulse must be her usual method of coping. "Yeah, I know what you mean. A little forethought goes a long way," Allison said.

"Shut the fuck up!" Harriet Ivers covered her ears with both hands.

"Careful with your gun. You might shoot yourself in the head."

Now, why did I have to go and warn her?

"Get on the Interstate and head toward Goodlettsville. Take the Long Hollow Pike exit away from town."

"All righty. What's in Goodlettsville?" Was the woman going to take her where she'd left Meryl's lifeless body?

"There's a farm. Been in my family for four generations. I'm taking you there until I decide what to do with you."

"So, you're not going to kill me right away? Great." She turned right on Old Hickory, aiming to cut through Bellevue to I-40. "Any chance I'll get to attend my future sister-in-law's bridal shower? I'm hosting it, along with my sisters. They're going to know something's up when I don't show up for work, but they're really going to freak if I miss the shower."

"Consider them freaked, then," the Ivers woman muttered, ramming the gun back in Allison's side. "Just drive."

What else could she do? She drove.

Nick sped down Hwy 100, moved into the left lane, then whipped into the Nature Center's parking lot. Sure enough, Allison's silver Camry was parked at the back of the lot. He pulled in beside it and braked. He got out and walked around to the Camry. The sight of the open driver's side door shook him.

Her purse on the seat and the keys still in the ignition. His heart hammered, the blood rushing in his ears. He glanced around the lot. Lying a few feet away, her cell phone—what remained of it, anyway.

Someone had taken her at gunpoint. There weren't any obvious signs of blood loss, so she could still be alive.

Fuck it. Why had she gone off half-cocked on her own? She knew better.

He called the office and gave Scott a sit-rep. "They have two security cameras. Get O'Malley working on a warrant for the camera footage."

Scott agreed and hung up. Nick sprinted over to the Nature Center and burst inside. A young woman with long dark hair and wearing a park employee uniform glanced up from her iPad. "May I help you?"

"A young woman was abducted from your parking lot this morning."

"What?" Her eyebrows rose.

"I need to review your camera footage." Might as well try, since there was no telling how long it might take going through official channels.

"Are you a police officer?"

"Former. I'm a PI now." He pulled out his ID and a business card. "But I can get a warrant if I really have to."

"No need," she said, a look of alarm across her face. "I want to help."

"I need footage for the camera facing the back of the lot."

"Sure thing." She nodded, opening the door to a small side office. Three monitor screens lit up the darkness. "One is aimed toward the back of the lot, one at the entrance, and one toward the front of the lot," the park volunteer said.

He'd noted two of the cameras, but three was better. "The back lot and the entrance. They'd have to leave the way they came in—right?"

"Right." She slid her hand over the mouse. "What time frame do we need to look at?"

"Anything after ten this morning." He paced as much as he could in the tight office. "Can we save it to a disc or a flash drive? The detectives on the case will need it."

"Sure. Actually, I can copy and save the part of the file you need and email it to the detective if you have his email address."

Nick hovered over her shoulder while she reversed the feed. "Wait. There's her car pulling in." He watched Allison while she sat in her vehicle and placed a phone call.

Must be when she called Caroline. Then a woman—*a woman*—emerged from a Cadillac Escalade, walked over to Allison, who was still chatting on her phone and oblivious to her surroundings. Dammit, he'd warned her. Horrified, he watched the kidnapping unfold.

His mouth dry, he said, "Now the one pointed at the entrance. We can get her license plates." He had a helluva good idea who the woman was.

Short, squat. Mean as a snake. And angry as hell.

None other than the good doctor's wife, Harriet Ivers.

Allison was right all along. The Iverses were involved, after all. The article in the paper this morning had definitely rattled their cages. And now, they—or at least *she*—had Allison.

"Now the footage of the SUV leaving. For the tag number."

The young woman complied.

"Can you enlarge the focus on the plate?"

"I can try. I'm not exactly an expert with this stuff."

"You're doing fine." He zeroed in on the plate.

Gotcha.

He gave her O'Malley's email address, then pulled out his smartphone and texted the tag number and Harriet Ivers's name to O'Malley and copied it to Justin at the office. "That should do it. Thank you."

"Glad I could help. I hope you find her."

He ran from the Nature Center, making a beeline for his vehicle. Allison's kidnapping was in the hands of the authorities, but no way was he gonna sit around and wait. Best head back to the office, and try to figure out where the Ivers woman had taken the woman he loved.

He was pulling out of the park when his phone rang. "Vitelli."

"BOLO is on," O'Malley said, "and search warrants are being served on the Ivers' condo and the doctor's office. We're also obtaining warrants for their phone records."

"How about a search of tax records—Davidson and Sumner Counties. The Ivers couple might have other property we don't know about."

"You think Mrs. Ivers might take her to the same area outside Goodlettsville where Ms. Litton's body was found?"

"There's some reason they chose that place for a body dump. I don't believe it was random. I'm heading that way," Nick said. "Call me if you come up with a location."

"Don't be a hero, Vitelli. Wait for backup."

"Discreet surveillance—nothing more."

"Better be," the detective warned, then disconnected.

He hit speed dial for the office.

Justin answered. "Got your email. Whatcha need? I know you haven't found her yet."

"You're right. On a hunch. Scan the tax records for any property owned by the Iverses. Davidson and surrounding counties, especially Sumner." To get technical, Goodlettsville, TN, was split between Davidson and Sumner

Counties.

"Will do."

"Call me and O'Malley when you find something. I'm working on a hunch and heading to the farm where Meryl Litton's body was found. I'll be close at hand...if you come up with anything."

"Yes, master."

Nick broke the connection. Now if he just didn't get stopped for speeding.

In a full-on panic, Caroline had left the office and driven home. No point in working when she had the bridal shower preparations to handle. What break in the case had Allison referred to? Drat it. Her younger sister was too impulsive for her own good.

Devastated, Caroline entered the house on Richland. Allison was missing. Who on earth had taken her? When Caroline left the office, Justin had pinged Allison's cell phone to no avail, but the GPS navigation unit on her Camry recorded her last location as the Warner Park Nature Center. What was she doing there?

At least Nick was on his way to the park. Hopefully, she'd hear from him soon, but would it be soon enough?

Allison's disappearance aside, Caroline had eighteen phone calls to make to cancel the bridal shower. She reached for her phone when it trilled. She pulled it from her purse and saw Nick's name on the caller ID.

"Have you found her?" she asked without giving him a chance to answer.

"I found her car and cell phone at the Nature Center. Her purse was still in the car. I've seen their security camera footage. She was taken by a woman at gunpoint. The transplant doctor's wife."

"Oh, God." Her heart racing and knees weakening, Caroline sank into a chair. "It's two o'clock and we still don't know where she is."

"We're gonna find her. I've already emailed the camera footage to Tess at Metro and to Justin at the office. There's already a BOLO out on Harriett Ivers's vehicle and her husband's as well."

"Is there any chance you'll find her?" *Before it's too late.* Her hands shook as she held the phone.

"I'll find her," Nick said. "Stay at the house, in case someone calls."

"Like for a ransom demand?" If only the situation were that simple.

Over the phone, she heard Nick clear his throat. "Uh, yeah."

"You *will* find her—won't you?"

"We'll find her. I promise."

It didn't take a genius to hear the fear and the doubt in his voice. And he wasn't making any promises about what kind of condition she'd be in when found. At least the woman hadn't killed her outright. It had to count for something.

So, Nick was scared. And now Caroline was even more afraid than before.

"Look, I gotta go. Traffic's getting heavy."

Numb with fear and her hands shaking, she touched the screen to disconnect.

All right. Start making calls. Couldn't have eighteen of Tess's nearest and dearest friends showing up for a bridal shower when one of the hostesses and the guest of honor were bound to be MIA.

Chapter Twenty-seven

"Go on. Get inside." Harriet Ivers jabbed Allison in the ribs. "In case you've forgotten, this thing is loaded."

"Oh, I haven't forgotten. You've been quite diligent in reminding me." Allison brushed aside a cobweb hanging from the doorjamb and shivered, then stepped gingerly across the rotted wood threshold and found herself inside a terminally dusty farmhouse. "You really should speak to your cleaning service."

A low growl emanated from her kidnapper's throat. The woman muttered something too indistinct to make out. But Allison guessed it wasn't anything good.

She picked her way across the littered floor. It looked as if someone from *Hoarders* had carted everything out but left the dirt and several old crates. "You *have* to understand my family runs a PI agency. They're good at finding people. They'll find me."

"Tough. They won't have a clue where to find you."

"They'll already be scanning the tax records for any property you and your husband own."

The woman smiled. "Good luck with that." She chuckled as she picked up a frayed coil of rope. "Sit."

Allison shrugged. "Chairs seem to be in short supply."

"Sit on the crate, smart-ass. Sit on the fucking crate." Ivers shoved Allison in the middle of her back, causing her to stumble and fall on her knees.

A swear word exploded from Allison's lips.

"Right where I want you."

"No problem. I'll sit on the crate." She scrambled to her feet. Being on her knees was a definite downer. What was next—a bullet in the head? Her stomach roiled at the thought. The woman had already killed once and wouldn't hesitate to kill again. Why couldn't she just keep her smart mouth shut instead of popping off and antagonizing her?

Was this sick feeling in her stomach anything like what Meryl felt before a butcher's knife plunged into her abdomen? Had she pleaded for her life and that of her baby? Had she even had time? No point in reliving what her friend had gone through. Although, the way things looked, she hadn't had much time.

"Have you thought this through? Shouldn't you check with your husband? He might not appreciate having to help you dispose of two bodies."

"Shut up!" Ivers shrieked. "I need to think." She waved the gun around unsteadily. "*Don't* tell me what to do. My husband's good at that. This is *my* problem, and I'll solve it myself."

"Really? You haven't seen controlling until you meet my brothers. I'm the youngest at home, so everyone tries to tell me what to do too. I really understand how you feel, and I hate it as much as you do." She'd say anything to build a bond with her captor, however tenuous.

"Shut up!" The semi-crazed woman put her hands to her head, then seemed to remember one of them still held a gun. "He's going to be so mad. He was furious last time I went out and did something spontaneous on my own."

"And were your spontaneous efforts productive?"

"Yeah. Your friend—that nurse—was on him about his transplant case statistics. But killing her wasn't a good idea. Besides, that's not why I killed her. It was an accident. A mistake, y'know?"

"A mistake?" Allison's stomach heaved, but she managed

to swallow back the nausea. One of life's cruelties.

"He was playing doctor with the other tall blonde. He couldn't fool me about that. She wasn't his first either."

"I've never been one to poach other women's husbands. I don't blame you for being upset. It just isn't right."

Ivers got down in Allison's face. "Oh, butter won't melt in your mouth now. I see what you're up to, but you're worse than your stupid friend. The hospital administrators are digging into his records now. If he can't talk his way out of it, he'll have to go to some godforsaken place like Mexico or some third world country to practice medicine after this. Singlehandedly, you've ruined his career."

She continued to rant. "We had a nice comfortable life here. The children are settled on their own and..."

The woman seemed to lose her train of thought but then recovered. "It's all your fault. But I think he'll want to be the one to take care of you himself. When he saw the paper this morning, he was so mad I thought for a minute he was going to have a stroke. I've never seen him so mad, except the day when I told him about my little oopsie."

Allison squared her shoulders and resisted the strong temptation to rush the woman for the gun. "You call murdering a woman and her unborn child an oopsie?" Figuring she'd said too much, she clenched her jaw to keep from saying something else which would get her killed. And if Harriet Ivers would just call her husband... He was Allison's last chance. If he had any sense at all, he'd have the sense to keep his wife from becoming a double murderer. Then too, maybe someone could ping the crazy woman's cell phone and get a location.

"Yes. Call him. Let *him* make the decision."

"I get it. You think he might be more reasonable? Forget it. You're not his type."

"No, I'm not a tall blonde—that's for sure." His wife

wasn't his type either. She'd had money. No doubt about it. Too bad the woman was nutty as a pecan pie and getting nuttier by the minute.

The sky was dark and getting darker by the minute as Nick took the exit onto I-440 and immediately regretted it. All lanes were blocked. He turned up the volume on his police scanner and discovered a semi had jackknifed, blocking all but half a lane over the Cumberland River overpass. To make things worse, a tornado watch had been in place all afternoon.

"Fuck!" He was a mile from the next exit. With no way out, he swore under his breath. Crap. Stuck in the far left lane, he was in no position to work his way over to the next exit. Instead, he pounded the steering wheel.

That crazy bitch had taken Allison. No telling if she was still alive or not.

Why in hell hadn't she called him or one of her brothers to go meet the doctor's wife? Why hadn't she used her common sense? Screw it. He was getting nowhere fast. He flicked on his right turn signal and started inching over into the next lane of nonmoving traffic. The nearest driver laid on his horn.

"Shut the fuck up!' Nick jammed his middle finger in the air.

Next thing Nick knew, the driver was jumping out, ready to fight. Nick jumped out too. Hell, the cars weren't moving. Might as well take care of this joker here and now.

"I'm in the middle of an emergency," he said, trying to reason with the red-faced semi giant before using his fists.

"Fuck you. And your emergency." The guy swung. Nick ducked and landed a fist in his opponent's gut. The guy staggered back a step, then lumbered forward.

"Listen, bozo. My girlfriend's been kidnapped, and I'm trying to get to her. So, unless you want to take this downtown, you need to let me over."

The guy took another swing, this time landing a glancing blow on Nick's chin. Apparently, clearer heads were not going to prevail.

"Look, dude." Nick clenched his fists. "I don't want to hurt ya, but I will if I have to."

Before the hothead could respond, Nick heard the *woop-woop-woop* of a patrol car. Another blue light was easing onto the scene along the far right shoulder. Two unis emerged. Nick took a step back and held up his hands, showing he wasn't holding a weapon.

"Just so you know, I'm a PI and licensed to carry," he said. "My girlfriend's been kidnapped, and this guy didn't want to let me over. I've got to find another route to Goodlettsville."

"Kidnapping?" the younger officer said with a skeptical frown.

"Check with Detective O'Malley. Allison Lackey was kidnapped an hour ago. Should already be a BOLO on the kidnapper's vehicle."

The younger officer nodded. "Right. So, what've you got to do with it?"

"She's my girlfriend."

"And Goodlettsville?"

"I'm working a hunch," Nick admitted. "But gridlock and"—he nodded at the not-so-gentle giant—"this guy, in particular, are holding me back."

The older of the two officers, a tall and burly sandy-haired man, scowled at the hothead. "You ready to cool off? Or do you want some help with that?"

The other driver's gaze shifted from one uni to the other. He took a breath, then ducked his head. "Sorry."

"We'll get your vehicle over to the shoulder and escort you to the next exit."

It took a good ten minutes just to work his car to the shoulder and another five to the 28th Avenue exit.

Fifteen minutes felt like an hour and could make all the difference in life or death for Allie. Finally. He accelerated down Jefferson, heading for the Jefferson Street Bridge.

All he had to do now was keep from getting pulled over for speeding.

Allison crossed her fingers, hoping Harriet Ivers would place the call to her husband. Even if he couldn't talk some sense into his demented wife, at least either Justin or Metro would be able to ping her cell phone. That way it wouldn't take too long for the authorities to find her body...if matters progressed that far. And she was anything but certain of how far the Ivers woman might take things. She'd already killed once.

She cringed as the woman reached her husband and began yelling, "I'm doing this for *you*. She's the one who's responsible for ruining your reputation. She deserves to *die*." The last word ended with a piercing shriek.

Allison's mouth grew cotton-ball dry. She tried to control her breathing but wasn't having much success. Panic mode had taken over.

"All right. All right. I'll wait until you get here. But, Morty, she's getting on my last nerve. She's a real smart-ass, and you know how I *hate* people like that."

He must've been trying to calm her down because she stopped her tirade and took a couple of deep breaths. "Okay, are you happy? I'm calmer now. Much calmer."

She might claim to be calmer, but from Allison's point of view, it didn't appear to be the case. The woman was still red-faced and tense. She clomped around the room, her fat, Nike-clad feet stirring up clouds of dust in her wake.

Perspiration started to trickle between Allison's shoulder blades. At the end of summer, Nashville was freaking hot, and the lack of any air circulation made for a stifling setting. Perfect. The conditions were ripe for her captor to whip herself into a menopausal hot flash if she wasn't careful.

Whether *Morty* could get here in time to talk his wife out of another murder... Well, it wasn't anything Allison would want to bet money on.

And once he got here, would he even try to keep his wife from killing her or go ahead and assist her with another body dump? The doc couldn't be as nutty as his wife. The man might be arrogant as all get-out, but he'd have to see reason and talk his wife down from her high perch on Hysteria Lane.

"Okay. Thanks, Justin." Nick punched the Disconnect button and eased the Bronco onto the I-65, I-24 strip. Keeping to the middle left lane, he aimed his vehicle for the spot where the two Interstates split. Left to I-24 and Clarksville, and I-65 to the right, his destination. At the beginning of the Friday afternoon rush, traffic was already getting heavy. The heat of Nashville's summer sun beat down mercilessly on the black roof of the SUV. He reached over and shoved the AC as high as it would go. High wasn't high enough, but it'd have to do.

He glanced in the rearview mirror. Behind him, however, the sky had darkened. Storms in Middle Tennessee had a nasty habit of turning into tornadoes when a cold front moved in on top of a hot and humid day, like today.

His phone rang, or rather his phone sang—country-western tune, of course.

"Vitelli," he answered, keeping his gaze on the road ahead.

"The doc has skipped out on us," Tess said, "just ahead of the search warrant. We haven't found anything incriminating in his office, but forensics is going over all the office and home computers."

"If you'd just let him, I'm sure Justin could give them his undivided attention."

"Yeah, but that's not going to happen. Chain of evidence, et cetera." Tess paused, then asked, "How's Justin doing on the country tax records?"

"He's making some headway. Ivers owns several rental properties in Williamson County, in addition to Davidson, but they haven't found anything in either of their names in Sumner."

"Tell Justin to check for property owned by their relatives or under the wife's maiden name."

"Will do."

Sweat collected between Allison's shoulders and ran down her back into the waist of her jeans. More and more, the longer the two women waited for Dr. Ivers to arrive, the old farmhouse resembled a not-so-easy-bake oven.

Still holding the gun, Harriet reached with her free hand into her huge designer bag and pulled out a bottle of water. Smiling, she managed to twist off the cap, then lifted it to her thin lips and guzzled half the bottle at one go. Allison tried to moisten her lips but was too dehydrated to work up any saliva.

"I bet you'd like some of this, wouldn't you?" Harriet sneered and set the bottle out of her reach.

She shrugged. "Whatever gave you that idea? I'm fine."

"I might give you a swallow if Morty says to let you go.

But he won't—you meddled in his business once too often."

Without warning, the room darkened. Allison heard the wind pick up as it rustled through the old oak trees surrounding the farmhouse. Was it going to storm? An afternoon storm wouldn't hurt. At least it might cool off the house a bit.

"How much longer?" Allison asked. Someone had missed her by now. Hopefully, Nick and her family were turning over every rock in Davidson County to find her. Too bad she was in Sumner County.

"If he left when I told him to, then he should be here in forty-five minutes or an hour. Depends on the traffic." Harriet's upper lip lifted. "Why? Are you so anxious to meet your maker?"

"The sooner your husband gets here and tells you to let me go, the better. He won't want to get into any more trouble than he already is with the transplant program...and the police. Actually, I guess he's not guilty of anything too awful."

She continued babbling, "Mainly, there's his mistreatment of a corpse and, of course, being an accessory after the fact. They can't make him testify against you since you're married. *You* might even get off with manslaughter." Not likely, but if Allison could talk her way out of this situation, she was determined to give it the old college try.

Nick had just driven past the Madison exit when his cell phone rang again. Using the phone's Bluetooth receiver, he answered.

Without wasting words, Justin gave him an update...and an address in Sumner County.

"Thanks."

All right. Things were starting to move. Justin Lackey

was worth his weight in computer chips. The agency's computer guru had discovered Harriet Ivers's maiden name, Covington. Further research had determined her paternal grandmother was still alive and owned a farm in Sumner County, less than a mile from where Meryl Litton's body had been dumped. He entered the address into his GPS navigation system. According to Justin's digging, Mrs. Ivers's grandmother was in a Hendersonville nursing home, and the farm was deserted. The property was listed as containing a barn, several outbuildings, *and* an old farmhouse.

If Allison was still alive, that was where she'd be. He'd bet his life on it.

No. The stakes were higher. He was betting *her* life.

Overhead, the sky darkened. Rain pounded the top of the Bronco, sounding like flamenco dancers having a field day. Visibility sucked. Nick slowed and stopped. Shaking his head, he beat the steering wheel with his fist.

At this rate, he'd never make it to the Covington farm.

Allison was depending on him. He had to find her before it was too late.

A sharp crack of thunder shattered the oppressive quiet. Allison jumped. "That was close," she murmured, remembering the large grove of oaks surrounding the small farmhouse.

"Scared of a little storm?" Her captor lifted her lip in an Elvis-like snarl. On the late singer, it had worked. On Harriet, not so much.

"We *do* live in tornado alley. And there was a tornado watch announced for this afternoon."

"The weathermen don't know anything. They just guess."

"They track these storms on radar." God. The woman was

dense.

Rain started pelting down. No, it sounded more like pellets of hail.

Another flash of light was rapidly followed by a crash of thunder. "Really close that time," Allison said. Expecting lightning to strike her freaking kidnapper was too much to hope for. Yet such an occurrence would take out her unfortunate victim as well.

Harriet walked over to the grimy window, rubbed a spot clean, and peered outside. "Doesn't look too good out there. The sky's really scary. Morty, where are you?" the woman muttered.

Allison couldn't resist. "What's the matter? Afraid of a little storm?"

"Shut up!" Harriet stomped over to Allison, who was still perched on the orange crate. "If he wasn't already so mad at me for killing that stupid nurse, I'd have gotten rid of you before now."

"Good for old Morty." Allison crossed one leg over the other. "He's just trying to make the best out of a bad situation. You're the one who's really screwed the pooch. You're going to prison, for sure."

"Not if I leave you here to rot and get out of the country." Ivers nodded and smiled, her beady brown eyes alight with anticipation. "Yes, I can go to one of those countries without an extradition treaty. People do it all the time."

"Maybe the people you know do." Allison shrugged. "Personally, I don't think you have much chance of getting out of Nashville, much less the country."

"I've had enough of your smart mouth." Harriet waved the gun around so crazily there was a good chance she'd shoot herself.

Or me.

Chapter Twenty-eight

The wind blew, rattling the windows in their frames. Continuous flashes of lightning brightened the darkening sky. Allison cringed with each crack of thunder. The rain came in gusts so fierce it sounded like a small hurricane was imminent. She glanced around the room. She would've loved to have something to duck under in case the weather got even worse.

"How about checking your phone for a weather report?" Allison suggested. No surprise her captor was unprepared for such eventualities as a tornado. At that, she shivered. This ramshackle house wouldn't provide any kind of protection.

For a moment, Ivers continued staring out the window, then turned to Allison and glared. "Why bother? Before this night is over, one of us is going to be dead for sure."

It wasn't difficult to figure out which "one" Harriet meant. "I advise waiting until your husband gets here. I bet he wasn't any too happy with your last escapade." Escapade? Call it by its right name. Murder.

"So what?" She smiled. "He's my husband, and he still helped me get rid of the body."

Before Allison could form an appropriate response, the front door crashed open and Dr. Ivers staggered inside, the water pouring off his clothes onto the floor. The wind blew so hard, it took all his strength to shut the door. "We've got to get out of here. There are tornado warnings all over."

"Good afternoon to you too, Dr. Ivers," Allison said.

"Believe it or not, I'm glad to see you."

He turned from his wife, giving Allison a sharp look. "The feeling isn't mutual, Ms. Lackey. Your inquisitive nature has made things a bit difficult for me at the hospital."

"Imagine that. Sorry." Okay, she lied, but it was time to play nice with this couple of psychos.

He strutted from one side of the living room to the other. "Nurses talking to reporters. Unconscionable."

"What *you* were doing was unconscionable but pales compared to what your wife did. Murder. And now kidnapping. This won't end well for her."

The physician who supposedly believed in "First, do no harm" clenched his fists. "Keep your mouth shut or it won't end well for you either."

"Morty, don't listen to her." His wife waved the gun around, inadvertently pointing it at him.

"Watch what you're doing with that thing. Here." He reached for her gun. "Let me have it."

Clutching the weapon to her chest, Harriet backed away. "No. It's mine."

"Harriet, give it to me *right now.*"

At least the doc wasn't going to put up with his wife's craziness. Hope blossomed—okay, it was a tiny blossom—in her chest. Maybe she would live through this after all.

"Fine." Harriet stomped over and shoved the gun into his ribs. "You know I ought to shoot you too. I'm tired of your playing around."

The doctor grabbed his wife's wrist and twisted the gun from her hand.

"Ow! You hurt me." Her bottom lip went out in a pout.

"Don't you *ever* threaten me again." He kept hold of her wrist. "You're in trouble. I barely got out of the office before Metro descended on it. While I can't be *forced* to testify, I can *agree* to."

"Morty, you wouldn't." She tried to pull away.

"I would."

Allison groaned. "For Pete's sake, can someone please change the channel? This soap opera you have going on is starting to get boring." Okay, why couldn't she keep from spouting off just once? Honestly, they were the most dysfunctional couple she'd seen.

The physician snapped his attention from his wife to Allison. "I was of a mind to just leave you here while my wife and I made a speedy exit from Middle Tennessee."

"Was? That's past tense."

"*Now* I'm of a mind to shut you up for good."

Despite the sick sensation gathering in the pit of her stomach, she couldn't resist offering a bit of advice. "Don't be too hasty. If the weather gets any worse, you might want to take cover, because this old farmhouse might just blow us all to kingdom come or Oz, whichever you prefer."

The doctor stopped and cocked his head, appearing to listen to the increasing pitch of the wind.

"Unless I'm mistaken," she continued, "that train-like sound only means one thing." Aiming to get away from the window, she hit the floor and crawled toward the wall, pulling the orange crate with her for whatever shelter it could provide.

The wind intensified to an earsplitting screech. Windows on the west side of the house blew in, raining shards of glass all around. Ducking behind the crate, she covered her head with her hands, but not before a sliver sliced her cheek with a beelike sting, and another pierced her arm. She winced. The backs of her hands stung from a fine shower of glass splinters. Blood trickled onto her neck, leaving a trail of warmth. The farmhouse shuddered on its foundation. With a torturous groan, the walls seemed to suck inward. Her eardrums popped while the walls exploded outward.

The ceiling collapsed, timbers falling like toothpicks. The last thing Allison heard was an eerie scream from the doctor's wife.

As more and more motorists pulled off the road, Nick took his chances and stayed on the Interstate. As he drove by the Rivergate Mall exit, the rain began to let up. More traffic, but visibility had improved. Just ahead was the Long Hollow Pike exit.

Closer. So much closer to finding Allison than he'd been before.

After taking the exit, he turned right and headed over the winding road toward Gallatin. Another seven miles and he'd reach the Covington farm.

Overhead, the sky was a dark, murky green, the color often associated with tornadoes. Grimacing, he turned on the police scanner he'd installed in his Bronco when he was still in Atlanta. *Brief tornado touchdown in West Nashville near West Meade Elementary.* Damn, a school. *No serious damage.* He breathed a sigh of relief. At least it wasn't Ben's school.

Before he could hear more, his phone sang again. "Vitelli."

"It's Tess. We've notified the Sumner County sheriff's department. They've dispatched backup, but they're being held up by the storm. And if there's a touchdown, all bets are off."

"What you're saying is there's no backup."

"Basically." She sighed, "They'll get there eventually, but the roads and traffic are a mess."

"You're telling *me*? I just left I-65. I'm on Long Hollow Pike." Without warning, a tree blew down ahead of him, blocking part of the road. Slamming on his brakes just in time, he managed to skirt it. "My ETA depends on the weather too." For the time being, he still had cell service.

"Careful. This mess is headed your way," she said. "Gotta go. Got another reported touchdown."

"Roger that."

Tess disconnected.

Focus.

Without warning, the sky blackened as if it were night. Holy shit. The wind built into a steady scream. The clouds enveloped his vehicle. Tree branches flew overhead. Debris hit his windshield along with the loud rattle of hail. He braked and jumped out. Leaping into the nearest ditch, he covered his head with his hands. And waited.

The crack of trees falling. Glass breaking. Crap. His Bronco must've taken a hit.

After what seemed like an hour, the wind diminished to a dull roar. Nick raised his head and surveyed his surroundings. Trees had been flattened, and those not flattened had no leaves.

The Bronco lay on its side in the opposite ditch. He swore. He'd never get it upright without a tow truck. Unsure how far the farm was from his current location, he blew a puff of air. No point in calling 911. Emergency vehicles would be involved with accidents and injuries. His royally fucked-up SUV wouldn't be high on anyone's priority list. He'd just have to hoof it to the farm.

He patted his holster. At least he still had his weapon. Better check the Bronco for more ammo.

He picked his way through storm debris to cross the road, climbed on top, and yanked open the driver's side door. He slid down into the vehicle. There was another box of ammo in the glove box. Shoving the box into his jacket pocket, he turned on the motor to see if the GPS was still working. Luckily, it was. Another three and a half miles as the crow flew, but he wasn't sure enough of his map reading skills to go cross-country. Another five miles at least if he followed the road.

He grabbed his Maglite and, as a precaution, two pairs of zip-tie cuffs, then climbed from the SUV and jumped down. If anything had happened to Allie, he'd never forgive himself.

Get it done. Time's a-wasting.

By the time Nick reached the Covington farm—or what he hoped like hell was the Covington farm—night was falling. He'd followed a trail of devastation as he headed to where he expected he'd find Allison. If she wasn't there, he doubted he'd find her tonight. He pulled the Maglite from his pocket and lit up the road ahead. He could just make out a mailbox, but the likelihood of it being anywhere near its correct address was slim. He kicked it over to read the address.

Just as he figured. It listed a Madison street address, a bedroom community between Nashville and Goodlettsville.

He shuddered. She could be anywhere. Minute by minute, the chances of finding her seemed more remote.

Sweat drenched his back. He slowed his pace long enough to wipe the salty moisture dripping into his eyes.

The landscape was utterly changed on his left, while on the right, he could just make out the outlines of an occasional house or barn against the darkening night sky.

In the distance, a dog howled. Somehow, the creature had survived the storm. It stood to reason Allison could've too...

According to the GPS on his phone, the farm was nearby. Just beyond the range of his flashlight, he caught sight of a chimney, half blown down by the storm.

His heart rate shot up. Up ahead, a tree had fallen over a couple of vehicles. He picked up his pace, running for all he was worth. He pulled back the branches and revealed one vehicle he didn't recognize, but the other he knew. It was Harriet Ivers's Escalade, the one she'd forced Allie into earlier.

"Allie!" Where was she? He climbed over the old oak and shined the Maglite light over the rubble. "Allie..." His heart felt as if it might rip from his chest.

There was no way she could've survived. Not a single wall stood. Part of the chimney jutted upward. He propped his flashlight on the oak's trunk so it would illuminate the scene. For digging, he'd need both hands.

She had to be alive. Had to be.

He threw brick after brick to the side, then lifted a section of roofing. About half the structure was missing, blown who knew where.

A rusty nail scraped his hand. "Shit." This job needed heavy gloves. He wiped his bleeding hand on his jeans. He'd worry about tetanus later.

He heaved another beam and discovered Allie's body lying in an open triangular space created by the falling ceiling.

So still. So quiet.

He placed two fingers on her neck, feeling for a sign of life. A weak but steady pulse. "Allie," he said, more gently this time. He glanced around. Where were the Iverses? Not that he gave a crap if they survived, but if they were alive, they could still cause him grief.

He gathered her limp body into his arms and pulled her from the rubble. In the beam cast from his Maglite, he noted a bump on her forehead, in addition to her other cuts and bruises. A concussion at the least. "Allie, darlin'. Wake up."

No response. His heart bottomed out. He swallowed

back the bile rising in his throat. He had to get her to the ER. Still cradling her in his arms, he straightened up, then climbed over the farmhouse debris.

Someone groaned, but it wasn't the woman he held so carefully in his arms. Another groan. This one deeper—a man's voice. Dr. Ivers?

The doc could rot for all Nick cared, and his freak-ass crazy wife as well.

Damn them both. Skyline Medical Center was miles away. And without an operating vehicle, he'd never get her to the ER on foot. She could die right here, right now, in his arms.

"Help. Please help me." A woman's plaintive whine came from somewhere under the rubble.

He stopped. "You're shit out of luck, lady." He spat the words. Who did she think he was—emergency services? He was just a man whose best girl might be dying. But his old vow to "protect and serve" ran too deep to ignore the other two victims, no matter what they'd done or who they'd done it to.

"Help's coming," he said, hoping he spoke the truth.

But first, he had to take care of Allie.

Chapter Twenty-nine

Back in the Holt Investigations office, Caroline paced back and forth, stopping to peer out the window. The worst of the storm seemed over. A light rain was falling and the sky seemed clearer, given a twister had hip-hopped over most of downtown on its way east. "Why haven't we heard anything?"

Leaning against the doorjamb, Justin brushed back his longish hair. "My guess is Nick's stranded somewhere on his way to the farm. Tess said the last time she heard from him, he was somewhere on the Long Hollow Pike. The twister ripped through the area right after that." He glanced over his shoulder at the TV in his office.

"So, no one's looking for Allison?" Scott emerged from his office, shaking his head. "That won't do. Let's close the office. We'll have to find her ourselves."

"The authorities are overwhelmed with calls. There's no way they can focus on finding our sister," Tamsyn said.

"We'll split up," Scott said. "Tamsyn comes with me. Justin, you go with Carrie—I don't want to risk her getting lost out in Sumner County all alone. No telling what we'll face. Looters even."

Caroline bristled at her brother's patronizing statement. "Hold on. Just because I have trouble remembering a few things, I can still find my way around Sumner County just fine." Her ex-fiancé's parents had lived in Hendersonville.

Scott flushed. "Sorry. I didn't mean anything by it. I just don't want any of my sisters out alone in the aftermath of this storm.

Caroline nodded. "Apology accepted."

Justin warned, "Cell phone coverage will be spotty. I have a couple of sat phones we can use to communicate."

"And we'll need first aid supplies in case anyone's hurt," Tamsyn said, voicing the least of their fears.

"Right. Check the storeroom," Caroline said. "Allie stocked us with enough medical supplies to outfit an ER. She's a bit of a survivalist in that respect. I just hope..." She faltered, unable to go on. Allison was tough. But tough enough to withstand a kidnapping and a tornado in the same freaking day?

Tamsyn returned laden with two large bags bulging with supplies. "Each group will take one," she said, handing one to Caroline.

"Are we going armed?" Caroline asked, thinking more about Allie's kidnapper than looters.

"Does a tornado always hit a trailer park?" Justin quipped.

"Justin," Caroline groaned. "How can you be so callous? Who knows what's happened to Allie or Nick."

Justin's reaction was a shrug and an eye roll.

"Yes. We're going armed," Scott said in his usual no-nonsense manner. "At least Justin and I are."

"Hey. I'm licensed to carry too." Tamsyn patted her sidearm.

Justin gestured. "Let's roll."

Nick laid Allie on the most solid section of the roof he could find. He covered her slender body with his jacket to protect her from the light rain still falling. "Allie? Open your eyes. Enough playing around. You're starting to scare me."

A muscle in her face tightened, then another. Her lids

fluttered. He blew out a sigh of relief. "That's my girl. You're gonna be all right."

"I take it you're no longer a PI. You're a doctor? Good deal."

"Now I *know* you're going to be all right."

She pushed up to her elbows. "Ouch."

"Where are you hurting?"

"All over."

"Try not to move. You have shards of glass in the backs of your hands. Your face is cut."

"I'm okay. Nothing's broken except maybe my head. Man, it hurts like a son of a bitch."

From behind him, Nick heard the sounds of one of the Iverses trying to dig out from the rubble. "Hold on," he ordered. "The police are on their way." He hoped this statement was true too.

"I've got to get you out of the rain."

"Yeah, I might catch my death," she quipped, shivering.

He didn't mind her smart mouth. As long as she could bust his chops, he knew she'd survive. "Try not to move. You'll just embed those splinters deeper."

"Yes, sir. Detective, sir."

He clambered over the remains of the farmhouse and examined the two vehicles. The doctor's Jag was crushed beyond salvage, but the Escalade was in much better shape since only the upper, outer branches had fallen on it. True, the window screen was shattered into a crystalline web of safety glass. He could fix that all right. He wrapped his jacket around his hand, punched through the safety glass, pulled it from the frame then tossed it on the ground.

The key was still in the ignition. Would it run? With luck, he'd be able to back it out. He opened the door and started the motor. On hearing the engine's steady purr, hope surged in his chest, then plummeted. No response when he turned on the headlights. Fuck. No way could he drive on dark, storm-littered streets in an unlighted vehicle. But if on foot was the only way to get her to the hospital, he'd have to chance it.

In the meantime, he could at least get her out of the rain.

He ran back to her side. "I'm going to put you in the SUV. It's not drivable, but at least you won't *catch your death*," he teased.

He picked her up and started toward the Escalade. Her body shook in his arms, whether from shock or chill, he didn't know.

The doctor rose from the rubble, weaving unsteadily, faced Nick, and raised his fists. "You're not taking her anywhere."

Nick assessed the smaller man and shook his head in disbelief. "Seriously?" He raised his knee and *encouraged* the physician with his foot to have a seat.

"Morty, help me." The plaintive cry came from beneath the wreckage.

"Great. Another country heard from." Nick continued with his original mission—getting Allie somewhere dry. He opened the Escalade's passenger door and eased her inside the vehicle. "You're gonna be all right. I've gotta deal with these two." More than anything, he wanted to just hold her in his arms, but there was still too much to do.

"Don't worry," she said. "I still can't believe you found me. At first, I thought I was dreaming."

"It's no dream, more like a nightmare. I'll be back."

Nick shut the car door, then walked back over to Ivers. "Hands behind your back," he ordered, then pulled out a pair of zip-tie cuffs and proceeded to restrain the doctor.

Ivers gave a rude grunt. "I don't know who the hell you think you are, but you have no right to treat me like this."

"I'll tell you who the hell I am. I'm Nick Vitelli. I'm a PI and a former cop. And what I'm doing is making a citizen's arrest."

"What charges?" the doctor demanded, bristling with anger.

"Kidnapping. You and your wife both."

"But I didn't—" the other man protested.

"The police can sort out what you did or didn't do."

"But I'm injured. Glass all over me. I could bleed to death from all these cuts."

"And as soon as I can get hold of 911, you'll be attended to."

"What about me?" Mrs. Ivers asked with a whimper. "I'm hurt...bad."

"Hold on, ma'am." He whipped out another set of zip ties. He made his way to the spot where he heard her voice, dragged away another part of the roof, then stopped.

Holy shit.

"Ma'am, don't move. I'll get you some help right away." He slipped the cuffs inside his back pocket. The woman wasn't going anywhere—not with a large shard of glass protruding from her gut.

Allison reclined in the Escalade, on the verge of dozing off now that the heater was warming her chilled body.

Nick rapped on the side window. "Allie, the doctor's wife has a foot-long sliver of glass in her belly. What do I do? Remove it and apply pressure?"

Alarmed, Allison straightened. "No! She'll hemorrhage." Not that the bitch didn't deserve to bleed out. Fitting. Karmic even.

"You *have* to go for help," she said. "What about your cell phone?"

He glanced at his phone. "No bars."

"You have to find some way or someone who can get her to the hospital. It sounds like she really needs a level-one trauma center. And in Nashville, that's Vandy. What happened to your Bronco?"

"It's lying on its side. I had to abandon it when the twister struck and jump for cover in a ditch. Barely made it."

She struggled to open her door, but a wave of dizziness hit her. She collapsed back in the seat.

"You're not going anywhere."

"But Mrs. Ivers needs my help." Like Meryl needed help but no one came to her rescue. But Allison was a nurse down to her DNA. She couldn't just abandon the woman to her fate, no matter how much she deserved it.

"Some of the houses I passed are still standing. They don't look like they took much damage. I'll have to borrow one of their cars. Steal one if I have to."

"And worry about it later? Sounds like a plan to me."

"You have to do something for my wife," the doctor shouted. "She's dying."

Nick shouted back, "I'm going to find another vehicle."

"That's the best you can do?"

"'Fraid so."

"Then remove these handcuffs," the doctor begged. "I won't leave her like this. I need to hold her hand. No matter what she's done, she's still my wife."

"Even if he runs, he's finished as a doctor," Allison said. "Let him go." Actually, she didn't feel quite so humanitarian. But apparently, there was still some feeling—call it love, whatever—between the two.

Nick left Allie and clambered over the debris once more and cut the disposable cuffs, releasing the doctor so he could comfort his dying wife.

He watched the doctor, tears streaming down his face, hold his wife's hand. Nick clenched his jaw. How fair was it the doctor's wife had someone to hold her hand while she died when Meryl Litton and her baby had died without so much as a sorry-wrong-nurse apology? He'd given up on finding any kind of grand scheme in life. He'd seen too much. Basically, all it boiled down to life wasn't fair. Sometimes—too many times—the bad guys won, and the good guys didn't. But as long as he could, he'd keep on trying to even the odds.

"Morty, help me. Do something," Mrs. Ivers pleaded, her voice growing weaker.

"I wish I could," Ivers said. "If we could just get you to a hospital, but it's too dangerous to move you."

"So, I'm just supposed to die here in the middle of nowhere? I'm wet, and I'm so cold."

Definitely, everything was about *her*. The doctor patted his wife's hand and looked up, his eyes pleading. "Help may come in time. Hold on, hon."

"I'm sorry I got us in this mess."

But was she sorry about killing Meryl Litton and her baby? He'd never seen such a self-centered woman.

"You went off your meds again, didn't you?"

"Y-yes. But you had no business fooling around with that nurse. It was too late when I realized I'd stabbed the wrong one. I had to finish her off." She moaned. "I'm such a screwup."

Still, everything was all about her, and not a single expression of remorse for killing a mother and her unborn baby. Nick clenched his fists at his sides, almost wishing he were the kind of person who could just reach over and yank that piece of glass from her belly and watch her bleed out.

Chapter Thirty

"Thank God for GPS," Caroline said, straining to see in the blackest night she'd ever experienced. "I can't believe how different this all looks now." While most of Nashville's downtown was still flooded with light, out here in the boonies...

"You're doing fine with the GPS," Justin said.

"Yeah, as long as I don't run over someone or power lines...or hit a freaking tree." Her mind raced with the possibilities. None of which were pretty.

"Just calm down, sis." Justin patted her shoulder.

"No road signs. No lights. No nothing."

"We're almost there. The GPS says it's less than a mile to the Covington farm."

"But I don't know if we can make it another mile. The closer we get, the worse the damage is. I just can't imagine how that old farmhouse could withstand a tornado. You saw the place in the satellite photo. It looked as if it were being held up with paper clips and Elmer's glue."

"Allie's tough. She'll be all right. You'll see."

"You're just saying that. Call Scott on the satellite phone. I can't see their lights behind us anymore. Make sure they're okay."

"Yes, ma'am." Justin chuckled, though what he found so amusing, she didn't know. "Holt car two, come in."

Justin chuckled again. "Carrie thought we'd lost you. What's your twenty?" He listened for a moment, then said,

"They're a half-mile back. Don't worry, they're still on our six."

"Honestly," Caroline said, still straining to see ahead. "Stop fooling around like you're military special ops. Six? Twenty? Please translate for this civilian."

"Twenty means what's your location. They had to wait on some local LEOs directing an ambulance through the last intersection. Just keep your eyes on the road and don't worry about them."

"What the...? Something must be wrong with the GPS. It says we're here and there's nothing but... The farmhouse is gone," Caroline wailed.

Hands trembling on the steering wheel, she pulled into what was left of the driveway, braking to a stop.

High beams from an approaching vehicle cut across the periphery of Nick's vision. Hope surged. They might get Mrs. Ivers to a hospital after all.

In the still of the night, Caroline's voice rang out shrill as the chime of a church bell. "Where's Allison? I don't see her."

Allison's sister jumped from the Ford Explorer. A second car door slammed, and Nick made out Justin's lanky frame in the beams from the headlights. "Dude, where's Allison?"

Nick jerked his head to his left. "She's in the Escalade."

"Where?" Caroline cried. "A tree fell on her?"

"I'm all right," Allison called from the Escalade. "It's not as bad as it looks."

By this time, a second vehicle had driven onto the property. Scott and Tamsyn, no doubt. Finally, enough help. "Sure am glad to see you guys. Mrs. Ivers needs a hospital in the worst way."

"She needs to be life-flighted to Vandy," Allison yelled.

Small chance of that happening, Nick thought. Time to take charge. He turned to Caroline. "Why don't you stay with Allison. We've got to get Mrs. Ivers into one of the Explorers. We can move her on this section of the roof."

"These the people who kidnapped Allison?" Tamsyn set her hands on her hips. "Why on earth are we helping them? I'd like to—" She fisted her hands and planted her feet apart.

Caroline interrupted with a calm, "Tam, you'd better stay with Allison. I'll help with Mrs. Ivers."

Justin ambled around the Explorer, holding out one of the satellite phones. "Since cell service is out, we've been using these. Now that we have a location, we can contact the Tennessee Emergency Management Agency, if that woman's really hurt as bad as you think."

"She is." Nick nodded, then pointed at Justin. "Fine. You take care of communications with TEMA."

Justin gave a quick nod of agreement and walked several paces away, distancing himself from the action.

"Now let's get Mrs. Ivers out of the rain and into the back of one of your vehicles."

In tandem, Nick, Scott, Caroline, and the doctor moved his wife onto the makeshift stretcher and slid her inside the back of Scott's SUV. "Keep an eye on him." Nick jerked his head toward the physician.

"Will do," Scott said, then added, "Then move Allie into the other SUV, will you?"

Caroline nodded.

Justin returned to the group, beaming. "I reached TEMA. They'll send an EMS unit and a chopper."

The Goodlettsville patrol unit showed up first. A tall police officer, who was pale, drawn, and overwhelmed, exited the patrol car. "What's the trouble here?"

Nick and Scott took turns explaining about Allison's kidnapping. "Contact Detective Tess O'Malley at Metro."

Officer James nodded. "We were aware of the BOLO, but I've had a hell of a time getting here. We've had an entire subdivision wiped off the map."

"We also have a kidnapper who's been impaled with glass," Nick said. "Once she's on the way to Vanderbilt, we'll take Ms. Lackey to Skyline ourselves. She needs to be checked out for a head injury."

"No, you won't," Allison called, now from the backseat of the Explorer. "All I need is for someone to wake me up every two hours and ask me a series of questions. Check my pupils and all that. Skyline is bound to be swamped. I'm not about to compound their problems with my simple concussion."

"Nurses and doctors make the worst patients," Scott said, shaking his head. "All right, home it is. We'll take care of you, but the first wrong answer and you're going to the ER. Deal?"

"Deal." She nodded.

The EMS unit arrived and set about stabilizing Allie's kidnapper. By the time the IV was hooked up, the air overhead filled with the unmistakable sound of a helicopter. As soon as it landed, the Ivers woman was loaded inside.

After the chopper took off, Nick breathed a sigh of relief, glad he no longer bore any responsibility for her well-being. He headed over to check on Allison, the one woman he cared about—now she was another basket of fruit. "I'll sit with her all night, whatever you all need," he told Scott. After coming so close to losing her, he wasn't about to let her out of his sight anytime soon.

Allison smiled, holding up her bloody hands. "But what about all these splinters? Are you going to play nurse with them too?" she teased.

"I'll take care of those," Caroline said, giving her a reassuring hug. "I have more experience with tweezers."

Nick nodded. "I won't argue the point. But I'm sitting up

with her tonight. Y'all can rest easy."

Taking care with her hands, Allison slipped her arms around his neck. "I'm just so glad you found me. How did you?"

"It was all Justin. He carried the main load. He found Mrs. Ivers's maiden name in the county records. Then he located the deed for this property still owned by her grandmother. All I did was follow my gut. This place was too close to where they found your friend not to be the one."

"My hero." She closed her eyes and lay her head against his shoulder.

His heart surged with an emotion he hadn't felt in years—love. Finding her before it was too late had been a miracle. Just as finding love again was another miracle.

"No place like home." Allison slipped between the cool, lavender-scented sheets in her entirely too girly bedroom and let out a big sigh.

Nick pulled up the light blanket, covering her with gentle care.

"Don't worry. I'm not going to break." She held up her bandaged hands. "Carrie and Tam did a fine job with the tweezers and dressings. They'd make fine nurses, don't you think?"

"How could they've done anything less with you directing them every step of the way?" The corner of Nick's mouth kicked up. "I'm just glad you're all right." He caressed the side of her face, carefully avoiding her cut forehead. "Your poor face."

"It won't scar," she said to reassure him. "The butterfly bandage is all it needs."

"If you say so, Nurse Lackey. Your sisters certainly came prepared for anything. I figure you could've done field surgery if it came down to it."

"You're exaggerating." She yawned. "It's been a long day."

"It's going to be a long night too. Open your eyes." He shined the flashlight in her eyes.

"Are my pupils equal and did they both constrict when the light hits them? That's what you're supposed to see."

"Well, can't rightly say for sure. Looks to me like the left pupil is a lot bigger than the other."

"What?" Allison sat up straight. "Give me the mirror." She pointed to her dressing table.

"Just kiddin'."

She frowned, giving him her most serious expression. "You're not nice. This is serious."

"Then we should've taken you to the hospital."

"No, I mean it *could* be serious *if* you were telling me the truth."

Gently, he took one of her bandaged hands in his. "I'm not about to let anything happen to you, darlin'."

Her heart sped up but then settled down into a steady rhythm as she relaxed under his tender care. She yawned again. "Sorry. I keep doing that."

"Go to sleep. I'll turn off all the lights except for this small one here." He looked askance at the lampshade with dancing poodles.

"Have you called Ben to see if he's okay?" she asked, feeling guilty she'd taken so much of his time.

"Getting ready to, as soon as I get you settled."

"Consider me settled. Call your son."

He stood and turned off the overhead light and switched on the small lamp. Then he settled into the rocking chair Tamsyn had earlier dragged into the room.

She tried not to listen, but it was clear from his side of the conversation his ex-wife was giving him grief.

"Where am I? I'm at Allison's."

The evil Eva wouldn't like hearing that, she thought.

"Of course I care about our son. But I heard on the scanner it wasn't anywhere near his school. I'm at her house because she'd been kidnapped and was held in a house destroyed by the tornado."

Give him a break. After all, his ex was the one who wanted out of the marriage.

"Fine." He disconnected, unable to hold back a quick "Crap."

"She's upset. Why?"

"She doesn't need a reason."

"I shouldn't mean mouth your ex, but she sounds immature and selfish."

"I gave up on figuring her out a long time ago. If it wasn't for my son, I'd never give her another thought."

"I hate that our relationship makes it more difficult for you to spend time with him. I don't want to ruin what you two fellas have."

"Eva's my problem, not yours." He took her hand in his. "As much as she drives me crazy, Ben will never hear me say anything bad about his mother."

"You think she affords you the same courtesy?"

"Probably not."

"Well, Ben won't ever hear a bad word from me either. I just want you to know."

"Appreciate it. Now it's time you got a good night's sleep." He reached over and patted her thigh. "Not that my waking you up every hour is gonna help."

"I'll sleep better just knowing you're here. I'm so grateful you followed your gut. Of course, we were both wrong about who killed Meryl. It wasn't her husband or the doctor. Mrs. Ivers actually confessed she killed Meryl by mistake. But she *never* expressed a single regret. The only thing that crazy bitch regretted was the inconvenience it caused *her*."

"Allison Lackey, shut your big brown eyes."

She did as requested, but she couldn't shut off her brain. She'd been so close to death. There wasn't a single doubt Harriet Ivers would've killed her if the tornado hadn't intervened.

And Nick... She'd thought she was dreaming when she'd first opened her eyes and seen his handsome face leaning over her. Such a sweet dream too.

Still, as much as she cared about him, she wasn't about to get between him and his darling little son.

Saturday morning, Allison opened her eyes, and for once, the bright light shining in her eyes was the morning sun streaming through the voile curtains. She gazed over at Nick asleep in the rocking chair. True to his word, he'd spent the night with her, waking her every hour and checking her pupils. Oh, he'd be so stiff when he woke up.

She kicked the covers off and eased from the bed. Her bandaged hands were itching, and she needed to pee. Tiptoeing past his sleeping form, she made it to the door.

"Where do you think you're going?"

"Bathroom, doofus." She reached for her housecoat, slipped it on, and tied the belt.

"Can you manage?"

She snorted. "I've been managing for some years now."

"I mean with your hands," he said, rubbing the sleep from his eyes.

"Yes, I can manage. And after that, I'm going downstairs for coffee. I think I heard the doorbell. That's what woke me up. I want to see what's going on."

Nick stood and stretched. "Remind me not to ever sleep in a rocking chair again...if you'll promise you won't have any more concussions."

"Promise."

"Now, about that coffee."

Downstairs, they found Caroline and Scott sitting at the breakfast bar along with Tess.

"Sorry for barging in on y'all so early," Tess said, "but I thought you'd like an update."

Allison poured two cups of coffee and handed one to Nick, then seated herself at the bar. "So, spill. Did Harriet Ivers make it?"

"Made it to Vanderbilt and through surgery...barely. I've been told she arrested on the table a couple of times."

"I just hope she lives long enough to pay for killing Meryl." Allison stirred sweetener in her coffee.

"What about the good doctor?" Nick asked.

"Arrested, charged with various minor felonies, especially improper disposal of a corpse, accomplice after the fact. He'll also be investigated for his part in the black-market organ trade. Naturally, he's already been bailed out by his attorney. And get this, he's indicated he will testify against his wife."

"Figures," Allison said, shaking her head.

"As for the wife, if she survives and is deemed competent to stand trial—there might be some doubt about—"

"No!" At the thought of Harriett Ivers not having to stand trial, Allison almost choked on her swallow of coffee. "That woman—she knew what she was about to do was wrong. She just didn't care."

"I don't disagree," Tess said, "but the woman's a long way from being medically stable enough for a mental evaluation."

Resigned to the slowness of the legal system, Allison took

306 | Marie-Nicole Ryan

another sip of coffee. "Not to change the subject, I'm really sorry about screwing up your shower."

"Yeah." Tamsyn giggled. "It was a lingerie shower too. Poor Scott."

Scott beamed at his fiancée. "Guess you won't wear any on our honeymoon, then."

Caroline held her hands to her ears. "La-la-la. I didn't need to hear this."

Allison laughed, beginning to relax. "We can just let everyone know to bring their shower gifts to the wedding. There's no time to set up another one. And there are two dozen cupcakes in the fridge. Anyone for breakfast?"

"Cupcakes it is."

Chapter Thirty-one

Later that afternoon, the sun beat down, the late summer heat warming Nick's arms. The heat felt good after last night's cold rain. Scott had his nose in a book, and Justin was firing up the grill on the sunny side of the deck. Under the deck awning, the girls sat, drinking iced tea or lemonade. A Rascal Flatts tune poured out from Tamsyn's iPod. Nick took a long pull on his beer. Frankly, life couldn't get any better.

To his relief, Allison's injuries weren't as bad as they'd looked initially. Each of her hands now sported a small dressing. The other wounds were superficial—so the nurse herself said—and would heal quickly.

Ready to doze off, he heard the front doorbell.

Scott raised his head. "Anyone going to get that?" When none of the girls appeared to hear, he dragged his body from the lounge. "Guess not."

A minute or two later, he returned with a wary expression. "Nick, someone wants you."

"Me? No one knows I'm here except my ex."

"Unless your ex is six feet tall with a mustache, it's not her."

Nick pulled himself from the lounge chair and trudged inside. So much for the perfect afternoon.

As Scott had described, a man with a mustache stood waiting on the front porch. Nick opened the door.

"Nick Vitelli?"

"Yeah."

Mustache man whipped out a blue-covered form. "You've been served."

"What?"

The man nodded and took off.

Nick opened the form and— "Son of a bitch!" Eva was suing for full custody along with a request to have his parental rights terminated due to his being an unfit and abusive parent who was associated with undesirable people.

He walked back onto the deck and handed the papers to Allison. "You're not going to believe this."

She glanced over the document. "She can't do this." She turned to Scott, who'd almost finished law school before the untimely death of their parents. "Can she, Scott?"

"Let me see the complaint." Scott held out his hand. Nick took the papers from Allie and handed them over to his boss.

"This is a nuisance suit," Scott said, frowning. "I'm surprised any ethical lawyer would take the case. We just need to figure out what she really wants."

"What does she *really* want?" Nick shrugged. "I wish I knew."

"Oh, that woman," Allison said with a growl. "She wants him to stop seeing me."

"Or anyone," Nick added.

She got to her feet and slipped her arms around his waist. "I told you I won't be the reason you don't get to see your son. You shouldn't have to choose between us. Ben is your priority. He has to be. I don't matter."

"You do matter. She has to learn she's not gonna run my life."

"I agree," Scott said. "She can't, but she can make you miserable and drive you crazy if you let her. Your best bet is attorney Ted Lindsey. He's a specialist in family law."

"Thanks." Just when he was getting on his feet financially, Eva had to hit him with this. No matter how frivolous the suit was, it'd cost him in the long run. "I'll go talk to her. She has to see reason."

"I wouldn't advise it," Scott said. "It could make things worse."

Before the discussion could go any further, Tess walked outside onto the deck. "I'm off the rest of the day, barring any shootouts on Broadway or the like." She smiled and leaned over Scott, giving him a kiss on the forehead. "What's going on? Sounded like quite the brouhaha."

Allison spoke first. "Nick's ex is suing him for full custody. She even wants to terminate his parental rights." She pulled her feet up and hugged her knees, seeming to withdraw from everyone.

"I'd say she's acting out." Tess gave a knowing nod. "Rumor at the house says the new chief's marriage isn't going too well."

"This is exactly the kind of situation I know how to fix." Allison's wry tone caught him by surprise.

"Really? What've you got in mind?" He caught her gaze and tried to hold it, but she looked away.

"We'll just stop seeing each other."

"Now hold on." Nick strode across the deck and sat on the foot of her lounge. "We're not going to let her ruin what we have."

She folded her arms across her chest, her chin set. "She has no inkling of boundaries."

"Let's discuss this privately." No point in entertaining her family with his ex-wife turmoil.

"We can do that, but I won't change my mind." Her phone chimed.

"Let it go," he said, eager to talk her down.

She glanced at the number. "I don't know who this is. I'd better answer it."

He waited, the toe of his shoe tapping.

Her face growing redder by the second, Allison walked inside without a word.

What the hell?

He followed Allison inside and heard her let go with a string of swear words that would've done an Atlanta cop proud.

Then she punched the Disconnect button. "Your ex is freaking crazy. And if you think I'm going to deal with her for the rest of my life, you're mistaken. You're free, Nick. I can't deal. I'm sorry I've caused her to go off the rails, but seriously, she needs medication or psychiatric help...or both."

"What did she say?"

"Doesn't matter. I didn't believe her."

"What'd she say? Dammit, tell me."

"She said the last time you brought Ben home, the two of you had words and you hit her. She said she has the bruises to prove it." Allison's phone dinged. "Oh joy. Now she's sent me the photo. How did she get my cell phone number anyway?"

"Beats the hell outta me." He held out his hand. "Let me see. If I supposedly hit her last weekend, that mark doesn't look like a week-old bruise to me. You?"

"No, it doesn't look like an old bruise. The coloration is that of a new bruise *if* it's a bruise at all. More than likely, it's a makeup job."

"I'm sorry you're so upset. I don't want you to think I could do something like this."

"I don't. In fact, I'm sure you didn't hit her, but I'm not going to be the cause of turmoil in your life. If you're going continue having a relationship with your son, I have to bow out..." She threw up her hands. I can never thank you enough for saving my life." Her eyes grew shiny with tears.

"I don't need your gratitude, Allie. I thought we had

something. You don't strike me as the type to throw in the towel and bail at the first sign of trouble."

"I'm just not going to—" She broke off. "That's all. I'm not going to discuss it anymore."

"So, it's over...before it ever really began?" His mind whirled with disbelief. "No," he said, not ready to accept her flat statement.

"Yeah. *So* over." She whirled and ran upstairs.

Oh yeah? You're not the only one who's stubborn in this relationship.

Nick clenched his fists. Damn Eva for an interfering witch. As angry as he was, he refused to call the mother of his son a bitch. Witch was as close as he would go.

How had he ever fallen in love with her? The answer was simple. He never was. They'd married because she claimed she was pregnant. Conveniently enough after they married, she'd had a miscarriage. Then two months later, she turned up pregnant again, this time with Ben. Maybe her dishonesty was the reason he'd allowed the job to take over his life. Maybe he'd just used it as an excuse. But his son was another matter. He loved Ben with all his heart, and no matter how difficult his ex was, he'd never disrespect her in front of his boy.

He walked back onto the deck and faced four pairs of raised eyebrows Everyone had raised eyebrows from Tamsyn to Justin. "Guess I'd better be going. Allie needs some time to cool off." At least that was what he hoped.

Caroline stood. "I'll go check on her. Don't worry. It's just her redhead's temper you've seen. She's quick to spark, but she'll mellow out soon enough."

"Not so sure about that. She says we're done." Nick shrugged. "Sounded definite to me."

Scott stood and walked to Nick's side. "Listen, buddy, just don't do anything rash." He clapped a hand on Nick's back. "Carrie's right about Allison. She'll see reason soon enough."

Allison threw herself on the bed and sobbed. How dare Nick's ex-wife call to spew more of her vicious lies? Dealing with someone like Eva frequently was a nonstarter. No doubt the woman would intensify her machinations the closer Allison and Nick grew.

Nick. It wasn't his fault. But poor little Ben. Would his mother try more dirty tricks to turn Ben against his father? If the woman was subtle, which she didn't seem to be, her scheming would be more damaging. Big lies the boy wouldn't believe, but little ones could breed insidiously in a child's mind until he didn't know what to believe.

She pounded the pillow. "It's just not fair."

"No one said it would be, hon."

Caroline's calm voice sent Allison into a fresh round of tears. She sat up and hugged her sister. "Have I done the wrong thing?" she asked between sobs. "I don't want him to lose his son entirely. And she's trying to make it happen."

"It's not your fault the bitch is self-centered and hateful."

"How could he have married someone like her anyway? I don't understand it."

"Men aren't known for thinking with their big brains. They tend to use the little brain between their legs, especially when they're young."

Allison nodded and wiped away her tears. "Ben is such a neat kid. I think he really liked me."

"That's the problem right there. She's jealous. And if what Tess heard at the station house is true, then his ex is worried. Take my word for it, she definitely sees you as a major threat."

"Maybe *I* could talk to her." Allison finger-combed her hair behind her ears. "I could convince her I'm not trying to take her place in Ben's life."

"No way." Caroline waggled her finger. "You can't talk sense to women like her. Don't waste your breath." She patted her younger sister's shoulder. "Now tell me true. Are you in love with Nick?"

Allison met her sister's steady gaze. "Yes. I am. I know it's awfully soon, but I *do* love him."

"Then give him some time to straighten his situation with his ex. But give him some hope too. I've never seen such a pitiful guy as the one who left just now."

Allison glanced at the door. "He's gone?"

"He is."

"Then I'll wait until after the wedding." She nodded. "I'll talk to him then."

"You don't want to wait too long. He's a great guy. Someone could just snap him up. Where would you be, then?"

"Right where I am now, I guess."

"Just don't wait too long."

Chapter Thirty-two

The next week had seemed to drag. Every night since she'd ended things with Nick, she'd held her breath, hoping he'd call and yet hoping he wouldn't. She'd gotten so used to having him around. She'd avoided seeing him at the office by staying home and searching the Internet, trying to find another job.

So far, one field looked interesting: litigation nurse consultant. No more hospital hours. True, she'd need additional training and have to sit for another certification exam, but exams had never been a problem.

Yes, that was what she'd do. She bookmarked the web site. No more moping about her lost job. As a litigation nurse consultant, she would have more control over her career. Greater flexibility in hours.

Good. Now that she'd made a decision about her future, she still needed a date for Scott and Tess's wedding. And no, she wasn't ready to talk to Nick yet. But who? Could she tolerate Rick's frat brother, Pauley, long enough to get through the wedding and reception? Of course, she could.

She'd give him a call and make it clear this was about his escorting her to the wedding and reception and nothing else.

"Yeah, that'll work."

Nick gulped down the last of his coffee and frowned. Stuff was strong, but strong was what he needed to keep going. He couldn't remember a worse week, other than the week

Eva had asked for a divorce and kicked him out of their condo. While he couldn't say he was surprised, leaving his son had been torture.

He'd spent Monday morning meeting with the family law attorney Scott had recommended. Now that the appointment was over, he felt more in control. The attorney agreed it was a nuisance suit, pure and simple. Maybe not so simple, since she'd asked for complete termination of his parental rights in addition to the assault accusation.

The assault charge aside, for Allison to dump him... Just when he'd thought they were working toward something good. For the first time, he'd envisioned a real future with a woman he truly loved. It hadn't been a long relationship, but it'd been intense. They'd grown close working together while Meryl Litton had been missing. When the young case manager's body had been found, emotions had skyrocketed.

"Nick?"

Startled, he looked up. Scott stood in the doorway of his office. "Sorry, my mind was a million miles away."

"You're still on board with being a groomsman, right? Don't let this thing with Allison keep you from the rehearsal dinner and the wedding."

"You sure?" He pushed back from the desk. "I don't want to make anyone uncomfortable."

"*Anyone* meaning Allison?"

"Who else?"

Scott frowned and hesitated as if not sure what to say next. "And by the way, you should bring a date. Allison has one."

Already has a date. "Who?" He squared his shoulders, ready for battle.

"Pauley—I believe you met him?"

"Short dude? He didn't seem like her type."

Scott laughed. "Believe me, he's not."

"I'll be your plus one," came Caroline's voice from the hall, then she hip-checked Scott, moving him from the doorway.

"What? You don't have a date?" Surprising, since the firm's office manager was tall and slender with green cat's eyes and could've passed for a runway model any day.

"Nope, not a single one." She gave him a cat-in-the-cream smile. "And if you're really lucky, I'll keep Pauley out of her way. Maybe you can talk some sense into her."

"She said it all the other night. We're done."

"Not by a long shot, sweetie. Just you wait. I have a feeling your lady love has tempered a bit."

"Sure hope you're right," he said.

"I've known her all her life. You'll work things out."

He couldn't keep a smile from tugging at his mouth. "She's done a helluva good job of avoiding me this week. Is she all right?"

"Oh, she's been doing some soul searching, trying to find a new job. You know the kind of thing. Personally, I don't think she's cut out for the PI biz."

"Not with her temper." But looking for a new job... What if she found one that took her out of town? Away from Nashville. Away from him.

Ominous thoughts aside, he stood. "I'm checking out. I need to pick up my tux for tomorrow. Dress code for tonight?"

"Nice suit should do at the country club."

"Tie?"

"Yes, darlin', you need to wear a tie," she said with a condescending smile. "Sorry, but even though we're paying for this shindig, Tess's mom requested a more private venue. Scott and Tess would've been happy with a pizza place—isn't that right?"

Scott nodded. "Yeah."

"But Tess's mother is old money, don't you know? She wanted Belle Meade, but Scott belongs to Hillwood, so they compromised."

Nick threw up his hands. "Man, who needs all this fuss? I give up."

"Didn't you and your wife have a big wedding?"

"Too big to suit me," he said. "But I wasn't consulted. She and her mom just told me when and where to show up."

Caroline laughed. "That's as it should be."

"Funny."

"Just kidding."

Caroline might be kidding, but the last thing he ever wanted was a wedding like Scott and Tess's. No way would he be making that choice anytime soon anyhow.

Nick circled the table at the Hillwood Country Club, noting the place cards, meaning to make sure Allie was seated next to him. He smiled. Someone—maybe Caroline—had already taken care of the matter. He caught her eye across the room where she was talking with Tess's parents and pointed at the name cards.

She nodded. He smiled his approval.

Tess's mother, the one with old money, was tall and slender, had fading red hair and bright blue eyes. Her father didn't look much like a police captain with his wire-rimmed glasses and his salt-and-pepper hair. He had a scholarly air thing going on.

Nick kept looking around the private dining room, hoping to catch a glimpse of Allison and her plus one. Caroline motioned discreetly for him to come over and meet Tess's parents. He walked over and—finally—caught a quick look at Allie as she walked into the dining room looking like a midsummer's night dream in a peach dress that stopped a couple of inches above her shapely knees. The top of the dress was tied around the back of her neck with two ribbons, leaving her toned arms and shoulders bare. And he knew just how soft the skin of her back was.

Caroline nudged him. "Nick, this is Tess's mother, Regina Storm, and her father, Captain Michael O'Malley."

As he thrust out his hand, Nick's face heated up, signaling his embarrassment. "Sorry. Very pleased to meet you, Captain O'Malley."

"It's Mike," Tess's father said. "Likewise."

"No wonder your attention strayed from us old fogeys," Tess's mother added. "Allison is a lovely young woman."

"Yes, she is," he managed to get out without swallowing his tongue.

And she had come with that frat boy. Nick clenched his jaw. Frat boy's hands were all over her too.

Allison brushed Pauley's hand from her waist. "I told you this wasn't a date, Pauley. Keep your hands to yourself."

"Just acting as if I'm your attentive date. Thought you wanted to make the lumberjack over there jealous."

"I'm not trying to make him jealous," she said with an exasperated air. "I just needed an escort for dinner tonight and the wedding tomorrow. Are we clear?"

"Okay. I get it," he scoffed. "But I don't see what you see in him. I mean, his knuckles are almost dragging on the floor. All he needs is a banana."

"They are *not*," she said. "I'll have you know he's very intelligent." She walked over to one of the round dinner tables to check the name cards.

Pauley followed. "Yeah?" he said under his breath. "Reads a book a year, does he?"

She gritted her teeth then said, "When I was kidnapped,

he figured out where I was and saved my life."

"Great. He's a freaking hero. Can't compete with that."

"No, you certainly can't." She perused the next table. "This is my seat. You don't seem to be seated next to me. Let's find your table."

"You mean we don't get to sit together?"

"Yes, Pauley. That's what it means."

"I'll just exchange this one with mine." He snatched the card. "Now where was I supposed to be?"

"Pauley..." Caroline's voice rang clear over the buzz of the guests. "Don't you be messing with my seating arrangements. You're over here with me. You wouldn't want to hurt my feelings, now would you?" She batted her dark lashes.

Snort.

"Of course not." His cheeks darkened to a deep red.

Gotcha. Allison hid her smile. Her sister had maneuvered things just right. "I'll take this." She whipped the card bearing Nick's name from Pauley's stubby fist and carried it back to its original spot...right next to hers.

Then she favored her escort with her most sincere smile. "You'll enjoy dinner with my sister. She's quite intelligent and a great conversationalist. Why don't you hit the bar and bring me a nice semidry white wine?"

Yes, a little fortification was needed if she was going to get through this dinner with a glowering Nick at her side. Even though she'd tentatively agreed with Caroline's plan to seat her next to Nick, she remained uneasy. And if his expression as he walked toward her was any indicator of his mood, she was in for an uncomfortable evening.

"Allison," he said, acknowledging her presence. "If you want to change places and sit with your—uh, date, I won't be offended."

She smiled and gazed into his pool-blue eyes. "Not at all.

320 | M a r i e - N i c o l e R y a n

Caroline spent hours on the seating arrangements. I don't dare interfere."

"Okay."

He ran a finger around the inside of his collar, uncomfortable in his suit and tie. Indeed, he was more of a T-shirt and jeans kind of guy, but he sure did clean up well. And the navy suit enhanced his blue eyes.

"Surely we can act like two adults during dinner." If he but knew how much she'd missed him over the last week. Why did she always have to flare up and speak without thinking?

"I guess I'd better introduce my date to the O'Malleys. I'll see you when dinner starts."

His reaction was a nod.

Fine. Be that way.

Nick gazed around the room. At least forty guests, about half from Tess's family. Her parents. Three brothers and their families, and kids, minus toddlers. The other half of the group were the Holt-Lackeys, their friends, and dates. Tess's maid of honor and four bridesmaids and their dates. The three other groomsmen and their dates. What a pack. And all of 'em in a better mood than him.

He pulled at his shirt collar, then tugged at his tie. Damn ties, damn starched collar. And *damn* that short dude who kept doing his best to lay hands on Allison.

True enough, she didn't seem to like him and kept brushing his hands away. *Better mingle.* Better yet, he could use a drink.

Five minutes later and beer in hand, he made his way over to Justin. "Quite a crowd."

"Yeah. How long before we can blow this joint? There's a ball game I wanted to watch. Just not the same on the phone." The computer guru pulled a smartphone from his jacket pocket and checked the screen.

"What's the score?"

"Second inning, two to one, Yankees."

Nick nodded, noting the entrance of three waiters bearing trays of salad plates. "Looks like they're ready to start serving."

Justin flashed a wolfish smile. "Yeah. The sooner we eat, the sooner we can get back to the game."

On his way to his designated table, Nick chuckled. Leave it to the agency's computer whiz to have the game close at hand. Both of her brothers were sports nuts.

The scent of honeysuckle he'd noted earlier reached him. He turned...and smiled. "Allie."

"Nick."

Her throaty voice sent a hum of anticipation to his groin. In a daze, he pulled out her chair, wishing he could bury his face in her soft red-blond waves. Come to think of it, there was another place or two he'd like to bury his face. One of those would be between her full breasts. What a woman. She looked and smelled good enough to eat. What man could resist such a tempting dish?

Small talk. You're at a party. Make small talk.

"Have you heard anything about the case against Dr. Ivers?"

"Just what I've read in the papers. It was as I suspected. He was bringing in people anxious to sell their organs, and they were being listed as relatives to recipients who were willing to pay for the privilege of skipping the waiting list. His percentage of living related donors was much higher than the local and national averages. Donors were paid half upfront and half after the procedure. The money changed hands away from the hospital, so apparently, the hospital won't be held liable for his underhanded ways. But the hospital's transplant policies are being investigated."

"And that's what Meryl was suspicious about?"

"Yes."

Nick took another drink, finishing his beer, then reached for his wineglass.

Allison picked at her salad, then took a small bite.

"Eat your vegetables. They're good for you," he said in a lame attempt at conversation.

"Yeah. I guess I'm not really very hungry." She reached for her wineglass.

She stirred in her chair, her thigh brushing his. An electric sensation zapped straight to his groin. His hand on the wineglass trembled.

"Sorry," she said.

He swallowed hard. "No problem."

Fortunately, their entrees arrived, serving as a momentary distraction. Steak with wine and mushroom sauce, baked potato, and asparagus.

She took another drink of her wine. "I might've been hasty the other night."

He stopped in the middle of buttering his roll. "Really?"

"Really. I don't blame you for being upset." She covered his hand with hers. "I hope we can work things out with your ex. She has to see reason eventually."

"My attorney's hopeful she'll get tired and drop the suit, but he's prepared to sue for full custody if she continues slandering me."

Allison touched her lips with a napkin. "I never believed you hit her. You've put up with me all through the investigation, and heaven knows I'm not an easy person. I'm not a quitter either." She shot him a quick contrite expression. "I don't know why I got so upset the other night."

Relieved by her change in attitude, he breathed easier.

Things might just work out after all. "Could be the aftermath of your kidnapping."

"Sort of PTSD? I thought so too."

He cut a bite of his Porterhouse. "Caroline says you've been job hunting."

She flashed a smile. "Yes. I'm looking into training as a litigation nurse consultant. I'll have to sit for a certification exam, but the career seems like a good fit."

"Given you helped blow Dr. Ivers's fraudulent practices out of the water, I'd say you're well suited for it."

"Thanks."

Another quick smile. Tension started to ease from his body due, no doubt, to excellent food, plentiful wine, and Allie's good mood. He reached for his glass. Yes, there was hope for the future.

All through dinner, which Allison was unable to taste, she found it difficult to keep from touching Nick. Finally, she was relaxed and comfortable in his presence. Thank heaven for the wine that had flowed so freely throughout the evening. Her thigh was pressed against his, and she simply couldn't resist sliding her barefoot up and down his calf.

"Stop it," he hissed. "You're driving me crazy." He reached for his wineglass and downed it. "I'll make you pay."

"Really?" She squirmed in her chair. "How do you propose to do that?"

"Keep it up, and you'll find out." He removed her hand from his thigh. "Eat your dessert." Using his fork, he pointed at her double chocolate cheesecake. "I thought you liked chocolate."

"Oh, I do." She took a bite and licked it off the fork.

"People are beginning to stare." His cheeks flushed.

She put her head close to his. "I'm going to the restroom.

Wait a minute and then follow me." She held her forefinger to her mouth in a shushing motion.

"I can't—"

"I know a place."

She rose from her chair and left the table.

Allison then waited in the hallway. Surely he wanted this as much as she did. Almost ready to abandon her plan for a forbidden quickie, she spotted him.

"This way," she whispered. "There's a locker room down this hall."

Her head was swimming and her knees were losing their strength. Just in time, they reached the locker room. "There shouldn't be anyone using it this time of night."

"Sure hope not."

"Here we go." Turning to face him, she tiptoed closer and sneaked a look over his shoulder. "We're clear."

Once inside, he shoved her back against the wall and covered her neck with kisses. He untied the top of her dress and buried his face in the valley between her lush breasts. "God, you're beautiful. You smell so good." His words came in gasps as he took one of her nipples between his teeth and delicately raked it.

A thread of desire wove its way to her lower belly, weakening her knees until they were like overcooked pasta. Her head went back as she gasped for air. "Here, let me." She hiked up her skirt and inched her panties down over her hips.

Her heart started beating a wild tango as he slipped one hand inside her damp panties, cupping her sex while he fumbled with his zipper. "I love an ambidextrous man," she murmured.

He yanked her lace bikinis down the rest of the way so she could kick them aside. He stooped, scooped them up, and sniffed the crotch. "Essence of Allie," he said with a broad smile, then stuffed the flimsy garment inside his pants pocket.

"Never took you for a crotch sniffer," she said, holding back a giggle.

"I'm particular, though."

"You'd better be." She slid her hand through the zipper. "Roughrider—all right." His erection was thick and hot in her hand. "Let's give little Nicky some air."

With a groan, Nick pulled a condom from his pocket. "Not too much air," he said as Allison tore open the foil packet with her teeth and sheathed him in what had to be record time.

Giving a hitch and a jump, she wrapped her legs around his waist while his cock found her cleft. She wiggled her hips as he slid the head up and down her slick valley. Then he thrust inside, her body welcoming him home.

He cupped her butt, supporting her weight on his forearms. "You all right?"

She nodded into his neck. "Yes, cowboy. Let's ride."

He chuckled but complied. His first thrusts were slow, and she met each stroke for stroke, faster and faster. His lips on her neck, each kiss scalding her skin. She clung to his broad shoulders as she gripped his cock with her inner muscles.

Faster and faster until they spun out of control.

A scream gathered in her throat, but he clamped his hand over her mouth, muffling her response.

"No doubt about it. You're a wild woman," he said, removing his hand from her mouth.

"Sometimes I surprise myself."

Slowly releasing his hold on her, he kissed her neck and set her feet on the floor. "God, I love you. You're crazy. Reckless—"

"And wild." She poked his ribs. "Don't forget *that*."

"As if I could." He nuzzled her neck. "As bad as I hate to, I guess we'd better cover these beauties." He took the dangling ribbons of her dress and retied the top behind her neck.

"You're such a gentleman." She held out her hand. "My panties, please."

Giving a wicked smile, he shook his head. "Nope. I'm keeping 'em."

"Ooh, for your collection?" She raised her brows and wriggled her shoulders.

"Like I said. I'm particular. I plan on remembering this night for a long time."

"Me too." She gave his crotch a glance. "Better check your zipper. We don't want to scandalize everyone."

He laughed. "We need a designated driver. Think Justin would give us a ride?"

"If he hasn't already taken off. I guess I *could* ride home with my escort," she said, teasing him.

He straightened and squared his shoulders. "No way in hell is that dude taking you home—you without your panties. We'll walk if we have to."

"Then we'd better find Justin or Carrie."

Allison waved good-bye as Nick headed home with Justin as his designated driver. She closed the front door and couldn't stifle the sigh that escaped.

Behind her, Caroline cleared her throat. "Well, young lady, what do you have to say for yourself?"

She gave her sister a broad smile. "I had a wonderful time at the rehearsal dinner. Great job, Carrie."

"I don't think I had much to do with your good time, except for keeping Pauley out of your hair. I must say he was none too pleased."

"Pfft. He'll get over it. He doesn't care anything about me. He's a player wannabe."

"You certainly had a healthy glow when you returned from the *restroom*."

"Did I?" She sashayed past her sister. "Must be my new blusher."

"Blusher hell. You had wild monkey sex. Don't deny it. I want details. I mean I *need* details. I've almost forgotten what it was like."

She wagged her finger in her sister's face. "No one's fault but your own."

"Don't change the subject. If nothing else, just tell me where."

Allison leaned back against the doorjamb. "Women's locker room."

"Risky. I *like* it."

"Suh-weet too." Allison waved away further questions. "That's all I'm saying." She yawned. "I'm going to bed. Big day tomorrow. Our brother's getting married."

"You mean today. It's after one."

"Even more reason to go to bed. Night." She climbed the stairs to her room, doubtful sleep would ever come. No matter how much she loved Nick, there was still his ex to deal with.

Chapter Thirty-three

On the Belle Meade Plantation carriage house porch, Nick leaned against one of the support posts and twirled the lace garter on his forefinger. He watched Allison come outside and look around until she spied him. "Some kinda coincidence, isn't it?"

With a fleeting grimace, she glanced down at the bridal bouquet she'd just captured and shrugged. "Yeah. I guess you could say that."

"I just did."

"You don't have to worry, it's just a tradition. Not an obligation." She worried her full bottom lip with her teeth. Those lips. Without warning, his mind flashed to the night before. Those lips had been all over his body. Like he could forget. Like he would want to. *Not.*

A smile spread across her face, lightening her countenance with amusement. "What?" he asked, a touch afraid of how she might answer.

Never taking her gaze from his, she moved very close into his personal space, the fabric of her blue bridesmaid's dress rustling as she brushed against him.

"Careful," he warned. "Wouldn't want to get embarrassed here in front of the wedding party."

"Scott and Tess won't notice. They've already gone to change." She scooted even closer.

An involuntary shiver of desire shook him to his core. Somehow he must convince her they belonged together. The way she fit in the curve of his arms. The way her body molded to his when they made love. Spending the rest of his life without her wasn't an option. Not a viable one, anyway.

Better do his best. Right here. Right now.

He dropped to one knee. Was he really going to propose? Risk rejection in front of everyone?

Hell, yeah.

His mouth grew dry. He looked up. Allie's eyes widened. Her lips parted expectantly, waiting for him to get on with it. A crowd was starting to gather around them.

The muscles in his thighs jittered. Somehow he had to get the words out. He opened his mouth. Nothing came out.

He swallowed. Or tried to.

Finally. "Allie—Allison Lackey, you're all the woman I'll ever want or need..." He swallowed again.

Smiling, she leaned closer. "Go on. You can do it."

"Making a real hash of this," he muttered under his breath. God. What an idiot he was. "Will you m-marry me?" he asked with a croak.

Allie—his Allie—dropped to her knees, wrapped her arms around his neck, and said, "Yes. Hell, yes, I'll marry you."

He felt the warmth of her tears on his cheek. Or were they his?

But who cared? She'd said *yes*.

Applause from the onlookers drowned out his stuttering avowal of love, but the warm, loving expression in Allie's eyes told him she'd heard. And that was all he needed to know.

"I love you too, Nick. So much."

He managed to get to his feet and pulled her up as he did.

"Where's the ring?" This came from Justin. "You better not be asking to marry my little sister without a rock to put on her finger."

Reaching for his vest pocket, Nick smiled as he extricated the small diamond ring he'd bought the day before. Hell, until last night, they hadn't even been on speaking terms, so he hadn't planned on proposing today. Not consciously. But after the way, things had gone last night at the rehearsal dinner... Perhaps it was a subconscious act he'd stuck it in his vest pocket...for safekeeping.

Smiling the beautiful smile he'd grown to love, she placed her trembling left hand in his. Her warm brown eyes glistened with tears as he slipped the ring onto her third finger. It went on without a hitch. Now that had to be a sign.

They were meant to be together.

She held her hand up in triumph. "I got my man too," she announced to the cheers and laughter of the surrounding wedding guests. Under her breath, she said, "I hope Tess won't feel like we purposely tried to upstage her wedding."

More applause and a few squeals from some of the young women who were also in the wedding party.

He nodded and smiled, acknowledging the congratulations. "She doesn't strike me that way."

"Well, she was having some true bridezilla moments in the dressing room when the accent flowers in her bouquet were two shades lighter than she ordered."

"Really?"

"Yes, really."

He grabbed Allie's hand. "As soon as they leave for their honeymoon, let's get out of here. I can't wait to tell Ben the good news. He really likes you."

"Oh..."

The dismay in her expression hit his stomach like a sucker punch. "What is it? Don't you want me to tell him?"

"Of course, but it'll mean facing your ex. I thought you might wait until your next weekend visit."

"I could. Truth be told, I'd rather get it over with."

"No point in putting it off. The sooner she gets used to the idea, the better."

"My thoughts exactly."

Rather than show up unannounced, which would definitely put Eva's panties in a twist, Nick sent her a text. That way he wouldn't have to listen to her scream until he arrived on her front porch.

He waited, then read her reply. *I was going to call you tomorrow, but this evening will do just fine.*

Puzzled by the lack of vitriol, he texted back he'd see her in twenty.

This time of night, Chief Mills would probably be home as well. Good or bad? Who the hell knew?

He parked in the long drive and walked up to the porch.

"Come in, Nick." Eva was calm and collected. And no sign of the bruise where he'd allegedly hit her.

"You all right?"

She nodded, motioned him inside. "Ben's in the den with Doug. They're watching a movie on Netflix."

"I have something to tell him, but first I want to say that you've got to stop harassing Allison."

"I won't be doing that anymore." She indicated he should have a seat, and she sat on the couch across from him, averting her gaze and smoothing the silky material of her slacks. "Doug overheard the end of that particular conversation, and he gave me an ultimatum. We've had some problems—but you don't want to hear about that. Just know I really do love him. Anyway, he made it clear my behavior was unacceptable. I've got to let you live your life. He made it very clear if I didn't focus on our relationship instead of yours, we wouldn't be together much longer."

Nick sucked in a deep breath and leaned back. All right, the chief grew some big ones. "I appreciate it, Eva." He took another breath, then continued. "I've asked Allison to marry me. There's no date set or anything, but soon. I want to share the news with Ben. I know it's not my weekend to see him and it's kind of late, but I'd like to tell him."

"Of course. Please make my apologies to Allison. I don't know what gets into me sometimes."

Okay, the new meek and mild version of his ex—freaky. Would it last? Doubtful, but he'd take advantage of her new personality as long as it did.

"Allison is a good person, and she made it clear she's not trying to replace you. But she'll take good care of him when he's with us."

Eva's chin trembled. "Thank her for me." She rose from the couch. "I'll go get him."

A minute later, he heard the rush of one small boy and dog running down the hall. "Daddy!"

After a giant hug that never failed to make Nick's heart swell with love and pride, he set the boy on his knee. "I've some news, buddy. Allie and I are getting married. I asked her tonight."

"Can I bring my puppy to live with us?"

"We don't have anything settled yet. But your puppy can visit and play with Allie's."

The boy leaned forward and whispered, "I think Papa Doug and Mommy are getting a divorce. They were yelling earlier. Mommy cried. Can she live with us after you all get married?"

Nick blinked. "Probably not. But Papa Doug and your mommy are going to work things out. Grownups have fights sometimes, but then they make up."

"I sure hope so. I like Papa Doug, but he's not around very much. He's real busy. That's what Mommy said."

"He's the chief of police in Nashville—that's a big job. An important job."

"Yeah, that's what Mommy said too."

"Okay, I'm going to let you get back to your movie. One more hug and I'll see you next weekend."

After the hug, Nick watched his son run back down the hall, his puppy nipping at his heels. The puppy might be small now, but the golden retriever wouldn't stay small very long. Wonder what Allie's rat—uh, Yorkie would think of it. He chuckled. At least someone in the Mills household had some common sense.

Outside in the Bronco, he called Allie. "You're not gonna believe this," he said, updating her on his conversation with Eva.

"She's become the Stepford version of an ex-wife. Cool," Allie said. "Just in time too."

Nick laughed. "I love you, Allison Lackey."

"Ditto, Nicholas Vitelli. Ditto."

Epilogue

"If we're going to do this wedding, we're going to do it up right. Follow me. I have everything all spread out in the man cave. We can make all our choices at one time, and then I won't have to bother you again."

Allison ignored Nick's bewildered expression, took his hand, and led him into her brothers' den, which looked like anything but a man cave. She spread out the last three issues of *Brides* on the coffee table. "What do you think of this dress? It's sort of sexy. Might not do for a church wedding." She pointed to a see-through lace-corseted Pnina Tornai mermaid-style gown.

Nick perched on the sofa arm, looking as if he might take flight any second. "That's some dress."

"Or I could go with something like this." She flipped the pages to a bookmarked spot showing a full-skirted gown with a crystal-jeweled bodice and sweetheart neckline. "Now this princess-style gown is more traditional, and the sweetheart neckline is *so* attractive. Plus, I love all the bling," she said. "Or I could go with something really fashion forward." She indicated a formfitting dress. "This one has a fitted silhouette with lots of ruching and a crumb-catcher neckline."

"Bling? Ruching? Crumb catcher? Seriously?" His eyes were already glazing over. How much further could she go before he broke? Her imitation of an obnoxious bridezilla was intentional. No. She wouldn't torture him too much longer, but it was fun to see just how much wedding talk he could endure.

"You'll be beautiful whatever you wear," he said, his voice husky with emotion, but his sky-blue eyes were darting here and there.

Such a sweet guy, but she couldn't resist teasing him a little more. "Now, I was thinking for the wedding cake, lemon pound with white icing covered in yellow cream roses and ribbons. And for the groom's cake, I thought red velvet with a chocolate cream-cheese icing. You'd like that, wouldn't you? Or would you prefer to do a tasting at the bakery? The shop is in Hillwood, and they do the most amazing cakes." Using her iPhone, she surfed to the specialty bakery's web site. "Here, see for yourself."

"Lotta choices," he muttered. "That—uh, red velvet one sounds pretty good."

"You know, I think we really ought to do a formal tasting. It would only take a couple of hours."

His gaze widened in—could it be horror? "A couple of hours?"

"And then there are the flowers."

"Hold on." Nick raised his hands in surrender. "Whatever you want, Allie. Just do it. Tell me when and where to show up."

"Well, if you have your heart set on a big wedding..." She let her bottom lip tremble just a bit. "Wait—I have it, a destination honeymoon somewhere tropical and romantic."

"Anything. Anywhere. I just want to marry you. The sooner, the better."

"I don't think sooner will work. This will take at least a year to pull together."

"A year? Are you serious?" The color leached from his face. "I don't know..."

"That's what I thought." She swept the magazines and travel brochures onto the floor, then stood and wrapped her arms around his neck. "Screw all this. I just want to be your wife. I don't need flowers or an expensive dress. I just want you."

His mouth broadened into a wide smile. "Now you're talking, babe. Any suggestions?" He stood, and his arms snaked around her waist, pulling her close.

Nodding, she beamed. "Gatlinburg. Sevier County. No blood tests. No waiting." Searching for approval in his gaze, she cupped each side of his handsome face. The face she wanted to see on the pillow next to hers each morning for the rest of her life.

"You've done your research." His eyes seemed to glow with passion and approval. "So, all this wedding hoo-hah was just to yank my chain?"

"You betcha," she said. "Now, it's true Scott and Tess had a beautiful wedding, and they'll have an album full of beautiful wedding pictures, but I don't want to wait."

"Me neither."

He dipped his head and pressed his lips to hers. Two thoughts, before all sanity fled. She had the love of a lifetime, and she owed it to Meryl.

Because of you, dear Meryl.
All because of you.

The End

ABOUT THE AUTHOR

Award-winning author Marie-Nicole Ryan writes spicy romantic suspense and sizzling erotic historical western romance. She's had a life-long love affair with books, so one could say it was natural she should write her own. She was born in Western Kentucky but lived in Nashville, TN, for more decades than she cares to admit.

When she has time, she loves to read murder mysteries, browse antique shops, and meet friends for lunch. She's also devoted to her Sheltie, Cassie, who tries to help write by walking on the laptop.

She loves to hear from her readers, and she's never too busy to respond. You may email Ms. Ryan at marie@marienicoleryan.com.

LINKS

Web site: https:/marienicoleryanauthor.blogspot.com
FaceBook: https://facebook.com/MarieNicoleRyan.author
Twitter: https://twitter.com/marienicoleryan/

DEDICATION

This book is dedicated to all the readers who have waited so long for the second book in this series. I hope you'll enjoy Allison and Nick's love story.

Also by Marie-Nicole Ryan

Music City Heat Series
Measure of a Man, 3
Because of You, 2
Love Me if You Can, 1
Beginnings, Prequel Short Story

Hill Country Lawmen
Hunted, 1
Threatened, 2

FBI Guys
Broken Promises, 1
Holding Her Own, 2

Love the Lawman Series
Mastering the Marshal, 3
Pleasuring the Pinkerton, 2
Seducing the Sheriff, 1

Stand-alone Romantic Suspense
Too Good to be True
The Man for the Job
See You in My Dreams

David & Miranda French Mysteries
One Too Many
Love on the Run

Holiday Interludes Short Stories
Valentine's Gift, 3
Pillow Talk, 2
Mistletoe & Mario, 1